She was beautiful, but cold and impassive. Soundlessly, she stepped into the room and walked in a direct line toward the table. They stood and watched in amazement, stepping back a little from her as she approached. When she reached the table, an antique scroll of parchment seemed to appear in her hand. She let it fall, then turned around. She didn't lift a hand to disturb the drapes, which enfolded around her as she stepped out into the air and vanished.

"That's impossible," Geraint said flatly. "The magical protections on this building would keep Lucifer himself out." The sound of rustling parchment, being carefully handled, came from just over his shoulder.

"This is a warning," Michael told them, dispensing with a complete recitation. "Written in medieval Latin. I can't translate the whole thing for you, but the gist of it is to keep our noses out or we'll be damned for all eternity."

"Colorfully put," Geraint said sarcastically, regaining his composure.

"No, I mean *literally* damned for eternity . . ."

SHADOWRUN

BLACK MADONNA

Carl Sargent
& Marc Gascoigne

A ROC BOOK

ROC
Published by the Penguin Group
Penguin Books USA Inc., 375 Hudson Street,
New York, New York 10014, U.S.A.
Penguin Books Ltd, 27 Wrights Lane,
London W8 5TZ, England
Penguin Books Australia Ltd, Ringwood,
Victoria, Australia
Penguin Books Canada Ltd, 10 Alcorn Avenue,
Toronto, Ontario, Canada M4V 3B2
Penguin Books (N.Z.) Ltd, 182-190 Wairau Road,
Auckland 10, New Zealand

Penguin Books Ltd, Registered Offices:
Harmondsworth, Middlesex, England

First published by Roc, an imprint of Dutton Signet,
a division of Penguin Books USA Inc.

First Printing, April, 1996
10 9 8 7 6 5 4 3 2

Series Editor: Donna Ippolito
Cover: Brooke Steadman

 REGISTERED TRADEMARK—MARCA REGISTRADA

SHADOWRUN, FASA, and the distinctive SHADOWRUN and FASA logos are
registered trademarks of the FASA Corporation, 1100 W. Cermak, Suite B305,
Chicago, IL 60608.

Printed in Canada

This book is dedicated to Lynn Picknett,
the Sherlock Holmes of the Shroudies,
without whom it really would have been impossible.
Thanks for everything.

History is an alliance of reality and lies.
The reality of history becomes a lie.
The unreality of the fable becomes the truth.
                    —Jean Cocteau

Prologue

The world was about to fall apart, but he could hardly have expected that to happen. Some things don't exactly happen every day.

Sam Kryzinski expected another boring, normal day at the office. Renraku had been paying him a comfortable salary as Coordinator of Matrix Security in their Chiba offices for four years, and that was as long as most good deckers lasted. Sam had stayed the course. It was a day just like any other; April 20, 2057, gray clouds and sixty-one degrees in the late afternoon, very comfortable for the time of year. There were no new wars of any significance on the globe, and no fool decker had tried anything more than flirt with the fortress-thick IC around the peripherals of the central Renraku system for weeks. It was also another day closer to his retirement and a good pension. Sam was thirty-four years old, already balding and slightly overweight, an American with the elevated coronary risk normal for someone of his age and profession. He divested himself of the jacket of his cut-price, Taiwanese rip-off Italian suit and dumped himself down on the titanium-chrome frame of the ergonomically designed chair in his office. Just another day.

Until midnight.

He was already looking forward to the company limo calling to take him home to his standard-issue, mousy, uninterested wife and two mildly hyperactive brats, with their range of behavioral problems resolutely average for American children of their age, when the brown stuff hit the fan with a vengeance. A real five-alarm frag up.

There was absolutely no warning at all. No IC activation, no alerts from the system's patrol of deckers. One second the system was operating perfectly and the next instant everything was shot to hell. Sam was idly checking some data on a laptop wired into the mainframe when the screen went blank with a soft clicking sound. He cussed and fiddled with the power cable. Then he realized something was seriously wrong. If his planner diary hadn't just crashed along with the rest of the system, he might have noticed his incipient coronary leaping forward a few months.

The blackout lasted fifteen seconds. Before the screen of his laptop flickered back into life he was already out of his chair, through the door and yelling bloody murder down the corridor even as the phones started ringing furiously on his desk. A white-faced technician almost ran smack into him, escaping from the computer labs and running around in a fair impression of beheaded poultry.

"What the frag is going on?" Sam yelled, clutching the man's arm. Any reply beyond the man's initial stammering was drowned out by a chaotic swirl of yells and shouts as Renraku's finest tried to figure out just what the motherrubbing hell had fragging happened to their megabillion-nuyen Matrix systems.

By the time some kind of calm had finally descended again, Sam was back in his office with his heartbeat still an unhealthy 105 and a gaggle of ashen scientists clucking around him. Feedback came mainlining back up on to his laptop and the larger displays in his office. He tried to take in the mass of data streaming into his senses.

"It wasn't a power failure," one of the whitecoats said helpfully.

"Brilliant, that was fragging obvious. That's what the quadruple backup systems are for," Sam snarled. "Frag, we've even got our own generators in the basement and more power stabilizers than you've had therapy sessions with your shrink. Surprise me more: tell me they worked too. Come on, come on. Tell me something I don't know yet!"

Nearly tripping over a wad of printout that cascaded down his legs as he struggled in with it through the half-open door of the office, Dmitar Radev finally arrived, and Sam thought he might at last get a sensible response out of somebody. Sam had a high regard for the Bulgarian, one of the top computer minds at Chiba. The Japanese made the best and cheapest hardware, but they'd never had the minds for programming and decking. Whether the incomers were from Europe, America, or elsewhere, fully seventy per cent of Renraku's best systems analysts and deckers were non-Oriental. The black-haired, fat-fingered, stooping Bulgarian with the vodka-rotted teeth and nicotine-stained hands was maybe the best of them.

"Massive system invasion and shutdown," Radev growled in his fifty-a-day rasp. "Someone got into the core CPU instantly. I mean instantly. No activation response."

"Im-fragging-possible," Sam stuttered.

"Sure. Unfortunately, when you've eliminated the improbable, all you're left with is the impossible. That's what happened. I'm telling you." Radev sat on the edge of Sam's huge desk and demanded some coffee from one of the lackeys.

"What are you telling me? We've spent four billion nuyen upgrading the IC in the last year and some fragger waltzed through it like it wasn't there?"

"You've got it," Radev said flatly, tapping the filter of a cigarette on the teak of the desktop. Sam threw a glance at the No Smoking sign on the nearest window, sighed with feeling and pulled an ashtray out from a desk drawer.

"Thought you gave it up," Radev said laconically, extending the pack to him.

"Picked the wrong time to do that," Sam replied with a grin, sensuously removing a cigarette from the proffered pack and accepting a light from the sweaty, saturnine Bulgarian. Then he had one of the smartest ideas of his life.

"Was this just us?"

Radev shrugged his shoulders as he inhaled, breathing out what was almost a neat smoke ring.

"What the frag does this guy want?"

"I think we may find out before long," Radev said slowly.

"Try Fuchi," Sam said urgently, his demand spraying out to cover his whole team. People started moving fast. "Get on it! I want to know if we're the only ones who got hit. And get me damage reports. And a full update on peripheral status throughout the system. Damn it, get me everything and get it now."

· 1:59 A.M.

It isn't the done thing to deck the frag out of another megacorp's central Matrix systems. It's virtually tantamount to a declaration of corporate war. But there are times when a little skirting around the edges is acceptable, especially if you've got reason to think something very strange is going down.

And when Kryzinski's deckers checked out the Fuchi system, they found proof that something way beyond merely "strange" had gone down. The entirety of the central CPU systems of Fuchi Tokyo had gone AWOL at midnight for exactly fifteen seconds. Having accessed the revealing data, the Renraku team got the hell out of the Fuchi system. The only casualty was a single decker who simply didn't get away from the trace and burn fast enough—a completely acceptable resource loss as far as Sam Kryzinski was concerned. It could be made to look like an accident of some sort. And even if it couldn't, Renraku could afford the few hundred thousand to buy off the guy's wife from making any claim. The data his team brought back told him instantly that the stakes were much higher than that.

"Fuchi?" Sam was incredulous. "At the same time?"

"Not even a millisecond later. Instantly, at midnight," Radev confirmed for him. "Just like us. Now, isn't that interesting?"

"Do we know if they've been decking into our system in return?"

"No, but they will," the Bulgarian said with a harsh grin. "We're on full system alert, of course. But then so were they."

The second hand on the old-fashioned clock across the office clicked one step closer to the hour. Sam had bought it on a trip to England, paying some ridiculous sum for a Victorian grandfather clock that was almost certainly a late twentieth-century forgery worth a fraction of what he'd paid, but the thing's bronze pendulums and its metronomic ticking could be soothing at those times when his stress levels shot through the roof. Hands folded on top of a huge pile of status reports on systems around the globe, Sam sat in reverie for a few seconds as the silver metal swept relentlessly to its zenith. Two A.M.

Tock.

Tock.

Every screen around him went blank.

Gravity switched off for an instant. Sam's heart rate spiked skyward and peaked at over 110. For a terrifying second he thought the chest pains he usually put down to too much caffeine and junk food were going to fulfill their grisly promise early. He was still young enough, and therefore stupid enough, to labor under the illusion of immortality that is the province of the youthfully immature. A sharp stab of pain radiating into his diaphragm gave him an intimation of approaching middle age. Next to him, Radev was jacked into the Excalibur on the desk, his teeth bared and his eyes wide like he was ready for a bloody fight.

God, just get me through this night alive and I'm out of here, Sam prayed. I'll jack out of this damn job and retire with Judith and the kids. Live on a remote Scottish island or in a beach hut in Polynesia, anywhere, just get me through this night still alive. *Please.*

By the time the stabbing pain had dulled and he was reaching for the analgesic shot in the bottom desk drawer, the screens were no longer blank but filled with static. Radev was absolutely still, blood wholly drained from his face. He didn't look quite like he'd seen a ghost. He looked more like he was actually shaking hands with one.

Sam had the flocculated hydrocodeine-methoxymorphine complex into the cannula and into his bloodstream by the time the image appeared on the screen. His pulse had just managed to return to double digits by then. When he looked, open-mouthed, at the extraordinary picture appearing before him, his heart skipped a few beats. The image was less than six centuries old, but it had more than two and a half thousand years of lies and history bound into it, and though he didn't fully understand it or its significance, its presence right here, right now, filled him with fear and dread.

There was a short text message accompanying the image. He didn't bother to take in the contingency clauses. It would all be recorded; he could review the details at his leisure. The part he did notice was the demand.

Twenty billion nuyen to be delivered by midday on the second of May 2057, or else every system Renraku possessed would be wiped and destroyed utterly, rendered completely useless.

Very slowly, hand flat over his heart to reassure himself he was still alive, Sam used his other hand to tap a key on his telecom.

"Get me Yukiano Watanabe," he spluttered in Japanese even before the image of the impassive Japanese secretary deliquesced onto the screen.

"I'm sorry, but Ms. Watanabe is—"

"This is Sam Kryzinski, Coordinator of Chiba Matrix Security," he said, deathly calm. "This has absolute priority. This is a Red-10 crisis. Now get me the lady, or the value of her stock will collapse to zero by morning. If the London Stock Exchange gets hold of this, it might be even earlier. Do it now."

The screen flickered and a holding pattern appeared, an incongruously tasteful and peaceful Oriental garden. Seventeenth century, but Sam wasn't into history at the moment.

Beside him, the Bulgarian had jacked out and his shaking hands were struggling to light another cigarette.

1

The Englishman was surprised to find himself in Chiba. He'd worked for Renraku before, of course—he numbered virtually all the megacorporations among his clients—but it was the first time he'd been obliged to travel from his Manhattan base to talk to a Johnson. Luxury suborbital was what he'd expected, but why did they want him in Chiba? The limo they sent to meet him had the usual darkened windows and armored paneling, even a life-support system built into its formidable carapace. He was met at the airport by four troll samurai, including the chauffeur, and even that seemed excessive. They know something I don't, he told himself.

Though almost thirty, Michael James Sutherland still enjoyed a reputation as one of the finest freelance deckers on the planet. Diplomatic and discreet, he got paid not just for what he could do, but for how he could do it and how he could keep his mouth shut afterward. A tall, blond, elegant man, he levered himself carefully into the passenger compartment of the limo, but it had more to do with an injury to his back than any show of dignity. Two years before Michael had taken a bullet to the spine that just missed paralyzing him for life, and he now had to wear a special corset for support. He'd briefly considered a silver-topped cane to ease the pain of walking. It would, certainly, have enhanced his carefully fostered image and his perfect Saville Row suit, but he'd eventually decided against it as just a little too over the top somehow.

Marveling at the absolute silence of the Phaeton's ride, Michael arrived fifteen minutes later at the door of a restaurant that must surely cost the better part of five million a year in rent just to keep the door open, given Chiba's overcrowding and the prodigiously wasteful use of space within. Each table was cocooned in its own curved-walled partition complete with cunningly designed acoustic shielding and sliding plastic and alloy doors.

I don't know what it costs to eat here, Michael thought, but it must be a few hundred just to draw breath.

"Sam Kryzinski," the balding man said to him as he entered the swishing doors of Space 17. "Coordinator of Matrix Security. Pleased to meet you." The handshake was a little limp and definitely sweaty. Michael put aside his dislike of the man. It wasn't relevant to the matter at hand. Whatever that would turn out to be.

"We have a minor problem," the American began, mopping his brow with a silk square as he perused the menu. Gleaming crystal glasses of absolutely pure water already decorated the crystal-topped, lacquered table. Orchids nestled in tiny, exquisitely decorated ceramic bowls.

"I assume so or else I wouldn't be here," Michael said evenly, sipping at the cool water and casually flipping open the menu. There were no prices. He hadn't expected to find any. If you had to ask, et cetera.

"Best sushi in Japan," Kryzinski informed him. "The seven-spiced seaweeds are something else, too."

"I'll take your advice," the Englishman said smoothly. "Now why don't we have a look at the contract?"

"There's a disclaimer and a confidentiality agreement," the American replied defensively.

Michael gave him a look that verged on the pitying. "If you really needed me to sign those, I wouldn't be here," he pointed out. "You know what I'm going to cost you, more or less. You know what you're getting for your money, more or less. Can we please dispense with the formalities?"

"It'll make me feel better," Kryzinski said fervently.

"If you wish," Michael said with a very slightly affected sigh. Accepting the documents, he plucked a silver fountain pen from his inside jacket pocket, initialed each page with his delicate, calligraphic hand, and signed the last page. Kryzinski was about to take them when Michael jerked the documents out of his grasp with a mildly theatrical gesture.

"Now I've signed them, I think I'll read the small print, old boy," he said mildly. "I've worked for Renraku before and I trust them, but it never hurts to know that one's trust is well placed."

For the first time, the American smiled a little and relaxed slightly. The doors swished quietly open and a Japanese waiter, clothed in incongruous and almost-perfect English butler's attire, silently appeared to deposit a tray of appetizers. Tiny portions, mostly seafood, perfectly arranged and with exactly the right array of microscopic bowls of dips and sauces; three types of chili, ginger, plum, two strengths of soy, and a creamed tarragon for those not wholly reconciled to Oriental tastes. Chilled saki and miniatures of Dom Perignon, with linen squares to swath the corks and silvered stoppers to preserve the aeration for the slower drinker, completed the service.

"I took the liberty of ordering appetizers," Kryzinski mumbled as Michael continued through the small print. The waiter had already vanished.

"Wonderful," Michael replied impassively, ladling a first small portion of bean sprouts and white fish with a smear of ginger and plum onto his plate. He ignored the chopsticks and settled for the silver spoon. If you can't do something well, don't do it at all, he thought. Stuff the chopsticks.

"We've suffered a certain violation of our computer systems," Kryzinski said carefully, watching in fascination as Michael, mouth still and eyes closed, allowed the contrasting textures of the crisp vegetable and soft fish to entice his senses. The sauces were perfect, sharp enough to stimulate the taste buds and smooth enough to warm the throat.

"Um-hum," Michael vocalized through closed lips as he allowed the last of the mouthful to slither down his throat. Whatever the job was, lunch was just fine. He set his spoon back on his plate and reached for the quarter-bottle of champagne. He wrapped the cloth around the cork and twisted the bottle to extract it slowly, with the proficiency of the habitual champagne-drinker. A gentle hiss of escaping carbon dioxide and the biscuity delight of Dom Perignon's bouquet prefaced the pouring of perfection into his fluted glass. He took a first sip of the drink and gave the sigh of the satisfied hedonist appropriately pleasured.

"An intrusion into the second-level CPU here at Chiba," Kryzinski continued. "An instantaneous system crash."

Michael was instantly alert. "For how long?"

"Some fifteen seconds."

"Any warning?"

"Absolutely none."

"I shall need a complete sysmon report."

"The system monitoring was rendered inoperative."

"Really?" Michael was impressed.

"Until the end-state of the crash. We have end-state reports for the systems and all peripherals."

"If there was no warning, you presumably have some end-state data. Did your decker leave any message or demand?"

There was just the slightest hesitation on the American's part. Though sensing it immediately, Michael hid it behind the act of spooning more food onto his plate.

"There's been a monetary demand. There was also an icon left within the system. A signature, if you will. Someone's ego getting oversized," Kryzinski said contemptuously. He handed over a chromalin, glossy and almost wet in appearance. The Englishman's eyes narrowed at the peculiar, strangely familiar image lying on the silk tablecloth before him.

"This is a rum do," he said finally.

"Unfortunately it's the only lead we have," Kryzinski said miserably.

"What?" Michael jerked his head up. "There must be more. Surely you must have gained something from system traces. No one could have gotten into and out of the system and promulgated a CPU crash, even at second level within your system, without *something* more than this."

"It's all we've got," Kryzinski said, an edge of irritation creeping into his voice.

"Fine. That's wonderful," Michael said through gritted teeth. Liar, he thought; you have more than this. You've got to. All those billions and a staff second only to Fuchi and you can't trace a crash? Bull.

His elegant fingers turned over the chromalin, and he gazed intently at the image. The body was naked, hands crossed over the genitals, the right hand gripping the left wrist; a man's body, lean and gaunt. The image was monochrome, and it looked odd, like a photographic negative. Startlingly, atop the body was the image of a face that was not in negative, or so it appeared at first sight. Then Michael realized that the oddly smiling face gazing out at him was that of a black woman. She seemed to have some kind of headdress or crown, and there were dark streaks on the forehead. Likewise, there were dark streaks, droplets, on wrists and feet and what appeared to be a ragged tear on one side of the chest of the torso, low down and near the hip bones.

"You must already have some data on this," he said.

"Not much. The crash was only twenty-four hours ago."

"Then give me what you have so far."

Kryzinski hesitated. "We want you to work up a report on what you can ascertain from it," he said slowly.

"Don't play games," Michael said angrily.

"I'm not," Kryzinski shot back. "It's simply that I have to be able to demonstrate to certain other parties that you have the investigative skills that are vouched for elsewhere in the company. Please bear with me. And I'm sure I don't need to remind you not to show this to anyone."

It sounded weak, but Michael was intrigued. His reputation was good with Renraku. They'd paid him nearly three and a half million nuyen over the last four years, and if someone was suddenly having doubts, it had to be up there at the highest levels. That told him he wasn't being given everything the corp knew, and that didn't mean just about the iconic image he was staring at. Second-level CPU systems? Maybe. Maybe not. I'm out of here to do some checking on my employer, he thought.

"Do we have a time limit?"

"The demand for payment specified the second of May," Kryzinski told him. "We need whatever you can get as fast as possible."

"Well, then, bugger lunch," Michael said amiably. "I'm sure they'll put it in a doggie bag for me. I'll eat on the hoof." He was about to get up from the table when he realized there was still a glass worth of champagne remaining. He fastened the silver stopper over the neck of the bottle and slipped it into his pocket, and then deposited the chromalin into his briefcase.

"I'll arrange it," Kryzinski said at once.

He's glad to see the back of me, Michael thought. This is a man under extreme duress. How interesting.

"Oh, and the advance on expenses, please. If you

would be so kind," Michael said smoothly as he carefully flicked some imaginary crumbs from his lap as he stood up. The American reached into his briefcase and handed over the credstick without a word.

"Ivory-handled, now that is tasteful," Michael said appreciatively. "I shall run out of pockets to store your largesse, Mr. Kryzinski." With the boyish smile that still somehow disarmed any irritation people might sometimes feel toward him, Michael Sutherland turned on his Italian-shoed heel and headed for the exit.

Within thirty minutes, he'd checked into a coffin hotel and slipped the seemingly featureless gray disk into the vidphone, canceling the vidlink and scrambling the signal and its origin hopelessly.

If Renraku tries to trace this, he thought with a grin, the decaying Strontium-90-based random switches will tell them I'm in Bogota one instant and Johannesburg a millionth of a second later. And while I was calling my Aunt Agatha in Peru to start with, it was my financial adviser in St. Petersburg that same split-second afterward.

The signal engaged and he heard the familiar rich Welsh voice of an old acquaintance, a member of the British House of Nobles; a politically powerful man, and one with financial interests pretty much everywhere in the world.

"Geraint, hello," Michael said affably. "How's Laura?"

"I have no idea. Don't you mean Dinah?"

"I can't keep up with your affairs," Michael lamented. "Look, I think I'm into something extremely interesting. Crashed Matrix systems. Big-time. I think we should talk."

"Where are you now?" The voice had just an edge of concern to it.

"Don't worry," Michael reassured his friend. "In Chiba right now, but I'll be back in Manhattan before you can say, 'Renraku hired me'. I'll call you from there. Oh," he added as if in afterthought, turning the chromalin over in his fingers, "Do we know someone who knows weird drek?"

"What type of weird drek, exactly, did 'we' have in mind?"

"Occult stuff. Obscure religious, hermetic. Who can we trust?"

"Well, there's Serrin," Geraint, otherwise known as Lord Llanfrechfa. "Of course. Where is he?"

"Just emerging from wintering in a castle I own in Shetland," Geraint told him. "With his wife."

"Ah, yes," Michael said, chuckling gently. "My own ex, I do recall. That was a most peculiar business. Still, it all got sorted out in the end."

"I don't think I wish to know the intimate details," Geraint said dryly. "Anyway, that's enough for now. Call me when you get back. No, leave it until tomorrow. It's the early hours of the morning here, you troublesome wretch."

"I'll leave you to get back to Dinah. Another blond, I presume?" Michael cut the connection before the Welshman could hurl an insult of his own. Grinning, pocketing the quantum scrambler, he called for a cab and began to make plans.

Money's good, he thought. When I get back I'll dial up that code Kryzinski gave me and collect the hundred thou deposit. They're buying me for the next couple of weeks, almost, and I'm worth it.

But it's a lot upfront.

Second-level CPUs?

Yeah, right.

2

Michael's body protested at the alarm call. Two suborbitals in a day were too much provocation for flesh that still had to cope with the effects of a long-term injury, and a sharp stab of pain in his lower back made him wince. He lay quite still for a few seconds and then negotiated his way off the futon, slipping off sideways and getting upright gingerly and with no little care. He rubbed his eyes, scratched at his disordered hair and took a long gulp from the steely mineral water with the chunk of fresh lime on the bedside table. The bitterness of the citrus made him shake his head like a dog emerging from a river, and he headed for the bathroom and the pleasant ritual of the morning shave.

The smart frames he'd set to work upon returning to New York had disgorged their usual mass of data. The icon left for Renraku had been matched very swiftly, and a two-version printout, one with keywords and a short summary and the other a lengthy document with references and appendices, were awaiting his attention. He picked up the précis as he waited for the squeezer to mangle the oranges and deliver his breakfast.

The torso was the Shroud of Turin, the summary told him. Allegedly the shroud that covered the body of Christ in Joseph's tomb, it had been established as a fake late last century by radiocarbon dating, which had placed the date of the cloth as somewhere between 700 and 850 years of age. The précis directed him to a technical detail regarding three-dimensional image-depth data in the longer printout.

Hmmm, he mused. I thought I recognized it, vaguely. There was a heap of controversy about it sixty, seventy years ago, but ever since the scientists had proved incontrovertibly that the Shroud was a fake, it had lapsed into obscurity. Yet the image was still compelling and powerful, even to a man with no devotion to the absurdities of religion.

By the time the orange juice was drained, leaving only an untidy tide-mark of fruit flesh lingering around the edges of the glass, Michael had found the referenced detail and was frowning over it.

There is an estimated discontinuity in image depth relating to the body and head, the text read. *Image integrity is not sufficient for further analysis.*

Well, big deal, he thought. The head is obviously a separate image anyway, and the whole damn thing is a collage. So what if there's different image depth on the head and body? At the back of his mind, though, was a vague apprehension, a feeling that he knew something intuitively that stubbornly refused to rise into his conscious mind. Then he spotted two key words lower down the page.

Mona Lisa.

The image of the face is a transformed image based on

the template of the Mona Lisa, painted by Leonardo da Vinci, the text stated simply.

He extracted the chromalin from the scanning peripherals and studied it closely. It was by no means apparent to him. But the familiar, indeed over-familiar, image of the Mona Lisa was so well-known in its normal form that his brain refused to perceive the same face as a photographic negative, which was how the black woman's face appeared. The confusion was even greater given that the image of the man's body was itself rendered in a photographic negative, just as Shroudman had been by his creator.

Then he jolted back for an instant. Wait a minute. How do I know this is the face of a black woman? If this face is in negative, like the torso, it would be the face of a white woman, wouldn't it? Yet I *know* that she's black. How do I know that?

He looked again at the impassive smile and for a moment indulged a flight of fancy, musing over how many millions of men had fantasized and wondered about the Mona Lisa's enigmatic almost-smile. Dissatisfied with himself, he replaced the chromalin and keyed in instructions for enlargements, enhancements, and various image transformations. While the system began its work, he made a swift decision and initiated some archival work by his frames.

Crossref Shroud/Leonardo, he instructed. It took the intelligent analytical program barely five seconds to flash the answer up on the screen.

One theory of the creation of the Shroud is that it was manufactured by Leonardo da Vinci in the first half of the 1490s at the probable behest of Pope Innocent VII. The process of manufacture employed a primitive, quasi-photographic technique using the principle of the camera obscura and light-sensitive pigments available to Leonardo at the time. Recreations of the suggested technique by British and South African researchers have been regarded by critical authorities as lending support to this theory, initially suggested in 1994. Consult the following references . . .

Michael skipped the listing that followed. So I have a decker with a Leonardo fixation, he thought. Well, he's

only the latest in a very long line. There must be more viruses named after da Vinci than anyone or anything else,
and I've lost track of the number of deckers I've seen
masquerading as him in the Matrix.

One final hunch made him key in a final query.

Crossref 2 May/Leonardo da Vinci.

Leonardo da Vinci died on 2 May 1518.

Well, there we are, he thought with a grin. Now, let's
get the frames to work on every Leonardo-wannabee documented by sysops, deckers, and corporate sources in the
last five years. Then we can start sorting the wheat from
the chaff and offer Renraku a list of possibles. They almost certainly have the same list themselves by now, or
will have shortly. This is elementary stuff, but I have to
jump through the right hoops to get to the next stage and
some serious money.

His thoughts turned to more difficult tasks. The next
step was to jack into the Renraku system and find out exactly how much damage had been done to them. There
was an element of real cat-and-mouse about this; he
guessed that Renraku might well expect him to do precisely this. What he didn't know was whether they would
treat his intrusion as acceptable—and evidence of his
skill and ability to define his own goals for himself—or
whether they'd be seriously slotted off.

Well, stuff it, he thought. I'm going to get right down
deep into their data stores and see just how heavy this
drek is. And I'm going to need some help.

He called the London number. Within an hour, he had
a reservation for another suborbital flight, and his body
was already groaning at the prospect.

Big Ben was chiming ten when the limo delivered Michael to the House of Nobles in the Westminster District
of London. He stepped out of one limo and straight into
another, this one upholstered with ermine-trimmed crimson silk and satin, and with the crest of His Majesty on
all available surfaces, or so it appeared.

He gave his friend a grin. "How's tricks at the Foreign
Office?"

"Much as usual," Geraint said laconically. "The wars
are small and the sterling deposits are stable, and the
French aren't any more or any less a pain in the rear than

they are all the time." He sank back into his seat, wrapping his luxurious Burberry coat around him as if warding off the cold. He looked tired, and had the beginning of gray circles beneath his eyes.

"Thank you for your help," Michael said ingratiatingly.

"I haven't actually agreed to help," Geraint pointed out. "I'm just putting you up for the night, as I recall."

"I think you'll be rather intrigued by the whole thing," Michael coaxed.

"Sounds like a crock to me," Geraint said in a rare lapse from King's English. "Some barmy nutter with a Leonardo obsession."

"A nutter with a Leonardo obsession who managed to paralyze Renraku's CPU cores twice inside two hours," Michael said as if it were of no more consequence than the usual British observations about the weather. Geraint startled, his sharp eyes turned on to Michael like those of a predatory sea eagle from one of his own estates.

"Did I hear that correctly?"

"You did," Michael said. "I rather thought the details might be of some interest to you, given your business connections. Of course, I trust you to treat what I tell you with absolute discretion." He didn't wait for the deprecatory hand gesture with which Geraint reassured him. "But given your many business concerns, which even I am hard-pressed to keep track of, I thought it would be only fair to let an old friend in on the secrets."

The Welshman grinned and let out a low, ironic chuckle.

"You cunning bastard," he said approvingly. "You always were a manipulative devil."

"I took lessons from observing you," Michael responded coolly.

"So you want some help in return for letting me in on the deal," Geraint mused. "Sounds fair enough. Actually, it'll be a relief. Life's been as dull as ditchwater here lately. Manchester's been away touring the colonies, I mean the Commonwealth Nations, for what seems like forever, and absolutely nothing of any consequence has turned up during his absence. It's been just the usual round of endless paperwork."

Michael had not met the legendarily crusty Earl of Manchester, Geraint's superior at the Foreign Office, but from Geraint's descriptions of him the man's absence wasn't cause for any great sense of loss. He looked down at the faded, scratched red box briefcase that Geraint's chauffeur had lugged into the back of the Phaeton and considered that it could probably hold a very great deal of paperwork indeed, and said so.

"You'd think they could buy you a new one sometime," he said.

"What?" Geraint sounded almost shocked. "This has been the property of the unfortunate junior minister in my position for the best part of seventy years. It's tradition, how can you say such a thing?"

"A more modern and comfortable one might not hold quite so much paperwork," Michael observed dryly.

"Well, I think I'll let Jenkins do it," Geraint said dryly. "Little bugger needs some drudgework to keep him quiet. Naked ambition in an underling is such a lack of style, don't you think?"

They laughed gently. The limo prowled its way toward the heart of Mayfair.

"This is very beautiful," Michael said approvingly.

He was being honest. The Mayfair apartment must have cost several million to decorate and yet the total effect was modest and self-effacing in its classic simplicity. After years in New York, Michael found the contrast striking. Geraint said nothing, just shrugged off his coat and switched on the OC player. As he headed, almost in the same movement, for the huge kitchen, the first few quiet voices filled the spacious room and the polyphony began to spiral around the first phrase.

Magnificat anima mea Dominum, my spirit doth magnify the Lord . . .

Michael sat down wearily in the plushly upholstered sofa and let the timeless music build slowly around him, waiting for the exultant *in Deo salutari meo* of the introduction. He closed his eyes and smiled, peaceful and quiet.

He had just re-opened his eyes and was taking in some of the fine art on the walls by the time Geraint reappeared with a silver tray and coffee service.

"This is very good," Geraint said as he poured the fragrant brew into the perfect porcelain cups. "Jamaican blue mountain. Costs the earth and they don't produce much of it these days after that damn hurricane two years ago."

"Always wanted to visit Jamaica," Michael mused.

"I wouldn't," Geraint said sharply. "Murder rate ten times higher than New Orleans and an average life expectancy of thirty-four for indigenous males. Go to the Leewards or the Windwards if you want a Caribbean holiday."

"It isn't exactly a pressing concern right now," Michael said with a smile as he lifted the cup to his lips. "Crikey, you're right. This *is* good."

"Well, here we are," Geraint said. "Enough of that to get us through the night and I have nearly sixty opticals of Palestrina and Josquin, which should keep you happy."

"Thank you," Michael said again. The Welshman had an excellent memory for the likes and tastes of others and was an unfailingly generous host. "What about Dinah?"

"In Paris for another collection," Geraint said slightly dismissively. "She's a fashion writer." His tone said one of them was probably a fashion accessory for the other; more likely both were. Michael did not press the point further.

"And Serrin?"

"I'm hoping he'll be here tomorrow," Geraint said. "The weather's appalling on Lewis, but the forecast for tomorrow is better and he should be able to fly down. I thought we could have dinner here."

"Sounds good to me," Michael replied. "I may be sending him off on a wild goose chase, but I've got a whole caseful of arcane drek and he might be able to give me enough leads to come up with a psychological profile of our nutter. Our very talented nutter, I should probably add."

Geraint smiled and sank an ivory-handled knife into the blue-veined Stilton cheese, extracting sufficient crumbly chunks to liberally coat one of the thin wafers just before the *Magnificat* reached its final *Amen.* There were a few moments of silence before the Kyrie of the following Mass rose gently from the small but powerful speakers secreted around the room.

"Port?" Suddenly Geraint's look was different. There was an element of mischief on his angular, handsome face, a look that said, in effect, "I haven't seen you in years. We may have work to do, and time may be pressing, and these may be very elegant surroundings, but we're going to get smashed anyway, horribly hog-whimperingly smashed." There was also the undercurrent of *That way you'll tell me everything I might be interested in.*

"Which vintages are you currently recommending?"

"I thought we might start with the 2002 and work our way forward, although we could always start with the agreeably nutty 2033 tawny and work backward," Geraint suggested.

Michael bit into the cheese-smeared cracker, wiped a crumb from the side of his mouth, and smiled back at his host. "Mix them all in a bucket and bring me a plastic straw," he said.

"Peasant," His Lordship laughed and set off for the mahogany cabinets on the far side of the apartment, "So, tell me what happened to Renraku."

Michael waited for Geraint to return with the first bottle, the lead-foiled cork crusted into the neck, before giving him a copy of the chromalin.

"What the frag is this?" Geraint said.

"That's our nutter's signature. Now I'll tell you what Renraku said he did, and then we should consider how we're going to go about finding out what he *actually* did." Michael got up and unlocked the first of the small steel cases he'd brought in with his suitcase. Geraint's eyes widened at what he saw when Michael threw back the lid.

"Very, very nice," he said approvingly.

"Modular Fairlight," Michael said. The cyberdeck was worth well over a million nuyen, and it had taken him some months to modify it to accept the vicissitudes of travel. The cases had traveled on their own first-class seat during the flight. The idea of putting them in a cargo hold simply never entered his head.

"It'll take me an hour or so to set up," Michael said. "Then we should go a-prowling."

"Oh, thank you so very much," Geraint said dryly. "So that your work can be traced from here. What an ungrateful guest I have."

"Come on, you know me better than that," Michael

said swiftly. "We'll be operating from a different location every thousandth of a second, unless there's someone specific you'd like to be nasty to, so that I can leave a traceable signal from their location instead."

"Now that is tempting," Geraint said with a clear intake of breath. "Perhaps young Jenkins . . ."

Michael laughed, the cork was drawn, and the deck components began to take shape on the teak table while the light port was decanted and left to stand for a while. The Englishman and Welshman began to talk, of old times, college days, drunken sorties, shared acquaintances, and all the things friends say when they haven't seen each other in many years.

Midnight approached. Outside, in a car bearing diplomatic plates and therefore not subject to the irksome parking restrictions of the ultra-exclusive neighborhood, an Italian took his first sip from a flask of a coffee far humbler than that his Lordship could offer, and settled back to keep an eye on the place. He was understandably nervous, as all in his organization were tonight, and he didn't know what to expect.

He certainly wasn't expecting to be shot by the Inquisition before the week was out, but then, as any Englishman with a sense of humor and history could have told him, nobody ever expects the Inquisition.

3

"Very, very nice," Geraint said again. "Can't get these on any market I know of."

"Cute, isn't it? I got the personamorph program from certain corporate contacts. Lets us slip into their sculpted system and become an absolutely integral part of it," Michael said as he worked to complete the cyberdeck coupling. It wasn't easy connecting his Fairlight to Geraint's humble Fuchi Cyber-7, and there would be delays in communication, but it was a far better option than his friend just jacking in for the ride.

"I think that's done," he said finally, standing back to admire his handiwork. "Now for the monitors. Green lead on the datajack, blue lead over your heart, old man."

"What are these for?" Geraint said, somewhat apprehensively.

"Cardiomonitors. We're headed into IC thick and deep enough to sink a whole flotilla of Titanics, and if you get zapped by bad black stuff this will jack you out before your brain can fry or the T'n'B rips your heart out of your chest," Michael replied with bloodthirsty relish. "Saved my skin a couple of times."

"I'm not really sure I should have let myself in for this," Geraint said disapprovingly. "Good job we kept the port down to two glasses."

"We'll finish the bottles later," Michael replied, settling himself down in the Chippendale chair and flexing his arms.

"Let's get down to it. Hello, Chiba."

"What the frag is this?" Geraint said unenthusiastically. "What a ghastly, tacky pinstripe suit you have there."

Michael checked out his own persona, the icon that let him navigate the Matrix even as his own meat body sat jacked into his deck. He looked rather like a cheap gangster from a bad black-and-white trid from way back, the kind where the main character calls everybody 'Blue eyes' or 'Sweetheart'.

"We appear to be someplace like Nebraska," Geraint said disapprovingly. "That is, somewhere entirely devoid of interest or value."

Michael peered up the long gray road ahead of them. "This is more fascinating than it seems," he mused. "We're not even into their system yet and there's a radiating sculpted effect. This shouldn't happen. Renraku's been doing some very interesting things."

"Never mind the interesting things they've been doing, let's find out about the interesting things someone's been doing to them," Geraint retorted, adjusting his fedora and setting off down the highway. There was a roadblock before them, a gaggle of 1930s black American autos and a group of policemen awaiting them at the system access node.

"Since when has Renraku sculpted their system to look like an old gangster movie?" Geraint whispered.

"Since now," Michael replied. "This must be a direct response to the system invasion."

"A bit tacky, if you ask me," Geraint said. "Oh, well, get that sleaze program working." They advanced on the police squad.

"Ain't nobody goin' up that road without authorization, bud," the barrier program instructed. Michael put a hand into his pants pocket with exaggerated slowness, so as not to activate any alert IC, and flourished a badge with the symbol of Chicago's finest on it.

"Authorization from the mayor himself, Mac," he said, palming it again swiftly. The policeman looked a little dubious and then waved them past the platoon of armed goons standing behind him.

"That was easy," Michael chuckled as they headed down the road and on to the dataline junctions.

"Great when we have to go back and get past that attack IC," Geraint said plaintively. The goons had been carrying disagreeably large heavy machine guns. Renraku had gotten heavy since the system invasion.

"Not to worry," Michael smiled. "We'll be leaving in an armored car, old boy."

They sidled into the outskirts of town, and down the narrow road saw a series of fortified buildings.

"The bank, I would think," Michael said. "Time to send off a browsing probe." He opened his violin case and a slightly mangy pigeon circled out into the skies above, coming briefly to rest on a distant roof, then hopping from one to the next. From one of the buildings in the middle distance, a sheriff emerged, wearing his badge of office and wielding a machine gun that made the weapons of the SAN IC look like popguns.

"System decker," Michael said dismissively. His armor program, and that of Geraint, had already equipped them with bulletproof jackets, and the Englishman had other surprises in store for the Renraku decker prowling the system. What worried him was whether this was just a random appearance, or whether the system was already alerted to their presence, and how long it would take the decker to alert it now.

As the sheriff leveled his weapon to fire, smoke exploded around him and a harmless burst of gunfire chattered off somewhere into the skies as the two intruders ran down the other side of the street to the bank. The stumbling figure barely emerged before they'd shot the locks off the bank doors, and above him the pigeon had already been replaced by Geraint's eagle, a scanner program searching for reinforcements. Michael's smart frame had already given the sheriff something else to worry about as they ran into the building.

"Hold it right there, lawman," the frame-persona drawled, "or your guts will have more holes than a Swiss cheese."

"Love it," Michael grinned as he activated the evaluate program and switched to sensor mode. Geraint covered his back, gun leveled at the swinging bank doorway. "Now, Tracey my dear, crack that code," Michael said.

The second smart frame got to work on the encrypted barrier, decoding and analyzing, Michael desperate to get at the data in the vaults. He got through just as the evaluate program gave him the final feedback.

"Bugger, it's not here," he growled. "We're going to have to wait for the dove to fly back. Well, let's face it—it would have been too easy to find it here."

Obligingly, the bird flew back into the room, as a confused system decker exchanged attacks with a smart frame in the road outside.

"I think I hear sirens," Geraint said anxiously.

"Bollocks," Michael said flatly as he took the tourist map from the bird's beak. "Down the high street and make for the travel agency. Travel agency? I like that! Very eccentric humor. They must have an Englishman on the programming staff."

"Not that I know of," Geraint said. "Listen, there *are* sirens."

"So there are, old man. Well, let's get moving. The back door, I think."

They got out of the datastore and raced down the side road, into the commercial district. Cars sped along the highway, data packets headed along the vast freeway of Renraku's innermost computer systems.

"Look, never mind subtlety," Michael said, extracting a grenade from his case and lobbing it at the doors of the travel agency. "No more sleazing. Let's just frag everything that moves."

"Sometime I wonder whether you haven't been living in America too long," Geraint muttered, keeping his gun leveled at their backs. The doors blew off the building in a splendidly agreeable cloud of dust and debris. Michael was already halfway into the place.

"Find it, find it!" he urged on his evaluate program. The customized program, specifically instructed to search for data on system intrusions, was already scurrying to the locked cupboards. It took the form of a rat in the sculpted system. Halting before one securely fastened cupboard in the distance, the rat raised up on its hind legs, sniffed, and twitched its whiskers.

Michael pried the lock off the door, and began shoveling files into his voluminous case. The first gunshots began to splinter the windows.

"Get to the fragging back door!" Geraint urged as he let off a flurry of his own shots at the advancing figures just visible outside. "The armor won't last forever." He scooped up a last handful of files as they blew their way out the back door and found themselves in an alleyway.

"Whoops," Geraint said as he looked at the cul-de-sac. A platoon of police were running at them from the far end.

"This program cost me half a million nuyen and it had better bloody well work," Michael muttered grimly as he yanked open the doors of the mechanic's shop opposite and raced into the gloom. He opened the door of the vehicle and started the ignition. Geraint had already flung himself into the passenger seat and flattened himself as close to the floor as he could. The armored car advanced into the street, performed a tire-screeching ninety-degree turn and raced toward the policemen. It scattered them far and wide, sprays of bullets bouncing off its armor as Michael raced the thing toward the outskirts of town again. Then, extraordinarily, he stopped and opened the driver's door. A policeman was approaching from the side of the road.

"What the hell—"

"Trojan horse, old man," Michael said as he handed over his case to the smart frame. "They almost certainly have special locks on data loss, and we may have trouble getting out with the data not ending up degraded. But Simon here won't have any problems."

"Simon?"

"Give them names, helps me remember what does what. Simple Simon—simple to get data out with."

"Doesn't make any sense to me," said the mystified Geraint.

"Doesn't have to, it only needs to make sense to me," Michael pointed out. "Now we have a roadblock to get past and, by the sound of it, half of Renraku's best are on our tails." The sirens got louder behind them.

"Now, let's go knock down that barrier!"

"Well, it wasn't traceable of course," Radev said consolingly as he lit another of his endless chain of cigarettes. "But then we wouldn't expect it to be. If it had been, we'd have been very disappointed. After all, we do pay him to get into other people's systems without being traced, so at least we know he does what he does for us rather well."

"Fine," Kryzinski growled. "And the data?"

"The data in the proximity of the invading personas was transformed by the morphic encrypters at one hundred percent efficiency," Radev smiled. "He will learn that what we told him was almost correct. If it had matched exactly he'd have been suspicious, of course. Now he'll think we had a slightly more serious system invasion than we told him we had, and we won't have to worry about being compromised by our own operative."

"Good." Sam sighed happily. "He's good, we're good, everything's just fraggin' hunky dory. Apart from twenty billion nuyen or you can all expect to wear brown pants for a fortnight."

"We'll have to see Sutherland's initial report," the Bulgarian replied. "It should conform to the initial assessment we have and then we can proceed from there."

Kryzinski yawned and looked at the clock. He resented having to work beyond his normal shift to be on hand when Sutherland's anticipated system intrusion occurred.

"I'm going home to get some sleep," he sighed. "That's enough excitement for one day."

"Our bosses will be pleased," Radev said consolingly, giving him a nicotine-stained smile.

"They'd fragging better be!" Kryzinski said fervently.

Michael keyed in the final instructions for the frame-analyzers and sat back triumphantly. Getting out of the system had been easier than he'd expected. The tar pit program that had nearly trapped their car had been the least he'd expected and the attack utilities barking gunfire at the roadblock had been almost disappointingly easy to fend off. Now it was five in the morning and dawn was still an unfulfilled promise. Fresh coffee was just arriving, and gleaming dark bottles of port seemed to be making suggestive invitations to him from the table opposite, but after two days of slotting around with his body clocks, certain minor visual hallucinations were entirely acceptable. Geraint, having already used some minor booster or stabilizer through the cannula implant in his neck, took a shot of something psychoactive to prevent that happening, but Michael preferred a less direct route. Caffeine and alcohol into the gut would do fine, and he lit one of Geraint's gold-banded cigarettes to add to the cocktail.

"They never saw it. What a bunch of dodos!" he smirked.

"Don't get arrogant," Geraint warned. "Wait to see what the discrepancies are. Don't celebrate the data haul until you've seen it."

"What we came out with was vanilla," Michael protested. "What the Trojan horse will come out with is—"

Text was already filling the thirty-inch auxiliary screen. It scrolled through the initial sections of the inhouse Renraku evaluations in synchrony with the accelerated lasprint output until Michael keyed the screen to hold. He read fast. The blood drained from his face.

"Holy Mother of God!" he croaked, his hands grasping the edge of the table as if it were the edge of a cliff and he was about to fall off. "Look at this."

Geraint leant over his shoulder, taking in the formal, emotionless language of the Renraku summarizer.

Total system invasion and collapse has been evaluated from corporate core systems with the following probabilities: Renraku, 100% known and evaluated; Fuchi, 100%

*with no error; Shiawase, 99% with error estimate +/–
1%; Saeder-Krupp, 99% +/– 1% ...*

"Total system invasion and collapse?" Michael said disbelievingly. "The whole enchilada? *Everything?*"

"Look at that," Geraint said, his finger tracing down the
rows on the screen. "They were instantaneous. Right on the
stroke of 00:00, Chiba time, and again two hours later. Boy,
that takes some doing to go back two hours later when the
corps must have had everything cranked way beyond max-
imum alert. Impressive."

"Someone invaded and collapsed every single
megacorp at the same instant?" Michael cried out, hands
falling into his lap as he leaned back in his chair. "No
way. Utterly, absolutely no sodding way!"

"It appears to have happened, however," Geraint
pointed out.

Michael was already scrabbling through the printout.
"Nothing here on the guy leaving the same icon anywhere else, and nothing on what he wants," he complained.

"There is for Renraku," Geraint observed. "He wants
twenty billion."

"Twenty *billion*?" Michael almost leapt from his chair.
Then his voice became slightly manic and humorous.
"Well, I mean, why not? Might as well ask for a fur coat
for the missus and a bike for the kiddie while you're at
it."

"If he can crash every Matrix system on the globe at
the same instant, twenty billion is probably about the going rate," Geraint said thoughtfully.

"He? There must be a whole flock of them," Michael
said. "Working together, one at each system. There's a
whole gang of these people out there."

"Now that *is* impossible," Geraint replied. "Are there
eight or so people in the whole world capable of doing
this?"

"No," Michael said, suddenly brought back to earth.
"No, there cannot be eight megageniuses sprung from nowhere to conduct such an operation. But how one decker
could do it ..."

"Look at what you do with frames," Geraint said.

Michael shook his head. "Couldn't do this with a frame."

"Couldn't do this at all." Geraint chuckled. "Let's face it. Whoever did this could construct frames to act synchronously with his own handiwork."

"How the hell am I ever going to find this guy? I had no idea. This isn't anyone known in the community," Michael lamented. "No way I can trace him."

"Indeed," Geraint said. "Well, old boy, looks like you're just a has-been now. This guy could have you for breakfast."

Michael bristled. "I'm not ready for a bath-chair yet," he said slightly feebly.

"You couldn't do this, though, could you?" Geraint said impishly, looking through some of the printout himself.

"Maybe not." Michael's voice had a definite edge.

"What do you reckon Renraku would pay you if you found out who this was in time?"

"Well, considering that I'd be saving them twenty billion . . ."

Geraint laughed appreciatively. "I'd say it would certainly be enough to keep you in appalling luxury for the rest of your indulgent life, at a conservative estimate."

"Yes, well . . ." Michael began in a suddenly perceptive tone of voice. "That's all very well—but why are you so keen?"

"Why do people climb Everest?"

"Because they're fragging idiots who ought to stay home and enjoy a comfortable existence instead!"

"No, laddie." Geraint wagged an admonishing finger at him. "Because it's there. This rather interests me, I must say. I need hardly point out that I've got a lot invested in various corporate interests around the world, and if this chap crashes everything on the planet, things could get a little ugly. And as it happens, I've grown rather fond of the creature comforts you so rightly appreciate yourself.

"One more glass and then I think we should get some sleep," the nobleman suggested. "We're going to have a lot of work to do tomorrow." His attention was finally caught by the winking light on his telecom, and he poured himself a last glass of tawny port on the way to pick up the message.

"And Serrin will be with us by teatime, if we can manage to wake up by then," Geraint said with a smile when he came back. "Dinner tomorrow will be even more interesting than I'd planned."

4

"I've just realized that we only have nine days," Michael said glumly. He sat looking out over the quiet London street, absently noting the handful of overdressed and over-wealthy socialites and their attendant lackeys staggering down the sidewalk with bags filled with the fruits of overindulgent shopping expeditions. In his hands was a copious listing of every documented decker with a Leonardo-fixation from the last twenty years. He'd decided that going back five might not be enough, but that hadn't helped much. Scanning the names and data told him what he expected: they were mediocrities, trying to puff up inadequate self-esteem by taking on the mantle of the genius, rather like suburban housewives convinced by some two-bit charlatan hypnotist and conman that they'd been Cleopatra or Catherine the Great in a previous life.

"Time to put a call through to Renraku Chiba, I think," he sighed, parking himself in front of his Fairlight. Geraint was musing over some stock transactions coming through from Hong Kong, his first cigarette of a hungover day spiraling blue smoke into the air next to him.

"You really should give that up." Michael waved an ostentatiously offended hand to dissipate the smoke. "You smoke far more than I do."

"Yes, I know, but I've had gene therapy to boost the enzymes that degrade all the tar residues," Geraint said cheerfully, "so it's no big deal. You lose more brain cells from one bottle of wine than I will from a year of these. Planning to stop drinking, were you?"

"The way I feel this afternoon, it had crossed my mind, yes, actually," Michael grumbled. "I'd forgotten how much you drink."

"Ha! Had to twist your arm, did I?" Geraint retorted

snappily. "You drink the best part of a thousand quid's worth of superb port and then whine about it. Have you no gratitude, sir?"

Michael laughed, poured another cup of coffee and made the link. Within five minutes he was preparing to jack in to examine the image that had been downloaded to him.

"I'm not sure I want that traced here—" Geraint began before Michael's frown stopped him in his tracks.

"This has been rerouted through just about everywhere on the planet, and no way can it be traced. Come on, lay off that stuff; you know how I operate. Renraku sent it to a holding bureau in Florence anyway, I've just acquired it from there. Now, let's have a look around this thing in full 3D. Want to come along for the ride?"

"Don't mind if I do," Geraint said, reaching out to plug into the hitcher jack.

The image inside the Fairlight's datastore was still haunting, despite the verdict of history and science. Shroudman stood upright, the image appearing to rotate as they shifted their viewpoint, the enigmatic woman's head and face making the icon more eerie than ever.

"There's a join down the middle," Geraint observed.

"Sort of. The original image was a couple of inches taller at the back than at the front. The haziness must be down to that. It's generally thought that the front and back were created from different torsos," Michael informed him. "The head—there's something different. There's a different degree of precision about it, the image is clearer and sharper. Well, anyway, that's our one clue. Let's let the systems get on with image analysis and the frames with their archival research. Hey, we have an incoming flight to meet, don't we?"

"I'll see to that," Geraint said. "I've already made arrangements with the caterers for dinner. They won't be here for an hour or so. I thought I could leave you to this while I go and pick them up."

"What's Serrin doing these days?" Serrin Shamander had been a rootless wanderer the whole time Michael had known him, and to have settled quietly on the inhospitable, stormy west coast of Scotland with a young Azanian wife didn't fit Michael's image of the man, but Geraint had known him for far longer.

"Not a lot," Geraint said. "Resting, mostly. He's rather quiet and we don't really see much of each other, to tell you the truth."

There was a diffidence in Geraint's voice that told Michael he wasn't hearing the whole story. There was apparently some distance, some barrier, between the Welshman and the American mage.

"So he just holed up in your castle for the winter. Nice place to be."

"It's hardly a castle," Geraint protested. "Just a fortified manorial house. It's very quiet and, as I say, they seem to like being alone."

"Rather a rum do that a girl from Cape Town likes the Scottish winter," Michael mused. "Seventy all year round and lots of sunshine and then transplanted to the Hebrides. I wouldn't have thought she'd be happy there."

"Cape Town gets enough rain," Geraint smiled. "Much the same on that count. Anyway, she's there because of him. They're actually very happy together, so far as I can see. Nice to see her happily settled with her second husband."

He laughed and grinned at his guest. "What on earth did happen with all that business? What were you thinking of?" Michael had never given him the full story of his exploits with Serrin, Kristen, and the others in Azania two years before, when they'd been exploring a trail of clues that led them to Germany and an elven nosferatu with the modest aim of wiping humanity off the face of the Earth and leaving it for his own race to inherit.

"Well, it was the only way to get her out of the country," Michael said. "To be honest, it was obvious she was devoted to him. I thought it would ruin it if I suggested that Serrin marry her, given that he's such a tortured soul and everything, so I did the decent thing. I did take precautions, though. Got her to sign a contract agreeing not to make any claim on me after we were divorced in glorious Sun City."

"Nothing like safe sex," Geraint observed wryly. "So you did it purely out of the goodness of your heart, then?"

"Um, well, yes, actually," Michael said, almost shamefaced.

Geraint looked full at him for a few moments and then

laughed aloud, stubbing out his cigarette. "Hardly something to be ashamed of, old man. Unless things have taken a real turn for the worse, I think they really and truly are a happy ending and the world doesn't have too many of those."

"Anyway, how did the chaps at Renraku respond to your little request?"

"They didn't bat an eye," Michael smiled. "All part of the chess game. They know I busted into their system. I'm sure they expected it and didn't give us as hard a time as we'd have had otherwise. They know I know it. We all keep quiet about it. Par for the course, but a necessary exercise before I get the next juicy credstick. For which I have to prepare an initial report about old Shroudman here and what leads he gives me."

"Going to drop a hint that you learned more than you should have?"

"Not at this stage, but there is something else I need to do," Michael replied thoughtfully. "I'll have to deck into the central system of at least one other megacorp so I can report that more than one system was hit. Renraku will expect that."

"Why bother? You know they have. You can improvise the details."

"Yes, but it will look better if I actually do it."

"Never mind that," Geraint said sharply. "It's a pointless risk. As you say, Renraku may deliberately have backed off from giving us real heat last night. Shiawase or—God forbid we even try—Fuchi would be another matter entirely. You know they've all been hit. You know it was synchronous. You also know that the other corps don't seem to have been given the Shroudman clue. That'll do for Renraku.

"By the by, why do you think only Renraku got this image?" The first enhanced chromalin was already slipping shinily out of the Fairlight peripherals.

"I don't know," Michael said slowly. "That's interesting. Maybe, just perhaps, Renraku's own deckers didn't get deep enough into enemy territory to get at data saying that others got hit too. If the others ultraclassified it, that could be the explanation."

"I don't think so," Geraint said. "There can't be anything classified tighter than the basic data relating to the crash. That has to be tighter-than-a-duck's-arse tight."

"Hmmm," Michael intoned, drumming his fingers on the teak. "You're right. Well, ninety-nine percent likely to be right. I have to scan it out on the off chance of that one per cent."

"Not now," Geraint said sternly. "Not alone, and not until you've recovered some. Your reflexes are too sluggish right now. You really should get one of these cannula implants, old boy. If you were me, we could have you fighting fit in ten minutes."

"Leave my brain alone," Michael protested. "It was bad enough pissing in flasks for you in the biochemistry classes. You're not tinkering with the fluids in my head as well."

Geraint laughed and pulled his overcoat from the coat rack, then tapped the comswitch to call his chauffeur. "See you shortly. And, really, don't go jacking in until I get back. A man in my position can't afford a corpse in his apartment."

"Well, thanks for the concern," Michael said sarcastically and turned back to his printouts. There had to be something here for Serrin to hook into, and he wanted to find it before Geraint brought the elf back from Heathrow.

"Unless I'm much mistaken, sir, we're being followed," the troll said impassively. There wasn't even the slightest inclination of his peaked cap to emphasize the observation.

"Oh, really?" Geraint perked up in the back of the Phaeton. "What by?"

"A Eurocar Westwind, sir, license plate DFR 336. It has diplomatic identification, sir," the chauffeur said. "From the Tuscany Republic."

"Now why would some obscure little Italian city-state send someone to follow me, Harold? Are we sure about this? I mean, he could just be making for the airport after all."

"Well, sir, he's been following us through central London, and as a matter of fact he was parked outside the flat all night. Not that I gave any thought to it at the time, sir, but the on-board computer's given me a match. Looks as if he has a definite interest in you, sir.

"I have the tracking systems locked on, sir, and we're recording."

"How extremely incompetent of our new friend," Geraint chuckled. "He really ought to know about the surveillance systems on ministerial vehicles. Well, well. Good work, Harold."

"Do you want me to send a coded signal to the Met, sir?"

"No, I don't think we'll call the police in yet," Geraint said after a moment's reflection. "Let's do a tour of the terminals, shall we? Make for Terminal Six by mistake, and then we'll backtrack to Terminal Four. See if our chummer follows us."

"Very good, sir," the troll growled as he headed down the road to the vast complex of the world's busiest airport. Geraint sat in silence and looked in a cursory, disinterested fashion at the papers on top of the pile. Shared military maneuvers with the Spanish around Gibraltar were not really of major fascination to him right then. Leave it to the Ministry of Defense, he scrawled on top of the memo. The limo swerved around the endless circular road system and headed past Terminal 2, where most transcontinental suborbitals landed, and made for the much humbler landing field for internal flights.

"Still being followed?"

"We are, sir. Do you want me to display the vehicle on the screen?"

"Please, Harold, and I think you'd better alert airport security just in case the bugger decides to take a pot-shot at me when I get out," Geraint said, grim-faced. "Nothing over the top, just the usual."

"Very good, sir," the troll said. "I'll cover you."

"Thank you, Harold," Geraint said dryly. The troll would make an excellent shield against bullet fire, not least on account of the armor beneath his immaculately pressed uniform. Geraint remembered the boffin from MoD telling him the stuff would stop antitank shells, and since Harold had a lot in common with a tank there was a certain appropriateness in that.

He stared at the car on the screen, monitored by the limo's own spy cameras. Even as he did, his chauffeur asked if he wanted a link into the airport's security cameras. As Geraint considered that, the Westwind veered off toward Terminal 5.

"Ah, well, there we go." Geraint breathed a sigh of relief. "No need for anymore shenanigans, I think. Let's just pick up our guests and go home."

Serrin and Kristen were just tumbling out of the terminal, as disorganized as ever, when Geraint climbed out of the limo, blinking in the afternoon sunlight like a surprised owl. The dark-skinned woman gave him her big, wide smile and a ferocious hug, immersing him in the scent of sandalwood and frankincense and warm wool. Behind her, the gray-haired elf looked healthier than Geraint remembered him. He still walked with the slight limp from an injury that had shattered his left leg, but when Serrin shook Geraint's hand, the old tremor seemed to have gone and his grip was firm, his gaze steady.

"Good to see you," Geraint said cheerfully. "Hop into the limo, hmmm?"

"Our luggage—" Serrin began.

"Harold will see to that," Geraint said a little hurriedly. The elf's eyes narrowed. "Something wrong?"

"Not really." Geraint decided that he wasn't quite up to lying and it wouldn't be the ideal start to a visit anyway. "We were followed by a car with diplomatic plates for a while. Nothing to worry about, he beetled off over there," he added, waving vaguely into the distance.

"So what's going on?" Serrin asked with a mischievous smile. "Michael arrives in town and right away you're being tailed? What game's afoot, to paraphrase one of your best-known detectives? You said you had something that might interest me."

"Let's get home first," Geraint said. "We can talk there."

"What are you discussing?" Kristen bounced back to the pair after having checked the baggage. "Boys' talk already?"

They turned and stared at her together. She wasn't much more than half the age of either of them, and the reference to "boys" seemed both incongruous and appropriate at the same time.

"Nothing important. Just world domination and the collapse of civilization as know it," Geraint said laconically. Kristen looked uncertainly at Serrin, who just smiled and ushered her toward the waiting limo, shooting a reproving look over his shoulder at the nobleman.

Actually, I was just being honest, Geraint thought, but then we've time yet to go through it all. Several days, in fact. Now let's get into the car and get a trace on those number plates.

As the limo sped away with the nobleman and his guests, a Frenchman got silently into the back of a much humbler vehicle parked outside Terminal 5 and exchanged little more than a grunt with the Italian who'd driven it there. Had he known that the man had tracked Geraint to the airport, he might very well have been tempted to shoot him then and there, but there were other things on his mind. He knew how little time was left, and that it was absolutely essential to close off the leads to the returned Master—not to mention getting rid of that troublesome individual. If shooting people was on his mind, he had not as yet included his driver on the list.

"Get moving," the man said in his even, humorless voice. "And is the Circle prepared?"

"Yes, sir," the Italian replied dutifully.

"Then take me to it," the Frenchman spat back.

5

When the limo returned Geraint, Serrin, and Kristen to Mayfair, it was a pale and drawn Michael who got rather unsteadily out of the armchair to greet the trio when they exited the elevator. Geraint was angry, and almost lost his temper and shouted at his foolish friend.

"I told you not to do anything until I got back," he said firmly.

"Sorry," Michael said meekly. "But we've only got nine days, after all. It doesn't look like Fuchi got the image, so far as I can see. The frames are still sifting through the data."

"You got into Fuchi?" Geraint's anger evaporated

slightly as it mixed with admiration. The Fuchi datacores were the hardest to crack on the planet.

Michael grinned. "No persp. Had to stage a decoy, though, and I may have fried one of my frames." He glanced at Serrin and Kristen. "But let's not talk shop already. We can go into that after dinner."

"So Geraint really does have some work for me," the elf said thoughtfully. "Well, we've been living off his hospitality long enough."

"Nonsense, you're welcome to stay as long as you want," Geraint protested, and again Michael had the sense that something wasn't quite right between the nobleman and his elven guest, but he said nothing.

They began to chitchat, starting with the matter of the weather, and before the pleasantries were completed the caterers had arrived with their boxes and cases and had set up camp in the kitchen. The skies darkened and Geraint clean forgot to check the data on the registration number as he busied himself with mixing cocktails and relaxing into the bonhomie of the early evening. If he'd done it, of course, the evening's unexpected and most unwelcome guest might not have arrived and he'd have saved his insurance firm a small fortune in the cost of repairing his apartment.

Serrin stared at the chromalin, turning it over in his short-nailed, chewed fingers. Opposite him, toying with the remains of the filet mignon, Michael awaited his response.

"So, what do you think?"

"You told me what your data showed," Serrin said, "and I don't think I could add anything. But you're not telling me exactly why you want to know."

Michael hesitated. "I told you it was left in a corporate Matrix system after an induced crash," he said defensively. "Let's say it was a big crash. This is the signature of whoever did it. I just think there's more to this image than I've been able to find out. I'm good at trawling through Matrix data and operations. This is a little more on the arcane side. You've got contacts. I was hoping you could tell me more."

"I'll do what I can," the mage said thoughtfully. "I take it you don't want this to get too public, but if I start asking questions, word is going to get around."

"That's inevitable," Geraint said as he refilled their glasses. Given the confidentiality of what they were discussing, he'd dispensed with waiters from the catering outfit. "There's so little time left anyway that I don't think we should worry about that too much.

"Anyway, that's for tomorrow," he continued cheerfully. "Tell me what you've been up to on that godforsaken island of mine."

Serrin grinned. "Making friends with the druids, mostly," he said. "Wandering along the seashore. Being happy. That sort of thing."

He exchanged swift glances with the dark Azanian woman next to him. They shared a kind of secret smile before he returned his gaze to the other two men.

Well, well. He really is happy, Michael thought. That makes a nice change.

"I'm grateful," Geraint said carefully. "The druids can be difficult at times. I leave the place to them to run, but some of them still get prickly about the issue of ownership sometimes."

"Well, they say it's been a sacred place to them for several thousand years and you can't buy that with money," Serrin said tartly. "But there aren't any real problems. The wiser of them hold sway and they're content that you leave them undisturbed. It took me some time to gain their trust, and I'm still learning. But they're good people."

"They're improving the value of my real estate," Geraint said mischievously. "Thanks to them, the marine wildlife around the coasts has flourished. The fishing rights have tripled in value these last five years."

"Don't give me that," Serrin mocked him. "You're not in it just for the money."

There was a short silence, broken by the chink of chromed steel against porcelain as Geraint began a coffee-pouring ritual. If anything, the tiny sound made the situation more uncomfortable because it was so easily discerned, underlining the silence.

"Oh, for Pete's sake, what is it with you men?" Kristen burst out suddenly. Frustration sparked in her brown eyes. "You're so good at not saying anything that matters." Michael turned and stared at her, one eyebrow raised.

"There's something wrong between you, and you talk about fishing rights!"

"Kristen—" Serrin began in a slightly weary voice, but she would not be stilled.

"You're very good to us," she said to Geraint, "but there's something wrong. You don't look at Serrin straight on. You look guilty. And you," she continued, giving Serrin an accusing stare, "you've been edgy ever since Geraint asked you to come. It's because of Michael, isn't it?"

"I have no idea what you mean," Serrin said flatly. "And you're spoiling a very pleasant dinner."

"Is it because of what happened? Because he married me to get me out of Cape Town with you, and you didn't? That's so bloody silly! You'd know why he did that if you weren't a man," she said exasperatedly.

"Actually, we all know why I did it, and sometimes men just do things and don't talk about them," Michael said firmly, but not unkindly. "Things are just understood, Kristen. Maybe you're making something out of nothing."

Her eyes flashed angrily, but she sat back a little in her chair, unwilling to pursue the point. Michael knew that she *had* touched on something; he too had sensed the awkwardness between Geraint and Serrin, in their over-politeness and slightly strained exchanges. He also felt that it was something better not brought out into the open.

The returning silence was disturbed by a sudden rustling sound from the heavy, silk-lined drapes at the far end of the cavernous dining room.

"What the—" Serrin began, and then his eyes grew as wide as the dinner plates set before him. He shot out of his chair, fumbled for a medallion about his neck, and began a hurried, rapid recitation.

He's spellcasting, Michael realized. He can't, not in here, the building has a hermetic circle better than—

The windows blew in with a rush of flying glass, and a storm-force gale howled into the room. Plates and glasses went flying from the table, and Geraint, being closest to the windows, was nearly flung from his chair. Michael lunged across and grabbed his arm even as Kristen clung to Serrin. Geraint freed himself from Michael's grasp and with a Herculean effort managed to struggle to a chest of drawers two meters behind him and wrench a drawer open.

Michael saw the gleam of gunmetal as he clung on to the solidity of the huge dining table for support. That's not going to do you any good here, he thought. It seemed like the massed legions of Hell were about to arrive in person at any moment.

The howling winds suddenly stopped, absolutely and in a split second. Everything was shockingly still. The drapes didn't even flutter back to their initial positions, they just hung in space, frozen in time. Then they parted and the figure strode into the room from the night air outside. There was no balcony outside for the woman to have climbed in from, but then she wasn't exactly flesh and blood.

"Get behind me," Serrin hissed and Michael guessed he must have created a magical barrier around himself. He needed no second invitation. What was left of the crockery on the table went flying as he threw himself across the table and went sprawling at the elf's feet. Kristen was at Serrin's side, hugging him close. Geraint had no time to make that safety, and stood facing the figure with the machine pistol in his hand and a determined stare. He didn't even bother to shoot.

The woman was clad almost head to toe in plate mail armor, and carried an ornate kite-shaped shield lacquered with white, a red Maltese cross adorning its face. A slender, scabbarded sword hung at her side. She wore no helm, and her long dark hair tumbled down her back. She was beautiful, but cold and expressionless, her blue eyes seeming to stare through and beyond the scene of mayhem before her. Soundlessly, she stepped into the room and walked in a direct line toward the table. She didn't even seem to acknowledge their presence. They stood and watched in amazement, stepping back a little from her as she approached. When she reached the table, an antique scroll of parchment seemed to appear in her hand, bound with red silk and bearing a wax seal. She let it fall onto the table, then turned around, walking just as silently back toward the blackness of night. She didn't lift a hand to disturb the drapes, which seemed to enfold themselves around her as she stepped out into the air and vanished.

Geraint's gun dropped from his hand and he gawked

disbelievingly at the place where she'd been. Michael, getting to his feet, was the first to recover his senses and reach for the scroll.

"That's impossible," Geraint said flatly. "The magical protections on this building would keep Lucifer himself out." The sound of rustling parchment, being carefully unfolded, came from just over his shoulder.

"That was a powerful sending indeed," Serrin confirmed, giving Kristen a reassuring squeeze. His eyes were like a raptor's. If he'd been uncertain about what Michael had asked him to do, his curiosity and stubborn determination were roused now. The arrival of the spirit, and whatever it was that Geraint and Michael were involved with, could hardly be coincidental.

"This is a warning," Michael told them, dispensing with a complete recitation. "Written in medieval Latin. I can't translate the whole thing for you, but the gist of it is to keep our noses out or we'll be damned for all eternity."

"Colorfully put," Geraint said sarcastically, regaining his composure.

"No, I mean *literally* damned for all eternity," Michael said wryly.

"And keep our noses out of what, exactly?" Serrin enquired.

"Doesn't say," Michael said offhandedly, putting the scroll back on the table.

"Maybe not, but *you* know and I think I'd like to know everything too," Serrin said pointedly. Kristen nodded emphatically for her share of revelations as well. "But first, I'm going to see if I can trace that spirit. Excuse me a moment." He wandered off toward Geraint's study, away from the confusion and animated voices as the others began to discuss what had happened.

Geraint looked at the scroll closely. It was entirely written in Latin, and he couldn't comprehend it. "Get a full translation in the morning," he said.

"Is that a good idea?" Michael said. "There might be something there we don't want anyone else to know."

Geraint looked wearily at him. "Are you kidding? The Foreign Office translators spend their entire lives translating documents filled with information we don't want other people to know. No problem there."

"Hmmm," Michael mused. "Look, there's something I need to do. My version of a head camera. Be back in the world of the living inside a few minutes." He walked over to where his computer system sat safe and undisturbed due to the security bolting and cables that had held it firmly to a table weighing a couple of hundredweight, and jacked into the Matrix.

Geraint used the telecom to call some fast-response building and repair firms he'd dealt with when government security installations had been hit by terrorists, animal-rights maniacs, or other disgruntled factions. Dealing with the interior decor could wait. The police might need some reassurance or insist upon a call to the Metropolitan Commissioner, but he could do that later if the need arose.

Once he put the phone down, Kristen ushered him into the kitchen and steered him purposefully to one corner.

"What's happening, Geraint?" she demanded.

"I have no idea," he said truthfully. "That was a bolt from the blue."

"Not just that. What is it with you and Serrin?"

He avoided her gaze and said nothing. Her right foot tapped on the floor. She was much smaller than him, but for all the world she looked like a feral predator and he like hapless prey unable to escape.

"You're getting into some kind of trouble here and I need to know what's happening," Kristen insisted. She stood with hands on hips, defiantly awaiting a reply.

"It's before he knew you," Geraint said quietly and a little hurriedly, hoping that Michael and Serrin were still busy with their own self-absorbed activities. "Something we were involved with."

"When you got involved with some murders here, something to do with the Royal family," Kristen offered.

"Yes."

"He wouldn't go into details," she said.

"Neither will I," he said firmly. "It's just that there was a certain . . . aftermath. Something later. Something that he doesn't know, and I can't tell him about. Please . . ." Geraint was all but pleading. "It's nothing he needs to know. It doesn't compromise his safety by not knowing. It would hurt him if I told him. Believe me."

Kristen stared determinedly at him for a time before

she judged that he was telling the truth. She made her decision. "Very well," she said grudgingly. "But you'll have to come clean about what's going on here."

"Oh, I think we will," Geraint said fervently. "I very much think we will."

Half an hour later the four of them sat around Geraint's study, drinking dessert wine and port and waiting for the repairmen to finish fixing the windows.

"Couldn't trace the spirit," Serrin said glumly. "That's not really my forte anyway and the masking was excellent. The trail petered out almost instantly. Nothing to sense in the astral and there's a lot of interference around here."

"I'm not surprised," Geraint said. "Anything strong enough to bust through the hermetic barrier here has to be good enough to mask its departure. I'm going to have some serious words with the house mages tomorrow morning. We'll have to improve security here. I could ask if the watchers saw anything, though."

"Better not," Serrin advised. "Let's not get too many people interested."

"Very well," Geraint conceded. "And so what has our genius decker come up with?"

"I was using a little program I composed myself," Michael said. The port was very, very good and he was really more interested in another glass than in reflecting on his discovery, since his frames were still busy analyzing correspondences and associations. "It translates recalled perceptions into objective form and makes a range of corrections based on our understanding of errors in perception and recall. Basically, it tries to take something I've seen in my mind's eye and asks, 'What did this guy really see if we strip away all the bulldrek inside his brain?' "

"So what did we really see?" Kristen asked, intrigued.

"Well, the analyses aren't complete and—"

"Cut the drek," Geraint put in. "What did we see?"

"Joan of Arc," he said simply.

Geraint's jaw dropped. In comparison, Kristen, brought up in a culture where the name meant nothing, registered no response at all.

"God, you're right," Geraint said. "I realize now. What the frag—Oh, idiot, idiot!" He thumped a clenched fist into midair. "There was something I forgot. Better late than never, I hope." He began frantically keying in instructions to a souped-up laptop sitting demurely beneath the lowlight lamp on his smaller study desk, rapping in passwords and ID. Within a minute or so he had his answer.

"Our pursuer this afternoon can be found in Chelsea," he said cheerfully. "One Monsignor Giovanni Seratini, a cultural attaché for the Tuscany Republic. Something of a coincidence, wouldn't you say? I was followed by this chappie on the way to pick up you two, and before the day is out an icon of the Holy Roman Church comes waltzing in to say, 'Rakk off, chaps, or it's a thousand years of purgatory for you.' "

"Eternal damnation in the flaming fires themselves, actually," Michael said laconically.

"I rather think we should visit Monsignor Seratini and make some enquiries of him," Geraint said.

"The car had diplomatic plates," Michael pointed out.

"Oh, yes, well, I wouldn't have got the woodentops of the Met in anyway. If you want something more complicated than knowing the correct time these days, you do *not* ask a London copper," Geraint replied. "However, one of the fringe benefits of working with the MoD most days is that one gets access to some very interesting personnel."

"MoD?" Serrin wasn't familiar with the British acronym.

"Ministry of Defense," Geraint explained. "Now, the MoD has a long list of ex-military personnel who work in, shall we say, semi-official security. They won't do anything that actively messes with officialdom, but they don't worry too much about what currently passes for the law. Especially when it comes to diplomatic immunity and dastardly foreigners. I know of some ex-SAS men who should be just the ticket. They even have enough sense not to kill our Italian term on sight and to realize that we'd like to talk to him, which is a lot better than you can get from most military lardbrains. Excuse me while I put through an encrypted call from my bedroom phone."

"Isn't this a bit premature?" Michael said. "I mean, it could be just coincidence. Not much to base a raid on."

"I don't think so. Our friend's car was parked outside the building all last night. Harold got him on the security cameras. He's had the place under surveillance, and then followed me. Dammit, we can't have one of His Majesty's ministers being spied on by a representative of a foreign power, can we? Have to put a stop to it. It's my patriotic duty," Geraint replied in a suitably, not to mention deliberately pompous tone of voice. "There's also an easy way to cover our tracks, as it happens. There've been suspicions concerning alleged elements of the Tuscan embassy in London regarding certain art thefts in recent years. Nothing the Met specialists could prove. But the word is that no one would be terribly surprised if some, shall we say, competing criminal element, ahem, took a shot at finding out if there are any tasty Old Masters on the premises. Especially since Seratini has an interesting Interpol file implicating him—nothing proven, again—with certain smuggling operations in the Italian states. I'm sure my associates will be able to dress things up to look as if that's what will have happened by the time they're through.

"How long have we got anyway?"

"Nine days," Michael said. "Didn't I already say that?"

"Right, then. Would you like to spend a few of them digging on our friend Seratini or shall we take a reasonable chance and go say 'Howdy' to him now?" Getting only a nod in reply, Geraint turned and left the room.

"This is going to be interesting," Michael said after the Welshman had left them to their drinks. "Midnight rambling again."

"Just like old times," Serrin grinned. "This time yesterday I was peacefully examining some shellfish down by the rocks. Now it's magical assaults, Latin warnings, and trolls with big guns in Chelsea.

"It's all right, *lekker,*" he added as an aside, hugging his wife to him. "We'll be fine." She looked a little anxiously at him, and nestled into his warm side. But for all her apprehension, Kristen could never have survived so many years as a street kid in Cape Town's predatory culture without strength and resourcefulness to spare.

"You know, I think it's about time we got the whole story," she suddenly demanded of Michael. "Everything you know, from the top."

"You're right," he said. "It's overdue."

He began at the beginning, and told them the full works. By the time he was through, Geraint already had the guns.

"The repairmen have gone. I'm expecting half a dozen very large gentlemen with military weapons and attitude to appear in the parking lot in a black van very shortly," he said as he offered them the latest range of hardware. "Coming?"

"Couldn't keep us away," Serrin said cheerfully.

6

Just before three in the morning, the black van rolled quietly into Cheney Walk, and Geraint lowered the window to reassure the resident security patrol. His government ID seemed to pull slightly less weight than the leader of the goons with him, who knew the senior guard on duty.

"We have a little semi-official business with a certain foreign gentleman, Charles," the man said meaningfully.

"Sure, Jim," the ork security guard said impassively. "Try not to disturb the neighbors, eh?"

The van rolled another few meters forward, and the rigger parked it a little way down a side street.

"Now, lads, let's get this straight," Jim said to emphasize the final briefing. "As little noise as possible and keep the casualties down. Disable at all times. Use the grenades and the trank shots whenever possible, and let's keep this nice and quick and painless. For us, anyway."

A dry laugh came from a dark-haired elf toying with an elaborate weapon that appeared to combine a grenade launcher, integrated taser, and trank-shot barrel all in one, and that was before the manufacturers had added stabilizers, IR sights, and whole range of other gizmos. Geraint had been impressed by the size of the elf's muscles to even carry the thing, though the gyromount harness was obviously helping with that. That he could still move with amazing swiftness when encumbered by the monstrosity was a testimony to his wired reflexes.

It was a well-balanced squad, Michael thought. Two trolls for strength and power, two elves for speed and re-action, a dwarf who appeared to be a combined engineer, quartermaster, and tactician rolled into one, and a single human who looked as big as the trolls and as fast as the elves, not even counting the chromed rigger. Judging by Serrin's thoughtful look, Geraint guessed that one of the elves was a magical adept at the very least, probably assensing even as they were approaching the building. The team ordered the nobleman not to come in until they'd disabled anything that moved inside number 16, and he was only too happy to comply. The flag of the Tuscany Republic hung outside, but that wouldn't do the occupants any good. It wasn't the official residence of the ambassador. Geraint had reassured them that while a raid might cause a slight ripple, it would be nothing he couldn't handle.

The black-swathed, armored figures slipped out the back of the van and merged effortlessly into the night, leaving the rigger behind to monitor the scene from a dozen different angles and taking downloaded data from the head cameras of two of those approaching the building. Within seconds, the familiar tinkle of breaking glass announced that a gas grenade had hit the first floor of the building even as rope lines were being fired to enable the elves to strike at any targets upstairs.

"Good, aren't they?" Geraint whispered as they watched the monitors' grainy image of broken windows and black figures darting into the building. "I think we can venture forth ourselves now. Right through the front door. Do you want to wait here?" He looked at Kristen, who shot back a look of disdain.

"Don't be patronizing," Serrin admonished him. "She once saved my skin by shooting someone in the head."

"As you wish," Geraint said mildly, climbing out of the van. Like the others, he wore light body armor, and Serrin had already locked a bullet barrier spell around himself and Kristen. They raced around the side street and made for the front entrance, already opened by one of the trolls who had a supercharged taser hefted at the ready.

"Not much resistance," the troll growled rather disap-pointedly as they approached. Then the sudden chatter of handgun fire came from the basement of the building.

"You spoke too soon," Geraint said as he made for the inside of the building, gripping his machine pistol more firmly with one hand while fastening his respirator with the other to ward off the effects of the trank gas billowing down the stairs. Passing through the hallway, he dimly took in the large reception room to his right, where the dwarf had three terrified clerks bent over a table while he toyed with the trigger of a Predator and began hand-cuffing them. Geraint made for the stairs where the elf with the integrated arsenal masquerading as a single weapon stood, casually dumping a grenade down the stairs and standing back to blow open the doors at the bottom. The explosion was less than Geraint anticipated, the door flimsy and easily blown apart, with debris mostly flying into the underground garage rather than back up toward them. By the time he reached the stairs, the elf was already through the shattered doorway, hunting the prey that had escaped and sought to flee by car.

The whir of a taser line hummed through the semi-darkness at the figure racing toward the parked vehicles. Geraint could just see the man duck and the line whiz over his head; the elf cursed and decided to dispense with precise targeting. A second gas grenade went flying into the parking lot, but the man pulled something up around his neck that looked to Geraint like a respirator. Then, from above them, it seemed for a moment as if the entire building shook and reverberated. Geraint had never been in an earthquake, but he imagined this must be what one would feel like. It really did seem like the entire place might fall down around their ears at any moment. He stepped smartly out of the stairwell behind the elf, who let off a burst of gunfire to scare his target, then began to run at him like a cheetah with a jalapeño enema up its tail.

A deep, grinding sound like two rock faces trying to sandpaper each other to dust came from upstairs just as their quarry managed to get into the car, start it up, and steer the vehicle toward the garage doors, with the elf still in hot pursuit. The SAS elf dropped to his knees and launched another grenade shot as the car veered crazily toward the exit. It didn't look as if the doors would open properly before the car got to them, and even if the elf missed, Geraint judged that the driver would quite possi-

bly get his head ripped off together with the roof of his
Westwind.

The cacophony of sound made the Welshman turn and
take the risk of making his way back up the stairs, leaving the fleeing car and its passenger to their elven pursuer. Upstairs, it seemed as if half the roof had collapsed.
Plaster, wood, stone, and a once-fine chandelier lay
strewn in the hallway. Geraint gripped his gun again and
advanced up the stairs. Of the others, save for the dwarf
completing his work, there was no sign.

When he got to the landing, the scene was astounding.
Every door leading off it was open, and in one bedroom
that approached palatial splendor he could see one of the
trolls laid out cold with a seeping pool of blood spreading
from his back and neck. Incongruously, in the bathroom
someone had seemed to take serious objection to avocado
green bath fittings by blowing them into ceramic shrapnel, but it was the scene in the large sitting room that
caught his eye. The place was filled with broken glass
and smashed furnishings, and there were at least three
prone bodies in it. Of the ones moving, Serrin and the
other elf were engaged in what appeared to be a desperate
struggle. Michael was lying slumped in a corner, but
there was no blood on him and it looked as if he were
merely knocked out cold. Kristen had her Predator
gripped in both hands, waiting for a clear shot.

Serrin was standing rock still, engaged in a magical
struggle with a bizarre figure, a human-like form that
seemed to be shaped of muddied clay, trying to claw its
way toward him and Kristen. The other elf was flinging
himself, long serried knife in hand, at a suited, dark-
haired man crouched across a table from him, his gaze
fixed on the clay figure. Even as Geraint approached, the
clay figure managed to force its way to Serrin and strike
him with one of its limbs, knocking the elf to the floor.
The other elf leapt over the table and buried his knife in
his opponent's right shoulder blade only a hand's length
from his heart. As Kristen and Geraint poured bullets into
whatever it was that had struck Serrin senseless, the man
screamed and the clay creature wavered and began to top-
ple. As it fell backward, almost as if in slo-mo, its form
dissolved into a wave of rolling, liquid clay, pouring into

a huge puddle of formless, slimy mud that seeped over the Persian carpet.

A haze of blue static began to shimmer into form in the center of the room. What Geraint had taken for simply a design in the weave of the carpet he now sensed was some kind of magical design, a ritual inscribing, though he knew little of such things. The knife-carrying elf, however, knew a lot more.

"Get the frag out of here! Move!" he screamed, grabbing the inert form of the group's leader as he retreated. Mercifully, the man seemed only stunned and was already able to move with the elf's help. Geraint didn't have to be told twice. He reached down and drew Michael up under the arms, dragging him back onto the landing, leaving the slighter form of Serrin to Kristen. The three of them struggled out with their burdens, the elf going back a second time to pull out his troll comrade as well. The static was forming into what looked like ball lightning and was beginning to spin in a crazily off-kilter orbit around the epicenter of the room. The man in the suit lay groaning, barely conscious, flowers of blood blooming down the front of his once-perfect white shirt. Geraint rushed to help the elf, and they managed to drag the heavy troll out of the room and slam the door shut in time.

The room exploded. Its contents spewed out over the length and breadth of one of the wealthiest, most exclusive, and generally quietest streets in all of London, and the detonation was enough to send them all flying across the landing. Geraint hit the door frame of the bathroom and just missed getting his hands sliced up on the porcelain fragments from the broken toilet bowl. Serrin managed to roll with the punches and came to rest a meter away from him, but not before hitting him hard and winding him. Up the stairs, the dwarf and the second elf were rushing to their aid, and after them the rigger—responding with amazing speed—was there too. Conscious, unconscious, and walking wounded managed to stagger into the street. Lights were beginning to appear from every building around them.

"Anyone dead?" Geraint said desperately.

"No, but that's a minor sodding miracle," the elf he had assisted said grimly. "We hadn't expected so much magic in the place. Serrin and I had our work cut out just to bloody contain it all. Let's get the frag out of this drekhole and worry about the details later."

The group's leader was just about conscious, and the ork from the security patrol was advancing on him with worry etched into his face.

"Frag it all, Jim, I said keep it quiet!" he complained bitterly. "How the frag am I going to explain this?"

"You know the drill," Jim said, grunting with pain, and handed the ork a grenade.

"Fifty thousand," the ork said. Geraint handed him a credstick, but the ork refused.

"Not now. The police will be round any minute," he said. "Tomorrow. Jim'll bring it round."

"Fine," Geraint shrugged, struggling to help everyone into the van. The first curious onlookers were just opening their doors. The ork marched off, summoned his group, and dumped the grenade. He and the other guards reeled away from the anaesthetizing gas and were all slumped on the ground within moments. Sirens were beginning to raise their howl of protest from the surrounding streets. The van's rear doors shut, and the rigger raced the vehicle like a bat out of the abyss.

"Well, I think we've certainly done enough damage to bugger any cover story that we were after their Old Masters," Geraint complained. "Did we get our man?" he howled above the noise of the accelerating engine.

"Bastard got away," the elf said impassively.

"Where's Gungrath?" Geraint went on, trying not to fall out of his seat.

"Took a couple of hostages away in one of the cars," the elf replied, explaining the absence of the second troll, who had recovered with astonishing speed. "Look, we've got to get to our repairman."

"You got it," the rigger yelled.

"There's something wrong with the van?" Geraint said anxiously.

"Nah, 'im," the elf said, jerking a thumb at the troll samurai with blood coating his chest and back. "Stopped some very heavy-duty AP. I've patched him, but we're going to need serious surgery here. And that'll cost you, term."

"Whatever it takes," Geraint agreed.

"Drek it, I've got four fast-response police APVs in the

radar locks and we're going to be lucky to get out of this," the rigger said desperately as he cajoled more speed out of the vehicle. "Get out of my way, you dumb frag!" The car in his path narrowly managed to swerve out of the way of the racing van.

The elf grinned at Geraint. "Don't sweat it, he's never crashed yet."

Serrin started from his stupor and looked dumbly around him. "Didn't quite work out, did it?" he said stupidly.

"Not to worry," Geraint said soothingly. "We got some people we can talk to. Unfortunately, our Monsignor Seratini appears to have escaped."

"Managed to stick a bug tracer on him," one of the elves said happily. "Roger here can track him down within a hundred klicks. Where's he now, Rog?"

"Somewhere off the Old Kent Road," the driver said after a momentary glance at his array of monitoring panels. "Jeez, we're being hauled in here. They've got locks on us and there's a chopper on the way. Mister, I mean Your Lordship, you're going to have to do some fast talking pretty soon. Can't evade this lot. There's another one every second."

"Don't forget, if we end up in jail it's a hundred thou a year for our families," the dwarf growled.

"You haven't got family, you stunty bastard," one of the elves said. "Born from a test-tube, you were. Face like that couldn't have a mother."

The dwarf hit him playfully in the groin with the barrel of his gun. The elf groaned with much feeling and rolled over in a ball, cursing. The van began to slow and came to a halt. The sirens behind them sounded like the Hounds of Hell.

"Well, this is it, Lord Llanfrechfa," Jim said casually. "Bulldrek or bust. You'd better have the connections they say you do or it's twenty years in Parkhurst for everyone—and that's going to cost you every last penny you've got."

Geraint groaned. This was going to be a very expensive evening.

And it was. Exhausted and bleary-eyed, they reeled out of the elevator and waited for Geraint to go through the array of scanners and decide it was safe to go in. They'd spent hours locked in the holding cells until Geraint managed to pull strings at the highest level to get them free. Geraint would have to foot a sizable bill, in terms of political favors owed as well as money, to pay for the night's exploits. He was also uncomfortably aware that he'd have to do a hell of a lot of careful explaining to senior figures in the British government, and he didn't have the best of cover stories to present to them just at the moment.

"Coffee, anyone?" he asked as they dumped their armor and gear in the cloakroom. Serrin shook his head and opened the far door of the room to make for the bathroom, sticking his head under the faucet and splashing cold water over himself. Kristen, pale and wild-haired, followed him anxiously with her eyes. Michael, having woken a lot later in the day than the elf, strolled into the huge central room and looked for the message he expected. The telecom and the faxbuffer store were both winking their warning lights at him. He began the data and message dumps, rubbing his sore back after the indignity of having been thumped senseless into the wall by the guardian they'd encountered inside the house at Cheney Walk.

"What have you got?" Geraint said as Michael began tearing paper from the printers.

"They work fast. They've downloaded the image data from the head cameras and it's being processed right now. However, the gentleman in the suit upstairs was one Monsieur Jean-Francois Serrault. You'll be interested to hear that the data pertaining to him cannot be found in Sûreté or French social security records, because he doesn't officially exist."

"How intriguing. Where did you get it?"

"That's my business," Michael admonished. "He's a mage, as it happens. Freelancer. Get some more data on him later. Has some interesting friends in occult circles, according to this. Enough to keep us interested, I should think."

"So what's he doing in the residence of the Tuscan attaché?" Geraint asked.

"Good question," Michael replied. "Hopefully, I should have the answer to that shortly. We really should have done more homework on our friend Seratini before we went trick or treating, I think. Oh look," he added, as an updated message came pouring onto the screen, "Good news. Our troll friend will be fine, which will save you a bundle. And our chappies have subcontracted the work of finding Seratini to some of their mates, who are on their way to collect him from somewhere in Brent."

"Brent?"

"Yes, it's rather down-market, isn't it?" Michael agreed. "Well, anyway, we've got him and if we want to go and talk to him, we can." They exchanged glances.

"Are you tired?"

"Absolutely exhausted, old boy, but I think we'd really like to know as soon as possible how our Italian friend comes to know a French mage who can blow half a house up even as he's popping his clogs."

"Won't the police be keeping a watch on us now?"

"No, I don't think so," Geraint said. "It cost a lot of favors, but, no, they won't. Not unless we do something terribly similar all over again."

"Well, hardly," Michael protested. "I mean, all we're going to do is go and talk to someone. We can hardly end up in a pitched battle doing that, can we?"

Geraint had already gone to get his coat for another evening excursion. Had he known how totally, horribly wrong Michael was, he would have thought twice about tempting fate so blatantly.

7

They parked the car a safe distance from the Brent address they'd been given and, pistols in pockets, walked quietly across the concrete parking lot. It was still night, with the promise of a morning chorus just beginning to insinuate itself, though it was yet to grow light. The street lights were erratic here, as much because of vandals as because the power company wasn't always supplying juice. The local council was notoriously adept at misplacing public money, and not even street lighting could be taken for granted.

"Are you sure about this?" Michael said for the fifth time.

"I checked with Jim twice. He's not a man you slot off by asking three times," Geraint replied tartly.

"It's a housing project," Michael said dubiously.

"What did you expect? A mansion? Have you ever been here before?"

"This is a part of London I was never in the habit of frequenting," Michael said. "Seems incredibly down-at-heel for a cultural attaché."

"That's the point, isn't it? A safe bolthole where no one would go looking for it?" Geraint said.

"I suppose so." Michael still seemed dubious. They walked across the concourse toward the looming concrete monstrosity, which betrayed rather less concrete-rot and acid corrosion than might have been expected. Unlike many of the surrounding edifices, it didn't look in danger of imminent sudden collapse, but then appearances were definitely deceptive in this instance. The only human decor in sight were a couple of junkies splayed around in the entrance doorway of one of the smaller satellite blocks, a small pool of already half-clotted blood testifying to their nocturnal habits of despair.

The elf slid silently out of his nonexistent cover. Even in the erratic lighting, there seemed to be nowhere anyone could hide, but he'd managed it.

Goes with the training, Geraint thought once his first instinctive alarm subsided. Might as well get that if you pay what I did for these guys.

"There's been a slight cock-up," the elf said quietly.

"Oh, wonderful," Geraint sighed. "Tell me about it. At least there hasn't been a firefight, since everyone's sound asleep hereabouts."

"Dead drunk, more like!" the elf chuckled sarcastically. "Well, you're going to owe us blood money."

"What?" Geraint was astonished.

"Jim's throat was cut from ear to ear. Cheesewire and strangulation," the elf said with a slight hint of disturbing relish. Geraint guessed he hadn't liked the team's leader all that much.

"What the hell—"

"There were some visitors ahead of us," the elf said. "Jim must have surprised 'em. He weren't expecting any grief, so he went in while we covered him. Forgot basic routines, though I did warn him."

"You said you had Seratini," Michael groaned.

"I said no such thing. Jim told you we were on our way. We didn't know someone would be lying for us. By the way, Gungrath's waiting for an order to let those hostages go. They're just office grunts—secretaries and clerks—and they don't know anything."

"Okay, okay, let them go then. You saw who did it? Here, I mean?" Geraint demanded impatiently.

"Sort of," the elf said.

"Sort of?"

"Look, the bastard was bloody fast," the elf shot back. "Ran like a Derby winner on methoxy. Seemed like he knew his way around. He went 'round the corner and next thing I heard was a bike heading off south. Must've been him."

"What did he look like?"

The elf shrugged. "It's dark, chummer. And he was wearing a long black coat and you might as well ask what the ace of spades looks like down a mine shaft at midnight on a moonless night. But the troll had a little run-in with him."

Ah, *the troll,* Geraint registered. No love lost here. At least Jim was Jim, even though this one doesn't seem to care that he's dead. But the troll—well, he's obviously just "the troll".

"Cut him," the elf said with a grin of relish. "Slashed him in the side with his knife. Got him on head cam. No way the troll could have followed him, of course. He's far too slow and there wasn't a blood trail to follow. Could have used IR on his footprints, but he still couldn't have kept up with him."

Geraint hadn't even noticed that the troll samurai had cybereyes. Behind them, implanted inside his skull, was a tiny camera that would have recorded the events of the struggle.

"Downloading it right now, back in the van," the elf said.

"What about—"

"Your Italian term? Dead, Your Lordship, dead as a

dodo with its giblets in an oven-ready pack." The elf grinned. "Throat job, just like Jim. The bugger must have been inside the apartment when we arrived. Nice work, too. Very professional. A trained professional, you know what I mean?"

Geraint looked at him hard. The elf was saying that this was not even an ordinary hit-man; this was military work. When an ex-SAS man called someone a "trained professional", that's what he meant.

"What if this was down to his dabblings in the illegal art trade?" Michael asked Geraint.

"Hardly." The Welshman's mind was racing. Something important was going on out of the frame, something that had led to a very professional assassination of a man who'd been tracking him, and maybe had a magical assailant invading his home that very night; and Geraint didn't like that. He was too used to being in charge, of calling the shots himself.

"Wanna take a gander?" the elf said, his South London accent seeming to get broader with every minute. "Scene of the crime? Make sure all those heavy nuyen you paid were earned?"

"What if the police arrive?" Michael said anxiously.

"Frag me, what a spoilsport," the elf spat out with an expression of barely contained disgust. "Look, do you wanna see the stiffs or don't you?"

Geraint's mouth felt dry, and he badly wanted a cigarette, but this was hardly the time or place. He nodded assent and they entered the building through the stark, bare foyer and approached the elevator. To his amazement, it was working, and the smell of urine inside stopped just short of overwhelming, which was a bonus.

The cramped and drably painted apartment was as starkly functional as one could imagine. Beside the basic kitchen utilities, a battered trid unit, and some bedding, there were but a few scraps of furniture. The only thing any of them had in common was that they all looked as if a pack of psychopathic and crazed felines had sharpened their claws on them, more or less continuously, for twenty years or so.

"I didn't touch a thing, inspector," the elf said dryly.

Almost despite himself, Geraint was beginning to

warm to him a little. Suddenly he realized he didn't even know his name.

"You can call me Streak," the elf told him. "Now get your arse in 'ere before someone else gets interested." He almost dragged them inside and shut the door carefully behind him. His dwarf fellow was standing guard within, a com unit half-sticking out of his pocket, awaiting the obviously desired signal to get out.

"They're here, Thumper," the elf said needlessly. "We can get our cred and blow soon. Show them the stiffs."

"Thumper?" Michael couldn't help but splutter.

"Named after some rabbit famous for its kicking," the elf told him. "Kicked me in the bonce once over a minor disagreement. I had double vision for the best part of a week. Gave him some respect for that."

Streak pushed at the corpse of his sometime leader just inside the doorway. "Here's the first one. If you want to get the slash close up, you'll have to turn him over."

"I think we can dispense with that," Michael said.

"We're going to bag him and get him out," Thumper said. "Can't leave him here for the filth to find."

Surprising that an ex-soldier should use such a term for the police, Michael thought, but said nothing of it. As the elf and dwarf sheathed the body in a resilient plastic body-bag, he could see the amazingly thin, smooth, deep cut in the man's neck. There was less blood somehow than he'd expected, and the pale corpse face looked oddly peaceful. Not what one would have anticipated from the victim of such an attack.

"Your Mr. Seratini is in the bathroom," Streak informed them. Geraint hardly needed telling; the flat was so small that it was the only place the as yet unseen stiff could be. He needed only a few seconds to take in the scene.

"How about that when you're just about to have your annual bath?" Streak said. "Such a waste of that pine fragrance too. Costs a fortune, that Luxo stuff. Made from real trees, apparently. None of your chemical crap."

"I'm afraid not," Geraint told him, giving in to his cravings at last and lighting up, to the obvious disgust of the dwarf. "It contains three coloring agents, one of which is probably carcinogenic, at least to metahumans, and two rather noxious scent enhancers."

"What are you, a scientist?" Streak enquired as he tugged at the zipper of the bag.

"I'm a director of the company that owns the people who make it."

"Well, that's the last time I sink myself in that crap then," Streak said. "You want to give us a hand with this or you going to stand there like a plonker till lunchtime?"

"You're taking him down in the goddamn elevator?" Michael said, surprised.

"Nah, you dumb git," the elf said. "We'll do what the locals do—chuck it out the window."

For a moment Michael thought Streak was joking, but then the elf and dwarf dragged the bag to the window. They hefted the body into a sitting position, opened the window, and on a count of three jerked the black bag and its contents out into midair.

"I don't believe this," Michael said, turning away.

"It'll hardly hurt him now," Streak pointed out. "Look, our terms have just picked it up. No one saw. Much the fastest way. Thumper sent the signal."

"How?" Michael was astounded. The dwarf had said nothing.

"Cybercom," Thumper said. "Thought-to-sound unit. Wired to radio. Paired with the rigger." Clearly, he didn't want to waste any time on superfluities like connecting principles or verbs here. "Told him, special delivery. In the van now. That's three hundred thou, mate."

"I'm not carrying that much," Geraint said, perfectly reasonably. "Come back to my apartment. You'll have the cred in five minutes."

"Fine by me," Steak said. "But it will be going to his family." The elf looked deadly serious for a moment. Behind the joking and facetiousness, and the seemingly awful fact that he barely seemed to care that a comrade had been killed in this place and his body treated like refuse, the elf had some honor remaining. He would see the man's family right, at any rate.

They were just about to leave when Michael spotted the slightly out-of-place cushion and told them to wait. Underneath the red wine-stained cover he found a small padded envelope stashed there, and pocketed it. He wondered whether to search the whole place, and then realized that apart from the wardrobe there was precious little to search. A quick check eliminated the wardrobe as an object of suspicion. Streak was beginning to get jumpy; the coast was clear and he wanted to get out now. Michael obliged and went down in the elevator.

"What did you get?" Geraint asked him.

"UPS package," Michael said. "Non-standard packaging, but they delivered it. The sticker with the ID is gone, but we could trace it easily enough."

"So, come on, what's in it?"

Michael fumbled with the packaging. It was, as courier deliveries usually are, rendered impossible to open without recourse to a sharp object of some kind. His nail-file didn't quite come up to scratch. By the time Thumper had offered him a combat knife, the elevator doors were about to open.

Standing before them was a large clutch of Metropolitan policemen. They even had riot shields and were obviously expecting some serious trouble. The electric stun batons they carried were further evidence of that, if any were needed. The two at the front of the wedge were orks, and they looked as if the police had recently taken to recruiting from hospitals for the criminally insane. Or perhaps doing so more openly and with less pickiness than usual. Michael's heart almost stopped dead and it was all he could do not to gasp aloud.

After twice catching Michael and company at the scene of a murder in a single night, the police weren't going to look at them any too kindly. They wouldn't get out of this again.

Michael and the others stared at the police, who stared back at them.

There was something horribly wrong.

"Rather fine gentlemen to be in a place like this," one of the orks said in an obviously assumed semiposh accent. He was staring at Geraint and Michael.

"Well, officer," Streak chimed in before either of the men could open their mouths, "that's because they were kidnapped and brought here. I'm glad to say we've just now persuaded their 'hosts' to release them, without any due trouble. Ransom job. Quietly and efficiently dealt with. No harm done, nothing to frighten the horses."

Geraint was amazed at his quick-wittedness. He was even more amazed at the response of the ork.

"I see, sir," he said, continuing with his brave attempt to sound like a BBC newscaster. "Well, then, we need not detain you any further."

"I assume you have other business here, officer," Streak said mischievously. The ork looked very uncomfortable. "Well, we won't get in your way. These places," he said, shaking his head, "such hot-beds of depravity and crime. Good to know London can rely on you brave fellows." He led them out, past the shifty-looking uniformed squad, and into the safe anonymity of the night. When they were a safe distance away, and the police safely inside the building, the elf almost doubled up laughing.

"I don't know how you got away with that," Michael said, shaking his head.

"Got away with it?" the elf hooted. "Police, my arse. They were local slints. Disguised as coppers. Gets them in the door and that's half the battle when they're out on a job, steaming a flat or thrashing some poor tosser senseless. There's been a rash of it lately. Good outfits, though. Not bad gear. Probably bought it as knock-off from some sub-station somewhere."

Geraint shook his head ruefully. The ork's attempt at posh English had been so absurd, but he simply hadn't thought of the possibility. Understandable, really. Few people, exiting from the scene of a murder, would have thought of it.

"Funny thing is, one look at a real toff and they go all slobbery and weak at the knees. The old hand starts tugging at the forelock before they know it," Streak said, still chuckling. "They knew you were class, Your Lordship. Tangling with you would be trouble. Get the real cops in, right? Not what they wanted at all."

"Makes two of us," Geraint said.

"Come on, let's get to the van, get those pictures for you," Streak said to Michael, "and then our cash. It's been a long night."

"It certainly has," Michael said in fervent agreement. Too long by half.

By five A.M., back in Mayfair and with their unexpected guests long gone back into the anonymous dawn, Geraint and Michael sat down to a brandy and waited for their over-stimulated systems to calm down to where sleep might be a possibility. Michael was painfully stiff across the shoulders and of course there was the permanent weakness in the small of his back. Whenever he exerted himself too much, he felt as if he'd spend a day on a rack. An image flitted across his tired mind of being tortured by devilish hooded figures from some historical Inquisition. Maybe it was coincidence, maybe it was psychic, but he dismissed it at the time.

Then he remembered the package he'd picked up in the apartment. He took a dagger-shaped paper knife from Geraint's desk and slit it open. Inside was a slim, leather-bound volume whose contents was written in Latin. He took in the long-winded title and shook his head slowly.

"Don't tell me, it's a book of fairy tales," Geraint said.

"Actually, you're not so far off. It's a treatise on undines."

Geraint looked thoughtful. "Go on. Refresh my memory."

"I'm not sure myself," Michael admitted. "Some kind of water spirit or something. Let me check."

A few quick recourses to dictionaries and a database had the answer before too long. Michael summarized the spew of words. "Yes, nature spirits in watery form. Often female. The Rhine maidens, that sort of thing. Want me to go press some macros and call up more detail?"

"I think it can wait," Geraint said, yawning at last. Finally, his body was telling him that it might be able to sleep after all. "But what does a—"

"—cultural attaché want with a book on undines?" Michael finished his sentence for him. "Indeed. What does it mean?"

"Maybe it was intended for Serrault?" Geraint suggested. "His mage friend? The one absent from public records?"

"Could be," Michael said. "Only one thing to do. Find out who sent it." His rubbed his hands together with the smug grin that prefaced any decking activity he expected to be very straightforward. "I think we've got to go trawling through the databases again."

"You do that, old man," Geraint said as he got up, rubbing his eyes. "I need some sleep like the Conservationist party chairman needs a punch in the face. Let me know what you find." He knew the expression in Michael's eyes from old, and guessed his friend would be busy for some time yet. Whenever they gambled with cards, or just played some game for the fun of it, Michael would always want one more. One more hand, one more twist, one more puzzle or riddle to crack. Because you couldn't have too much of a good thing. Geraint was just a couple of years older, and much less prone to riding waves.

"Later," Michael said, but his back was already turned and he barely registered the Welshman trooping off to the bathroom. The Matrix beckoned like a warm swimming pool after a long, dusty day. He dived in.

8

Breakfast stretched into an extended brunch as people woke, bathed, gathered their wits, and exchanged tales over a series of mugs of coffee throughout the morning. Geraint's kitchen became a virtual coffee fountain. His original claims for the excellence of his favored brand hadn't been exaggerated, which encouraged everyone to drink too much. A caffeine buzz settled on them well before noon.

"And so I found out the package came from Clermont-Ferrand, France," Michael finished. "It must have been delivered to the main office. The address is a false one. There isn't such a number on the street. And the name of the guy who sent it isn't in any provincial register."

"Rather remiss of them," Geraint said.

"Not really. I mean, what the hell, as long as someone isn't trying to send a bomb it's hardly feasible to run a retina-scan on every customer," Michael protested. "Anyway, Jean-Marie Muenières doesn't exist. Not in the area, anyway. So all we have is the topic." He looked at the elf.

"It's a genuine historical article as far as I can tell," Serrin said. "But in terms of content it's mostly a collection of fairy stories."

"What did I tell you?" Geraint grinned, another mug of fragrant Jamaican in his hand.

"Though it does have some rituals for summoning undines in an appendix," the mage continued. "Oddly enough, they're not all that different from some shamanic rituals. Or so I'd say."

"Are undines spirits or elementals?" Michael asked.

"I think the question is, are spirits or elementals what were know as undines?" Serrin said.

"I really don't know what you're talking about," said Kristen. She was bored, fidgety with a coffee buzz and full recovery from the tiring travel the day before. Too much talk and inaction was making her restless. Michael noticed, but ignored it. He had one surprise up his sleeve, but he was biding his time. Serrin set it up beautifully.

"I'm still not certain why you asked me here," he said doubtfully.

"To cover anything magical," Michael said. "There's an occult angle to this."

"You mean, you think there is."

"No, I mean there definitely is." Michael paused. In the end it was Geraint who fell for the lure and asked the question that pressed the button.

"The assassin," Michael said.

"You got an ID on him?"

"Not as such. Not an individual ID, that is. Of all things, he had face blacking," Michael said. "Such an old trick, but it stiffs any hope of a photofit even with the best enhancing programs I've got, because it really messes up all the face contouring. But there was something else. He was slashed, as our friends put it."

"So?"

"The knife cut his jacket and shirt. Judging by the lack of a real trail of blood—or so we were told—it must have been a superficial wound. No real harm done. But it did cut through his clothing and exposed some of his torso."

"So?" Geraint repeated.

"So," Michael said, retreating to the lounge and retrieving a glossy photo, "here's what the download of the head-camera film showed. Of course, I've enhanced it some, but the program says it's a ninety-nine point nine percent match with the library image, which are certainly odds I wouldn't bet against."

The photo was grainy and plainly an extrapolated enlargement of a small body area. The sternum was protruding in part; the man must have been somewhat shallow-chested. Lithe and swift rather than muscular. But the marking, revealed except for the extreme right side where the material of his shirt still covered it, was quite distinctive. Two hands clasped together at an angle of perhaps thirty degrees from the vertical, the right hand in foreground covering the left; seemingly cut off at the wrist, disembodied, eerie.

"What on earth is that?" Geraint said, peering intently, but Serrin's sudden paleness revealed that he, at least, already knew.

"Those, my friend," Michael said with relish, "are the hands of Ignatius Loyola, as rendered in the famous portrait of him. Poor dead Monsignor Seratini's nocturnal visitor was a member of the New Order of Jesuits, that enthusiastic body of fellows sometimes known vulgarly as the New Inquisition."

"Jesus Christ," Geraint said.

"Well, absolutely," Michael laughed.

"Was Seratini some kind of heretic?" Geraint said. "Oh, I wish I knew more about these people. Even the FO doesn't say anything more about these Jesuits than it positively has to."

"There's nothing in Seratini's history that I've been able to find to possibly explain why the NOJ would be after him. Oh, and don't just say 'Jesuits.' There are Jesuits and Jesuits, as I'm sure you know. The NOJ is, shall we say, the hardline faction."

"So how come they had him killed?"

"That has to be the reason," Michael said, pointing to the treatise sitting under Serrin's hands. "Or at least a pointer to the reason."

The elf pulled his hands off the book with a jerk, as if in some gesture of guilt or attempted expiation. "We need to know why it was sent, who sent it, who it was intended for, and what it means. I think this is out of my league. Serrin?"

"Yes, I can ask around," Serrin said thoughtfully. "I've got some contacts who should know about this general area. I did some field work with an Amazonian guy once, he'd know. Can I use your phone?"

"All day," Geraint told him.

"We get Joan of Arc, and our term with an interest in

tracking you gets the Inquisition." Michael smiled grimly at Geraint. "Reckon there's some kind of occult angle?"

"Point made," Geraint said. "I think I need to rattle some cages at the FO about the New Order bods. The Templars?" The last term was used questioningly.

"Somehow I don't think so," Michael said. "Seeing that the Inquisition had the real Templars burned alive for a variety of sins, real or imagined, and wiped them out almost to the last man. Burned nearly fifty of them in one day alone in Paris, I seem to recall. I know the term is sometimes used mockingly, but it couldn't be wider of the mark. A bit like calling the Pope a Satanist."

"You haven't been keeping up with affairs in Ulster lately, have you? There are plenty of people there who'd tell you he most certainly is," Geraint shot back with a rueful smile. "Anyway, give me the afternoon to see what I can pick up. I also have certain feathers to unruffle about last night. You can make your own fun while I'm away?"

Michael looked over at the glum Azanian girl and nodded after a moment. As Geraint went through the ritual of putting on his overcoat and adjusting the hat he'd taken to wearing, and then calling his limo, Michael turned to Kristen.

"Serrin's going to be busy," he said. "I can't do much until he gets some leads for me. But I guess you've seen the sights of London, haven't you?"

"Some," she said, but it was an invitation of sorts, and being confined within the four walls of the apartment, luxuriously appointed as it was, was beginning to lose its fascination.

"Then let's go out and see some more," he said.

"You mean they didn't bring you here?" he said as they munched the free samples in the food hall, taking in the sights and sounds around them. "That was remiss. I'm disappointed in Geraint, really I am."

They stood in the middle of Selfridges, consuming a new almost-caviar, which, in truth, had little to recommend it other than the fact that it was free as part of some promotion or other and was accompanied by tiny, thimble-sized crystal glasses of a very good frozen lemon vodka. The high-class emporium did its utmost in a world of synth-this and fake-that to sell only food that hadn't been forced into existence with steroids or boosters, on one hand, nor laced with pesticides or pollutants, on the other, and it almost invariably succeeded. The cost to the credstick was correspondingly high.

Then he realized he'd put his foot in it. It was Serrin, her husband, who should have been showing her around town. Furthermore, not mentioning Serrin was an implicit criticism that he wouldn't be thoughtful enough to do so. Irritated at his clumsiness, Michael tried to extricate himself from the faux pas.

"After all, he knows this city a lot better then old Serrin," he continued. "He's lived here eight years or so. Knows it inside out."

"It's all right, I know what you meant," Kristen said coolly. "Serrin's not a very worldly person, not really, for all he thinks he knows about things. But I saw a lot of the museums and galleries and I'd never been to places like that, and I did get to go to the best bagel shop in the universe."

Her face cracked in a grin, and Michael reflected that when she smiled she did look very pretty, not because her smile might have graced the cover of some fashion tridzine, but because every gram of her spirit was in it.

"Better than the mock caviar," he said ruefully.

"The vodka's great, though," she said, the smile taking on a wicked aspect. "Can we get another?"

Michael looked at the bags he was carrying. He'd spent enough to make a return to the freebie counter entirely reasonable.

"If I bring you back drunk in the middle of the day Serrin will never let me hear the end of it," he chuckled. "Can't have you consorting with an ex, you know. Even one who only existed as a technical formality."

"Actually," she said archly, "I think that's a very English thing."

He laughed out loud. The Cape Town street kid was doing a creditable impression of being very worldly indeed, even if her husband wasn't, despite his many years of traveling the globe.

Just before the second vodka, as they stood inhaling the splendid, biting aroma that rose even from the near-frozen liquid, Kristen finally decided to confide her concern.

"I can see why Serrin's here, but I don't feel very useful," she said. "I don't even really understand exactly what's happening, you know?"

"Neither do we."

"Yes, but I don't even know why I don't know why."

Michael looked at her standing there for all the world like a very serious child who has gazed up at the stars and thought to herself, "What is it with all this infinity and eternity stuff?" He wasn't in love with her and never had been, but he could easily understand how any other man might be.

"In a nutshell," he began, taking a deep breath, "some joker—some extraordinarily talented joker—says he's going to frag up every computer system on the planet and gives every indication that he's more than capable of fulfilling such a threat. He leaves an icon, a calling card, which is the most famous fraud in Christianity. He names himself after the greatest genius in the world's history. I'm asked to find out all I can and maybe find him. I no sooner start making attempts to do so than an awful lot of people start getting very interested in *that*. One of them sends our party guest last night. One of them tracks Geraint and ends up dead at the hands of Jesuits. At first I didn't know what the image meant, the face of a black woman, but now it looks as if some very weird occult or religious stuff is involved. And that's what Serrin's helping me with. And, oh, we have seven days before our joker pulls his party piece—the systems crash and the world grinds to a halt. Okay?"

He had hardly paused for breath and did so now, gulping down big lungfuls prior to swallowing the vodka. It hurt the throat and brought tears to his eyes and he shook himself in a shivery spasm right afterward, but ten seconds later his throat was warm, his stomach glowed, and he felt wonderful. Kristen had done the same, but somehow managed the operation without the cough and sharp intake of breath.

"All right," she said with that same serious-child look. "I don't know much about Jesuits. Where I came from there were Sunnis and Shi'as, and a few Rastas, and the Dutch Reformed Church, of course, and some Hindus, and a few others as well. But I never heard of any black woman in Christianity."

Just for an instant a chill ran down Michael's spine, and if he'd been the kind to pay more attention to intuitions—endowed with Geraint's Celtic genes, perhaps—he'd have stayed with the sensation. But he put it down to the vodka, which had made him just a little light-headed, and he missed it. People do sometimes. They miss things because what they know prevents them from seeing what else is there. Brains are designed to keep information out, and they're good at that.

Besides that, his stomach was running interference on his brain in any event. Being the last to get up meant scrounging up breakfast from what little was left by the time he got to the kitchen, so he hadn't really eaten, save the tiny scraps of caviar with some sour cream and crackers. He rummaged in one of the bags.

"Let's wander outside and eat these saffron biscuits," he said conspiratorially, and the serious child he'd been looking at turned into the larder-raiding variety. They made a swift exit back out into the bustling street to open the packet.

It was half-past four and Geraint had already retrieved his overcoat from the antique hatstand and was ready to leave with his familiar red box, when a bulky figure entered his office. Since he came in without knocking, it could only be one person.

"Llanfrechfa, glad I caught you," the portly man grunted. He parked his spreading rear in Geraint's own chair in an appropriating gesture. Geraint knew at once that this was going to be bad news. His boss, the Earl of Manchester, usually summoned him to his own offices. If he came to Geraint's, then there was trouble to be shared or delegated. It might be gout, it might be one of his wives demanding more maintenance for the noble offspring, it might be anything—but it would be trouble. Geraint sat down opposite him, dutifully.

"Wanted a word," the man continued. Geraint's heart sank. That was a code, long-established through use. It meant it was serious trouble and he was the cause.

"If it's about last night—" he began.

"Bugger last night!" the Earl said. "Not important. The

Commissioner of Police hasn't had to smooth anything over for some time, not since that idiot Earl and the scoutmaster, so it won't cause many ripples. Not, however, that I suggest you involve yourself in such nocturnal alarums and excursions on a regular basis," he finished in finger-wagging mode.

"I wouldn't dream of it, sir," Geraint said fervently, making sure he got the "sir" into the conversation right at the start.

"But it is about last night, in a manner of speaking." The Earl stopped there, and began the ritual of lighting one of his implausibly large cigars. Even in Havana, nimble-fingered artisans must have been appalled at the prospect of rolling one of these monstrosities. Bizet's famous heroine would have had thighs like a Sumo wrestler's had she been obliged to roll such cigars all her life. Geraint could do nothing but wait.

Cunning old swine, he thought. It's absolutely deliberate, leaving me to stew in my own anxiety until he chooses just the right moment to dump ten tons of stinking drek on me. Full-blown ministers need that kind of talent, I've learned.

"There are certain foreign interests to whom HMG does not wish to cause unnecessary offense at this particular moment in time," the Earl said slowly. Again he paused, using his free hand to check the time on the pocket-watch he fished out of his waistcoat pocket. Geraint waited further for the punchline.

"Those interests are unhappy regarding the nature of certain enquiries you and a certain associate appear to be pursuing," the Earl went on. "It gives them offense, I regret to say. And His Majesty's Government does not wish that to happen. And of course I am a servant of HMG, even as you are."

And of course we both know the other hold you have on me, Geraint added to himself. But he chanced something anyway.

"May I respectfully enquire as to whether you are familiar with the nature of the problem that has led to our undertaking certain enquiries?" he said, using the intractably long-winded language that was the lingua franca of professional British politicians.

"I may or may not be," the Earl said, "but I do know

where the interests of King and country lie. So I trust I can rely on your discretion in this matter. Perhaps we shall take dinner at my club, then?"

The invitation couldn't be refused. It was like a gentleman's handshake, a seal on the matter. To do so would implicitly reject the Earl's demand. Accepting it, of course, would mean that Geraint could not go back to Michael and the others and engage in any more mischief. Despite his irritation, Geraint admired the aging Earl. He knows the rules of the game and how to impose himself, he thought. And best of all, he reassured himself, he has no idea why we're doing what we're doing. Which gives me one loophole. If we're successful, I can argue that the end justified the means and he won't be angry afterward. But if we're not . . .

"Delighted to," Geraint said cheerfully. "Does Alphonse still do that wonderful sea bass?"

The Earl's face lit up with that expression of delight that can only be seen on a politician who thinks he's just gained the submission of an underling. When he rose to his feet, he didn't even fart, which he almost invariably did. Juniors at the Foreign Office had been known to refer to their minister as The Lemur, interpreting this behavior as some bizarre form of territorial scent-marking. Clearly the Earl was in excellent spirits, feeling entirely secure.

You don't know how wrong you are, Geraint thought as he picked up the phone to warn Michael of his impending absence while the Earl summoned his limo. Now I know that whoever's against us can get to you, which means we really are on to something big.

And if I can crack this one, maybe I'll get the monkey off my back that you put there.

It had been a standard black taxi like any other London taxi cab. The trip from Oxford Street to Mayfair was through crowded streets, a short enough haul, a small fare, and it could have been any taxi. Michael had barely glanced at the driver. Dusting the last of the cracker crumbs from his mouth, he'd climbed into the first one in the queue waiting for fares in front of Selfridges. After giving the address, he sat back with a yawn, a bit sleepy after too few hours of rest the night before and the lingering effects of the drink. He hadn't taken much, but it had been ferociously strong.

But surely not so strong, he'd thought while loosening his tie. He'd felt hot and sweaty, and light-headed, and then he registered that Kristen was tugging at his sleeve and looking at him with an expression of concern, an expression that turned to panic as the taxi began to run the red lights. After that it was a long enough stretch of almost-open road ahead to be able to pick up a little speed and minimize the chance of any passerby registering that two people were trying to clutch at the windows and not managing it, two people finally slumping back into their seats as the last of the gas billowed soundlessly into the sealed back compartment.

Black taxi cabs are not so unlike the cars that follow the hearse in a funeral cortege, after all.

9

"They're still out," Serrin told Geraint when he rang the apartment. "Not back yet."

"Oh, well, never mind," Geraint said. "I won't be back until eleven or so, I don't expect. Fortunately the old bastard usually nods off in his chair about half-past ten and the liveried servants carry him away to sleep it off. See you thereabouts."

Serrin was surprised that Geraint hadn't asked him how his own searches were going. He was already intrigued, and after a few more phone calls had gotten even more so.

While adding to his notes, he realized he hadn't eaten since breakfast and went to raid the fridge. He managed to put together some highly inept sandwiches from soft cheese and Parma ham, wishing the bread were a bagel, and went back to his writing. Finally, pausing at the last sentence, he caught the time on the carriage clock on the mantelpiece.

Ten minutes to eight.

He was astonished. Subjectively it felt around six at the

latest, and with the heavy drapes drawn in the room—Geraint's suggestion, since they had, after all, been subject to surveillance—he hadn't realized that it had long since grown dark outside.

Something was clearly wrong. Michael and Kristen had been gone for more than seven hours and they would surely have phoned in the normal course of events.

There was a knock at the door, and a whole host of paranoid thoughts and images leaped into his mind. He found himself walking over to get the Predator from his jacket, and then realized this was only bloody England, after all. Even in this day and age, there was barely one licensed gun for every hundred people—about the exact reverse of the situation at home—and there weren't *that* many illegal weapons on the street.

And those that were usually didn't make it north of the Thames all the way to posh Mayfair.

Opening the door a crack Serrin saw a uniformed delivery man standing outside with his clipboard and pen, awaiting his signature.

"His Lordship isn't home. Detained on urgent government business," he said.

The delivery man didn't look terribly impressed. "Has to be his signature," he insisted. "Says so on the paperwork. Look," and he demonstrated the fact with a thick, ink-stained finger.

Serrin shrugged. "He probably won't be back until midnight."

"Look, mate, this is well out of hours already. Special service extra delivery, know what I mean? Rakk me if I'm coming back at rakking midnight."

"Yes, yes, all right." Serrin was irritated at the man's foul mouth. "Look, I'll sign and everything will be in order."

"Rakk off. You're not a lordship," the man said huffily. "You can't even be one of his servants—you're a bloody sep, you are! I can't let you have this, guv. More than my job's worth."

Serrin fished into his pockets and located what he considered a reasonable sum in pounds sterling.

The man looked at the bills rather dubiously.

Serrin exchanged the sum for nuyen, and upped the ante fifty percent.

The man shrugged philosophically. "Just sign as 'im and no one will ever know the difference," he said casually. Serrin did as he was told.

"So where's the package?" he asked.

"Down in the parking lot. I'm not lugging it all the rakking way up here."

"Thanks," Serrin said dryly, wishing he hadn't upped the payment. Just as the delivery man turned to leave, a dark-haired elf dressed in black emerged from the elevator and fixed him with a stare by way of greeting.

"Lord Llanfrechfa at home?"

"Frag me, this is worse than Piccadilly Circus!" Serrin sputtered. "He's out and isn't likely to be back until midnight."

"Pity. It was urgent," the elf said quietly. Serrin appraised him. He was muscular of build, but very lithe and in excellent physical condition. A street samurai or a physad, he thought.

"You Serrin?" the other elf asked suddenly, to which Serrin nodded. "Streak. Maybe Geraint mentioned me?"

Serrin recalled the name from breakfast and said so, making the mistake of mumbling some thanks for the help the elf had given his friends. Streak took the advantage.

"Look, mind if I wait? It really is urgent," he said insistently.

"This isn't my place," Serrin began, but the elf cut him short.

"Look, brother, last p.m. I had five terms working with me on a raid for his lordship. By the time we shipped out again this morning, I had three and a half, with what was left of one of the trolls. Now I'm down to two and a half. Maybe, some time soon, one of my terms is going to find out he's down to one and a half." The elf drew his right forefinger across his throat. It was melodramatic, but he was dead serious.

"I reckon I could use at least enough explanation to keep from becoming another statistic myself. Frag it, brother, I'm not here to knock you on the head and take the family silver. Give me a sodding break, okay?"

Serrin decided to let the other elf in, then locked the door and drew the chain bolt as well.

"Not a bad idea," Streak said. From his amply padded

black jacket, he took the component parts of two folding-stock automatic weapons and began assembling them.

"I don't know if we're going to need this kind of heat," Streak told Serrin, who was studying him doubtfully, "but I'm not taking any chances."

"I've got to go investigate a package and I'm not leaving you here alone in the place," Serrin said.

Streak looked at up him with an intense stare and then nodded. "Fair enough, term. Fortunately for you, I've done some bomb disposal in my time."

"Damn, I hadn't thought of that," Serrin said. "Thanks."

"Only some, mind you. Don't get too grateful too soon. Anyway, the scanners should have picked up anything suspicious entering this building. They've got good security here."

"Let's be grateful for that," Serrin said with feeling, but Streak caught him out again.

"Not good enough to stop me getting in, of course, and if it's one of those experimental percussion-sensitive gel explosives that scans as biomatter, then we'd be buggered sideways whatever we did," he said with a laconic chuckle. "But then, live life to the full, that's what I say. Can't worry about being blown into bloody fragments every day of your waking life."

Streak put down the assembled LMG and got to his feet, taking in the look on Serrin's face. His own broke into a gleeful smile.

"Serrin, mate, you're a worrier, I can see that," he said, putting an arm around the other's shoulder. "I like that in a bloke, but don't let the bastards get you down.

"Now, let's go say hello to Mister Bomb."

The wooden crates were bound only with rope. They were not, apparently, even nailed shut, with sliding tops restrained by the thick ropes around them. Streak's diagnostics took a few minutes, and he looked reasonably content.

"There's a little metal content but very little indeed. Actually, I think it's probably a watch, and a ring. Oh, and a portable computer and one or two other little extras."

"What extras?" Serrin asked.

"There are two bodies in there."

"Spirits!" Serrin cried out. "How many dead people are we going to—"

"They may or may not be dead," Streak said. "Anyway I think we can risk this," and drawing out an evil-looking survival knife, he slashed clean through the ropes on one crate and slid back the panel top.

Kristen, apparently sound asleep, lay within. Serrin made a scrabbling attempt to lift her out, but it was impossible given the height of the crate. With Streak's help, he gently tipped the crate onto its side and lifted her into his arms.

"Know her?" Streak asked as he slashed at the ropes on the other crate.

"She's my wife," Serrin said, hugging the inert body close to his chest.

"Right, then I s'pose you do," Streak replied. "So who'd Father Christmas put in this one, I wonder?"

Serrin told him. Like Kristen, Michael was fast asleep and absolutely impossible to wake.

"Oh, look, one of the reindeers dropped a message," Streak said, extracting a waxed scroll of paper and handing it to Serrin. "Nicely done, eh? Dead authentic."

"Just stick it in my jacket pocket," Serrin snapped. His arms full of warm, sleeping body, so mercifully alive, he could hardly take the paper and read it there and then. Streak looked at him, stepped backward a few paces, and broke the seal. Serrin was furious, not wanting the other elf to know who had been responsible for this.

"No, I'll do the town crier act here, I think," Streak said imposingly. "Your terms are asleep, sep. Mine are dead."

Given the emphasis on the last word, Serrin couldn't really argue. He could only wait and listen.

" 'This is a reasoned warning'," the elf read out. " 'We kill those who shed our blood, but we do not kill without honor. Desist from your enquiries. This reasoned warning is also a final one. Our honor will not be impugned.' Phew."

"That's it?"

"That's it."

"No signature?"

"What did you expect, the Spanish Inquisition?" the elf

said with contempt. For the first time in their brief acquaintance, Serrin had him absolutely trumped.

"Well, actually, more or less, yes, that's exactly what I expected."

Streak's jaw dropped and he just stood and gawked. "You're fragging serious, aren't you?"

"You wanted an explanation and now you're going to get it," Serrin said with the triumph of an absolute advantage. "Just get Michael into the elevator and into the flat and we'll talk."

Geraint was entirely unprepared for the scene he encountered upon returning home sometime around midnight. Using his magkey to let himself in, he entered to find two elves sitting on his sofa so deep in discussion they barely even acknowledged his presence.

"Well, excuse me, but I just live here," he said tartly while hanging up his coat. "Where are Michael and Kristen?"

"Sleeping," Serrin told him.

"They retired early," Geraint observed casually.

"They didn't have much choice," Serrin shot back, then explained for Geraint's benefit. "Whatever it was hasn't worn off. Face slaps, cold water, we tried it, it didn't work."

"But they're fine," Streak put in quickly. "I scanned 'em. Not the same as a doc, but I didn't know if you'd want one summoned here and Serrin didn't either."

"What are you doing here?" Geraint asked. He hadn't expected to see the elf again; he'd just been someone useful commissioned for a job, to be paid and then forgotten.

Serrin told him that Streak had a right to know something, what with half his team either dead or incapacitated.

"Since whoever we're up against has it in for them as well as us, I thought we owed him something," he finished.

"Thanks for consulting me about it." Geraint was obviously not pleased.

"You weren't here to ask. And, be fair, he checked those crates. They could have been rigged. He opened them and took his chances."

"So he knows everything?" Geraint asked. Serrin

paused for the merest instant to let him know that no, the
other elf didn't know everything, but he could hardly tell
the Welshman what he hadn't divulged here and now. It
would have to await Streak's departure.

"So, another warning," Geraint concluded, after sitting
down and reading the missive Serrin handed him. "This
is getting ridiculous. They got to my boss as well; he
warned me off. That makes three so far—this, him, and
old Joan of Arc last night. These bloody Jesuits don't do
things by halves."

Streak asked him what he meant by referring to Joan of
Arc, so Geraint told him about the commotion of the previous evening. Clearly, Serrin hadn't gone into all the details on that score.

"Well, whoever sent the spirit—if that's what it
was—it wasn't the NOJ," Streak said. "I've come up
against these blokes before. Little job down in, oh well,
never mind. But I had to learn some stuff about them, and
I know enough to tell you that's hardly on the menu. That
wasn't them."

"How can you be sure?" Geraint asked.

"My sources say the same thing," Serrin added. "Joan
of Arc was, after all, a woman."

"Well, frag me," Geraint said, "I never knew that."

Serrin ignored the sarcasm. "It's just that, well, the
NOJ thinks of her as a heretic. A bit too florid. Catholic
politics, misogyny, rumors about Pope Joan, that sort of
thing. Anyway, they certainly don't care for her. They
wouldn't summon a spirit to take that form."

"Then you're saying that at least two groups, or a
group and an individual maybe, have been telling us to
sod off and stop doing what we're doing sharpish," Geraint said incredulously.

"It would appear so," Serrin said.

"How the bloody hell did they get on to us so fast?"

"Good question," Serrin said. "It's not one we can easily answer, since we don't know the second interested
party. As for the NOJ, well, they have people all over the
place."

Yes, but why would they be interested? We're investi-
gating a—" Geraint stopped for a moment, realizing that
he couldn't speak freely with Streak in the room. "Well,

a computer dysfunction. Hardly red-hot Catholic politics, is it?"

"Look, mate," Streak said with some feeling, "I know I'm getting the mushroom treatment here. Kept in the dark, blah blah. Why don't you level with me? You trusted me to watch your back down in Chelsea. That turned out to be life and death. And as it happens, if you're in deep drek I'm currently available for work. I also have a vested interest in finding out who's wasted some of the few people I could trust with my life. I'm not going to be blabbing anything to anyone."

Geraint thought long and hard. Serrin's expression was clearly urging him to come clean.

"Well, it was Michael's job originally," Geraint said truthfully. "A decker is threatening to do some heavy-duty sabotage to some corp systems. He left an identifying icon behind that seems to have some occult or religious significance. Not that we really understood that at first, but we certainly do now that people are taking an active interest in us and applying the thumbscrews. It's big corporate nuyen on the one hand, and some very odd occult stuff on the other."

"All right," Streak said slowly, still unsure that he was getting the full version. "So if it's sleeping beauty's job, how come you guys enter the frame?"

"We go back a way," Geraint said simply. "Michael thought I could help with the corporate angle and that Serrin could help with the magical, occult angle. Not to mention the money."

"That sounds hopeful," Streak grinned.

"We could use him," Serrin suggested, looking to Geraint. "We're hardly a bunch of street samurai, are we?"

"Maybe, maybe," Geraint said. "But we need to discuss it with Michael. It's his job, after all."

"That's reasonable enough," Streak said, satisfied, or at least content, for the moment. "Like I say, reasonable rates and I can scan bodies for damage, crates for bombs, shoot an apple off your head at half a klick and I have specialist friends available if need be. Easy terms. All major credsticks accepted."

"All right, all right," Geraint grumbled. "I got your CV first time round. We'll wait for Michael."

The phone rang, and after exchanging a few words, Geraint handed the receiver to Serrin. Whoever was calling wasn't willing to use a telecom. Serrin put the communication through the external speaker so the others could hear, and then realized that maybe he shouldn't have. Geraint he wanted to hear the conversation, but Streak ...

"Greetings, chummer," the Brooklyn-accented voice said cheerfully. "Did some legwork among the crazies. Not too much on the grapevine, but you know how it is with everyone being so interested in Chicago and Dee Cee and all that drek. Got some background and a name, though."

"Give me what you got," Serrin said.

"Well, chummer, I drew a blank on the Seratini guy. No real connections I could find. Must be small beer. Maybe just a contact man."

"Oh, well," Serrin said.

"But this Serrault turns out to be a bit more interesting. He may be—and I say may because if there's a membership list no one has access to it—a member of a hermetic group that goes way back. Take this down: the Priory of Sion."

"Don't think I know of it," Serrin said, even as he dimly sensed that he'd heard the name somewhere and completely forgotten it.

"Not sure how long they've been around. It depends on linkages—whether you believe one cult combined with another, that kind of thing. There's one version that says they go back to the time of those crusaders, the Knights Templar."

"I'm listening," Serrin said as the hair rose on the nape of his neck.

"Serrault's not a member of major importance, but word is he's a possible recruiter. He's a socialite and hangs around to see if he can turn up any interested, talented people the Priory can use in some way. Middling mage, by all accounts. Not drek-hot, but capable enough."

"Finding people he can use for what?"

"Well, now that depends. The orthodox heresy"—the New Yorker chuckled—"is that the Priory serves to protect the bloodline of the descendants of Jesus Christ."

"Oh great. More freak-show stuff," Serrin lamented.

"Maybe, maybe not. Maybe it don't matter. Maybe the idea is emotive enough that it's important as a myth in itself. Life's just a big myth, Serrin, you know that." The voice trailed away into a gale of laughter and then calmed down again. "Sorry about that. Anyway, the HQ of these boys is a place called Clermont-Ferrand in the Languedoc. Did I get that pronunciation right? Down south in France, virtually in Spain."

The room was deadly quiet.

"I've heard of it," Serrin said, and waited.

"Right. Well, before you head off to warmer climes, if you have some reason for that, and I'm not asking, I've got a name closer to home. You want to trawl MagicNet, you can get half a dozen bonehead stories on the Priory, conspiracy theories and the usual pile of drek. You know how mages just spin drek day and night, chummer."

"Spare me," Serrin said. "Just give me the name."

"Yeah, sure. Guy down in Glastonbury. All these quaint English names, love it. A German exile, name of Karl-Heinz Hessler. Keeps pretty much to himself, and it's not really a question of whether you want to see him as whether he wants to see you. Supposed to live in a little place close to the Tor. Serrin, what the frag is a 'tor'?"

"It's a small hill," Serrin said. "Now, anything else on him?"

"Not really, except that he's the man to speak to. Well, not man, elf rather. One of your people. Might help. He's an old guy, too, which makes him a bit unusual."

It certainly did. Elves had been born into the Sixth World for less than half a century and, with their as-yet-undetermined but definitely extra-human lifespan, they hadn't grown old yet. Serrin was intrigued.

"Oh, and he has a sense of humor too. He's got some kind of spirit about the place, an ally, I guess. Calls him Merlin. So be respectful. I heard he took up with a cat, too, or it took up with him."

"Any more trivial details?"

"The cat isn't trivial. It's one of those blackberry cats. Like I said, be respectful. OK, chummer, that's a favor you owe me sometime. Toodle pip, old chum, and cheerio and all that. Must pop over for some crumpet some time." There was more chuckling.

"You got it. Thanks, McCarthy," and Serrin placed the receiver back on the handset.

"Clermont-Ferrand." Serrin simply restated the name

and looked at Geraint. "There's our second interested party, then."

"I don't get it," Streak said as Geraint nodded. Serrin gave Geraint a full-on "Shall we tell him?" look.

"He was there, we'll tell him," Geraint said, and retrieved the package for Streak to examine.

"I think we should hire him," Serrin suggested.

"I think I might," Geraint said slowly.

"This is music to my shell-likes," Streak grinned.

"For seven days," Geraint said, "starting now."

"Seven days?"

"That's how long we've got, and that includes today, which is almost over, so we've got six days really. Before the systems crash. Oh, well, let's get this over with," Geraint sighed, and he told Streak the whole story. More or less.

10

Michael woke around five in the morning with a head full of murder. He felt like he'd had a head-on collision with the entire Giants defense, and his head throbbed horribly. Groaning, he tried to get out of bed and found himself tottering backward. So he stayed put for a few minutes, took a drink from the bottle of mercifully still-cool mineral water, and then stood up and poured the rest of it over his head. He managed to stagger into the bathroom, stuck his head under the cold faucet, and waited and hoped for the best.

By five-thirty, after two cups of Geraint's finest coffee extracted from the espresso machine, he finally felt able to peer out between the veins of his savagely bloodshot eyes. He went back to the bathroom, showered and shaved, and by six-fifteen, dressed in one of his best blue Saville Row suits, felt almost human. He was on the verge of contemplating getting something to eat, his hunger having finally overcome the residual nausea from the gas, when Kristen managed to hang on to the doorframe of the kitchen and focus her uncertain gaze on him.

"That is absolutely the last time I drink lemon vodka with you," he said with a weak laugh. "Kick like a pack of mules. Good morning. Want some coffee?"

She slumped into the chair opposite him, the effort of speech apparently beyond her, but she was just about able to lift a cup and drink. Her hair, which seemed to have grown thicker and more lustrous since he'd previously known her, was an untamed mane of frizz around her face. She was wearing only a short nightgown, and her silky brown legs stretched under the table, touching his. Her physical presence was imposing for all that she was small, still young, and having considerable difficulty engaging with reality.

"Give me a cigarette," she begged at last.

"Sure?"

"Don't ask," she said. "Just do it."

He didn't argue. She inhaled deeply, drank the cupful at a gulp, and sat back with her eyes shut.

"Wish I had the real thing," she said, looking forlornly at the cigarette.

"I don't think that would be a good idea this morning. What happened to us? I can't remember anything after getting in that taxi."

"Me neither," she said, and stretched like a jaguar in the sunshine. She hadn't bathed yet, and her scent was musky and sweet. But as he glanced at her, he saw a mark on her arm. Reaching out, he took her arm in his hands.

"Pinprick," he said. "Look."

Kristen stared intently at her arm, chewing her lip in concern. "How did you see that?" she said doubtfully.

"Don't know. It just caught my eye." Then he slipped off his jacket and rolled up his sleeves.

His left arm had the same tiny mark. He'd missed it while showering, the slight ache in his arm probably masked by the general feeling of fatigue. His head had still been full of cotton-wool at the time, the world a fuzzy haze around him.

"Drek," he said, shaking his head. "Someone's taken blood samples."

She looked alarmed. She didn't know what it meant, but she was probably wondering what else might have been done to her.

"Blood, maybe for ritual magic," he said. "It's not an

uncommon practice. They probably snipped off some hair as well. Not good. We're going to have ask Serrin about this. He's the expert."

Kristen wasn't reassured. She knew little of the art, and what things Serrin told her were hard to understand. The magically talented and the mundane walked different paths, with many points of simple incomprehension between them.

On cue, Serrin appeared in the doorway, a silk dressing gown draped around his thin form. The contrast with the graceful figure of his wife could not have been greater. Knobbled knees and a mass of scar tissue on the leg shattered during a botched run for a corp many years ago were visible beneath the garment. He took one look at the coffee machine dispensing dark fluid, and made for it like a polecat after a baby rabbit.

"What happened? How did we get back?" Michael asked him. Serrin told him. Michael was indignant at first, and then, despite himself, laughed. "Shipped in a crate? The bastards. Well, I can't say I take offense, not really. They could have killed us, after all." Then he told the mage about the pinpricks and the possibility that blood samples had been taken from them.

"Then we'd better get down to Glastonbury damn quick," Serrin said, rubbing at his short-cropped gray hair. "We'll have more to ask than just information. We'll need to be able to build magical wards around us too." He paused as he heard what he was saying. "What are we getting into? Two days ago I was walking the Scottish coastline. Now we're knee-deep in drek coming from all directions."

"Glastonbury?" Michael enquired.

"There's a lot to catch up on," Serrin said, and briefed them about the events of the previous night.

"So we've got someone else on board?" Michael said doubtfully.

"Look, we knew we should ask you first, but honestly there wasn't time, and after all the guy was here when you arrived and when I took a call and he'd seen half the picture already. There was little point in not giving him the rest. After all, in a week's time it's all going to be public knowledge if this doesn't work out," Serrin said reasonably. "Anyway, we didn't tell him everything. He thinks that someone's going to wreck one big corp system and he wouldn't expect us to say who we're working for. He doesn't know it's the whole works."

"Put like that I can hardly argue," Michael agreed. "We can trust him for a week, I suppose."

"Why is he called 'Streak'?" Kristen asked.

"A childhood nickname, apparently." Serrin smiled. "He was very thin as a kid and apparently the Brits have an expression for people like that—'a long streak of piss'?"

Michael laughed. "Well, I guess if he kept that moniker he must have a sense of humor."

"Oh, he has that," Serrin said with some feeling. "Often at our expense, I find."

"You were talking about me?" The elf had snuck up on them while they were absorbed in conversation, and walked past them to the fridge, as if he owned the place.

"My, this is good," he said, rubbing his hands at the delights within. "His lordship has real taste. You can't buy that, you know. That's one thing you Americans"—he grinned at Serrin—"never truly understand."

"Okay, okay, let's stop this now," Michael protested.

"Serrin says it's down to Glastonbury today." Streak was breaking eggs into a bowl. "Want some scrambled?"

Everyone nodded. Any original resentment at him treating the place like he owned it evaporated at the prospect of his acting as quartermaster-cum-chef.

"Best go out through the back door then. I assume we don't want to be tracked," Streak said. "Can you mask us against watchers, that kind of thing?"

"There's a very good hermetic circle protecting this building," Serrin told him.

"Yeah and I'm the Queen of bloody Sheba," Streak said derisively. "You'll have to do better."

"I think I can," Serrin said quietly.

"There are some service tunnels linking these buildings," Streak told him. "We can get out of here half a mile or more away. Best to take an underground route first, I think. Need to arrange the motor, though."

"We can't take Geraint's limo," Michael said. "Have to hire one, I suppose."

"Brilliant," Streak said derisively. "Traceable by anyone with a Radio Shack. Leave it to me. Unregistered ex-

cept on hot police systems so we can't be traced unless
someone can deck ice thick enough to cover Antarctica.
No names, no pack drill. Be here five minutes after I call
it in. You want a limo or an APV?"

"I think an ordinary saloon will do us," Michael said
with a grin.

"Have we got any way of warning this guy that we're
about to arrive on his doorstep?"

"I don't see that we can," Serrin said. "Anything we do
in that direction would be traceable. I thought of sending
a messenger spirit, but it would be detected as soon as it
left the area and there are ways of interrogating them."

"I can at least find us somewhere to stay," Streak said
thoughtfully. "Want some bacon with this?"

"Wouldn't say no. There are some mushrooms in the
cupboard," Michael pointed out.

"I can get a booking somewhere out of the way
through an intermediary," Streak said. "Hey, you want to
go as mellows? I mean, taking in the sacred vibes, all that
drek? I could get some wiz clothes for mellows. I know
some undercover people, drugs-and-chips guys, who've
got that kind of gear."

"That's probably overdoing it. Anyway, I don't think
Hessler would be any too impressed," Serrin told him.

"You know, you don't all have to go," Michael put in.
"I'm the one who should talk with him. There's no need
for anyone else to go, not really."

Kristen grabbed his arm and gave him a very reproachful look, but Michael nipped the idea in the bud anyway.

"Not a bad idea to stick together," he said. "We're a lot
easier targets in ones and twos. Ask any taxi driver."

"All right then," Serrin said. The bacon was beginning
to grill nicely now, and the smell was making Michael
and Kristen, unfed for the best part of thirty-six hours, almost drool.

"Voila!" Streak dumped the eggs into a serving dish.
Milk, just a little cream, and plenty of butter had made
them perfection. Kristen couldn't wait long enough to
scoop them onto her plate, but rammed a spoonful
straight into her mouth looking as if an angel had dropped
down from heaven bearing her own personalized chalice
of manna.

"This is better," Streak said, and emptied the second

serving, this time complete with melted cheese, onto a second plate.

"I told you we were right to hire this guy," Serrin mumbled between forkfuls of egg.

"I think I'd better call Geraint while there's still some left," Michael grinned.

By the time Streak had broken every last egg in the place to feed the eager breakfasters, Michael was already jacked in, data-trawling, getting every last piece of data he could before they set off on the short haul to the West of England. The problem was not that he didn't know what he was looking for, but simply that he didn't have the background knowledge to evaluate what he found. That was why Serrin was with them.

The downloads took a long time even for his Fairlight whose transfer speeds most deckers could hardly dream about—which this morning was just too damn long. He was impatient at having to wait for the archival material, and then dismayed by the sheer volume of it all when it arrived.

"This is the problem," he explained to the freshly shaved and dressed Serrin. "The printouts go on forever. I can get a trillion tons of data dumped down in an hour, but it still takes me a lifetime to read and evaluate it, even with Simon's filtering."

Serrin smiled. "Another of your frames?"

"Yeah, but I don't have the parameters to guide him as well as I'd like," Michael said. "I need your brain in there, Serrin. There has to be a way to do that."

"You leave my brain out of this. I'm very attached to it." Serrin was feeling unusually chipper right now. It was partly the excellent breakfast, partly the sheer relief that his wife had been returned to him safely, and partly anticipation of the audience he was hoping to get. He'd talked with a Scottish druid friend who'd spoken of the old elf they were due to visit with near-reverence, and Serrin was both intrigued and a little awestruck. In a cynical world, the latter was a nice feeling to have.

Michael pointed to the stack of material, the printers still dumping out text and pictures. Even a reader knowing what he was looking for would take days to find what he needed in the mass of data—and they didn't have days.

"I guess we can start reading this in the car," Serrin said, idly picking up a stack of chromalins disgorged from the optical printer. He leafed through them idly. "What's this, a rogue's gallery?"

"Known or suspected members of the Priory of Sion, and known NOJ agents in London, then England, then Britain, then France," Michael said. "Not that we could get all of them. Many will be unknown, many I couldn't get mug shots for."

"Don't see a face I recognize here. Oh, good holiday snaps." Serrin chuckled as he dropped the stack and picked up another.

"Various locations of possible significance," Michael muttered. "You see what I mean? It takes forever to discover what we're looking—Serrin, what's wrong?"

Serrin had suddenly gone even paler than usual and clutched the chromalin in his hands like a drowning man hanging on to a length of wood to keep himself afloat. Michael stopped in his tracks and went over to have a look.

"That's her," Serrin said in a whisper. "In every detail."

"Good Lord," Michael said. "What the—"

"You downloaded it," Serrin said, staring at him. "You tell me."

Michael checked the codes and was rattled when he found the source of the picture.

"It's a statue," he said.

"Obviously," Serrin said impatiently.

"In the chapel building at Rennes-le-Château."

"Go on."

"Rennes-le-Château is just up the road from Clermont-Ferrand. It's sacred to the Priory of Sion—well, sort of. It's a tiny little village. You want more details? The demon over the chapel door and the warning written in Latin?"

"A demon on a chapel?"

"You got it," Michael said. "This is no ordinary house of the Lord, not according to this." He handed over the relevant pages.

"I think you're going to have some background to take to Herr Hessler, Serrin."

11

"I had no idea this was here," Geraint said as he followed Streak through the narrow, hot tunnels.

"Course you ain't," Streak said reasonably. "It's people like me who have maps of such places. I could take you out in Bayswater if you wanted. Well, more or less. Will South Ken do? It's where the Westwind's waiting, so it's probably a good move."

They didn't argue. Serrin had done his best to protect them from magical surveillance with extended masking, and at last they found themselves ascending steps, waltzing past a security inspector Streak seemed to know personally, and into the underground garage. The sleek dark blue Westwind was to all appearances merely a slightly bulkier version of the standard model, but something about that bulkiness implied that it had certain extras they might not necessarily want to think about just at the present moment. It was certainly armored, which was reassuring.

"I still think you'd look great kitted out as mellows," Streak snickered.

"Don't push your luck," Serrin called out from the back. "Just drive us to the M-way and out of here."

"And watch out for any tailing taxis," Michael called out.

They were almost high this morning. Of the five, not one could be called a "shadowrunner." Serrin had been, some time back, but those days were recalled ambivalently. Good friends had been made and lasting associations formed, but he'd been rootless and left with a minced leg as a permanent memory of life in the shadows. Married now, and settled, he had no desire to return to his old ways, especially with a wife who, though a survivor, had no experience of such things and was far from her country of origin. Michael's work was strictly decking, almost always carried out from the high security of a Manhattan apartment in the city he had come to call home, and Geraint was a politician and businessman. Streak was the only one looking out for himself among the dangers of the street most days, but even he was an ex-military man.

They had an excitement about them, now they were on the move, which a team of seasoned runners might have buried under a veneer of experience and routine. And after the invasion of the apartment and the ambush in the cab, they felt almost like animals escaping from a trap. On the road as they headed west to the orbital and the huge freeway beyond, a simple sense of freedom lifted their spirits.

"Nice system here," Streak said approvingly. "Constant camera op, scans following vehicles, checks ID, checks for following vehicles, analyzes their motion patterns, all kinds of stuff. If they're gonna follow us, they'll have to use a convoy of the buggers."

"Where'd you get this?" Geraint asked.

Streak smirked. "Never you mind. You just paid the bill."

"I paid actually," Michael said. "It'll be on the corp's tab. We'll have to get something concrete today, Serrin. They need another update and report before they'll give me any more money."

"We'll get something," Serrin assured him. "I've brought the treatise on elementals with me. At the very least, it's an intro to get Hessler interested, and there's no reason I shouldn't give it to him if he is."

"Mind if I smoke?" Geraint asked.

"The filtration system can handle that," Streak told him. "It's not the full EnviroSeal job, but it's enough."

"What else do we have here?" Michael asked as Geraint reached for the lighter next to the ignition.

"We got ECM. We got signature masking. We might or might not have a little weaponry carefully concealed about the place," Streak said carefully.

"What?"

"Well, what's a little SAM between mates?" The elf laughed. "Hell, you'll be worried about the machine guns next."

"If we're stopped in this thing it'll be five years apiece," Michael said, exaggerating a genuine concern.

"No one's going to stop us in *this* thing," Streak said with real enthusiasm. "Drek, I hate these speed-trap camera systems. Putting the foot down in this monster is more fun than you can have with your clothes off, I tell ya."

"I just hope no one's decking into the camera downloads," Michael said.

"The ECM should slot that up just fine," Streak said. "But we can't be a hundred per, which is why I ain't burning up the rubber. Rakk it, can we take a detour through some wild land on the way back?"

"Just get us to Glastonbury, James," Serrin said, "and hold the horses."

"The hardest thing was finding somewhere safe to park Susan," Streak said when they reached their destination, not long after noon. "I don't want to park her out in the open."

Kristen wasn't listening. Glastonbury had impressed her from the first sight of the place; the dominating, imposing mound of the Tor, the small stone houses, old and weatherworn, which had mercifully resisted the temptation to become tourist attractions, the quietness of the place. The number of visitors to the area was strictly limited, and even Geraint had needed to pull strings to get them in. There were no police roadblocks, or anything so heavy-handed. It was just that no accommodation would be found for a visitor without the relevant documents, no shops would serve him, that sort of thing. Glastonbury valued its peacefulness. Power hung about the place like mist on a spring-morning river, and Serrin began to sense it even while they were still kilometers away.

They stood in front of the pub as Streak drove off to stash the car, their travel bags left dumped on the ground by the curb. The place was picture-perfect with its thatched roof, and yet it didn't have the look, so common in some parts of England, of having been deliberately crafted in that image to deceive gullible visitors. It had always looked this way. Michael signed them in and paid in full, in advance, with a service fee just a little above what might have been expected but below what would have been ostentatious. Flaunting excessive wealth would not have been in keeping with the town.

Their rooms were low-ceilinged, small but comfortable, and welcoming with the scent of fresh linen sheets and towels and a faint trace of lavender, which, for once, didn't seem like the scent of maiden aunts. By the time Streak returned they were already in the restaurant-bar, having ordered pub food and sinking the first of their pints of warm, malty beer.

Michael broke the dark brown crust on the steaming pie with an eagerness quite unjustified after his mammoth breakfast—but since that had, after all, been the only meal he'd had in a day and a half, the steak and kidney was exactly what he needed. He thought of ordering a second one, and guessed that at least some of the others might be of the same mind, but not wanting to draw undue attention, he settled for a pudding instead.

Kristen was wriggling in her chair, trying to stifle her giggles behind her hands. He looked uncomprehendingly at her.

"That's rude," she said, and even on her brown face a blush was apparent.

"What?" He was still perplexed until he realized what was happening. "Ah, spotted dick. Yes, well, it's a suet pudding with currants in it. Hopefully accompanied by a large amount of custard with satisfying lumps in it. Traditional English pudding."

She looked doubtful and slightly embarrassed until the dish arrived, and lived up to Michael's description of it, right down to the thick skin settling on the surface of the custard, which did, indeed, appear to act as a camouflage blanket for floury lumps lurking underneath.

"I had better go alone," Serrin said eventually, having dispensed with such temptations. He had no liking for sweet foods, and was impatient to be away. "Will you be all right?"

"I think we might be," Streak said, settling into a third pint. Serrin looked askance. "Don't worry, term," the other elf said pleasantly. "I can handle this stuff. Not something that can dull wired reflexes."

"Very well," Serrin said, getting up from the slightly uncomfortable wooden chair.

"When will you be back?" Kristen asked, fixing her eyes on his.

"I have no idea," Serrin said truthfully, checking that his small bag held the leather volume and the paperwork he'd done his best to assimilate during the journey.

"Look, let me come with you as far as the foot of the hill," Streak said. "Sure you want to go on alone, but let's not take any chances, right?"

"It's not a bad idea," Michael said.

Serrin thought about it for a moment, then nodded. "Come on, let's go. See you later, darling. Enjoy your, er, pudding, Michael."

"Sgreat," Michael managed to say through a mouthful of custard-lubricated heavy pudding. Kristen threatened to laugh again as the elves made for the low doorway, ducking their heads down to get outside.

Streak left him at the approach road. The cottage was plainly visible, with only a few trees around it, and Serrin was almost surprised at the plainness of the place. He half-expected a small mansion shrouded in some form of mist, with spirits all over the place. Assensing the place, he found nothing around, not even a watcher. Nor even any obvious ward or barrier, but that might testify only to the old elf's ability to disguise power.

Serrin paused along the short driveway. The obvious thing was to walk right up and tap with the brass door-knocker, but somehow it seemed wrong to do so. He was a little unnerved. He had the feeling of being naked, as if the old mage would see right through him even though Serrin had nothing to hide. Summoning his will, he covered the last few paces and knocked politely at the door with two short raps of the knocker.

It opened immediately, revealing a young, fresh-faced man with dark curly hair standing in the doorway. Behind him, the small hall showed simple carpets, a few brass and pottery ornaments, and an old grandfather clock ticking away sonorously, its giant pendulum swinging in its slow, steady rhythm.

"I hoped to make an appointment to see Herr Hessler," Serrin said. "Forgive me, but the matter is pressing. I have what I hope may be a gift in return for some of his time."

He had thought out the speech carefully. In response, the young man rubbed his chin and looked him over sharply.

"You're trouble," he announced.

"I beg your pardon?"

"Well, not you so much as your woman. Someone's got it in for her," the young man said, folding his arms across his chest.

"Oh, drek," Serrin said, his prepared polite introduction abandoned in the face of such an unexpected revelation. What could this youth mean?

"I think my master might be interested in you," the youth said. "But go back and bring your woman with you. She's going to need more help then you do. Oh dear, there's someone else too, isn't there? Sorry, the emotional bond isn't so strong between you and I couldn't see him straight away. Someone's got a sign on two people around you.

"Well, bring your woman anyway," the youth said at length. "One should be enough."

He'd been assensed already, Serrin realized, and it didn't much surprise or annoy him, it being only what he'd expected. But it was disconcerting to be so vulnerable to someone so young. Then he realized that this wasn't, of course, a youth at all.

"You are Merlin, I presume?" he said politely.

"You can call me that if you wish. He does." The spirit grinned. "And I'll call you Serrin. So I know your real name, but you don't know mine." The grin grew a little wider.

Serrin smiled in return. To know a spirit's true name was power over it, and only Hessler would know that information.

"I'll be back," he said.

"Make it swift," Merlin said, for the first time a truly serious expression settling over his face.

Serrin was halfway down the driveway, the door to the cottage closed behind him, when his senses dulled suddenly and he felt almost faint. A humming sound came from behind him, and he turned slowly—unsure whether he really wanted to do so—to see a black cat sitting by a bush, purring gently.

That must be his cat, he thought.

He got a distinct impression of resentfulness implanted in his feelings and corrected the error swiftly.

Sorry. You are his cat companion.

The purring seemed a little softer and the cat licked its paw, then used the back of it to wash its face. It looked wonderfully unconcerned while it was giving him the once-over.

An image came into his mind of four small, dark kittens accompanying a larger tom cat. Black like them, the tom had white socks and a bib and a characteristic mane of hair and long white whiskers.

Skita! Suki's cat, he thought. The tiny elven talismonger was among his few friends in London. This cat seemed to be saying it knew her cat. The image of one of the kittens grew and turned into the cat before him. The cat advanced and stood beside him, tail arched.

That's Skita's gesture, he thought with an inner smile. *Spirits, are you Skita's offspring?*

The cat purred more loudly. Serrin felt himself freed as if from some constraint, and on impulse took a small brown paper bag from his pocket. He had come prepared for this, and fortunately the delivery had reached Geraint's apartment just before they'd left.

He reached inside the paper bag and extracted the cloth mouse with its faint smell of catnip. He rubbed it vigorously to make the scent stronger, and laid it at the cat's feet.

The cat took one look at the mouse, which seemed to return the look, as if wondering whether this was safe. Then the cat seized the mouse in its jaws, ripped at it with its front claws, and finally rolled over on its back, savaging the mouse with all four paws. After a few seconds of mayhem it flung the mouse aside and rolled back over, giving Serrin a sharp look that did its best to mask embarrassment at its indignity.

Serrin dutifully turned and walked off, leaving the cat to its intoxicatory pleasure unhindered by human voyeurism.

I have a friend here, I hope, he thought. The thought cheered him as he walked back to the town to find a wife who did not yet know she needed the protection he so fervently hoped Hessler would give.

12

She was apprehensive, and the trim, simple, picture-book quality of a springtime English garden did not reassure her. As Serrin led Kristen up to the cottage, the enigmatic cat was nowhere to be seen, having doubtless taken its prize away to a hiding place safe from prying human—or elven—eyes.

"But why would he want to talk to me?" Kristen asked again.

"I told you, maybe he won't want to talk, just to see you," Serrin said carefully. "He may want to offer us some protection, that's all."

"But why didn't he want to see Michael as well?" By now she'd had time to think about this. The point hadn't occurred to her initially, gently mellowed as she'd been by English ale and surprised by the invitation.

"I don't know," Serrin said a little testily. "Perhaps he will. Later." To his relief, they'd reached the front entrance, without any need to knock for admittance since Merlin already stood just inside the door, which opened at their approach.

"He will see you now. Just go up the stairs," Merlin said pleasantly. "As to us"—he turned to Kristen—"I think he'll call if he needs us. Can I offer you some tea?"

"Oh, um, yes, thank you," she said, a little taken aback and giving her husband a nervous glance. Serrin had not been able to hide from her that this was a spirit taking human form. Streak had joked about it back at the pub, and Serrin had tried to explain exactly what Merlin was. Kristen had seen only one spirit in her life, a city spirit conjured by an angry Xhosa shaman, and it hadn't looked much like Merlin. This one looked deceptively mundane—mundane in the sense of flesh and blood—but his slightly crooked smile was open and friendly and she liked him.

"Tell me about the Rain Queen," Serrin heard Merlin say as he guided the young woman into the small kitchen, from whence issued the scent of toasting muffins and tea. He grinned, ducking his head as he climbed the tiny wooden stairs up to the landing.

The old elf stood waiting, framed in a doorway by afternoon light streaming through the windows. His appearance was in no way imposing; he was neither exceptionally tall for an elf, nor short of stature, and while lean, he wasn't thin. His silvery hair was long, but not unkempt, and his eyes were gentle, not piercing or sharp. He gripped a hazel stick in a way that said he needed its support, and not just as an affectation, and his clothes were plain and dark blue without any ornate decoration. Had he been seen in a photograph, the most perceptive of viewers would not likely have considered him anything out of the ordinary.

Standing a meter away from him and meeting his gaze was different.

Serrin remembered an old man, a human, he'd known as a child. The man had studied what had been known as psychic phenomena in the years before the Awakening, and he'd been the first to see that the young elf was no mundane. It was due to him that Serrin had been selected for hermetic studies at a young age. Serrin remembered this man telling him of his own youth, over a century before the current age, when he'd sat on his grandfather's knee and been told of his travels in the British merchant navy to lands unimagined: India, Africa, China.

"Hard to imagine, lad, but there wasn't any trid then. There wasn't even television—well, not in the homes of ordinary working people. So, I'd never seen a lion, or a tiger, or an elephant. And my grandpa told me such stories about them, and the places and sounds and sights, and the way the women bore baskets and water urns on their heads across the deserts, and the way the people dressed and how the stars were different in the southern skies. And I used to sit there speechless, not wanting him to ever stop telling me. I loved the old man in a different way to anyone else I ever knew, or ever could have known. These days, I see wonders around me that make me feel like I did when I was a child on his knee. And they're going to be your wonders in this new world."

Serrin remembered that old man, his grandfather's close friend, and how he had been enthralled by the man's firm sense of awe and wonder even in his late eighties. When he looked at the old elf, it all came back to him.

It was not the first time Serrin had been in the presence of someone imbued with unusual, or exceptional, power before. It wasn't usually a comfortable experience. In his limited experience, such individuals were usually aloof and arrogant, or simply withdrawn, not people to make others feel at ease in their presence. The old elf, who was peering at him intently, was none of these things. Shaking, Serrin realized with a sense of profound shock that what he felt in the other elf's presence was deep and intense love, a yearning realization of the goodness of this person that he'd never even seen until now. He felt faint, and when the old elf turned and took a shuffling step into his study, it was all Serrin could do to take a couple of faltering steps after him.

The room was too large, of course; that was obvious as soon as Serrin entered it. Every last centimeter of wall space was covered in hardwood shelving, crammed with grimoires and books of all kinds. There had to be thousands of them. From outside, it was obvious the room couldn't possibly hold so many.

Hessler smiled at his wondering look. "Oh, that. It's nothing. I just like this little old place and I had to get them all in here somehow. Takes Merlin an age to find things from storage and sometimes he's busy. Won't you sit down?"

It was a relief not to have to remain standing any longer. Serrin almost fell into the hard-backed chair across the desk from the gently smiling elf.

"There is a powerful mark on her," Hessler said in his drowsy, gentle, delicately accented voice. It was obvious who he was talking about.

"Yes," was all Serrin could think of to say.

"She could be killed at any time," Hessler continued, even-voiced still.

"I imagine so," Serrin said weakly, still trying to orient himself. Hessler's presence was so powerful that it rendered him utterly passive, almost unable to speak.

"However, you did not come for my help with that, at least not initially," Hessler observed. He took up an old-fashioned quill pen from his teak desk and toyed idly with it.

"That is so," Serrin said, at last beginning to gather his wits about him. "Though now that I know how serious that is, it's the most important thing to me."

"I think we can deal with it," Hessler said pleasantly. "So, now, why don't you tell me why you came in the first place?"

He knows, Serrin thought, but for once, he was wrong. The old elf did not know in every respect, but by the time Serrin had finished, he certainly did.

"So you came to ask me about the Priory of Sion," Hessler said thoughtfully, turning the quill over in his fingers as Serrin's story trailed off. "That's a very large question, Serrin. We could be here for a week and, from what you've told me, you don't have a week to stay and listen to the answer."

"True. We wondered why they'd be interested in what we were doing, why they'd have sent the spirit to warn us off."

"Go on."

"I can't believe that a hermetic organization can have any direct interest in Matrix activities and computer-system sabotage," Serrin said slowly. "Perhaps some individual member or members might. But not the organization. At least, I can't see how they could."

Hessler's eyes were glinting slightly. "That seems reasonable."

"So I thought," Serrin said tentatively, the pieces beginning to fit together even as he spoke them, "that they must be taking an interest on one of two counts. One, they know the decker who's threatening to bring down the house of cards. Or two, the icon he left is some kind of danger to them. Perhaps it threatens to implicate them. I can't really understand the logic there, but that's because I don't know exactly what this organization does. There's a hell of a lot of books, a huge mass of data, but there are a dozen different stories, and without detailed knowledge we can't know which is true."

"So you come to me," Hessler said, and waited.

"Yes," Serrin said simply and, in return, waited.

"Well, then, I can tell you that the Priory wouldn't care a damn if every computer system in the world disappeared into thin air overnight," Hessler told him. "Completely irrelevant to them."

"Then it's the decker," Serrin said at once. "They know . . ." He stopped. "What do they know? Do they want him? Are they afraid of him? They must know who he is."

"Logical," Hessler said with the hint of a smile.

"Then why are they afraid that we might find him? They must be, surely, to have warned us off."

"Perhaps," Hessler said, "they want to find him themselves, and they don't want anyone else to do so first."

"And the Jesuits?"

Hessler's eyes hardened. "That might apply to them also."

"An awful lot of people seem to want to find our decker."

Hessler laughed, a soft, musical peal of sound. "Including a lot of very wealthy corporations, by your account."

"He must be one hell of a guy," Serrin said, the older elf's laughter becoming infectious.

"Makes one wonder how he hasn't been found, doesn't it?" Hessler said it almost as if the statement were no more than a throwaway observation. Serrin looked up at him and his mind was suddenly completely concentrated. It was as if he were suddenly sober after an evening of intoxication.

"You know who he is," he said, just managing to keep it from sounding like an accusation.

"I might," Hessler said evenly. "That is, I might have my suspicions."

So how does this mage know who an exceptional decker is? It can't be because he's a decker, he must be more . . . Serrin's mind was racing.

"Michael's employers would pay a fortune to know," Serrin said.

"Come now," Hessler said in a gently reproaching voice, "You must know that money isn't the kind of thing that matters to me."

"And you won't tell me," Serrin said miserably.

"It's not as simple as that," Hessler said. "If my suspicions are right, then I want to know why he's doing this. It's not really like him."

"So it's a him," Serrin said. "Well, that eliminates half of the population at least."

Hessler laughed again.

"Why won't you tell me?" Serrin's voice was urgent now.

Hessler looked gravely back at him. "Serrin, it really isn't as simple as all that. I'm not the only one who'll be interested in why he's doing this. There are certain ... certain rumors I have heard, that others of us have heard, which might explain it. I need to know for myself about those things. The matter of the Matrix is unimportant to us."

"Unimportant?" Serrin was incredulous. "Every business system on the planet might crash overnight. The consequences are unimaginable. The Great Crash of 'Twenty-nine all over again but magnified a hundredfold. Thousands bankrupted, millions thrown out of work—unimportant?"

"Relatively, yes," Hessler said quite firmly.

"Relative to what?"

"I don't think I can really discuss that," Hessler continued. "The decision is not mine to make."

"Thanks so very much," Serrin shot back. "My friends and I are getting attacked by spirits, traced and tracked, drugged and dumped in crates, and our associates killed because we're stumbling around in something, and it would really be good to have some idea of what that might be, you know."

"You have enough leads to follow," Hessler said. "Judging by what you've told me."

"You can give me something, surely," the younger elf said plaintively. He was almost begging.

"Then keep away from the NOJ," Hessler said sharply. "They, too, have an interest, which is obvious. But they're killers pure and simple, as they have always been in their various guises over the centuries. Avoid them. Consider some form of understanding with others. That will suffice.

"Now there is another matter. There will be ritual magic needed. I must send a spirit to destroy the tokens taken from your friends. It will have to be strong to breach the defenses of the enemy, and must not be traced. This will not be easy."

"Don't I know it," Serrin said uneasily. He'd never been much at practicing ritual magic, but the scale of the enterprise was clear enough to him.

"I can do it for you," Hessler said, "but there will be a price."

Serrin nodded. "Of course."

"It's not for me, you understand, but for Merlin," Hessler said.

"Merlin is ... an ally?"

Hessler sat back in his chair and laughed loud and long. When he was done, he wiped at an eye with his right hand, and smiled almost forlornly.

"Ach, dear me, no. It would amuse him to hear you call him that. Merlin is a free spirit. He has simply chosen to be my companion. He is curious and loves this world and the people in it. That is why he will help you too. The reward should be his."

Hessler paused and gave Serrin a long look before speaking. "I want karma from you, for him."

Serrin had half-expected it. It would drain him, for weeks even into months. Some of his own spiritual strength and power would be gifted to the free spirit, who would use it to develop its own powers and talents. It was the price free spirits always required for their services. And while mundanes could yield a little for such assistance, a magician was always the most effective donor of such energies and power.

"Whatever it takes," Serrin agreed. It was for Kristen, after all. After a winter of cold, snowbound Scottish nights spent around warm log fires with her, walks into a gray, almost Arctic horizon, after uncounted thousands of words shared and spoken or not required to be, he would have given up anything that was demanded of him. And he trusted the older elf.

"It should be soon," Hessler suggested.

"Soon as possible," Serrin said fervently. "We've got less than a week."

A black cat strolled into the room, tail raised to the heavens, and leapt into Hessler's lap. Absentmindedly, he stroked under the cat's chin, where felines have oil-secreting glands and love to be cosseted. The cat purred and closed her eyes.

"I believe you've already met Hathor," Hessler said.

Serrin grinned. "I'm on very good terms with her father." He genuinely liked cats, and they took to him readily. He also knew another ailurophile when he saw one, and the older elf's way of pleasing the cat was clearly born of experience. The first knuckle of his index finger knew exactly the right spot to rub under the cat's chin, and she was already threatening to roll over to have her belly rubbed.

"Better ask Merlin to come up," Hessler said thoughtfully. Serrin took the cue and left the elf to his thoughts.

To his surprise, Kristen was bright-eyed and enthusiastically, even volubly, talking to a young man clearly hanging on her every word. Serrin paused at the foot of the stairs, surprised and even relieved to hear her so animated. The sound of a chair scraped along stone punctuated the monologue.

"Then they move like *this*, you see." Serrin could suppress his interest no longer and walked into the kitchen, to find her in a swaying dance before the enraptured spirit-man.

His smile was broad, but she stopped and looked a little bashful.

"I didn't mean to—" he began.

"My master wants me?" Merlin said at once. "Well, please excuse me, young lady. This has been wonderful! I have learned so much."

He got up and nodded his head a little to her, an almost subliminal gesture, and smiled at Serrin as he walked past him and up the stairs outside.

"And you were apprehensive about him," Serrin said gently, trying to avoid the impression that he'd broken in on something pleasurable for her.

"Well, I didn't know what a spirit was like, I mean, not like him," she said a little defensively, and sat down in her chair again.

Serrin was hurt; it felt almost like a reproach. He sat down beside her and took one of her hands in his, cupping his palms around her warm hand.

"Hessler will help us," he said, looking her full in the eyes. "There's just something I have to do for him. It isn't much."

Her pupils dilated a little and he could see she was alarmed.

"It really isn't much," he said again.

"What does he want?" She was clearly worried, maybe even frightened.

"Nothing for himself. It's for Merlin. Spirits need power, karma, to grow. He wants karma from me."

She didn't really understand the concept, but she knew it was part of his nature and power, the core of him, and she opened her mouth to protest. He raised a hand and placed an index finger over her lips to quiet her.

"I said, it isn't really so much. I'll regain it in time. It's a fair price. No, it's better than a fair price."

"Why can't I do it? It's because of me," she pleaded.

"It's better coming from a magician, and it isn't because of you. Not really. It wasn't you who started us out on this trail. So don't worry about it."

It was only a momentary gesture, but he saw her suck back her lower lip and bite a little at the inside of it, to keep it from trembling. He wrapped his arms around her and held her close, and they stayed that way until they heard Merlin's footsteps coming back down the stairs. When the spirit returned, Serrin was not surprised by its more serious countenance.

13

"I think it's clear what he's saying to us," Michael offered.

It was well into the hours of darkness now. They had discussed Serrin's conversation with Hessler at some length, and Michael, as ever, was trying to do some logical summation work.

"He's saying keep off the Inquisition. Well, that sounds good to me. How did he put it? 'Consider other understandings'?"

" 'Consider understandings with others', I think," Serrin said.

"Which logically means the Priory of Sion," Michael suggested. "I mean, it can't refer to anyone else, can it?"

"That sounds reasonable." Abandoning his usual filter cigarettes, Geraint had taken refuge in a modestly sized and surprisingly fragrant Cuban cigar. Sweet blue smoke gathered just below the ceiling of his room, where the five of them had cloistered themselves after dinner.

"There's a certain problem. I mean, one of their people was following you and shadowing us. And he's dead now. Not to mention their mage, who's also dead. Doesn't leave us with any real contacts, and you must admit they might be a bit, well, suspicious after two deaths. Wouldn't you be?"

"Depends exactly why they were tracking us, and why they had such an interest, doesn't it?" Geraint said reasonably. A very respectable smoke ring rose slowly to dissolve among the remains of its predecessors.

"I have an idea," Michael said slowly.

Everyone waited.

"We don't know any other of their people—well, I've got a list of suspected members, but we can hardly go around knocking on their door saying, 'Excuse me, got an interest in some decker about to bring the world crashing down, have you?' "

"Agreed," Geraint said wryly.

"Then we could go and say hello to them in their own back yard," Michael said. "Serrin says he forgot to give Hessler his little book."

"It just went out of my mind," Serrin confessed. "I'd still like to offer it to him, though."

"I'd rather you didn't," Michael said. "It gives us *something*. It gives us a foot in the door. 'Excuse me, we've got something that belongs to you. Would you like it back?' "

"Yeah, right," Streak said sarcastically. "They'll bloody love that one."

"We don't have to walk right up to their door," Michael pointed out. "We can go as sightseers. Rennes-le-Château gets a reasonable number of fruitcakes and nutters turning up to see the diabolic doorkeeper and all the other weirdness. Not many, but, slot, we could be researchers for a trid company. Or anything. We can at least scan it out and decide our next move from there. We can keep our research on the rails if we base ourselves in Clermont-Ferrand. Hell, we'd only have to go on a day trip. And there's one other thing: it would get us out of London and keep us on the move. Away from those not-terribly-pleasant people keeping an eye on us."

"We can be tracked," Geraint said.

"Well, of course, but that's better than being a bunny staying down a hole and waiting for the ferret," Michael said sagely.

"Ferret?" Kristen asked. It didn't feature among African fauna.

"Polecat," Michael offered. That she'd heard of.

"He's got a point," Streak said thoughtfully. "It's a good principle, to keep on the move. Especially when there's more than one bunch of hostiles out to box us. They do keep muttering about final warnings."

"I'd better see about flights," Geraint said.

"Can you wangle airspace permits?" Streak asked him.

"I think so, yes, I'm sure I can," Geraint said after an initial hesitation. "Barnaby Smythe over at the MoD owes me a favor on a business deal I cut him into last year. Why do you ask?"

"I can arrange a slamming 'chopper deal with a pilot who's the dog's bollocks," Streak offered. "Fly in real comfort."

"Including airline food?" Michael said, chuckling.

"Including some of the very wizzer weaponry available," Streak said gleefully. "That's what I mean by comfort."

"What do you think?" Michael looked at Geraint. "We'd need to make for Toulouse if we could, that would be nearest. Or even Andorra and we could nip over the border."

"Let's go for Toulouse and cut the border crossings down by one," Geraint said. "One fewer database with any information on it. We don't have time for fake ID, not for everyone. I had better set the wheels in motion for that in case we have to hit another place later.

"How long will you need, Serrin?"

"Allow all night," the elf said quietly.

"Can you have the chopper here by dawn?" Geraint asked Streak.

"Given your credstick codes, yes, no probs. Pick it up at Taunton, I think."

"Taunton? Taunton has an airport?" Michael said doubtfully. The small English country town wasn't a likely candidate for such a facility.

"Airport? Who said anything about a bleeding airport? Since when did a chopper need an airport?" Streak replied pointedly, adding a choice selection of tutting.

"All right, all right," Michael said, raising a hand as if to ward off an angry hornet. "We'll get there as soon as we can pick Serrin up and drive down. It's going to be an early start, then. What time is it now?"

"Half past ten," Geraint told him.

"I think I can sleep now," Michael said. "I slept long enough last night, but it wasn't exactly restful sleep. And as for Kristen . . . "

They looked at her in the corner. She was curled up on the sofa, one arm bent under her body a little crookedly, already fast asleep. Serrin walked over and, with an effort, picked her up in his arms.

"We won't be needed, then?" Michael said, reassuring himself once more.

"Thanks to your second recent blood donation and that lock of your hair, no," Serrin told him again.

"Tell me I won't feel a thing," Michael invited him.

"You won't feel a thing. Honestly. Apart from the ever-present possibility of instant but agonizing death evaporating from your aura," Serrin grinned. With Kristen asleep and wrapped securely in the protection of his arms, he felt able to jest. He was certain that Hessler would be able to deal with the problem. The joking was a way of defusing his own anxieties about the ritual, and what it would cost him.

"Spirits bless you," Michael said with some feeling. "And now I'm going to get some sleep. Polish up my French."

"Drek, that's a point," Serrin said. "How many of us actually speak French?"

"No self-respecting Englishman speaks French, other than deliberately badly," Geraint pointed out.

"Good job for you I got no self-respect then, ain't it, mate?" Streak grinned.

"You speak French?"

"I can tell you to rakk off and die or your mother was a no-good alcoholic whore who serviced rottweilers in five different European languages, not counting English," Streak said with some pride. "S'a legacy from intelops work. Got a gift for languages, I have. I can even handle Languedoc dialect, too. Been down Toulouse and worked in Marseilles, of course. I mean, who hasn't, in my line of work. Even picked up some Arabic down there."

"Who'd have thought it?" Michael said incredulously. Serrin grinned and took his burden to their room. A yawning Michael was already shrugging off his tweed jacket as he followed him out.

"That leaves just you, me, and your credstick," Streak said purposefully to the room's only other occupant. "You don't know how refreshing it is to work for someone with an unlimited budget, Your Lordship. I always said the aristocracy was class."

Geraint was beginning to warm to the elf. The pun was neat enough and his straightforwardness was refreshing, especially to a politician.

"I never said 'unlimited'," he pointed out.

"Whatever," Streak said. "Just tell us when the dosh is about to run out. Now, did you want chemical weapon grenades or will you settle for the ordinary gas and frag varieties on board?"

"Wait a minute. We're planning on *talking* to people, Streak," Geraint protested.

"Of course, but I always find backup is so useful when discussions just won't come out right."

"Well, anything that's capable of neutralizing large numbers of the French will be altogether welcome, I must admit," Geraint joked.

"I'll see to it," and the elf was gone into the night. A few minutes later Geraint heard the car speed away. He went to his room and undressed, then opened the small, high window and lit a good old-fashioned candle at his bedside.

He had just a little of the talent himself, though it wasn't something he knew how to master or make answer to his call. He knew that one or two of his speculative business deals had been startlingly successful because of that old Celtic gift, and he was superstitious enough that when it served him well, a good chunk of the money found its way anonymously to what he considered to be worthy causes. And sometimes, when the gift came uncalled and unlooked for, it guided him to other benefits.

He opened the mahogany box carved with the images of dragons; dragons of Wales, the dragon land itself. Unwrapping the silk bundle, he shuffled the large cards a little awkwardly and his thoughts naturally concentrated themselves on the theme of a dominant image, here and now.

The Heirophant. The open-handed symbol of wisdom and understanding stands as a guardian and advisor to the seeker and initiate. This is Hessler, Geraint thought. The one Serrin will soon be with. I would like to meet with him, sometime. When this is all over, perhaps.

What are we being guided toward? he wondered. We think we know who our enemies are, out there. But of the central figure, this decker, we know nothing. All we have is icon and enigma. Show me something.

A card slipped easily from the oversized deck. *Ace of Swords.* The brilliant emerald of the runesword glittered at him from the candlelit card, the tip of the blade piercing a crown of yellow rays, the sword bathed in the yellow sun and blue-tinged clouds of the heavens. The beginning of some great new idea; genius. But not a person. An inanimate object revealed itself to him. Of the person he sought, the deck gave him no sign.

What does he want? What is his goal, then? What drives him to the Ace?

Adjustment. In most decks, Justice. The beautiful, grave splendor of the masked female figure, the alpha and omega, beginning and end of all things, balanced in the scales of Justice on each side of her tall, taut body. Her strong hands rested on the hilt of a great sword driven into the ground.

Geraint knew that, for once, the deck's designer had deeper understandings than most. Justice was not the answer here, not truly. The meaning was deeper, a rebalancing, an establishment of a deeper equilibrium, the revelation of a Truth.

What *is* this man seeking? he thought. I knew, I *knew,* early on that this was more than it appeared to be. The interest being taken in us only confirms that. So, it began as a potential hijack of the Matrix and, heaven knows, that would affect me enough, but what it's leading to . . .

He wrapped up the deck in its silk and yawned, leaving any further intuitions to insinuate themselves into his mind from the realm of dreams.

They hadn't known what to expect, not really. Michael had had fanciful notions of bolts of lightning breaking in a great storm around the cottage in the distance, of distant rumblings under the ground and thunder from the heavens. Of the four of them, only Geraint had uneasy sensations as they waited by their car in the pre-dawn chill. Unable to assense the astral, he still registered churnings within his guts from the struggles of power so near and so far from them. At moments he felt like an animal sensing the first dim seismic shocks of an impending earthquake and felt panicky, longing to run from the place. Cigarette followed cigarette into the promise of daylight. He paced up and down like a caged beast.

Serrin came shambling up the driveway a few minutes after dawn began to break. His jacket collar was pulled up around his neck, and his usual limp was more exaggerated. He looked as if he could barely make it as far as the gate. Kristen broke ranks and ran forward, flinging her arms around him, helping him to the car. The others stayed silent, unsure of what to do or say.

Geraint took one look at him and offered him his silver hip flask. Serrin didn't speak, just raised the flask to lips that seemed as bloodless as his face and took a huge draught of the brandy. When he had mostly stopped shaking, he drank the rest.

"Are you all right?" Michael said lamely, just to say something. Serrin's gray eyes looked dully up toward him.

"I will be. I think," he said in a voice as shaky as his legs. "Yes. Maybe. What are we doing?"

They looked at him blankly.

"He's disoriented," Streak said helpfully. "Get him into the back. Roll the window down. Fresh air will do him good."

"I mean, what are we doing?" Serrin said urgently. Kristen clung to him tightly, gently murmuring words of comfort. He was wild-eyed now, staring around in all directions.

"It's all right," Geraint said, taking the elf's face in his hands and staring intently into his eyes. "We're going to take a short drive, and then a flight, and we'll be out of here. You can sleep, and you'll be all right when you wake."

"Sleep. Yes," Serrin said blankly. He had to be helped to the car, Kristen getting in beside him, cradling his head on her breast as he slumped over toward her.

Down the driveway, a young man wearing a nondescript overcoat approached them with long-legged strides.

"He'll be all right soon," Merlin said affably to Geraint. "He'll be confused for a bit, and then he'll be amnesic. My master thought that was a good idea. The struggle was quite powerful and it's better that he not remember it. Not that he'll suffer any permanent draining or damage from it."

"You'll be safe now," he continued, bending down to look at Kristen through the lowered back window. "Keep well. I did enjoy talking with you, very much. I hope you will come back to us when this is all begun."

"Don't you mean all over?" Geraint asked.

"I meant what I said," Merlin said coolly and placed a hand on the girl's forehead.

Sometimes, rarely, people experience something that could be called, for want of a better term, a quasi-Eureka moment. It isn't that thing that made Aristotle leap out of his bath. It isn't the answer. It isn't there in black and white, in everything but the fine detail. What it is is a sudden switch in the way some problem, or things in general, are perceived. It's the *possibility* of Eurekas to come. It's the realization that there's an entirely different range of options available from those one knew existed until that very moment.

The touch of Merlin's fingertips had all that. Kristen's eyes shone in surprise and wonderment, and she did not shrink back from him. He smiled gravely, but with a little touch of mischief in his own eyes, and then he blew her a kiss and wrapped his woolen scarf about his neck.

"Thank you for the Rain Queen and the tales and stories," he said. "They helped me. Come back soon."

As he strode back up the driveway, she had no idea

what he meant by her helping him. She knew the night had too many mysteries only half-hinted at to think it through now, and thinking wasn't the answer anyway. Instead she wrapped herself around the pale, forlorn figure of the elf beside her, and waited quietly while the others buckled themselves into the car and Streak started up the engine. Streak turned and looked at Geraint, Kristen, and Serrin in the back.

"This is weird drek, isn't it?" he said, eyes narrowed and his face very serious.

"This is, indeed, weird drek, as you so eloquently put it," Geraint agreed.

"Fine by me," Streak said, guessing that those would probably be the last words spoken until they reached the chopper, and he was dead right.

An hour later, an elf considerably older than any of them had imagined stood staring up into the sky, leaning on his staff for support, a much younger figure standing quietly beside him. He could hardly see the chopper headed for the English Channel, and he wouldn't have risked any assensing. It had been a long, hard struggle to find the well-masked body tokens, and the spirit he'd employed, though formidably strong and with the benefit of his own masking and concealments, had perished very shortly after it had done its work.

"I wonder whether they'll find him, Merlin," Hessler said quietly.

"They're looking in the right place," the spirit said amiably.

"Perhaps. It will depend on the reaction they receive when they get there."

"Well, that you can do something about," Merlin pointed out. "After all, you've been a member of the Priory for some time."

"There is that." The old elf smiled. "And my voice has not gone unraised in the current debate."

"And your messenger is already gone before them," Merlin said. "All in all, I think they have every chance. I do hope so. The girl is a happy spirit, and I would like to see her again. She is happy when she smiles and dances. I like people when they are like that."

"Merlin, there are times when you lighten the heart,

you really do," Hessler said gently, and turned back to his home. At his feet, a black cat purred over the remains of an unfortunate field mouse.

14

Serrin fell asleep in a car in England and woke up in one traveling through the south of France. Squinting at the sunlight, he rubbed his stubbly chin and tried to focus his vision. The delicious aroma of hot coffee offered itself to his senses. He grabbed the plastic cup and drank greedily while Geraint resealed the flask.

"Oh, spirits, that was good," Serrin said with real gratitude. "Where are we?"

"Ten minutes out of Clermont-Ferrand and what looks like a pretty decent rural chateau, judging by the trid picture library," Geraint told him. "You've been asleep since the night with Hessler."

"Right," Serrin said doubtfully, trying to marshal his thoughts. "Er, right."

"What happened?" Michael spoke with an artificial cheeriness that Serrin didn't detect.

The elf rubbed his chin, sat up and stretched to get the stiffness out of his back, and smiled at Kristen.

"Hmmm?" He thought deeply for some seconds. "Frag me, I can't remember a thing. Honestly. It's a complete blank."

He turned back to Kristen and, ignoring the rest of them, leant and kissed her on the lips.

"Ugh, morning breath," she giggled, then grabbed his face with both hands and kissed him long and hard.

Merlin was right, Geraint thought to himself. Whatever magic Hessler had used to banish the memories, he must have added something to stop him worrying about the amnesia too. That was good of him.

"Stop shagging in the back there!" Streak berated them jokingly. "Puts me off my driving. I have this horrible tendency to voyeurism."

"Frag off," Serrin said cheerfully, giving Kristen a hug.

He was in unusually good humor this morning. More after-effects of whatever magic Hessler used on him, Geraint thought. From what he knew of Serrin, mornings were usually good candidates for avoiding his company.

"Here it is. Must be this whitewashed one at the end of the road," Streak said happily.

"That's not whitewash," Michael complained, peering through the windscreen.

"Well, whatever it is, we're booked into it. Now give me a hand with the guns and grenades in the back," Streak said as he unbuckled himself and opened the driver's door.

Seeing the look on Michael's face, he laughed. "Only kidding, mate. Honest."

"That's a relief," Michael said. "We came here to talk, not wage war."

"Nah, I mean I can handle 'em myself," Streak said with an evil grin and hefted the first of the metal cases.

Within the hour they were close to the small village, their hired car—much humbler than the Westwind that Streak had left to be collected in Taunton and returned to the rental firm—negotiating the narrow roads with no little difficulty. The rockiness of the hilly terrain was stark, even with the green coat of spring on the hillsides. The land looked, somehow, as if reluctant to allow the new growths of the season. There was something unforgiving about the hills and mountains, the ragged treeline, the harshness of the light here.

Their plan was for Michael and Geraint to take an initial stroll into the village, to climb the ascent to the place that had come to be known as Sauniere's chapel, and to observe what they could. They would formulate further plans on the basis of those observations. Serrin didn't want to risk any astral assensing, since he'd been forewarned of the likely presence of mages watching for anyone doing just that. Kristen would stay with him. As for Streak, they didn't plan to need his French for conversing much with the locals at this stage.

Sauntering into the village, Michael and Geraint chatted casually about the weather and the grandeur of the scenery as they headed toward the road up to the chapel. They didn't get far. Half a dozen sturdy French peasant farmers, each bearing a walking stick that looked very like a club, or else a spade or pitchfork, slowly congregated together from various directions and barred their way.

"Excusez-moi, c'est le chapel de Sauniere?" Geraint said cheerfully, waving his cheap camera in a fair impression of the Idiot British Tourist in Europe.

The men just stood in their way and said nothing. Geraint and Michael took a step forward and one of the Frenchmen did the same, raising his spade and driving the metal into the ground beside the stony path. He spat on the ground before him, and the others stood with arms folded, clubs at the ready.

A further reasonable impression of the British Idiot only got Geraint the grunted statement that the chapel was closed to visitors. An enquiry as to when it would be open got no reply, only a hostile stare. There was nothing for it under the circumstances but to beat a retreat while trying to appear disappointed but unconcerned.

"It could just be paranoia," Michael said when they were out of earshot. "On their part, I mean." The men were still standing together halfway up the path. There was no sign of anyone else attempting to ascend it. Oddly, there seemed to be little sign of anyone else in the village, though by now, mid-morning, the houses should have been showing some signs of life and activity.

Stymied, they returned to the car, where the group discussed their options. Michael wanted to retreat to Toulouse, rescue his portable cyberdeck, and get some more research done, leaving Serrin more bookwork to get through. Streak, unsurprisingly, thought the terrain was fine for a covert approach and blasting his way past any obstacle that presented itself.

"Something's going on up there," Geraint observed. "They're not protecting nothing. And we need to see what it is."

The sound of an automobile engine began to swell behind them. Their car was pulled just off the road, with enough tree cover to disguise if not conceal them. Streak slipped out of the driver's seat and vanished into the trees like some predatory woodland animal. A few moments later, a flash of black and silver moved behind the trees and continued on into the village. They ate their bread, paté, and cheese and waited.

Streak did not reappear.

They were getting nervous by the time the black-and-silver reappeared, this time moving in the opposite direction, and not long afterward the elf emerged from the woodland.

"Now I wouldn't want to get you alarmed," he said gleefully as he climbed into the driver's seat and broke himself off a sizable hunk of hard cheese, "but I think someone else was observing the village. Some interesting dark-suited gentlemen with no little in the way of chrome about them, unless I'm much mistaken.

"They just drove in, took a look around, and drove back out again. Couldn't see much of them with the window tints, but I saw enough. Heavy rakkers. I doubt they came out here for nothing."

"They just drove around the village?" Michael asked.

"Didn't stop," the elf confirmed.

"We've got to get into the chapel," Michael said. "Who knows when they'll be back—whoever they are."

"We've got their book," Kristen pointed out.

"Let's go for it," Streak said.

The second time, all five of them marched up to face the line of peasantry with their crude weapons. Streak inched ahead of the others and conversed in French, Michael explaining to Serrin and Kristen the gist of what was being said. Streak produced the slim leather book and gestured with some animation at the impassive, hulking Frenchmen, pointing to the chapel and appearing very nonchalant.

"He says we just want to return some property that was stolen, and surely someone could come to collect it," Michael translated.

The men's hard-lined faces looked puzzled, uncertain. Streak's request was certainly reasonable enough. At length, the largest of them leaned his hands on the handle of his broad-bladed shovel and grunted simply, *"Non."*

Streak's smile exceeded the determination of the man's frown as he hefted his Predator squarely at the man's head.

"S'il vous plaît," the elf said pleasantly. The man didn't budge a centimeter. His knuckles went a little

white on the wooden handle he gripped, but he didn't flinch.

The impasse was broken when a slender man appeared from the front doorway of the chapel, ducking his head as he emerged, even though he was not tall. Everyone looked at him as he descended the stony pathway, a tousle-haired man wearing one of those Italian suits that cost a fortune but don't advertise the fact. He had the Mediterranean complexion of the other men here, but was otherwise utterly unlike them. As he drew closer, his expression broke into a casual lopsided grin. He shambled up to them, scratching at the crown of his head.

"Do we have a misunderstanding here?" he asked in perfect English.

"We only came to return some lost property, and I'm afraid these gentlemen took exception to our altruism," Streak said.

The man stared pointedly at his gun. Streak lowered it.

"Altruism down the barrel of a Predator," he said dryly. "An unusual expression of that all too rare and noble emotion, wouldn't you say?"

"To whom are we speaking?" Geraint enquired.

"You may call me Gianfranco," the man said pleasantly. There was a short pause.

He did not ask who they were. The implication was obvious: he already knew.

"We had hoped that a conversation to discuss some matters of mutual interest might not be too much to hope for," Geraint suggested.

"Then you have hoped in vain," Gianfranco said, still quite affably.

"There is the matter of your Mr. Seratini and the men at whose hands he died," Geraint fired back.

"There is also the matter of our Monsieur Serrault and the people at whose hands *he* died," Gianfranco replied sharply. "Now, if you will excuse me, there are several very well-armed and well-trained men at my instant beck and call and if you don't turn around and get out of here this instant I will, with some little regret, have to ask them to blast you into a large number of bloody fragments, which my friends here," he concluded, with a glance back at the surly band of peasants, "will be able to feed to their dogs. Good day."

He turned on his heel and marched back up the path. They watched his back until he disappeared through the doorway, slamming it shut behind him.

They looked at each other, at the still-impassive Frenchmen, and back at each other again. With a shrug of his shoulders, Geraint led them back down the path and to their car.

"So much for that," Michael said glumly. "Now to Plan B."

"Which is?" Streak asked.

"I'm working on it," Michael told him. "I think a strategic retreat is in order."

Serrin suddenly looked alarmed and clutched at Streak's shoulder. "Get us out of here!" he said urgently.

"What the—"

"I said, *get us out of here!*"

Streak fired the ignition, reversed out of their parking spot, and made haste down the road. He was five klicks away by the time the white-faced mage decided it was safe again.

"There was a summoning," he said simply. "Another minute and the whole hill would have flung us over the rocks and into the valley. Trust me on this one."

"Fair enough," Streak said without any trace of his usual bantering. "Back to Clermont-Ferrand?"

"For now, yes," Michael said miserably. "I don't see we have any choice."

Back in their villa, with a large pot of Streak's preferred tea being dispensed into the cracked cups that came as part of the furnishings, they considered their sharply reduced options.

"Almost all of what we've got points here," Michael said at length. "We have to talk to these people somehow. We're hardly likely to get anywhere trying to talk to the Inquisition. The Priory know something. I think they know who the decker is. We've got to get into that place."

"Why did the bloke refuse point-blank even to talk?" Streak asked him.

"Because we don't have anything they want," Michael guessed. "They know everything we do and they don't want us getting involved."

"Then this"—Serrin clutched at the book he'd retrieved from Streak—"isn't of any importance to them."

"Which means—"

"Which means what's in it doesn't matter," Serrin mused. "I don't understand that. It has to matter, somehow."

"Great. Let's slot around worrying about textual analysis when what we need to do is talk to Gianfranco down the barrel of a gun," Streak said. "I can get a couple of guys from over the border. Not that I put much store in the Spanish by and large, but I did merc work with 'em and they might be able to get here by nightfall."

"I can deck into their Matrix system and close down every alarm, servo, and automatic protective device they've got in there," Michael said. "Hell, I can even get into the French grid, arrange it so they haven't paid their bills for ten years, and get 'em disconnected. Turning off the juice is very simple, and the effects can be devastating."

"They'll have a generator," Streak pointed out. "Everyone around here does. But we could take those rakkers."

"Oh, sure," Serrin said sarcastically. "Bullets and grenades aren't the problem. You're forgetting something. I felt the power they've got up there. They could crush us like bugs with magic. Try using your pistols and grenades against that."

"You can buy us enough time," Streak cajoled.

"Right. I can make you a paper parasol for when the ten-kilo hailstones rain on your head," Serrin told him.

"Look, I've got disabling stuff. Paralyzant gas grenades. Tasers. Smoke canisters. If we get surprised, we can buy enough time to get in, get one guy out of there— it's all we need—and run like frag. What else have we got?"

"You can make your phone call," Geraint said slowly. "Get those guys you trust. Then we'll see."

Streak was up and out of his chair before Geraint had even finished the sentence.

"Are you sure about this?" Michael asked earnestly.

"Of course I'm not bloody sure," Geraint said, taking refuge in another cigarette. "But we don't have any time, and it's obvious they're not going to talk peaceably. If we're going to see this through I don't think we have any other option. Why don't you start getting into that data in earnest? If Streak's bringing people over the border, that gives you a couple of hours at least. About time you and Serrin came up with more than bulldrek from all that stuff."

His voice was reproachful, and Michael wondered about that as he retreated to his deck. It's almost as if he's more motivated than I am, but it's meant to be my show, he thought, not with resentment, but with curiosity and some puzzlement. Is it only that his own fortune might be threatened if our decker brings down the entire Matrix? Hardly. Not with all the land and property he owns. So why . . .

He forgot all the idle speculation as he began preparing the analytic frames. By the time the heavy raps came on the front door, it had long grown dark and Michael was completely oblivious to everything around him.

15

Streak had only been able to recruit two samurai, but they looked as if there were six of them. The ork, Juan, had shoulders that would have put a troll to shame. His skin gleamed. Looking him over, Michael guessed that he had dermal sheathing, which would explain his relatively light body armor. The ork's matching cyberarms, one with a gyromount installed in it, must have cost a fortune. Juan couldn't have gotten it without being very, very good and very successful somewhere along the line. And probably more than once. But his cybereyes were dark and cold, and Michael noted how Kristen in particular gave him a very wide berth. He did, truly, look to be more machine than meat.

His human colleague was equally imposing. Xavier came clad in full body armor, and moved with the strange and unnatural lightness, which, when it accompanied excessive size and weight, screamed "wired reflexes." Michael sensed, though, that there was something more. The samurai had an occasional twitchiness in his muscles, around the eyes, that suggested the wiring was deeper and more powerful than usual. Streak has some over-powered friends, he thought.

"So you want to take a captive," Juan said in a deep voice, richer in tone than the inhumanity of his appearance. He seemed almost disappointed.

"We need someone to interrogate," Streak said. "That's essential. That's the mission goal."

"What about corollary damage?" Xavier asked, in much better English than Michael would have expected.

"Irrelevant," Streak said with relish.

"Wait a minute—" Geraint started.

"Look," Streak said exasperatedly, "you want a prisoner or not? You say you've got five days. Now if you want someone to talk to, we do it our way. How many tactical raids have you mounted on reinforced installations packed with samurai and mages?"

"Okay, all right," Geraint said testily. "But in this country, I can't get us bailed out if we get into big-time trouble."

"Which is why we're not going to ponce around like a bunch of pansies," Streak asserted. "And we're going to use disabling approaches."

"Pity," Xavier said thoughtfully. "I've got some Byelorussian fire gel that could immolate the entire place inside five seconds. Wonderful stuff. Burns like crazy for that time and then, wham! The shrapnel cakes go ape and spray the firezone. It could take out a wizworm, honest. Well, with a depleted uranium boost it could, and I've got some of that too."

"We said disablement?" Geraint said incredulously.

"Yeah, right," Streak said. "Okay, terms, you know the deal here. You also know what their strengths are likely to be. How's that Matrix work coming along, Mikey?"

"Nothing difficult," Michael told him. "I can disable the system exactly when you want it done."

"And you, brother?" Streak said to Serrin, who grimaced a little at the overfamiliarity.

"I've prepared us as I can," Serrin told him with a shrug. There was little point in going into detail on the spell locks he carried, the rituals he'd prepared, the barriers he'd primed as best he could. They would hold for a while, but that wouldn't be long. To hide his irritation he made for the kitchen. After a moment Kristen padded after him on bare feet.

Streak and the other samurai pored over the map spread before them. "We come in from the south, I think," the elf said. "Divide up. Juan and I will go in first. Michael and Geraint can cover us. Xavier, you're gonna hang back and use the ranged stuff, and cover Serrin here as well. Yeah?"

"I want to be on elevated terrain to be able to provide auxiliary cover if you need it," Xavier said. "Not to mention that I don't want to do everything with IR and laser sighting. You've been up there in the daylight. Where's the best spot?"

"You want to be up high, with cover as well?" Streak grinned. "Don't we always want everything? Here"—he stabbed a finger into the map—"looks about best to my way of thinking. Should be enough green drek to cover your arse. And you've got some magical camouflage from Serrin."

Serrin was arguing with Kristen in the kitchen, their voices growing increasingly audible.

Streak chuckled. "I think the girlie doesn't want to stay barefoot in the kitchen."

"I've seen her shoot a guy in the head and save someone's life," Geraint informed him. "So not so much of the 'girlie', please. She can look after herself. She wouldn't be here if she wasn't a member of the team."

"Keep her back with Serrin and Xavier then." Streak was serious now. "She may have guts, but she ain't got no smartgun link and she shouldn't be up with the professionals."

"Fair enough," Geraint said. "Time to get that body armor on, Michael. Are you sure you want in on this?"

"I've done enough night work with firearms," Michael said. "Hell, I live in the Rotten Apple. It's the second thing you do when you arrive."

"What's the first?" Streak asked.

"Practice shooting in daylight," Michael told him.

Streak laughed, then hefted his LMG and pack. "Let's get this show on the road. We've got an hour in the car to go through every step. They're going to be crying in the chapel tonight."

Michael looked puzzled.

"It's an old, old song," Streak told him. "You want to get some culture, term."

"When I hear the word culture—" Xavier burst out laughing.

"Yeah, I know. But you don't need to hear that word, you psychopathic fragger, you just love reachin' for your gun anyway." Streak threw back his head and laughed along with him.

They parked the cars a couple of kilometers out. They had a time persuading Serrin to risk any assensing, but he found no trace of either watchers or other similar precautions at this range and it looked as if the Priory mages weren't expecting them back.

"I can't risk it when we get closer," he said. "We'll have to trust that the barriers work."

"Then we'll have to move fast," Streak said. "Can't risk getting any closer in the cars. They'll be detected too easily."

They crept along the uncomfortable path with its stones and undergrowth straying on to the walkway, the cloudy night giving them no helpful moonlight to see by. They were halfway to the hill when the sound of a heavy engine began to approach from the south. They were well away from the roadway, and Streak dived off into the night to see what was coming.

They were nearing the hill when the elf returned. In the dark, the alarm on the elf's blackened face wasn't entirely obvious. When he spoke, though, his concern was all too tangible.

"I don't want to worry you," he whispered, "but there's one seriously big fragger of a truck riding up to the hill. Looks like a twenty-tonner. Black as sin and completely sealed. I could hardly even see the thing. Can't get any scan on what's inside it."

"Reinforcements?" Michael said, fretting.

"What for? Frag it, you could get the entire fraggin' Inquisition into the back of—"

The elf's voice trailed away into the eerily quiet night.

"Nah. Don't be silly," he said hurriedly. "Just a figure of speech. Let's move it."

They were thirty meters further along, within fifty more of their planned forward positions, when the truck rolled into view and stopped. Black figures appeared from the back of it like chitinous insects swarming out of a disturbed nest.

The first shell hit the building atop the hill two seconds later, lighting up the night like Times Square. Only Streak and Juan, with their flare-compensating cybereyes, didn't have to turn away in pain and blindness.

"We got gate-crashers," Xavier grunted. Juan swiveled and his laser designator focused on its target.

For what had been planned as an extraction operation, the ork was carrying some mighty potent weaponry. The shell screamed through the night at the truck, and rammed straight into the side of the massive vehicle. It should have ripped a hole right through it. Instead, it seemed to bounce off and disappear in a vast fireball somewhere to their right.

"Madre de dios!" the ork exclaimed in fury. "What the hell kind of fraggin' armor has that fragger get on it?"

Geraint had kept his attention focused on the chapel building. At first it seemed little damaged despite being struck by a shell, then suddenly a wave of fire began to form around it, seeming to immolate the chapel even as he watched. Then, the fire-ring coalesced into a pillar and rolled down the hill toward the truck. The Priory mages aren't taking this lying down, he thought. By God, I'm glad that thing isn't coming our way.

The elemental swept to within thirty meters of the truck before it was snuffed out like a smoker's match dropped in the rain. The chatter of automatic weapons began to fill the night, almost mundane in comparison. Dwarfing it, a fireball burst above the chapel and began to expand even as Geraint looked on, mushrooming until it encountered an invisible hemispheric barrier. It cascaded down the sides of the barrier, spluttered, and died.

And they've got their defenses readied too, Geraint thought.

"Hey, you want me to frag the truck or frag the chapel?" Juan yelled at him. It was a pretty fair question under the circumstances. Geraint was still considering how to reply when the arriving mages, unseen in the back of the huge truck but very evident by their handiwork, pulled the stunt they'd been waiting for.

A vast pair of spectral hands, clasped together as if in

prayer, appeared like some nightmare borealis above the chapel. They hovered thirty meters above it, suspended in the air, shimmering with magical power, and from the tip of an index finger a bolt of lighting crackled down and struck the hermetic barrier. When the irresistible force met the immovable object, the gates of hell were flung open—then slammed shut again.

The detonation flung everyone into the air, and then heavily back down onto the rocky ground. Michael groaned as his weak back was flung against a particularly unforgiving mass of rock, and he rolled over, yelping with pain. Even Juan was flung off his feet, though the immensity of the ork had seemed capable of defying gravity. Streak alone stayed on his feet, and managed to keep his Ingram leveled at the figures suddenly advancing on them. Two of the dark shapes fell before his arc of fire even as tracer rounds screamed through the night and, unbelievably, the howling of dogs came from the vicinity of the chapel. It was utter mayhem.

Fifty meters away from them the Priory mages and their unseen assailants were engaged in a titanic struggle of will and power, and Serrin suddenly switched his focus. He had to add to the spell lock and cover his friends, and the barrier came up just in time to save them. Streak would have been carrying half his own body weight in flaming lead from the advancing samurai if he hadn't. The elf gawked a little as he didn't die in the field of fire, then emptied his clip just as Xavier pumped the first of the gas grenades into the samurai threatening to take him apart.

"The bastards have respirators," he growled. "Come on, you stinking fraggers, let's see how you take stun." Another grenade hot-fired, landing just behind their front line, and more were being frantically slammed into the launcher.

"How do you like this, you fraggers!" Xavier laughed as the first grenade landed right on target and blew the dark samurai backward. Streak hadn't even bothered to slam another clip in. He just switched weapons and scythed down a few more of the previously advancing samurai. A fortunate shot from Geraint finished off one of those he'd wounded.

Juan had learned his lesson from his previous assault

on the truck, and started launching at the chapel, but Geraint told him to stop and concentrate on the unknown assailants beginning to fall back to their vehicle. The ork grinned and fired a canister grenade at them. The effect was horrifying: the shell burst in midair and a great web of sticky strands covered them, setting them alight on contact, the corrosive acid of the strands burning through armor and flesh as surely as the flame it generated. The screams of the dying were appalling to hear.

The hands in the air moved. The fingers were now pointing at the four men, and no longer at the chapel. Serrin saw it before the others did, and he knew they hadn't a chance against the power of the mages. He'd known this would come some time, and had just enough time to grab Kristen's arm and shout a few words to her.

"Cover me," he said. "I'm not going to be up to much after this."

She nodded once, grim and determined, and hefted her pistol, sliding the top of the barrel back to slip a round into the chamber.

Serrin had dutifully learned a lot about barriers and wards in the previous few months. He had enough anxieties about highly powerful mages with an interest in him, and a naturally paranoid nature to match. He'd spent more time practicing the centering rituals than he cared to think, and now he was going to find out if he'd gotten it right. If he hadn't, the drain was going to kill him. It was either him or his companions. No contest.

He clutched the focus in a white-knuckled grasp and began the incantation.

The finger seemed to dip just a little. The four men were scattering. Even the monstrous ork samurai knew that whatever those hands were going to deliver in the way of chastisement, his samurai's killing weaponry was going to be about as useful as papier mâché armor.

The blue arc of energy left the fingertip. Serrin spoke the last words and fell back into Kristen's arms. Xavier only had time to launch a frag grenade to discourage anyone from getting too close to him before he looked around to take in what had to be the mass funeral to his left.

The power struck the barrier and arced around and across it, great ripples of force thrashing at the invisible ward like breakers against a rock cliff. And the barrier held.

For a moment.

Then there was a deafening, nerve-shredding screech, like a thousand fingernails being dragged down a hundred blackboards, and the power bolt grounded itself—fifty meters away, to the left of its target.

Michael didn't remember much after that. This time, his head landed where his back had the first time, and he was lucky to get away with concussion and mild amnesia. After a few moments, Geraint was also blasted off his feet, then managed to pull himself up onto all fours. In his swimming, hopelessly unfocused vision, he saw shells bursting into the chapel and, this time, disintegrating stone and thatch, smashing at the fabric of the building. Towering above him, an ork tottered around with his gyromount arm swinging relentlessly around to its designated target.

Not the chapel, bonehead, Geraint prayed. Don't let him waste energy on that. *Please.*

The shell smashed into the truck. This time it did a lot more damage than the first. The side of the vehicle ripped open like a tearing flap of skin, and a rain of bodies was flung into the night, screaming and groaning. A second later, Xavier's frag grenade changed that to silence.

Unbelievably, the truck's engine groaned into life and, unsteadily, the vehicle turned itself around. Juan was staggering around, trying to focus his senses on a last shot to send the truck and its surviving occupants to final oblivion. Then, of all things, a monstrous black dog sped across the terrain toward him, its eyes afire in the flame-streaked night.

Geraint leveled his pistol, prayed, and emptied the clip.

The dog rolled over and didn't get up. The truck made its away down the hill and into the night. Geraint dropped to his knees and tried hard to keep the nausea down; two shock waves had wreaked havoc with his body. A thin stream of blood trickled down his chin from his bitten lip.

Striding jauntily over to him, Streak looked like a walking nightmare. The elf was wide-eyed, his face a manic grin, and both face and body were covered in fresh blood. Horribly, his guts seemed to be spilling out of his abdomen, and he didn't even seem to care. Geraint stared at him, stupefied.

"Nah, it's not me," the elf laughed, looking down. "One of their bloody dogs. Ripped 'im," he added, flourishing his serrated knife with pride. "Always the best way. Nothing like hand-to-hand, I always say."

"You're mad," Geraint said incredulously.

"Barking, mate, fragging barking!" the elf laughed. "Not like poor old Lassie. He's barked his last bark, I can tell you." He looked around at his companions. "Rakk me, this is a mess. *Como está,* Juan? Okay?"

The ork grunted. Streak took that as an admission of good, rude health.

"Looks like matey here is a bit fragged," Streak said, kneeling down over Michael and scanning him. "Pulse okay, bit febrile. Banged his head, though. Ouch! Look at that lump. Patch job should be okay." He kneeled down closer, and then shrugged his shoulders. "EEG's okay. More or less. He'll be all right." The elf took a trauma patch and applied it to the unconscious man's wrist.

"Not much left up there, by the way," Streak continued, gesturing to the remains of the chapel. Now that Geraint had recovered most of his wits, he could see that the Inquisition—for it surely must have been them—had, at the last, succeeded in flattening Sauniere's historic chapel. Anyone inside it would surely be dead. Streak seemed to read his thoughts.

"I wonder who's in the basement," the elf said thoughtfully. "Let's check on—ah, here he comes now."

"All dead and gone," Xavier said cheerfully. "I let the survivors have some frag and newt and there's nothing left now."

"Newt?" Geraint was unfamiliar with the term.

"Nerve gas. Deadly, but it decays inside five seconds. Absolutely lethal. Packed in a cloth- and armor-dissolving unstable gel base. Squelch. No more Mr. Bad Guy. I've scanned, there ain't nothing and no one left alive, Your Lordship."

Geraint suddenly realized that the burden the man was carrying was Serrin. His face changed expression.

"Reckon he saved your hides from those hands in the sky," Xavier told him. "Fainted away. He'll be okay. Want to scan him, Streak?"

Streak took a few seconds to make his diagnosis and confirm that the unconscious elf was not in any immediate danger.

"We'd better go in," he said to Geraint. "Xavier, you want to stay and take care of these terms?"

"Fine by me," the elf said cheerfully. "Frag, that was a lot of fun. Thanks for the invitation. Some party!"

"Not bad, eh?" Streak grinned. "All right, Your Lordship, let's see if the boys at the chapel have learned some better manners. Better put that respirator on, we may need trank gas just in case they're still a bit lively."

"I wish Serrin could check it out first," Geraint said anxiously. "Those mages up there had to be good."

"Past tense is dead right," Streak replied. "If they were still up and firing on all cylinders, I don't think the chapel would be doing a good impression of Dresden right now. Let's get in before they recover, if there's anyone left to recover."

Before they moved off, Geraint went over to the forlorn figure sitting with her gun held loosely between her knees and put his arm around her. Kristen was shaking, but her eyes were dry.

"Don't worry. He'll be right as rain in the morning," Geraint reassured her.

"I know," she said in a voice stronger than he'd expected. "He told me what he was going to do."

He hadn't told anyone else. Geraint tried not to look surprised.

"Stay and look after him," he said.

"No, Xavier will be with him, and I trust him. He's okay."

"What do you want to do then?"

"I'm coming with you. I want to know what's happening, and you say the answer is up there. Since Serrin isn't awake to hear, I'll be able to tell him all about it. Whatever it is."

Geraint looked askance at her, and then a smile spread across his face. "Good for you. Come on, then. Let's not keep Streak waiting. You know how impatient he gets when us civilians dawdle."

She took his arm and they walked up the hill to the ruin.

16

It wasn't easy trying to find any sign of a place of access beneath the rubble. Most of the walls had been shattered, and heavy stone lay everywhere. There were bodies, badly mangled, and Geraint had to look away from them. To his surprise, Kristen seemed less squeamish, though she obviously disliked what she was seeing. Her previous life on the streets of Cape Town must have been far harsher than he'd ever fully comprehended.

"Ah, here," Streak said at last. "Here are the steps leading down into the dungeons, master."

The trapdoor had been shattered and rubble was piled up in the stairwell below. A haze of dust and vaporized plaster gave the depths the impression, indeed, of some macabre Victorian underground labyrinth or prison straight from a Fuseli drawing. The twin flashlights of Geraint and Streak lit the gloom. They showed the first of the bodies at the foot of the steps. Stepping carefully over it, Streak led them on.

They found him within moments. His perfect suit covered in dust, the man lay sprawled on the floor, groaning. There was no blood visible on him, but his left leg was crooked at a horribly unnatural angle and it was obviously broken. He looked up at them, pain distorting his face.

"You murderous bastards," he spat at them.

"It wasn't us, matey," Streak said cheerfully. "It's true we came to, well, force a way in. But we never fired a shot at the place. Sure, Juan here blew that truck full of Jesuits back down the hill. But if not for us, it would be them talking to you now. And somehow, I don't think they'd be offering you the morphine shot I'm considering giving you for the pain. That leg looks terrible."

The man looked at them with the eyes of a frightened animal, exhausted and in agony, but with an even greater pain than the simply physical; the painfulness of hope in an impossible situation.

"You're lying," he said.

"Sure we are," Geraint said. "You know who we are, I'm sure of it—you didn't even ask who we were when we met. You think we could create that magic that smashed your barriers? You think we're that powerful?"

Gianfranco looked full of doubt for an instant, and then a spasm of pain from his shattered leg made him cry out. "For pity's sake give me that shot," he begged.

"After you talk," Streak said implacably.

"No." Geraint was adamant. "Give him the shot."

"Are you crazy? He'll talk. With that pain, anyone would. We'll get what we want!" Streak protested. Gianfranco could say nothing. His arms moved to clutch at his agonizing, smashed limb, and then drew back since the pain of clutching it would be even worse than the pain of just lying where he was.

"Tell me what I want to know and you get the shot," Streak said urgently, kneeling over the man.

"Give him the shot, man, and do it now!"

"Frag off!"

"I'm paying you and you'll do what I damned well tell you to!" Geraint yelled furiously, his face reddening in anger. He rarely lost his cool, but when he did the Celtic temperament was fearsome to behold. Streak stared back at him defiantly, and then gently put the patch on the man's throat. Within seconds, the cocktail of opiate, endorphin, and anti-trauma colloids was surging through his jugular, into his heart, and spreading sweet relief into the tortured flesh of his leg. Geraint knelt down to see how he was.

"The Lady bless you," the man said fervently. He gripped Geraint's hand in his own and sighed in relief.

"Fragging bleeding heart," Streak snarled. "We could have had what we wanted by now."

"It wasn't us," Geraint said. "It was NOJ. Those hands above the building—you know their sign."

"I know it," Gianfranco whispered, his head dulled with the drug. "I couldn't be sure who you were with. You could have been in with them."

"Why would you think that?" Geraint asked.

"You're a member of the British government and you ask me that?"

It was true, Geraint thought. Even his own boss seemed

to jump at their call. It wasn't so surprising that
Gianfranco should think that.

"We have to get him out of here," he told Streak.

"There's no rush," the elf said. "There aren't going to
be swarms of French police or army up here for a while.
This is the back of beyond. Slot, there are even border
bandits in this region. It's virtually Sardinia up here.
Ain't that right, guys?"

"Sure is," Juan said laconically, picking at his teeth
with a match.

"Just do it," Geraint said wearily. Streak looked resigned and flipped open the top of his comm unit.

"Let's get the cars up here," he said. "It'll be faster that
way. He's in no shape to be carried three klicks or more."

"Who are you calling?" Geraint asked. "There's no one
left outside, only Xavier, and he's no nearer the cars than
we are."

"No, but he's got the remotes and you didn't travel in
his car." Streak grinned suddenly. "Computer mapping,
topology analyzers, autopilot, and his machine'll be here
in five minutes. We can put the sleepers on the roof rack
until we get back to ours."

"Like I say then, just do it," Geraint said. Though it
was still not yet midnight, his body said it was five in the
morning after a very, very bad day.

The car turned up, gliding driverless up the hill, as
swiftly as Streak said it would. As they shambled out toward it, Geraint's eye was caught by a flash of color
among the blackness of shattered stone under the lightless
sky.

"Well, I'll be damned," he muttered, staring down at
the statue. Incredibly, it had somehow survived among
the ruins of the conservatory. Knocked from its pedestal
by the force of the blasts that had demolished the building, it seemed remarkably pristine and unmarked. The
paintwork was oddly gaudy, and it looked like a cheap
curio sold in those shops that vend plastic icons and bottles of Lourdes water to the faithful and those bereft of
intelligence or aesthetic discernment.

"That's the very figure. Just as we saw her."

He remembered the spirit who'd invaded his flat and
delivered the warning to them. Lying at his feet was a

replica of that figure, staring back at him as if defying the might and brutality of all those who had destroyed her shrine.

"Joan of Arc."

He almost crossed himself. He felt somehow compelled to make an apology to her, a sign of appeasement, but he stopped himself because he knew it was wrong. Not wrong to make an apology, but wrong to make the sign of the cross.

He didn't understand that, and he knew it mattered; and when he turned away, he was troubled by it. But Streak was trying to squeeze everyone into the car, and he had to walk away and involve himself with that.

But he did not forget it.

They decided to risk staying in Clermont-Ferrand for the night, not least because they didn't want their unconscious and injured to have to make the trip to Toulouse at this hour, and arriving in a major city in the shape they were in would surely attract attention. The risk was that those who'd raided the chapel—or their companions— might come looking for those who'd defeated them, and Clermont was too close for comfort.

"We can't move this guy," Streak said. "We probably shouldn't move Michael either, not with a bump to the head; and I always get uncomfortable around mages who get drained. They always tell me not to frag around with them. I don't like staying here, but I reckon we have to. Until Michael comes around, at the very least."

Geraint left the elf to organize matters here and went to tend to Gianfranco. A second painkilling shot had left the man dazed and confused, but it was obvious he needed serious medical help. He would be permanently crippled, or even die, if he didn't get expert medical help shortly.

"Gianfranco, we're going to get you to a hospital," he said quietly to the Italian. The man nodded and clutched Geraint's hand again to express his thanks.

"But look, you owe us, really you do. You would have been killed like the others if we hadn't turned up here tonight. And we really only wanted to talk peaceably. You turned us away."

The man said nothing for a few seconds, and then looked up in absolute torment.

"I cannot talk," he said wretchedly. "You don't under-stand."

"I understand quite a lot. I understand that you had me tracked and sent a spirit to warn me off, smashing its way into my own home. Just for starters."

"We didn't harm anyone," the man protested. "You killed Serrault, our mage."

"That was an accident," Geraint said, aware that the man had a fair point. "Serrin says he was heavily drained from ritual magic and shock killed him."

It wasn't true, but he had to lie. Time was short.

"We saved your skin. You can give us something."

The man said nothing. Geraint thought of another tack and guessed that this time, he just might have some luck.

"And look, Gianfranco, Streak would have made you talk before the shot. And you would have talked. Yes, you would."

The other man's eyes met his and confirmed the truth.

"So, you owe me twice over. The Inquisition came af-ter us. Kidnapped two of us, drugged them and took blood for ritual magic, threatened to kill us. We need to know why. They killed your people, and they'd have killed us too. We want to know how to stop them when they try again. It's not an unreasonable thing to ask."

The man groaned again, the last residues of pain numbed by doses of the drugs that were weakening his resistance. Geraint hoped they weren't also making him unable to explain himself.

"I'm not a senior figure," he pleaded in a cracked voice. "There is much I don't know."

"The book. You sent the book," Geraint guessed. "Why?"

"As a message."

"How was it a message?"

"It was a clue. To the nature and location of the man Seratini was seeking. The one you seek," Gianfranco managed to say.

"How was it a clue? I don't understand," Geraint said plaintively.

"The topic. Water . . ." Gianfranco's eyes were begin-ning to flutter now, the drugs obviously taking over his mind and senses.

"Who is he, Gianfranco? I have to know," Geraint pleaded.

For a second, the man's vision cleared and a mixture of base cunning and intelligence shone out at the Welshman.

"There is one statue left in the city," he grinned, and his grip of Geraint's wrist relaxed as he fell into a narcotic slumber.

"Damn," Geraint cursed. He got back to his feet and turned away. The scent of coffee greeted his senses. It wasn't his newly discovered favorite, but at this time of night it smelled awfully good.

"If you want to get him to a hospital now, we've got to leave at once," Streak said. "We go to Toulouse, dump him at the airport, ring security from the plane, take off and get home. We can't risk anything else. If I drive him to Toulouse they'll ID him, get a trace to Rennes-le-Château, and then the police will descend on Clermont."

"Actually, given what's happened up there they'll be doing that anyway," Geraint said. "Think about it. There's a village up there. Someone must have noticed that the place has been flattened by now, not to mention all that magic lighting up the night sky and a few score corpses littering the farmlands."

Streak's eyes widened. "Frag me! I never thought of that. These bloody French villagers. What a damned nuisance they are!"

He was absolutely serious. Geraint almost doubled up in laughter, and the elf saw the funny side and laughed himself.

"Well, then, we'll have to pack up and move out whether we like it or not," he said briskly. "Come on, people, time to book. Back to Blighty. Job done. Game over."

The other samurai were already packed and ready to leave. Juan cheerfully waved the credstick Geraint had given him.

"A pleasure," he said. "Work for you any time, Your Lordship. You can always trust a British aristo, I say."

"That last fragger stiffed us," Xavier growled.

Juan shrugged. "Yeah and look what we did to his boyfriend."

Geraint started checking through his mental files for

who they might be referring to, then decided he really didn't want to know. The pair of samurai left, with one last goodbye and a complicated handshake with Streak that seemed to portray torture as some kind of friendship ritual. At least, it would have been torture if normal sinew and muscle had been involved.

"We're ready," Kristen said simply. Almost unseen, she'd packed everything they had, even weaponry, into their bags. Geraint had to smile. A clear head in a crisis was a valuable quality to have in a team member.

He looked doubtfully at the car, and then at Streak. "We can fit three recumbent people into that little thing?"

"Just. However, I hope you two are good friends. Either you're going to have to sit on his lap, missy, or you go in the boot." The elf avoided the playful kick the girl aimed at him. "No, honestly, I mean it."

Geraint got to the doorway of the bedroom just in time, or he'd never have known what happened. Hovering above the man on the bed was a ghastly imp-like form, a wrinkled creature of spirit and yet tangible, almost earthy. It drew a long pin from which some corrosive liquid dripped, and drove it through Gianfranco's ribcage and into his heart.

The imp turned, looked at him, spat, and disappeared. There was a smack as air rushed to fill the gap it had left.

To the Welshman's utter horror, Gianfranco suddenly jerked into an upright position on the bed. His eyes bulged in their sockets, and his tongue protruded from his mouth, blackened and swollen. Flecks of gray foam sputtered on his lips, and his hands clutched at midair in a final spasm of agony.

Then he screamed.

Clermont-Ferrand is in strange territory. Southwestern France has more than its fair share of tales of lycanthropes, hauntings, malign spirits, and other unseen horrors of the night. Grisly deaths don't really cut it, not on their own. It needs more than that to make tongues wag in this part of the world.

They say in Clermont, and in villages around it, that you could have heard the scream five kilometers away, and people who live that far out confirm it.

Geraint reeled back into the living room, his head full

of nightmare, guts churning, heart beating like a hammer
on an anvil in Vulcan's realm. For a moment, he actually
wondered if this was what it was like to die of shock. A
stunned elf was looking at him, white-faced, next to him
a girl whose face mirrored the expression, the two of
them clutching each other for support. They just managed
to keep each other from falling over.

When they began to calm down, the three of them tottered to the doorway and opened it to get the cold, fresh
night air into their lungs.

"Let's get the frag out of here," Streak croaked. "I
don't want to know what happened, man. I just don't
want to know. Don't tell me. I don't ever want to know."

He was barely coherent, but at least he could speak,
which was more than the others could. And, somehow,
they had to get two unconscious bodies into a car and
drive away.

The third body they no longer had to worry about.

17

It was a distinctly jaded huddle of people who managed
to bluff and shuffle their way through the apparently
equally tired and more than disinterested security at the
Toulouse airport. They'd already soaked Michael's jacket
with a generous dose of brandy and proclaimed him dead
drunk to account for his unconsciousness. Serrin, in contrast, had made a fairly swift recovery during the drive,
surprising them all, though he was still not entirely himself. He seemed vacant, not attending to his surroundings,
but he was able to talk coherently and seemed to be suffering no more than physical fatigue. Coffee from a flask,
and a nip of the brandy left over from anointing Michael,
had had a powerful restorative effect on him.

Streak talked them through without incident, and they
were just fastening their safety belts in the Yellowjacket
when a pair of airport security guards came racing up to
their chopper.

"Oh, drek," Geraint said. Streak frowned, but had no choice but to push open the chopper door again.

"You forgot to sign this," one of the men announced, proffering a form that looked as if it had outgrown "triplicate" and was now heading for double digits.

"Yes, and this," the other one grinned.

"Yeah, yeah, it's chill. Sorry, we were in a hurry. Guess I forgot," Streak said, managing to sound bored as he signed the top copy with a pen borrowed from one of the men. That pen, when it found its way back to the officer, was wrapped in a high-denomination French banknote.

The man smiled broadly. "That will do nicely, *monsieur*," he said, and the pair retreated slowly back to their concrete watch-house.

"I was so busy trying to be casual I forgot the bleeding bribe," Streak explained once he'd closed the door of the aircraft. "Sorry."

"Thank God that was all," Geraint said. He was overtired and jumpy. Of them all, he alone had seen the malefic spirit that had killed Gianfranco, and the sight had seared his nerves.

"London?" Streak asked again. Apparently no one had heard him the first time.

"Guess so. I'm too tired to think of anywhere clever," Geraint said feebly.

Streak turned briefly to his fellow elf, but Serrin had his nose buried in paper. With Michael still unconscious, the mage had apparently decided to take over the task of plowing through the morass of data he'd unearthed in his investigations. His brow furrowed, he ticked off something on one page, then resumed chewing the end of his pen absentmindedly as he scanned the next. Beside him, Kristen gazed absently out the window, apparently mesmerized by her light-spotted reflection.

"Can't go back to London . . . some mad Shi'ite ragheads have nuked it!" Streak announced loudly.

"Hmmm," Serrin said, chewing hard.

"Does he often get like this?" Streak asked no one in particular.

"Uh? What?" Serrin said, suddenly looking up.

"Never mind," Streak said wearily as he prepared to taxi off. "It doesn't matter." He pulled on his headset and hailed the tower, asking for clearance and a runway. The engines kicked into life, straining and purring like barely house-broken leopards.

When they were airborne, and heading up above the lights of the night-shrouded French city, Geraint turned to Streak with a look of real gratitude.

"Thanks," he said simply. "Seriously. We weren't in too good shape back there."

"All part of the service, mate," Streak said amiably, leaning gently on the stick to start the copter into a long turn toward the north. "I'll stick it on me bill for later."

They fell to talking then, Streak speaking of his mercenary life in hot spots around the globe, Geraint risking telling the elf something of the politics and intrigues that had created or exacerbated those incidents. A few times Streak whistled between his teeth at the mention of some exceptionally perfidious treachery or double-dealing behind the scenes. In the back, Serrin had his arm around Kristen, but his eyes and his mind were on the papers and images before him. His wife gazed away into the darkness, but it was difficult to say whether she was seeing her dark reflection, the occasional yellow light from far below that glided eerily through it, or anything at all. Michael slept on peacefully.

London seemed gray even before dawn, not needing the drab morning light to pronounce its grayness. Slowly falling rain reduced visibility to an uncomfortably short range, and Geraint's anxiety mounted steadily until at last they were safely back on terra firma.

"I don't like the idea of Mayfair," he said to Streak. "Who knows who's watching the flat now?"

"Yeah, I've been thinking about that myself. Do you know old Carney over at MagSec?" Streak asked.

"Certainly," Geraint said. The officious but highly respected midranking officer in the magical security subdivision of the Ministry of Defense was known to a lot of Foreign Office officials who had important foreign contacts they needed to keep hidden during their stay in London.

Streak smiled. "Well, your man Carney owes me a favor."

"Carney owes *you* a favor? Are you sure? Of course you are; ignore my stupidity. Well, well I never." Geraint

was dumbfounded. Was there no end to this elf's hidden
depths? Horace Walter Arbuthnot Carney never owed
anyone favors. They owed him. He had enough favors
coming to him to be king one day, or so went the joke.

"Just don't ask why."

"I wouldn't dream of it," Geraint said fervently.

"Carney has safe houses," Streak pointed out. "But it'll
cost you. Cashing in a favor with Horace means I'm losing a major fallback."

"Whatever it takes, Just make the call."

"You know, mate, you're getting to say that an awful
lot."

"It's because you're so damnably resourceful, my
man," Geraint was smiling now, his spirits lifted. If they
could find a bolthole in one of Carney's secure houses,
the Inquisition wouldn't be a problem. The Pope himself
couldn't get in.

Streak rubbed his chin, and then his eyes. "Jesus H, but
I'm seriously knackered myself. Any of that brandy left?"

"Just enough for the two of us to get steamed out of
our heads."

"Ahem." There was a small cough from behind them.
They turned to see Kristen grinning back at them, Serrin's
sleeping head in her lap.

"Don't forget me," she said quietly, glancing down to
make sure she wasn't disturbing her husband. "You got
any rags, Streak?"

"Not on me. But I'm sure I can rustle up the best toke
in town in fifteen minutes once we're through here."

"That would be really great, man."

"Lord, what kind of company am I keeping?" Geraint
said in a tone of mock wonderment.

They all laughed. It was pure relief, relief at getting
back safely. Arriving at Gatwick Airport, they climbed
stiffly out of the chopper and prepared to go through the
arcane and manifold rituals airport officialdom demanded
of all its new arrivals.

When Serrin woke at nine in the morning, at first he
couldn't remember how he came to be in what looked
like a high-security cell complex, with gentle lighting but
no visible windows to the room. The magical power
around the place all but screamed as it shimmered around

the edge of his senses. Around him, the gently sleeping bodies rose and fell in time to their breathing but gave no sound.

"Where the frag am I?" he wondered aloud, his voice cracked with sleep, and then the events of the day before all came rushing back. He glanced over at Kristen's sleeping form and smiled, then searched around for his stack of papers and was soon lost in their convoluted contents.

Michael was the first of the others to wake. It was around ten in the morning according to Serrin's watch. He rolled over, sat up suddenly, groaned and rubbed his forehead.

"Oh, frag," he moaned, delicately shaking his head in the manner of someone with a dropped parcel trying to determine whether the china tea service inside was in rather more pieces than it should be. "Frag frag fraggetty fragging frag! Some evil twisted bastard is drilling my skull open from the inside. This is becoming an almost daily occurrence. You know, I'm sure I can faintly remember some time in the far distant past when I didn't wake up sick."

"You fell on a rock," Serrin said helpfully, barely looking up from the papers.

"Wonderful. Hell, I need something for this headache," Michael said as he gingerly tested every last strain and ache in his body. A column of incipient pain seemed to run from the base of his skull to his tailbone. He felt dreadful. Then he took in his surroundings.

"Where the frag are we?"

"Some kind of safe house," Serrin murmured, moving another page to the back of the pile on his propped-up knees. "Magically protected. The barriers around this place are something to behold, I can tell you. Geraint didn't want to risk going back to the apartment, in case we had another visitor like Joan of Arc."

"Right. Yeah, right," Michael said dully. "Coffee. Give me coffee or I'm going to die. Now."

"Try the blue flask," Serrin said, his conversation still coasting on autopilot. His head was obviously full of what was in the printouts.

Despite the protests of pain from his aching body, and a headache that truly felt like an old-fashioned lobotomy had been inflicted upon him very recently, Michael tottered over, driven by his curiosity.

"What have you got?"

"Interesting. Did you know that Leonardo da Vinci was Grand Master of the Priory of Sion in the years immediately before his death?"

"Frag, why didn't I get that from all my cross-indexing?"

"Because you wouldn't have known to look for obscure connections when you're not familiar with the background," Serrin pointed out. He lit a cigarette, a habit he indulged in much less frequently than he once had. Michael had noticed the change, putting it down to the mage's new-found domestic happiness.

"And Victor Hugo too. And Jean Coctaeu. And even, maybe, Isaac Newton."

"Newton? Really? Tell me more," Michael said, and as the others slept on, the pair were both soon engrossed in the data. Soon, pens were jabbing into paper, words were being underlined, key phrases highlighted, and Michael almost managed to forget his headache.

The hours ticked away and Kristen, in particular, was developing the first signs of going stir-crazy. Indulging in Streak's special-delivery product made her a little less restless, but definitely more ready to complain.

She was doing her best to distract Serrin from his interminable note-sharing with Michael when a gentle tap came on the door. One of the guards answered Geraint's "Come in", smiling in a way that suggested he'd recently been the unfortunate recipient of a thorough mindwipe (or had just graduated from a Golden Arches managers' university; it amounted to the same thing), and told them they had a visitor.

The gun was in Streak's hand instantly, leveled steadily at the casually dressed visitor, but Serrin told him to drop it when he saw who it was. By all the odds, there simply shouldn't have been a visitor. No one could have known where they were, and no one should have been able to get past the guards if they somehow did. But then their visitor wasn't flesh and blood.

"Good afternoon," he said pleasantly. "May I sit down?"

"Who the hell are you?" Geraint said furiously. "Streak, I thought you said—"

"It's all right," Serrin said rapidly. "I know him. What on earth are you doing here, Merlin?"

"I'm acting on my own initiative, I'm afraid," the free spirit said with the sheepish look of a five-year-old boy caught perched on a high stool with his hands in the cookie jar. "I do consider that my master might have been a little more forthcoming than he was."

"Then sit down," Geraint said, waving the guard away. The man gave him a questioning look, then closed the door behind him.

Kristen already had a cup of tea in her hand, and offered it to the spirit. He took it in his right hand and took one of hers in his left, raising it to his lips to kiss it and bowing slightly as he did so. He caught Serrin's eye and smiled.

"Do forgive me," he said affably. "Please don't be jealous. I'm not even human, after all."

"Hmmmm," Serrin grumbled, but Kristen looked pleased.

"So," the spirit said as he sat down, crossing his legs at the ankles of his elegant cotton trousers, "I gather you've been abroad."

"Might have," Streak said suspiciously, gun still in his hand. "On the other hand, maybe we ain't. What's it to you anyway? And will someone tell me who this is, if he isn't human? He looks bloody human to me."

"He's a spirit," Serrin said. "Which is doubtless part of the explanation for how he got in here."

"That worries me," Streak replied. "If he can—"

"Ah, yes, well," Merlin said hurriedly, "it's rather easier to find someone when you've been involved in a hermetic ritual with them. The linkage is much simpler. Not an advantage the Priory or the Acquavivans would have."

"Acquavivans?" said Serrin, unfamiliar with the term.

"Those NOJ tossers," Streak said. "They're only one Jesuit faction, after all. Named after Claudio Acquaviva, devisor of the Ratio, their organizational code. Hard-nuts, the lot of 'em.

"So how does chummer here know about all this?"

"Please, please," Merlin entreated them all. He sipped

his tea and smiled at Kristen. "Most welcome and refreshing, thank you. It's been a long hard day and it isn't even teatime yet."

"I don't believe this bloke," Streak said to Geraint. "Are you sure he isn't related to you? He sounds just like you."

Serrin ignored him. "Tell us why you're here, Merlin?"

"I thought you could use a little help."

"That's putting it mildly," Streak said. "But like I just said, mate, what's it to you?"

"Look, Streak, leave this to me," Serrin said irritably. "I know Merlin."

"Why don't we go and have a gin and tonic, Streak?" Geraint said pleasantly, with just the slightest edge in his voice that clearly implied, "This is not a suggestion." Streak looked uncertainly at him, and at the spirit, and then decided that if Geraint didn't mind sitting it out, he'd settle for a secondhand summary too. They retreated to the kitchen.

"What does Hessler think of your being here?" Serrin said carefully. He was hardly party to the details of the spirit's dealings with the mage he had, after all, called "Master."

"He might not be entirely pleased," Merlin confessed. "But there are some things I think you really should know. Otherwise, you won't be prepared for some of the opposition you may encounter."

"Such as?" Michael ventured.

"The NOJ are hardly to be trifled with," Merlin said. "Not when a matter of such importance is at stake."

"But what can be so important to them?" Michael asked. "I mean, we're not planning to nuke the Pope or something."

"Well, actually," the spirit replied, "I think that's more or less exactly what they think you're planning to do. In a manner of speaking."

"What?"

"The problem is that the situation you're stumbling into is far, far bigger than you can possibly realize."

"Wonderful," Michael said. "You know, it always strikes me how funny it is that people say that when all they really mean is, 'I want you to stop being a pest and go away'."

"Perhaps, but I'm not people," the spirit said pleasantly. "I look at things rather differently."

"This isn't getting us anywhere," Serrin interjected. "What we know is that someone has been able to deck into big-time computer cores. He left behind a puzzling icon of religious significance. That choice wasn't accidental or trivial. It's the reason why the Priory and the NOJ are so interested in the entire affair."

"Good," Merlin said approvingly.

"And that icon holds the key to who he is," Michael offered.

"Absolutely," Merlin agreed.

"And to why he's doing this . . ." Serrin said slowly, wondering even as he said it why he did.

"Excellent!" Merlin was beaming with genuine pleasure.

Michael looked at Serrin with a mixture of respect and a little admiration. The mage's intuitive leap had struck paydirt.

"What's odd is that quite a few people think they know who he is," Michael said. "Even more odd is that Renraku is offering a very large sum of money for that information, but no one's telling. Now doesn't that strike you as peculiar?"

"Michael, you're British," the spirit admonished. "You should know that some things are priceless, simply beyond money. I do believe you've been bettered in this understanding by Serrin, who's American. How times change."

"Touché, all right," Michael said irritably. "But our decker is planning to cause the Crash of 'Twenty-nine all over again. Isn't that enough to make anyone speak up? Think about it for a minute. It will mean mass unemployment, social chaos and unrest, suicides, even revolutions and mass bloodshed in some lands if it's anything like 'Twenty-nine was. Doesn't anyone care about that, even if they don't worry about the money?"

"Yes, Michael, they do," Merlin said wearily. "That's why I'm here. I don't think we can let him do this."

"Then tell us who he is," Michael demanded flatly, punctuating each word with the slap of his hand on his knee.

There was a long silence.

"It's not as simple as that," Merlin said at length.

"Funny, it never bloody is," Michael snapped. "I shouldn't have thought that speaking the few short words of a name was so terribly demanding, not really."

"Don't be facetious," Merlin shot back, genuinely irked. Michael looked angry himself for an instant and then shrugged, sitting back quietly.

"You can appreciate that I'm not always free to speak of what I know," the spirit said to Serrin.

The mage nodded.

"And this is one of those times. If I told you who and where, I'd be snuffed out of existence permanently and instantly as soon as it was learned of, and I don't relish that prospect one bit, thank you."

"I had not taken your Master to be so vengeful," Serrin said, a little surprised.

"Oh, if it was only up to him, I'd be safe enough," Merlin said. "Yes, I'd probably have to clean the kitchen every day for a year, but I do that most of the time anyway."

Serrin couldn't help but smile a little. The contrast of such a homely detail with the scale of what they were discussing was comical.

"There are powerful people with an interest in this," Merlin said, "and there are those among them who could and would destroy me—and my Master, for that matter.

"And if I told you who is responsible it would ruin everything."

"Pity about that," Michael said.

"Look," Merlin continued, a hint of irritation coloring his voice once more, "if I told you who was responsible you wouldn't believe me. If you want to find him, you'll have to do it on your own. The only way to stop him, I think, is by finding him for yourselves and persuading him, coming to some understanding. He needs the money for what he's trying to achieve. He'll need to get it. Or at the very least, a large slice of it."

"That's going to take some negotiating," Michael said dryly.

"Understand that I, for one, agree with what he's trying to achieve," Merlin said sharply. "I have some sympathy for him. And that's just when it comes to the initial goal.

The deeper one I don't think you're ready to know about right now.

"Find him. He can be talked to, but you need to know how he thinks. There won't be any substitute for finding out yourselves. Trust me, when you find him you'll know what I mean."

"Is this like reading a story, a mystery, and not wanting to know the ending in advance?" Kristen said uncertainly, leaning forward to enter the debate.

The spirit beamed at her. "Almost exactly so," he said. "He will need to see that you feel as you should when you confront a wonder.

"Have you ever seen the Pyramids, Serrin?"

The question came from the blue. The mage stared back at the spirit, keeping steady eye contact.

"Yes," he said. "Yes, I have."

"What did you feel when you first saw them?"

"Wonder," the mage said simply.

"The Pyramids are the most accurate stone buildings ever made," Merlin told him. "Forget all the half-witted theories about why they were built. They were built to connect people to heaven, and to remind people forever of wonder. There is a saying, I believe"—the spirit smiled slightly—" 'Man fears time, but time itself fears the Pyramids'."

Kristen had only ever seen the colossal, mighty Wonder of the World on a scratched postcard, but the proverb made her spine tingle, though she didn't know why. Maybe it was the way the spirit spoke, maybe it was the element of eternity in the words. Unconsciously she began rubbing one arm with the other hand.

"Be prepared to wonder, Serrin, I haven't mentioned the Pyramids for nothing. But I'll let that pass for now. What did you learn abroad?"

Michael looked uncertainly at the mage, but Serrin wasn't in any mood to conceal anything.

"Not a great deal, I'm afraid," he said sadly, and began to recount the events of the previous night.

The spirit looked disappointed, but Serrin didn't have anything more to tell him.

"I'm sorry about Gianfranco," Merlin said, "though I knew him only very slightly. Did he say anything before he died?"

"I wasn't there," Serrin said. "I was out for the count. Unconscious. Geraint?" he yelled toward the kitchen. Within moments the Welshman appeared in the doorway.

"Gianfranco. You were with him when he died."

"I certainly was." Geraint shuddered at the memory.

"Did he say anything?"

"Famous last words? No, he was asleep at the time."

"Nothing? There must have been *something*," Serrin insisted.

"I'd given him drugs for the pain. Hang it, the man's leg was shattered."

That touched a chord in the elf. He could all too easily imagine what it must have been like for the man. "Oh, well." Serrin sounded resigned.

Geraint rubbed his chin thoughtfully. "Wait, there was something," he said. "Something that didn't make any sense at all. I thought at the time he was rambling because of the drugs ... he passed out just after he said it. Oh, frag, what was it?

"Something about a statue. A statue." Again he saw the statue of Joan of Arc lying, so impossibly perfect, among the smashed ruins of the chapel, and then he remembered.

"A statue in a city. There's just one statue in a city, that's what he said. No, I don't know what it means and I didn't have a chance to ask him." He waved away Serrin's puzzled look. "I couldn't make head or tail of it."

"Then you have all you need," Merlin said, getting to his feet. "There's nothing more I need say. You have your quarry and you will know where to look. He's moved on by now, I suspect, but you won't be far from him if you go to the obvious place. Besides, I believe you had no plans to stay here."

"We certainly didn't," Michael told him.

"I don't understand," Geraint said.

"You will," Merlin said. "If it takes you more than half an hour I shall be very surprised. Well, I hope we shall meet again some time in the none-too-distant future. I can see myself out." He stood smoothly and made for the door.

"That's it?" Michael said.

"That's it," Merlin told him. "I've seen all those notes you've got. If you can't learn what you need from them, you'll really disappoint me, and I have faith in people. I know you won't let me down."

He was grinning broadly as he opened the door and departed. The others looked at each other, bewildered.

"Statues," Michael said. Geraint told him about the statue at the chapel.

"Yes, we've seen it," Michael said, digging out the picture he and Serrin had found from among the piles of paper. "Is this the one?"

"That's her," Geraint said.

"He can't mean this," Serrin said.

"I'm sure he doesn't," Michael said. "Time for a fishing expedition." He made for his portable cyberdeck.

"I'm afraid not," Geraint said, putting a hand on his companion's arm. "We had a once-over done on you when we arrived, when you were still flat out. Absolutely none of that for twenty-four hours. It would be dangerous with you still somewhat concussed, and no more than an hour a day for a week afterward."

"Drek," Michael groaned. "How am I supposed to earn a living?"

"Use a laptop like everyone else."

"Oh, sure," Michael said between gritted teeth, unclipping the lid of his laptop instead. "Back to steam-powered technology, slow everything down, I hate this."

"He said we needed only half an hour." Geraint smiled at his friend's impatience.

"Yes, but that bastard already knows the answer. Me, it's going to take weeks."

Michael was wrong. It took him seventeen minutes.

18

"Oh, of course," Michael groaned as the answer came up on the screen. "I should have gone to this first. I'm obviously more concussed than I thought. Never mind the NOJ and the Priory and Joan of Arc and everything else I've tried." He turned the screen around to face the eagerly expectant faces opposite him.

Leonardo da Vinci, declared the global dictionary header. The subhead read simply, *Statuary works.*

"Here we go: 'Leonardo's best-known statue is the Sforza Monument, commissioned after lengthy discussion by the Duke of Milan in 1489,' " Geraint read aloud. He was ostensibly doing this for the benefit of Streak, lounging on a sofa with his second gin, but not knowing how Kristen's literacy lessons were coming, he thought it would also prevent her any embarrassment.

"Unfortunately it was destroyed by the French in 1494," he continued, summarizing the next paragraph. "Wouldn't you just know it? Bloody French."

"Somehow I don't think this is it," Serrin fretted, then scrolled the screen down. "Ah, but this—"

"Lady with Primroses," Geraint read. "Erm, ascribed to Andrea del Verocchio, circa 1475. In the Baptistery, Florence, having been relocated from the Museo del Bargello in 2048. Suggestions that Leonardo assisted his master with this work were confirmed by the discovery of working sketches and notes in a fragment of a Leonardo codex discovered in 2037 in the papers of a member of the Savoy family. Currently and for the last 150 years or more this work has been regarded as the only surviving statuary by Leonardo.

"So that's it," Geraint peered at the image that formed on the screen.

"Not much to look at, is it?" said Streak from over his shoulder. Curiosity had got him up to see what was going on. "Wouldn't have thought he was a genius from that."

"The hands," Geraint mused. "Look at the hands. That's remarkable work."

"They're too big," Streak said simply. "Women don't have hands that big. Look, they're longer than her head is tall."

"You know, you're right," Geraint said.

"The Shroud," Michael said suddenly with a dramatic snap of his fingers. "The Shroud is too tall."

"What do you mean?" Geraint asked.

"The figure on the Shroud is nearly two and a half meters tall. What's more, the front and reverse images of the torso are different sizes by about five centimeters. One of the reasons why it's hard to claim that it's anyone's winding-sheet, let alone that of a specific person."

"So?" Streak said laconically. "So our great genius can't draw proportion. So much for genius."

"There's more to it than that," Michael began, but he couldn't crystallize his thoughts. Something still eluded him.

"Then Gianfranco is telling us to look in Florence?" Serrin asked, squinting a little to study the image closely. With a mere laptop, the printer would take some time to produce a high-res printout of the archive photograph.

"Merlin says he may have moved on," Geraint added. "Somewhere close."

"Okay, but let's consider Florence first," Serrin insisted. "What's Leonardo's history in Florence?"

"He spent some four years there, if I recall correctly," Michael told him. "He wasn't happy. He had left his master's studio after he was, I seem to remember, accused of high-jinks with some seventeen-year-old. But the Medicis, effectively the ruling family, don't seem to have rated him much. He headed for Milan, where he spent maybe twenty years. After that, there were spells back in Florence, Venice, Milan again, and then he died in France. In the arms of the king, the story goes."

Geraint laughed. "You've been reading up."

"If someone's seriously into a Leonardo persona, it seemed like a good idea," Michael replied.

"So what now? We go to Florence and put ads in the papers and on the bulletin boards saying, 'Tasty bird wants to meet Leonardo for a bit of artistic experimentation'?" Streak said sarcastically.

"I don't think so. The seventeen-year-old wasn't female," Michael said sagely.

"Ah," the elf said.

"Not that anything was proved. Such accusations were often made for political reasons. Anyway"—Michael got up and gave his hair a distracted ruffle—"I've got a report to file for Renraku, but at least this gives me something solid to give them at last. I can say where we're going next and make up an ingenious set of lies to embroider the story a bit, and they'll send me a comfortingly large sum of money by return. At the very least, that'll pay for the neurologist I'm going to need if I get my brain scrambled by gas or falling on rocks again, or anything else. Coffee?"

"Please," Serrin asked.

"What amazes me," Streak said as Michael went into the kitchen, "is how come we're alone in this. There must be other people after this guy."

"Michael and I wondered about that, too." Geraint said. "There probably are. But Renraku was the only corp to get the icon. They've probably hired a couple of other teams, but they'd stick with the best. Michael certainly qualifies as that, and there aren't many, not for something on this scale. I bet we're a jump ahead of any other team. We're not alone, but we must be a short head in front."

"Eh?" Kristen was baffled.

"A horse racing term," Geraint explained.

"Geraint," Michael said innocently as he returned from the kitchen with a ceramic tray bearing mugs of steaming coffee. "I wondered why you mentioned our man moving on when Florence was suggested. You know someone there, don't you?" He grinned mischievously.

"I was rather hoping you'd forgotten," Geraint said, obviously ruffled and embarrassed.

Streak saw his reaction immediately. "Tell us," he said with an evil grin. "My Lordship, we have to save the world from the forces of chaos and discord and we need every friendly face we can find."

"Frag off," Geraint said pointedly. "I know a certain noble in Florence, yes."

"More than that." Michael twisted the knife.

"Very well, I had a relationship with a certain countess from the city some years ago," Geraint admitted to them all with an acknowledging sweep of his hand.

"Come now, my lord. So modest! There was a duel," Michael said grandly.

"That was blown all out of proportion," Geraint grumbled.

"The pistols were loaded," Michael continued with relish.

"He only suffered a flesh wound."

"I'm afraid," Michael announced to Serrin and Kristen in an excellent impersonation of a regretful English butler, "that our friend had an *affaire d'amour* with a married lady. The duel was at dawn in the garden at—"

"Yes, yes, all right," Geraint said irritably.

"And I believe her husband is dead, killed in a car

crash," Michael said. "So the lady Cecilia is a widow now. I'm sure she'd be more than happy to receive a visit."

"I'm sure she wouldn't," Geraint countered.

"Cecilia? That's an Italian name?"

"Lady With an Ermine," Michael said mysteriously.

"With what?"

"One of Leonardo's paintings. The woman was Cecilia Gallerani, a young Milanese—a teenager when Leonardo painted her. I recall vaguely that she had a somewhat interesting romantic life. Rather like your Cecilia, Geraint. Now there's a femme fatale."

Geraint shrugged wearily. "Yes, I had an affair with a rather tempestuous married Italian countess. I wasn't the first and I dare say I shan't be the last. We did part on good terms, but I will not use this contact to get us into Florentine high society."

Four pairs of eyes turned as one to look at him. Throats were cleared, voices prepared to go into cajole-and-beg mode.

He never would be sure exactly how they managed to persuade him to change his mind, but within ten minutes he made the call.

"We leave tomorrow," Geraint told them. "Fortunately, Cecilia is about to set off on one of her jaunts. She'll receive us for lunch, and then she's off to the mysterious Orient. Her words, not mine."

There was clearly some relief in his voice. Michael had had time to develop some guilt about digging at him. He now recalled the events of that time more clearly, and although he hadn't been spending much time in London then, he remembered that Geraint's entanglement with the Countess, whom he'd never himself met, had seemed to hit the nobleman rather hard. It hadn't been one of the litany of short-term affairs with glamorous, often aristocratic women that Geraint had these days. But Michael recalled that the woman was a dozen years or so older than Geraint, and despite his assuredly romantic leanings, the Welshman would have had the sense to realize that it could never have been anything more than an *affaire d'amour.* Didn't he?

"Time is running out," Michael said.

"The doctor said you need rest. He said you shouldn't be undertaking any exertions for four days at the least and absolutely no decking until tomorrow. More haste, less speed, old man." Geraint wagged a finger at him.

"Yeah, but we could go tonight," Michael urged. "Get some groundwork done."

"That's not what I arranged," Geraint said smoothly. "Serrin also needs rest."

"I do?" the elf said, surprised.

"Yes, you do," Geraint insisted. "And Kristen agrees with me."

Serrin looked askance at his wife, who gave him a grin and a raised eyebrow and that "Yes, we've been talking about you" look she could summon up impressively when the situation so required.

"But—" Michael began, and then couldn't suppress a big yawn. He looked surprised at himself, amazed that his body had betrayed him so easily. Fatigue and lassitude were, indeed, creeping up on him. His calves ached, and there was a stiffness in his shoulders and back that didn't help him deal with his residual headache too well.

"Well, stuff it," he said amiably. "It feels like my body's decided for me. Maybe you're right, Geraint. Time for a siesta." He shuffled off toward the bedrooms.

"I just might do the same thing," the Welshman said, yawning himself. "I'm whacked."

"It's only just past noon," Serrin said.

"It's all right for some people, they slept in the car on the way back from Clermont. Not to mention most of the flight home," Geraint observed.

"Oh, right, sorry." Serrin had already picked up a sheaf of notes from Michael's stack and was apparently beginning to contemplate searching through them. Kristen didn't look too pleased.

"Have a kip, Your Lordship, and I'll wake you for tea," Streak said, flipping open a Zippo to light a cigarette.

"I didn't know you smoked," Geraint observed.

"I don't," Streak said, taking a massive drag and holding it in his lungs for some time. His grin grew a little broader.

"Oh, I see. I think I'll set the alarm clock," Geraint said sagely and stretched his arms above his head.

* * *

Nearly a thousand miles away, a young man smiled broadly as he jacked out of the Matrix and turned to his companion with an expression of satisfaction.

"They've made reservations on a flight to Florence," he said.

"That seems about right," the older one said. "They should be in the right place at the right time, I should think."

"There may be others there."

"Then perhaps you should be there to meet them. They may need a little gentle steering. It won't be easy for them to make further progress. And, of course, they'll almost certainly meet opposition."

"I may need to return here in a hurry," the young man frowned. "I mean, Master, in a *real* hurry."

"That shouldn't be a problem, and no, Salai, I haven't forgotten that there are those who might seek to interfere with that. Nor what they can do. Be gone, then."

"Shall I take a direct approach?"

A pause. "Give them one day and see what they do," came the considered reply. "Then use your own initiative."

"Ah, you say that to me so rarely," the young man said.

"But you so rarely do what I tell you," he was gently chided in return.

"Which is why you keep me with you." The young man laughed happily. "Take care, then. It will be soon now."

"It will, Salai, it will indeed."

Give them a day? the young man thought as he collected his already-packed cases. I think not. We do have a very good idea of who's already there. No delays this time. I shall need to move swiftly.

Besides, I was told to act on my own initiative.

Within minutes, the chopper rose over the lagoon and headed westward into the darkness.

19

They gave up any hope of getting their biological rhythms synchronized. At midnight, Michael was wide awake and lively while Serrin and Geraint were tired. Streak seemed inexhaustible but was keeping his own counsel. Kristen was excited at the prospect of seeing the great city of Florence, so it was difficult to determine how tired she actually was. Further delay seemed pointless. Only slightly over eighty hours remained before Michael's deadline was up.

"At least Renraku seemed happy enough," Michael told the others. "That is, they're in a state of barely controlled hysteria. It's when the control breaks down that they'll start screaming. In the meantime I got the money. The reward's gone up, too."

"Reward?" Streak sniffed the air like a well-trained bloodhound. "Someone mentioned a reward?"

"If I play a determining role in keeping Renraku from getting wiped I get the reward," Michael grinned. "You're on a retainer. I may cut you in for some of the deal if we succeed."

"Very generous," Streak said with feigned nonchalance. "What're we talking about here?"

"I could stretch it to a hundred," Michael said.

"A hundred nuyen? Oh, wow, like, carry me out on a gilded—"

"A hundred *thousand,* slot," Michael retorted sharply. Before the astonished elf had time to reply, he'd picked up his suitcase and left the room.

They made the small local airport at two in the morning. A security squad had delivered everything they thought they might need from Geraint's apartment and a no-name, no-number, ex-SAS rigger was along for the ride in the pilot's seat, hitching a lift, as it were, on his way to other business in Italy. The small private jet rose into British airspace at two-fifteen A.M. and entered Florentine airspace at four-forty. The sky was just beginning to hint that the black of night was really only a deep blue deprived of light.

"Airport breakfast and we get collected at six," Geraint told them. "We have a villa at our disposal."

"What about security?" Streak asked.

Michael threw up his hands in amazement. "We're staying with a member of the de Medici family and you ask about security?"

"I don't know no de Medicis. I'll need to check it out when we get there."

"I don't think so," Geraint said in his best "We're paying you, so just for once do what I say" voice. Streak frowned and fell silent.

"There are one or two people I might talk to here," Serrin offered.

"Yeah?" Michael asked casually.

"Yes." Serrin apparently wasn't giving anything away. "And we'd better be careful. The NOJ has force in the city. We need to keep a very low profile."

"Actually, I'm not even sure what we're doing here," Michael said.

Serrin ran it down for him. "One, we're out of London, where a bunch of watchers are currently taking a very active interest in Geraint's flat. Two, as I said, there are people I can talk to here. Three, Merlin seemed happy about it. Four, why not? It's a lovely city."

"Okay. Just get me through breakfast and let me get my deck set up. I want to snoop around the corps today. Find out who else is onto this and what they've got so far."

"Breakfast in the airport," Geraint said as they disembarked, "is a depressingly imminent probability. Let's get it over with, shall we?"

The sky was bright and clear as the horse-drawn carriage took them along the convoluted Viale Machiavelli, through the riotous Boboli gardens, past the Belvedere fortress with its looming clock-tower, toward the Arno River. The air was clear and fresh, the scent of flowers and blooming trees sweet but not cloying. Unlike Venice, a city that had virtually rotted from within around its toxic lagoon and in the deep chemical-soup slurries at the bottom of its canals, Florence had remained more or less beautiful over the centuries. The carriage headed toward the old Roman gateway to the inner city, and then along the broad, straight Via de Serragli toward the Carraia Bridge.

"We're staying in a villa along the Via Cavour," Geraint told them, "not far north of the river."

"Not far from the Baptistery either," Michael murmured. "A place we should go and see, I think."

"I'd sure like to take Kristen there," Serrin said.

"Be my guest," the Englishman replied. "I'll leave you to it and stick with my deck. Just who're you going to see here, anyway?"

"I'm not absolutely sure," Serrin admitted. Michael looked curiously at him, but didn't press the issue.

"I'll leave you to your own devices," Geraint told them. "I decided to get measured for some suits as long as we're here. My appointment's at midday."

"You want me to stay with Mikey boy or tail Serrin and Kristen in case they're being tracked by any interested parties?" Streak asked.

Geraint looked to Michael. "What do you think?"

"Go with them," Michael said. "So long as the villa security is good enough." He looked out the window at the swift-flowing river down below.

"It will be," Geraint promised. "Trust me. I've been here before. Someone tries to kidnap a Medici every week of the year, or so it seems. Quite often it's one of the other Medicis. The descendants of Cosimo and Lorenzo have some exciting internecine feuds."

"They run the whole city?" Streak asked.

"More or less," Geraint said. "The city council is absolutely dominated by them and their proxies. It really isn't so very different from the fifteenth century—except that they don't have to worry about being invaded by the French or Spanish."

One of the black horses whinnied as the carriage halted outside the villa. The title was somewhat misleading; the house was narrow and several stories towered high above the narrow terraced street. If Serrin had imagined a small white building set off in its own gardens, he was disappointed. Liveried servants hurried to take the visitors' baggage off the carriage and ferry it indoors.

Geraint quietly and subtly handed one of the men a tip

as the others milled in the hallway admiring the paintings and various busts.

"Never mind those. There's a genuine Donatello in the dining room, apparently," Geraint told them, opening the double doors to that room with a sweeping gesture. His gaze passed over the superb mahogany dining table and chairs, over the gleaming silverware and crystal, to the carved alcove at the far end of the room.

The depiction was very unusual. No Mother of Christ stood facing them, but the Magdalene. It was a Magdalene to rival Donatello's most famous, and one that was alleged to be a first study for that later work. If so, it seemed even to surpass it. While the final version was a portrait of decay and dissolution, the artist influenced by Gothic tradition, this statue seemed serene by comparison. Ragged and poor though the figure was, the face of the Magdalene did not have the ravaged look of the later statue, and the clasped hands of the bronze seemed more relaxed, the pose more peaceful, than Donatello's final nightmare vision. The quality of the piece was stunning, simple and radiant, and the whole group stood staring in silence for a few moments.

Even Streak. "Now that really is something," he mumbled. In an odd gesture, he seemed to feel for a nonexistent hat as if to take it off his head, and then realized he wasn't wearing one. The effect was comical, but his sincerity was genuine.

Michael walked up to the bronze and stared at it intently. "A mysterious lady," he said wonderingly.

They could find little else to say. The great artist's work could hardly be done justice by hasty words. They carried their bags up the stairs, despite the protestations of the domestic staff who'd arrived belatedly on the scene. The scent of freshly ground coffee and baking bread wafted gently after them.

"I know we just scarfed up that breakfast," Streak said, "but slot if I don't half feel peckish again."

"I just saw the cook with a basket of cheeses," Serrin whispered to him conspiratorially. The other elf licked his lips.

"And prosciutto with melon," Serrin added. Streak flung his bag at a bedroom doorway chosen at random and scurried downstairs to the dining room.

Serrin glanced around at the others and grinned. "I'll be down later," he said. "Save some melon for me." He reached out a hand to Kristen and, with a nod, she took it. They closed their bedroom door behind them.

Michael winked at Geraint. "I don't think we should disturb the loving couple, should we?"

"I thought he'd lived in Britain long enough that his libido had waned by now," Geraint joked.

"Come now, Geraint, I think that you of all people can hardly subscribe to that old myth," Michael said tartly. "By the way, how is the Countess?"

"Just fine," Geraint said. "Let's have a second breakfast. That ham did look awfully good."

Kristen watched over Serrin's physical body as he breathed quietly, the rest of him utterly still. Quite unconsciously, her hands were clasped together and, if she'd lived in Donatello's day, something quite different might have stood in the dining room, the subject of admiring gazes from visitors of later centuries.

The spirit had not wanted to materialize. He was not entirely sure what place they were in, and he didn't want to enquire where the guiding watcher spirit had directed him.

"I shouldn't really be here," Merlin fretted. "But matters move so swiftly and I'm restless and troubled."

"I plan to go to the Baptisery," Serrin told him. Despite the endless immensity of astral space around them, their astral forms were huddled close together. They might have looked, in some far more mundane context, like a pair of third-rate spies exchanging secrets on some dingy, muggy street corner.

"Yes. That's good."

"Merlin, it's hard to play a game when I don't know any of the other players nor the rules of the game," Serrin said exasperatedly.

"I think he will come to you," Merlin replied slowly. "Or he'll send some message, some sign. He wants to see you make the right moves. Visit the Baptistery. Don't forget what it means to this city."

"I don't understand," Serrin said.

Merlin looked around him, as if fearing some menace or threat. His face was furrowed with anxiety and sadness. "I can't put it more bluntly. Consider what the Baptistery means to this city and consider how he has depicted it. Then you'll have more understanding of him.

"When you see him, take your wife," the spirit concluded, quite unexpectedly. "That is vital."

"What do you—"

"Just listen and do what I tell you." Merlin was, by all appearances, struggling to contain a rising anger, but then he calmed down and seemed filled with sadness again. "Oh, Serrin, when you understand all this, you'll look back and kick yourself for being so slow. Though that's not any consolation to you now. I must go. My absence will be noted if I do not."

The figure moved away with astounding speed. Serrin swam his way wonderingly back to his meat body, settling down into his physical shell, then roused himself to wakefulness.

Kristen saw his eyes flutter beneath his eyelids and smiled. When he woke, she hugged him and cradled his head against her chest.

"I met him," Serrin told her. "He says that when we finally catch up with whoever it is that's behind all of this, you must be there too."

"I told you he was wise," Kristen said, teasing but also pleased.

Serrin looked at her a little darkly.

"And I like that he makes you jealous. Well, I like it a little," she said, with the coquettish smile that at times drove him to distraction. This was one of those times.

They didn't make breakfast for a while.

The ornate carriage clock was chiming nine when they finally emerged, to be greeted in the dining room by the vulture-stripped carcass of what must once have been a massive breakfast. Michael looked distinctly as if he needed his corset for more than supporting his back.

"Middle-age spread" Serrin taunted him, threatening to poke his stomach. Michael groaned, unable to take evasive action. "You look like Hecate when she was a kitten."

"I what?" Michael said, inelegantly.

"Our cat. When she was a kitten she once stole a cooked chicken off a table and ate the whole thing. All of it. All she could do afterward was lie on her back and make pathetic mewling noises. She couldn't walk for a day and a half. You remind me of her."

"Thanks, friend," Michael said witheringly.

"At least I kept him off el vino," Streak put in.

"Good job too," Serrin said, sitting down and spreading some goat's cheese on a stray slice of bread. "Mmmmm," he purred through his first mouthful. "Swunnerful."

"Enough," Geraint clapped his hands together. "Michael and I are going to check out some corp systems for a few hours and then I'm off for lunch." He grimaced a little at the thought of any more food. "You're going—"

"—to visit the Baptistery. Where are my guide books?" Serrin made a dive for his bag.

"What do you need to know?" Michael asked. "I did some preparation, and Geraint's been here before."

"The Baptistery. I know it has some of the finest art in the city, but what's the most important thing about it?"

"Depends on what you mean," Geraint said. "The most obvious thing is that John the Baptist is the patron saint of Florence."

Serrin stopped searching through his bag for a moment. "Uh-huh," he said thoughtfully.

"Why did you ask?"

"No special reason," Serrin lied. He was still mulling over that interesting fact and remembering something he wanted to check out. There was a painting, wasn't there?

Geraint let it pass. The mage seemed even more absentminded than ever this morning. He wondered if the months in the lonely wilds of the Hebrides had accentuated the trait. He wiped the corner of his mouth with a linen napkin, then he and Michael made for their decks awaiting them upstairs.

Serrin quietly asked one of the maids who came to clear away the table where he could find a particular kind of store, and learned to his satisfaction that one was only a few minutes' walk away. He squinted a little in the now-brilliant sunlight as he stepped into the street, and followed the simple directions to his destination.

A little later, he walked slowly back, looking at the picture.

Ah, now, isn't that *wrong*? he thought.
And doesn't it have an extraordinary beauty?

20

"It's a girl, I think," Streak said doubtfully.

"No, it isn't. Look at the nose," Kristen said. "It's a young man, not much more than a boy."

Serrin moved the sheet of paper away from the body of the image. He'd occluded most of it, leaving only the enigmatic face for the others to see.

"Oh, it is a bloke," Streak said. "Them shoulders give it away. Funny. I could have sworn it was a woman's face, honest."

"But . . ." Kristen said, hesitantly.

"Yes?" Serrin waited.

"It looks just like the other woman. The smile. It's her smile."

"What other woman?"

"The picture you showed me before. The *Mona Lisa*."

"My God, it is an' all," Streak said, screwing up his eyes. "I tell you, mate, that's a really weird painting."

"Isn't it?" Serrin said softly.

"So what is it then? Who's our geezer?" Streak said.

"Our geezer, as you so charmlessly put it, is John the Baptist. As painted by Leonardo da Vinci."

"And why's he pointing his finger up like that? I mean, it's not as if he knows cricket umpire signals." Serrin and Kristen gave him the same look. "Sorry. So what does it mean?"

"I don't know," Serrin admitted. "But this is, well, strange. I don't know why. But something tells me it's important. We're in his city—the Baptist's, that is. We're chasing some freak with a Leonardo fixation. His only statue is here too, so I think we should go take a look at it. Coming?"

"Mikey and his nibs are still up to their arses in electrons," Streak said, picturesquely if inaccurately. "I think a stroll into town is on."

* * *

They approached from the east gates and stood before the remarkable work, the ten beautifully etched plates of biblical scenes that hung there. Above them a stone angel stood watching John baptizing Christ. Porphyry columns flanked them as they walked through the doors and made their offering of coins and notes at the small box placed just inside.

In the cool interior, Serrin consulted the little guidebook, searching for an illustration of the angel and directions to where it might be found.

"You are looking for something in particular?" a young, fair-haired Italian youth asked in perfect, barely accented English.

Serrin turned to look at the fresh-faced young man. He was handsome, slightly feminine in appearance, with high cheekbones and full lips. He smiled at the elf and looked expectant.

"Verocchio's angel, actually," Serrin told him.

"I think that if you head for the north gates and walk out there, and mingle with the crowds, then you should be able to make it very difficult for the three gentlemen in the piazza to shoot you as they intend," the youth said equably. "Get into a taxi and tell the driver to drive like crazy, I should think."

Serrin's jaw dropped.

"Jesuits are very resourceful. I will be seeing you later, I expect," the young man said with a pleasant smile. The trio were too stunned to grab him as he walked out the east doors and disappeared with startling rapidity into a knot of tourists enjoying the early-morning sunshine.

"I think we'd better do what he said," Serrin said, glancing around as calmly as he could manage under the circumstances. Kristen's nails were digging deep into his arm.

"I couldn't risk bringing any heat in here," Streak said, "though I've got a little something in my pockets." He patted his jacket and there was a dull plastic clunk.

"I'll never be able to cast a spell in here," Serrin fretted.

"On the way out?"

"We'll be sitting ducks in the doorway," Serrin said.

"How about claiming sanctuary?" Streak's eyes darted this way and that, taking in the scene outside. He couldn't pick out any potential attackers amid the milling crowds, but finally he caught the man in the suit eating ice cream.

"Ah, got one, I reckon," he said. "But who the frag was—"

"I have no idea," Serrin said with a wave of his hand.

"I don't feel well," Kristen said.

"This is no time to—" Streak began.

"I said, *I don't feel well*," Kristen insisted, tapping a foot irritably on the floor. "Do I have to wink too?"

"Go on, girl. It's now or never," Serrin said.

Kristen suddenly dropped onto the floor in a very convincing faint. Serrin fell to his knees beside her and Streak finally got the game. He jabbered in passable Italian to a young cleric who'd hurried over to see what was wrong, asking the man to call for an ambulance. It probably wasn't serious, but it wasn't the first time and. . .

The priest hurried away but was soon back, reassuring Streak that an ambulance was on the way and asking if there was anything else he could do. Streak reassured him, and gave him a small sum, asking him to offer a prayer for the afflicted. The young man bobbed his head and went off to light a candle, still keeping a wary eye on the apparently stricken woman. A small knot of people was beginning to gather around them. Streak noted the dark-haired man in the plain gray suit who hovered at the doorway. He guessed that there must be some kind of detection and alarm system at the doorway, and the man did not dare cross the threshold.

The man looked around him, then suddenly reached into his pocket.

Streak reached into his own.

In a split second, a Predator would have been fired into the Baptistery and a molded plastic throwing knife would have cut deep into the gunman's face.

It didn't happen.

What Streak saw, and afterward he wasn't at all clear just how he did see it, was the youth who'd warned them standing well behind, and slightly to the left, of the man in the suit. The youth had a broad grin, and was reaching inside his own powder-blue jacket. He drew a weapon from inside it with astonishing speed.

It was impossible. Not the speed of it, though that was swifter than Streak had seen even a move-by-wire cyberzombie move. It was the weapon itself that was impossible. It was utterly bizarre, an anachronism. What's more, it could never have been concealed inside the jacket and, even if it could, there was no way it could have been drawn, aimed, and fired with such precision.

The weapon looked like a huge laminated crossbow, but instead of the usual bridge for bearing the bolt there were perhaps a dozen smooth, very slender metal barrels spread out in an arc of maybe thirty degrees. Faster than was possible, the screw mechanism at the base of the barrels sank down into the weapon and a swirl of bubbles flew from the barrels.

Streak gazed at them like a helpless, paralyzed viewer watching a slo-mo film. The bubbles meandered lazily toward the man in the suit, who was frozen in mid-gesture, the emerging gleam of imminent metal just visible inside his barely open jacket.

The bubbles swirled around the man's head and back. His eyes rolled back in his head and he fell to the ground like a sack of vegetables dumped on a larder floor. The young man replaced the weapon inside his jacket and raised his left index finger to his lips. He blew on it, smiled at Streak, and then he wasn't there anymore. Streak felt a roaring sensation in his ears and everything seemed to return to normal.

The sound of an approaching siren came from somewhere along the piazza as Streak struggled to stay on his feet. He couldn't think straight. As yet, no one had noticed the man who'd collapsed behind the group of people around Kristen.

Streak kicked himself into action. It occurred to him that the man might get bundled into the same ambulance as Kristen, which wouldn't do at all. He shouldered his way through the crowd and knelt down beside the fallen man. As he bent over the body, he pulled a leathered flask from his jacket, thanking providence that he never traveled without some form of alcohol on his person.

The other men in suits were closing in, and people were turning to look now. Streak flicked off the cap and poured the whiskey over the man.

"Get rid of this drunk," he said loudly and with a fair semblance of disgust. "At this time of day and at the door of a house of God. What a disgrace!"

Tutting rose among the crowd. The two advancing figures halted, unsure of what to do. A moment before they'd been ready to blow the elf away, and their hesitation was fatal. The paramedics were within a dozen paces now. One of the men gave the other a look, then both turned tail and headed quietly away. Streak exhaled with relief. His Italian suffered a little as he thanked the paramedics just a bit too profusely.

The elves piled into the back of the ambulance and began to ask whether there was a paramedics' retirement fund to which they could make a serious contribution.

Michael's face was drained of blood by the time the three of them returned from the hospital, where the doctors were stunned by Kristen's miraculously swift recovery. A little implausible nonsense about witch-doctors and curses had soon persuaded them they were probably dealing with nothing more serious than a case of hysterical fainting. Kristen hadn't found Serrin's impromptu story terribly amusing, but all that was forgotten as Streak managed to gabble out what he'd seen.

They were excited as they rushed upstairs back at the villa, but the sight of their two white-faced and obviously exhausted companions immediately told them something was wrong.

"We didn't exactly blow it, but it was pretty bloody close," Geraint told them. A cigarette hung from his fingers, the smoke spiraling upward. "Mitsuhama wasn't a problem, they don't have much. But Fuchi—Fuchi's got something, and they're not letting anyone get close. Not even Michael could cope with the ice, and that means it's thicker than the walls of the Tower of London. I've never seen anything like it."

"Metasculpture," Michael muttered. "Sculpted system with covert implant viruses. Very neat, a constant assault and nonresponsive to anything I've currently got. It's going to cost me a lot of money to buy cover against that drek."

"We're only three days away from meltdown," Serrin observed. No one seemed to care.

"So tell us, how was your day?" Geraint asked eventually, stubbing out the cigarette. Gray circles were beginning to form under his eyes after days of strain, irregular sleeping habits, and constant adrenaline rushes.

"The NOJ were out as a welcoming committee," Streak told him.

"Fragging great," Geraint moaned. "How'd they get on to us so quickly?"

"Maybe they didn't," Serrin suggested. "They may have followed leads of their own and simply arrived in the same place. Interesting that they had goons around the Baptistery, though.

"Michael, could you crack their system?"

"Who knows? I have no idea where it is. It'll be a PLTG for starters."

"Pardon me?"

"A private local system. Just finding the bugger will be hard enough. I've got to admit I don't exactly feel up to it right now. That's the first time I've ever seen ice sculpted as a tank when it wasn't just a macho gesture. It wasn't kidding."

"We've got to get into something, somewhere, that belongs to someone who knows more than we do," Serrin said.

"I'd just like to talk to Blondie," Streak said pointedly. "That vanishing act was something else, real smooth."

Michael blinked wearily. "What are you talking about?"

Serrin looked at Streak, who proceeded to fill them in.

"It was that rakking gun," he said in conclusion. "The weirdest bloody thing I've ever seen. Straight up. It didn't fire bullets and it had about a dozen barrels, like I said. I mean, that's impossible. I've only seen things like that in museums, and then the barrels were all together, not spread out in an arc. There's a few in the Royal Armories, right?"

Geraint nodded. Among the exhibits at the Royal Armories at the Tower of London were some of the first German multi-barrel pistols and rifles, ungainly and unwieldy things. They hadn't been a notable landmark in the history of gun design.

Serrin's eyes gleamed and he suddenly left the room, apparently with some strong purpose. He was only gone a moment, returning with a book open at an early page.

"Did the weapon look anything like this?" he asked

Streak, pushing the book out in front of his face. The other elf pushed it back so that he could focus his eyes properly on the illustration. His cybereyes could have compensated, but the reflex was ingrained.

"Shee-it! That's it," he said wonderingly. "Well, I mean, it's as close as makes no difference. I didn't have very long to see it, don't forget. But, yeah, it did look just like that. Bugger me. What the frag is it?"

"Leonardo da Vinci's design for the *scoppietti*," Serrin told him. "I guess someone's really starting to play serious games with us now. It's begun."

"What's begun?" Geraint asked.

Serrin gave him the beatific smile of someone who thinks he's noticed something of major importance that has passed everyone else by.

"A game is being played out here," Serrin said, drawing up a chair and swinging his good leg over to sit on it straddled, his elbows draped over the chair-back. "Our target has a real fixation with Leonardo, right? The Shroud icon. The date of the Matrix meltdown. This weapon, whatever it actually was. And more as well."

"We knew that already," Michael reminded him.

"Okay, right. Now, Leonardo was the Grand Master of the Priory of Sion, and the current Priory has an interest in our quarry. Leonardo faked the Shroud of Turin at the behest of Pope Innocent—I forget which one."

"The eighth," Michael completed.

"Right. Thanks. And the hardline Jesuits out there serve the Vatican and they're certainly stirred up about what's happening. And there's an extra layer of depth to this. Leonardo may or may not have been gay, but the androgyne recurs again and again in his work. *Mona Lisa* is Leonardo as a woman, okay? His painting of John the Baptist is extraordinarily feminine—our man Streak here actually took the face for a girl's. There's more too. Verocchio's *Baptism of Christ* has an angel painted by Leonardo, and it's another androgyne—the figure is male but has a very, very feminine face. I looked at that after we'd seen the statue downstairs."

"Blondie was an interesting looker," Streak said.

"Wasn't he? Put him in a cocktail dress and a wig and

he'd make an excellent *petite jeune fille*," Serrin said wryly.

"Are we even sure he *was* a bloke?" Streak suddenly asked.

"Yes, he was," Kristen put in firmly. "His voice was too deep for a woman's. Just. And his posture was a man's. That can't be faked."

"You haven't been to San Fran," Serrin told her. "Yes, it can."

"We have cross-dressers in Cape Town too, dear," she countered icily.

"Whatever. Anyway, look at the Matrix icon. It's the Shroud, with the face of a woman. It's Leonardo's androgyne all over again, in a more shocking form."

"So?" Michael demanded.

"So I think that's at the root of it," Serrin said. "It recurs too often. And there's something about this we haven't worked out yet: why is the woman in the icon black?"

"Tell us," Michael said.

"I don't know," Serrin replied. "I've tried some digging but there's so much bulldrek about this kind of thing that without expert advice I couldn't begin to sort out the wheat from the chaff. I mean, we've both been through the 'How do you know God isn't a woman' drek and that kind of thing enough times."

Kristen looked pointedly at him.

"Sorry, lover. It's just that the people who make that argument are ninety-nine point nine per cent screaming flakes," Serrin said impatiently. "You spend a couple of days reading nothing but and you'll agree, trust me.

"There has to be something more than our decker merely adopting Leonardo's persona and having a Leonardo fixation. Otherwise, the Priory and the NOJ wouldn't be involved."

"I'll buy that," Michael said.

Serrin shrugged. "We can't know that. But I wonder. The official line on the Priory is that they serve to protect the bloodline of Christ, right? The old myth that Christ wasn't crucified but came to Europe, maybe with Joseph of Arimathea, had children and some still survive? The Gnostic gospels have stuff on this and there are almost as many files suggesting conspiracies along those lines hog-

ging the Matrix as there are on Trekker drek. But even by
the standards of flake theories, it's weak. I'm not buying
into it as the Big Reason behind all of this. But they're
protecting something. I just wondered if—"

"If this is a descendant of Leonardo?" Michael said,
doubtfully.

"That possibility has occurred to me," Serrin admitted.
"But it doesn't feel right either. I still think there has to
be *some* link to the real Leonardo. This isn't just a flake
doing impersonations."

"Whoever pulled that stunt with the gun Blondie had
was no flake, that's for bloody sure!" Streak said. "I have
no idea what took that guy out, but trust me, I'd give up
all the dosh I've got stashed to be able to buy one. If
someone can invent something like that, we're not dealing with an idiot."

"Not to mention the minor matter of crashing the entire
fragging Matrix," Michael reminded them.

Serrin smiled weakly. "We almost forgot about that for
a moment, didn't we?"

"What we desperately need to do," he went on, "is
somehow get one step ahead. So far, we've been following leads and there always seems to be someone waiting
for us around the corner. We have to find some way, just
one thing, for moving ahead of the game. And this is a
game, albeit a game with seriously high stakes."

Serrin hesitated. The pause told Geraint there was
something he wasn't revealing.

"Come on, Serrin, what is it? It's Hessler, isn't it? He
told you something you don't want to tell us. I guess I understand why, but—"

"No, it isn't Hessler. It's Merlin," Serrin said, gently
and sadly. The change in his voice was obvious. They all
fell silent and looked at him.

"Merlin is a better 'human being' than most people
are, I think," he said. "Well, elf, human, what the frag.
He's a spirit of people, I think. I don't know much about
his history, he hasn't told me about it. But he genuinely
likes people and he's troubled. He knows who we're after,
and can't tell because he'd be destroyed once people figured it out that we got it from him."

"Then Hessler must know," Michael pointed out.

"Yes, I think he must," Serrin agreed. "He's obviously

a member of some powerful hermetic order. His command of metamagic is something else, I can tell you. He can snap his fingers and do things I'd need a week of preparation to even risk attempting. He's impressive. And he's especially impressive because he doesn't make a show out of it, and he doesn't do things in ways other than are absolutely necessary. I'll never be anywhere near that good." He shook his head, but not sadly. "He's simply in another league. Whatever that is. I think there's some kind of game afoot among them. And our target is part of that game."

"So what's the point of the game?"

"Our target wants the money," Serrin said. "I do know that. He genuinely wants the money, though I don't know what for."

"You could buy a fair-sized country with it," Geraint observed. "So he could want almost anything. With that much, you could do almost anything, let's face it."

"Look at it from the other side," Michael said. "What could you want to do that *needs* that much money?"

"Settle Mars?" Streak said, shrugging his shoulders. "Frag it, you're talking that kind of scale."

"What would you want to do if you were Leonardo?" Kristen asked. They turned and looked at her. "Sorry, was I being stupid?" she said meekly.

"On the contrary," Michael said. "Serrin, can I borrow your wife for a while? Would you mind, Kristen? You have more common sense than I do and I think I have a lot of data you ought to be looking through.

"If this is deeper than just a Leonardo-fixation, then we should test the idea out. What would Leonardo have done next? What did he leave as an unfulfilled ambition? At least if we work on this theory we could do something. Something that could be a signal to that someone, out there, who's playing this deadly game. And we might just get a response."

"You'll have to continue this discussion without me," Geraint told them. "I have to go and bathe and change. Luncheon awaits."

"We won't expect you back too soon," Michael said sweetly.

"Frag off," Geraint said tartly.

"Actually, Geraint," Michael said as seriously as he

could muster, "if the drek hits the fan and you go broke, the Countess has a lot of property holdings. She's a very rich window indeed. And a marriage to a de Medici too. It would be so utterly, utterly romantic." He gave a horribly twee grin and then his face broke into a playful smirk.

"Welsh-Italian children. Imagine the tantrums they could throw!"

Geraint decided, on balance, not to throw the marble ashtray at him, but it was close for a time. He stalked out of the room.

"Kristen, my dear, you just made more sense in one line than we've managed in several days," Michael said with relish. "Now let's see what we can do on the basis of it."

"There's just one final thing," Serrin said hesitantly. "About the bloodline angle. And the androgyne."

"Mmmm?"

"I wondered, just wondered, if it might not be a woman, you know. Putting her face on Shroudman. Doing what her great-great-as-many-greats-as-you-can-count-great-grandfather did when he painted *Mona Lisa*. Wouldn't it fit?"

Most chains of reasoning break down somewhere. Serrin's just had. But as Geraint toweled himself dry after his shower and mentally checked the list of purchases he wanted to make on the way, and as the others discussed their options, it was a woman, somewhere, who looked down on all this and smiled.

But she was smiling upon someone else, and he was in another city.

21

She'd changed little. There were a few, just a very few white and gray hairs scattered among the thatch of black, but her blue eyes were as liquid bright and ocean deep as ever they had been. Geraint hadn't thought that eyes so dark blue could be found outside of Tír na nÓg, but he'd been mistaken. And he'd looked into them long enough to be sure, those many years ago.

"It's been a long time, Geraint," Cecilia said in her soft voice.

"I needed the time," he said simply.

Geraint took her hand and led her down the marbled corridor, into the conservatory garden. He knew every inch of the house, and it hadn't changed much in all this time. Some of the trees had grown more than he might have expected; the freak olive, with its cinnamon-edged leaves, had flourished and stood double his height now. He sat down with her at the bronze-topped iron table and presented her with his gift.

She opened the packaging, pushing back the layers of silky, pearl-colored tissue paper, and took out the dress. It was the simple, classic, small black dress that has always flattered the woman slim and small enough to wear it well. She was about to compliment him on it when her hand found the jewel box underneath it. Her eyes darted a glance at him, then dipped again as she flipped it open and took out the pearls inside. She smiled at him.

"These are truly beautiful," Cecilia said quietly. "You flatter me."

"Impossible," he said, returning her smile. He was indescribably relieved to find that he could gaze steadily at her and not feel as if his heart was about to burst. "Flattery is an untruth. They suit you. Nothing less would have done."

She put her elbows on the table and cupped her face in her hands. If her eyes had not quite cut him to the quick, the small, upturned nose, at least, gave him a pang that reached back through the years for his heart.

"You always were the perfect gentleman," she said, the same quiet smile playing about her face. "Ah, it is good to see you. You look well. But a little tired. What have you been up to?"

"Ah, well, Contessa, that is a long story." He grinned, lighting a cigarette for her.

"And like so many of your long stories, not one I'm going to be told," she chided him. "You British are always so."

He looked away with a rueful expression. "I'm not so sure of that, but in this case it's purely business."

"You are not married," she observed.

"You neither," he replied, wanting to get the ball out of his court swiftly.

"I said you were the perfect gentleman," she told him. "Men here, they want sex, or money, or a name, for reputation and wealth. And if they love me, it is swiftly over. I am no longer of such an age that I can summon that emotion so easily in a man's heart, nor keep it fixed there."

"I doubt that," he replied with feeling. Cecilia de Medici had not changed so very much after all. But he stiffened just a little as she poured a second glass of wine for herself, not more than a few minutes after the first, which had been waiting for her when she arrived. He had only sipped his. That had been the reason why he could not, after her husband Bernardo died in one of Italy's staggering tally of road accidents, come back to her. It was her fatal weakness, and if her face and body did not show the ravages as yet, it would not be so very long before they did. Not that that had worried him; it had been the effect on her emotions, the terrible black depression that settled on her when she was drunk, then remained with her for days stretching into weeks, further fueled by the endless drinking.

When she was like that, and she had been so very often, she drained emotion and life from all around her. Geraint hadn't wanted to end up floating down the river, as others had before him. Lovers died because of this woman. She'd told him once, when he'd found the bruises on her and was ready to rip Bernardo apart with his bare hands, that sometimes she deserved them. Geraint had been young then, and uncomprehending, but over the coming months had grown older and wiser very swiftly.

But it is bright here, he thought now, looking around at the sun-filled conservatory; and unless I am much mistaken that is Maria, her maid still, and by God she was an oasis of sanity in this household. And there are still the glorious paintings, and the sculptures, and the hoard of Medici papers the family discovered recently in some long-abandoned country house, so I am bound to be shown those . . . I can get through this. There should be enough to keep all the bad memories at bay. The trick will be not to remember the good ones.

"What did he leave unfinished?" Michael said. Serrin was flicking through books, print-outs, and piles of paper, and the Englishman was calling up archival and library material from everywhere he could think to look.

"There isn't really any single thing. There's nothing specific when he died," Serrin said. "But I came across something interesting here, from a biography. Listen to this.

" 'He had progressively purified the syntax of his work throughout his career, finally reaching one supreme emotion that contains all others—and since some element of his sexuality crept into it, reason cannot always resist the overwhelming impression it conveys. *John the Baptist* leads to every temptation. I like to think that this was Leonardo's last work—in some sense his final will and testament. His subject has ceased to be "a voice crying in the wilderness." He has reached the ultimate limits of human knowledge; he smiles and points at the source of everything, which amazes him but which is unfathomable'."

"And he has the Mona Lisa smile. The smile of the Shroudman Matrix icon."

"There's something else too. The writer says that *John the Baptist* was painted at the same time that Leonardo was drawing terrifying images of an apocalypse. There are some entries from Leonardo's diaries here about this.

"Ah yes: 'The submerged fields will display waters carrying tables, beds, boats, and other improvised craft, out of both necessity and fear of death; on them, men, women, and children, huddled together, will be crying and lamenting, terrified by the furious tornado that whips up the waves and with them the corpses of the drowned . . . The waves strike against them and repeatedly buffet them with the bodies of the drowned, and these impacts destroy those in whom a breath of life still pulses . . . Oh, how many people you will see stopping their ears with their hands, so as not to hear the mighty noise with which the violence of the winds, mingled with the rain and the thunder, and the cracking of the thunderbolts fills the darkened air! Others, losing their reason, commit suicide, despairing of being able to bear such torture; some hurl themselves from the top of ridges, other strangle themselves with their own hands, others again seize their children and kill them with a blow. Oh, how many mothers brandish their fists against the heavens and weep for the drowned sons they hold on their knees, howling curses on the wrath of the gods.'

"By the spirits, I had no idea he ever wrote anything like that." Serrin closed the book; he looked genuinely distressed by what he'd read.

"But it makes sense," Michael said. "It's the Biblical apocalypse, isn't it? And at the same time he paints John, the author of Revelation? For reassurance about deliverance? The Baptist may be a strange figure, but he looks incredibly serene to me."

"Does it occur to you that if this kind of apocalypse was in Leonardo's mind at the end of his life, that our quarry may be filled with something of the same horror and madness? And what could you do with twenty billion nuyen?" Serrin said, shaking a little.

"Oh, hell," Michael breathed, turning a little pale himself. "You don't think, surely—"

"I don't know. We could be following the wrong route entirely. We just don't know. And what did his biographer mean by saying that *John the Baptist* leads to every temptation?"

"Look, guys, I've had enough of this bollocks," Streak said suddenly, getting to his feet. "You two are talking out of your arses. How about finding me someone to shoot? That, I can do."

Michael had just opened his mouth to hurl some reply when there was a soft knock at the door. It was a maid, small and dark, holding a silver tray with a small card on it. When bade enter, she looked about her.

"You are English Michael?" she said, looking at the man.

"I am, thank you. That is for me?" he replied, puzzled.

"Thanyou," she said sweetly, putting the tray down on the table before him and sashaying out of the room.

"Who knows we're here?" Michael questioned.

"Don't touch it," Streak growled. "It could have contact poison."

"The maid isn't dead," Serrin said sarcastically.

Streak pulled a pair of tweezers from one of his many pockets and held up the card for Michael to read.

"A small token of esteem will arrive for you at five o'clock this afternoon," Michael recited. "Beautiful handwriting."

"That's it?" Serrin enquired.

"That's it."

"From whom?"

"I haven't the foggiest."

"Get that bloody maid back in here!" Streak snarled. He took a couple of paces to the doorway.

"Let me," Michael stopped him in a weary tone of voice. "I think I can handle this a little more diplomatically."

He left for the domestics quarters and returned within a couple of minutes, looking distinctly puzzled.

"She doesn't remember."

"Oh, great, someone called no more than five minutes ago and she can't remember what he looked like?"

"No. She doesn't remember *anyone* calling. She doesn't remember giving me the card. She says she's been stocking the linen cupboards."

"Did you get the right maid?"

"Give me a break," Michael complained. "I can tell the difference between a maid in her twenties, five foot one or so, slim and dark, and one who looks like a retired member of the Bulgarian Olympic shot-putting squad."

"Can you deal with it?" Streak asked Serrin. He drew the obvious implication that the maid must have had some memory-affecting suggestion implanted magically in her mind.

"Possibly, but why? He's going to be back at five o'clock, right?"

"I suppose so," Streak said, fidgeting. "I'll be waiting for the bugger when he gets here."

"We might actually want to talk to him," Serrin pointed out.

"I had tasers in mind," Streak said defensively.

"I think we might opt for something a little less aggressive," Serrin replied sharply. "Whatever, we'll wait for Geraint. He should be back soon, and we've got three hours before the little token turns up."

"Can we go sightseeing?" Kristen asked plaintively. "I'd really like to get out of here and look around."

Serrin was on the point of refusing, when he stopped to

think about it. "I don't see why not if we stick to a car," he said. "After this morning it would be best not to go about on foot. If they were prepared to take a crack at us outside a church, they'd take a crack anywhere."

"Okay." She was a little disappointed, and not able to hide it very well.

"Look, when this is all over we'll come back and see the place properly. And it'll all be over one way or another very soon," Serrin said soothingly.

"Yeah, and whether the Jesuits still want to kill you may still be up for grabs," Streak pointed out. "Sorry to be a party-pooper, but—"

"I think Geraint just got back," Michael said, looking out the window. "Keep any wisecracks down. I was winding him up before, but I think this won't have been much fun for him." He decided, on impulse, not to trust Streak's discretion in particular, so he got up and raced downstairs to the hallway.

It didn't look good.

"You okay?"

"Don't ask. It's no use. Nothing has changed. If anything, she drinks even more than before." Geraint's voice was filled with sadness, weariness, but above all resignation. "I want to be out of here tonight. I'll fix something with the consulate. Get packed."

"Someone is delivering something for us at five o'clock. I guess," Michael extrapolated wildly, "that it may be some kind of message from our target. From the blond man, probably."

"All right," Geraint said, too drained of emotional energy to argue. "Get packed so we can be out of here right afterward. I have some calls to make. See you later."

He didn't even ask about their continuing researches, just made his way to his room and locked the door behind him.

That's the difference between us, Michael thought after his friend had disappeared from view. We can both do the British gentleman act to a tee. Everyone looks for the deeper stuff behind that facade. I'm the lucky one. I don't have any depth. I *am* facade. It's a lot less stressful like that.

I don't end up locking myself in my room.

With a shrug, he turned and followed his friend up the stairs.

* * *

Across the city, three men stood ashamed before a seated figure, their heads held rigid but their eyes downcast. Their interrogator wore clothes akin to those of a Vatican cardinal, but simpler and more austere. Eyes the gray of granite stared out at them over the bridge of his hooked nose.

"So you failed," was all he said, speaking in harsh Spanish.

The men stayed silent.

"And now they may be one step nearer. Fortunately, we are ahead of them. We know where the heretic is now. And against my better judgment, I shall grant you a second chance. Not that I will trust you alone, needless to say. Nadal will command the unit."

The men did not look at each other, did not move at all, but their hearts sank. Juan Nadal was as fanatical as any commander they could have hoped to avoid. Formally titled an Assistant, nothing could have been further from the truth. Nadal was as powerful as the General himself and when he spoke at the Gesu, everyone listened. Those who had worked with Nadal in the New Inquisition didn't speak of it. His name itself was only whispered, and then in fear.

"I hardly need add that if you fail this time, you will have an eternity to pray that you might receive the blessed mercy of purgatory. Remember that the faithful who disappoint God are more damned than those who have never heeded his words. Do not fail Him again."

The men turned away and said nothing as they trooped quietly toward the unvarnished wooden door. The one to the left of the group twitched just slightly, a muscle in his left hand overtensed and dysfunctional. He balled his hand into a fist and said nothing.

22

Michael had shooed the others out of the room and was busy skipping through the electronic static. He knew the

LTG number of the Priory system at Rennes-le-Château, and now that he'd recovered he was finally doing what he should have done much earlier.

Somewhere there has to be a directory, he thought; somewhere, I can find who was connected to that system, who entered it, the records will be *somewhere*. Oh, I just *love* these blind hunts, and I don't expect the icons will be the obvious ones.

It took him a frustratingly long time to hunt down the numbers. When he did, what he found annoyed and frustrated him further. Nothing remained in either of the first two systems he cracked but a single icon in the stripped databanks: an icon of a plain stone throne. When he found it a third time, he jacked out and scratched his scalp in irritation.

To his surprise, the clock opposite him read four forty-eight. He went to join the others, but Geraint was not among them.

"I'd better get him," he said. "Leave this to me."

Slightly apprehensive, he hurried to Geraint's room and knocked gently.

"Yes, come in." The voice was still tired and weary.

Almost reluctantly, Michael opened the door. Geraint was sweeping away four cards from the table before him, back into the silk wrap in which he kept them. Michael knew enough of the designs to know what they were.

The Empress, The High Priestess, Queen of Cups, and lastly Art, the angel usually named Temperance. Not difficult to see what's on his mind, he thought. As Michael sometimes did with anything outside his own expertise, he made the mistake of taking the surface appearance for the underlying one. The explanation was too facile, but he wasn't going to ask about it in any event.

"It's nearly five. We're expecting a visitor, remember?"

"Yes, thanks." Geraint didn't look at him. He was lost in thought.

I may have to do my world-famous impression of an alarm clock with a snooze function in five minutes, Michael thought glumly. He retraced his steps.

Streak was polishing a gun barrel. Michael would have been disappointed if he'd been doing anything else. The elf hadn't been hired for his analytical intellect, after all.

"I'll take the front, you take the back," he grinned. "Serrin can sit up here and do the ju-ju all over the shop. We'll net the plonker, bet your life on it."

"Elegantly put," Michael said wryly. "I think I'll have to do some explaining to the servants, though. Excuse me one moment."

As the clock ticked on to one minute before the hour, they grew tense. Serrin was getting no signal from any of his watcher spirits, and Streak was almost twitching with apprehension. At last, a carriage meandered down the street. Remarkably, it didn't appear to have a driver.

"Here he comes," Streak said through clenched teeth to Geraint beside him. "Right, term, let's see more than your visiting card."

The carriage stopped precisely before the front door and Streak slipped into the doorway, taser readied, hawkish eyes scanning the scene.

The young man opened the carriage door. Streak didn't move.

He wore an ostentatious costume, a floppy dark blue cap, a silk doublet with gold threading, and powder-blue hose. His shoes were exquisitely soft leather, with gilded buckles. Whether he was smiling as he had been at the Baptistery was impossible to see: the gilded mask covering his face didn't permit his expression to show.

He stepped up to Streak without any undue hurry, and handed him the medium-sized wooden box he was carrying. The elf took it dumbly, and the man turned around and got back into his carriage. Leaving a motionless pair of men behind, the carriage moved at a sedate pace down the street and disappeared into the crowd at the crossroads beyond.

Streak snapped back into wakefulness and almost dropped the box. Very gingerly, he put it down in the doorway and reached for his scanners.

"What the—"

"I couldn't stop him," came Serrin's voice from behind him. "Couldn't touch him. He had enough power around him to bust right through the barriers. The watchers never even twitched. No trace either. I tried to have a watcher follow him and it looked more confused than I've ever seen. It's out there wandering around somewhere, but I don't think it's going to find anything."

"He pulled this same stunt at the Baptistery," Streak growled. "I'd like to meet Blondie again when he isn't expecting it, the little scumfrag."

"What's in there?" Serrin pointed to the box.

"Nonferrous metal," Streak said.

"Open it," Geraint ordered.

"I haven't finished—"

"If he wanted to do us any harm he could have cut our throats in the doorway," Geraint pointed out. "He's hardly going to bother with a bloody bomb, is he?"

"He also stopped us getting scragged this morning," Serrin added.

"Okay, you got it," Streak said, whipping out a heavy knife and prying open the wooden lid of the box.

"Oh, very slick," he said as he lifted out the item inside.

It was a clock, of sorts. A hand's length high, the gold filigree-decorated clock sat inside a glass case. A pair of exquisitely sculpted angels were bracketed to either side of the clockface and housing. Beneath the clock at the base of the case was a pool of liquid, and an intricate motor-driven mechanism rotated, lifting tiny buckets of the water to drive the clockwork mechanisms inside the housing.

"Exquisite," Geraint said softly. "It's worth a few nuyen, I can tell you. I don't think I've ever seen anything like it."

"I think I have," Serrin replied, amused.

"Really? Since when did you start taking an interest in antiques?"

"Since, oh, a few days ago. Unless I'm much mistaken, this is a superior working version of Leonardo's design for a water-driven clock. Let's go and check it against the sketches in the book I got this morning."

It took only a couple of minutes to confirm the identification. The clock continued to function perfectly and soundlessly, keeping immaculate time.

"Bet you a monkey the sodding thing goes bang at six o'clock or something," Streak said, grumbling.

"We've been through that," Geraint said laconically. "So why this? And why now?"

"Now, because we're here. As to why this," Serrin mused, "I really don't know."

"Well, we can worry about it at the villa I've found for us tonight," Geraint said. "I had some words with the consulate. You packed?"

"More or less. Michael still has to get his deck squared away. Did he tell you what he got?"

They walked slowly back up the stairs, Michael explaining to Geraint that the Priory of Sion's systems beyond Rennes had been stripped bare and closed down, leaving only the throne icon behind them.

"Some kind of message or signal," Serrin suggested. "But it's so general, it could mean anything. It must mean something specific to the Priory, but without someone to explain it to us we can't know what it means."

Idly, he turned on the trid. They had a few minutes to kill while Michael gathered together his equipment. The tail end of the local news was showing. Thick red and white smoke swept over the heads of a roiling crowd waving banners and gesticulating wildly.

"The Milan soccer derby," Serrin estimated. "Usually only two or three get killed each year."

"These Eyeties don't know squit," Streak growled. "Take 'em down to the Dogs, down Milwall. We know how to have a decent soccer riot down there. And look at that crowd, has to be a hundred thousand. Too many by far."

"The San Siro," Serrin told him. "Magnificent, isn't it?"

"Not bad," Streak said. "Oh! Ouch, look at that tackle. I'll give them that: their footballers really know how to break legs," and then he had no more time to expand upon the subject as the tridcast cut to an entirely different scene. After a few moments of trying to figure out what was being discussed, they dissolved into laughter.

"Oh, lovely icon that."

"The evaporating turd? Yeah, good one. What the frag is this?"

Florentine local trid was using some graphic icons to illustrate the tail-end news item. Since it concerned a rival city-state, it wasn't going to get better than last-spot status, but it was important enough that it couldn't, regrettably from the Florentine point of view, be ignored entirely.

Waterways were shown with icons of various toxic effluent, from the graphic pile of excrement to clouds of steaming vapor with skull-and-crossbones motifs, evaporating from them. The scene panned back to show the canals. Serrin sat bolt upright in his chair.

"What are they saying?"

"Can't make much out, he's jabbering too fast," Streak said.

"Call up the bloody subtitles," Serrin demanded.

"Don't know how, not on this," Streak complained.

"Give me the gist, then."

"It's about de-polluting the canals in Venice." Streak paused, listening hard to the next chunk of excitable commentary.

"Big change. Lots of drek disappearing. You can fall in and not be dead inside the hour now, apparently. Tourists come to Venice, that sort of spiel. This local commentator's getting right sarky about that."

The scene cut again to the advertisements. Apparently soap powder moved scantily clad young Italian females to implausible states of hopeless excitement.

"Venice! The bastard's in Venice," Serrin yelled.

"How can you—"

"The book. The book! Slot! Why didn't we see it? The book we found."

"See what?" Geraint demanded to know.

"The book was a signal to the Priory guy—Serrault, Seratini, whatever—as to where our quarry is!"

"What do you mean?"

"A treatise on water elementals, right?"

"And so?"

"We just got a water-driven carriage clock as a message. We had a clue about water elementals. Leonardo lived in Venice for some time, and he certainly spent enough time designing canal systems. Including the years just before he died. And what was that apocalyptic stuff I found earlier?"

"The Flood," Geraint mused. "It sounded like the myth of the Flood to me. All it needed was a bloke with a big ship and the old animals two by two."

"Merlin also told me he might have moved on," Serrin added. "I think we should try Venice. Look, it's barely an hour away and if we're wrong we can get back here damn quick. Not that we have any definite idea of what to do here next anyway."

"Can we find out how long this has been going on in Venice?" Geraint said. "The book was sent a week ago or thereabouts. If you're right, the Priory knew our man was in Venice then. If this detox work started at least that far back, that would be worth knowing."

"We must be able to check. What about the consulate?"

"Nice idea," Geraint grinned. "I think I may just have had a call from His Majesty's Department of the Environment that I must relay to the consulate officials with all due speed. Consider it done." He walked off briskly to his bedroom to make the call.

Michael returned with everything packed and they filled him in on the details.

"I'm not sure about this," he said. "The chain of logic isn't too compelling."

"It isn't compelling, but it's plausible," Serrin said, "and since Venice is so close we've got nothing to lose by a short detour. At least we can start checking something out there."

"Sounds good to me," Streak said, fondling an Ingram with his usual meaningful expression. "There's another reason why I like the idea of moving on."

"And what's that?" Michael asked.

"While you guys have been reinventing the Bible and up to your ears in clocks, I've been doing some peeking through windows. Our old muckers, the gentlemen in suits, are out there now, if you know where to look. The NOJ has, of course, tracked us here. Which I expected. Sometimes, Serrin mate, people *do* expect the Inquisition."

"Very droll."

"However," Streak said with a slight grimace, "unless I am much mistaken, I also saw a certain Mr. Raoul Huetzlipochtli taking the air briefly on the street corner. Always did hate that moniker, the pretentious git. His real name is probably Poxface or something—it would suit him, you could land an Apollo mission on old crater-face. But it's something of a coincidence."

"And who, pray, is Raoul Hootzlipockle?" Michael made a brave, if rather unsuccessful, stab at pronunciation.

"Top-drawer Azzie killer. Ice-cold snuff merchant. Top twenty, maybe top ten. Not surprising that other corps have their eyes on our clock-fancier. Bit alarming that Aztechnology's leading psychopath is eyeing up our villa, though. Made me wonder a bit. Of course, I may have been mistaken."

"You think you might have been?" Geraint asked, more casually than he was feeling.

"Nope." Streak finished packing the gun. "Might not be a bad idea to import one or two of Streak's little helpers into Venice, Your Lordship."

"Like who?"

"Like two Spanish amigos who helped us before."

"Maybe that's not a bad idea," Geraint said. "God, this is all getting out of control."

"Of course it is. I would be worrying if it wasn't," Michael observed. He seemed remarkably calm. "With so little time left, Aztechnology, Fuchi, MCT, and the rest must all be needing terrifically frequent changes of underwear. It's not surprising that they've got people out there. And hardly earth-shattering that some of them have found their way somewhere close to the right place."

Disturbing the flow of speech, Michael's portafax began chattering a message. He checked the screen ID, grinned, and read the short communiqué.

"Ah, Renraku has re-routed this through Mozambique. Cheeky buggers, that's been one of my tricks of late. They've upped the stakes, lady and gentlemen. We're now talking five million on the nose for saving their butts."

"Shee-it, that's a million each," Streak whistled.

"Not quite," Michael replied, wagging a finger at him. "Two million for me, since it's primarily my gig, and you guttersnipes can slug it out for the rest."

"It's a convincing reason for not just escaping and getting the hell out of here. Not that I was planning to," Serrin said hastily.

"Indeed not. Time, I think," Michael said as he flung a bag over his shoulder and then grimaced a little at the resultant pain in his back, "to live on the edge a little. Hell, why the frag not? Did you know, there were people dumb enough to pass up on the dessert trolley on the *Titanic*. Never forget that, friends.

"Venice it is."

23

They left later than they would have liked. Everything seemed to take longer to pack than they thought, and errands kept demanding completion. Geraint had to phone to order a parting gift for their hostess. Michael felt the need to call Renraku and let them know that, yes, he was aware that time was short and yes, they were closing in on their target and no, he definitely couldn't say more than that and also, to be quite honest, shouldn't they already know all that anyway? Streak had to leave several telecom messages, increasingly urgent, before Juan's resonant ork voice finally called back. The evening was turning remorselessly into night by the time they piled into the limo for the airport.

The small plane descended from the blue-black, starry night into Marco Polo Airport. With the low angle of descent, they could see the magnificence of the city lit along its canals and squares, the small moving points of light being not just the cars common to most cities but also gondolas ferrying people along the Grand Canal and its myriad tributaries. They seemed almost to skim the very waves of the lagoon as they glided into the runway.

"This brings back memories," Michael said as the light went out and he could unbuckle his seatbelt.

Geraint's reply was only a slightly curt, "Yes."

"It does?" Streak said with a raised eyebrow. He could see Geraint's response was not one of comfort.

"We spent a week here as students," Michael said gleefully. "I studied the art in the basilica, the Doge's palace, the Rialto. Young Geraint took more of an interest in other aesthetic forms."

The nobleman coughed. "I don't think we have time for trivia like this," he said, slightly pompously.

"Oh, but surely we do," Streak shot back.

"I don't pay you to take satisfaction in my discomfort," Geraint pointed out. "Come on, let's find a cab."

"Not a gondola?" Serrin queried.

"They do have bridges," Michael said gently.

"Yes, I suppose so," Serrin mumbled.

The usual backhander was required to get them through the formalities of customs, even on a Sunday night. Though resplendent in the Doge's livery, the opulence of the officials couldn't have contrasted more sharply with their manner. Then the five of them had to squeeze into a small cab, which demonstrated its supreme lack of any suspension as it coughed and wheezed its way southwest.

"Frag me, my arse feels like I just got a housebrick suppository. I've had more comfortable rides on the back roads of Pakistan," Streak grumbled. Hearing him, the driver pointed out in colorful language that the elf was more than welcome to get out and go there right now, preferably in a hearse.

"Yes, yes, we're sorry," Michael said soothingly.

"No, we're bloody not," Streak yelled. "We don't have to be so sodding English all the rakking time and put up with such crap. Listen, matey, this is a genuine English lord in the back seat here and he deserves better. So button your lip or I'll put some lead in the back of your head. Prat!"

Stunned by this rejoinder, the driver said nothing and even appeared to drive a little more slowly so that the vehicle didn't rattle quite so badly. Michael glowered at the elf, who, in a moment of reckless abandon, simply stuck his tongue out at him and raised a single expressive digit.

The journey took mercifully less time than they'd feared. Entering the city itself, they drove over the tiny bridges of the Castello and west into San Marco, the heart of the city, and into the Piazza San Marco itself, drawing up opposite the forbidding height of the Campanile with the mighty basilica just behind them. They got out of the car and Michael muttered some words of apology to the driver and gave him a thoroughly undeserved tip, much to Streak's disgust.

First out of the vehicle, Kristen hardly knew whether to look at the basilica and the palace to her left, or the great tower before her. She turned from one to the other and back again, and then to her husband, a look of sheer wonder on her face.

"This is incredible," was all she could manage to say. Serrin stood behind her and put his arms around her and held her, sharing her delight as she took in the splendor of the buildings.

"You say anything sarcastic," Michael said to Streak, "and I'll kill you. Get the luggage inside."

"Yes, Your Lordshipness," Streak grinned, grabbing a couple of bags and making for the noisy cafe.

It hadn't changed much in the decade or so since Michael and Geraint had stayed in Quadri's. The clientele certainly seemed the same: students nursing one last coffee; a cabal of down-at-the-heel artists doping likewise; some ill-disguised tourists, obviously wealthy and thus ripe for plucking by the local predators; and some off-duty officials and soldiery from the Doge's palace, the latter confident in their uniforms, enjoying the looks of respect the foreigners gave them and behaving rather less badly perhaps than soldiers usually do in any civilized location. The place was noisy, but not rowdy, and Michael smiled as he approached the bar to pay and collect the keys to their reserved rooms.

"You won't remember me, Claudio, but I haven't forgotten how good it is here," he said to the owner. The owner's hair was more streaked with silver now, and his waist a little thicker, but a decade of middle age hadn't changed him overmuch. His dark brown eyes narrowed a little as he scrutinized his guest.

"No, no, I do. Michael! It is Michael. But I forget your second name," he said apologetically.

"Your wife, I think, took our booking. How is Lucrezia?"

"Michael Sutherland! I remember you! And that nobleman friend of yours—he was not English, I remember, but he was as English as any Englishman." Claudio grinned widely. "Is he with you? I remember *him*. One or two of the ladies remember him too."

"Yes, I'm sure they do, and yes, he is with us, and he's a Welshman," Michael said all in one go. "It's good to see you again."

"And my wife is well," Claudio said.

"And I hope she'll be happy to receive this," Michael said, handing over a small cloth-covered box. The man looked a trifle suspicious and opened the hinged lid. Inside was a small replica axe, long-handled and fashioned in pure silver, with a small booklet accompanying it. He certainly hadn't planned bringing it. He'd discovered it in one of the zip-fastened pockets of one of his travel bags, forgotten entirely when or why he'd bought it, but it seemed to fit the bill.

"It's a replica of the axe that beheaded two of the wives of our King Henry the Eighth," Michael told him conspiratorially. "Created by the silversmiths of the Tower of London. The original axe was used," he said slyly, nodding his head secretively and barely managing to keep from winking, "to deal with wives who were not always as obedient as their husbands might wish."

For a ghastly moment he thought he'd mistaken Claudio's sense of humor, and the magnificent rows he had with his wife. Inside one week he and Geraint had seen half a dozen items of crockery flung by the fierce redhead at her husband before the delighted customers of the cafe. Then the man burst into a huge laugh and reached across the wooden counter, grabbed Michael by the shoulders and kissed him on both cheeks.

"You are a wicked, mischievous Englishman," the man laughed. "She will be delighted with it. I will see to it."

"I hope so." Michael was laughing now too, ignoring the intense garlic aroma that lingered from the man's greeting.

"Ah, so here is the lordship now, yes." Claudio beamed as Geraint, Serrin, and Kristen pushed past Streak as he struggled with the last of the bags. "Hey!" he announced to the multitude. "This is an English lordship staying at my place! What you think of that?"

"Oh, shit," Michael said between clenched teeth. Anyone who managed to trace them to Venice wouldn't find it hard to locate them now. English nobility visiting Venice would hardly be unusual, but staying here would be. That was the whole point of coming here. Geraint glowered at him, and then had to force himself to smile as various comments, some respectful but most ribald, were hooted at him from various quarters of the cafe. Doing the only thing he could, he bowed to the customers, who cheered him and then returned to their wine.

"Thanks for that," he snarled at Michael as they climbed the rickety wooden steps. "Why not put up a poster and advertise our presence?"

"It would have been less effective," Michael said sadly.

When they got to the landing, Geraint was still visibly seething. Kristen took a determined step forward and faced him squarely, hands on her hips.

"You're not angry," she told him. She grabbed him by the arm and half-dragged him over to the small window facing south. "Look," she said.

"It's the piazza," he said, wondering what she meant. She stared at him. He almost had to look away; she was very intense, her body stiff.

"I said look, *pampoen*," she repeated, using the Afrikaans for idiot. "Look at it, look at it. Look at those horses, they're almost alive." She was pointing to the gilded bronze horses of St. Mark prancing above the huge central doorways of the basilica. "And look at that tower, it reaches up to heaven. Now don't you dare to be angry when this is so beautiful."

Geraint understood what she meant and what she was feeling, and for a moment he felt a tinge of some small sadness that he couldn't feel the same about the place. But he had forebodings about the city after what he'd seen in the Tarot cards, and besides that he carried his own troubles. He didn't have eyes to see the wonder of San Marco right then.

"I'm sorry." He gave a slight shrug. "You're seeing all this for the first time . . . Of course, you're taken with it. Why not go out and stroll around the square? I'm sure it's safe."

'I will," she said, a little deflated. Something wasn't quite right with Geraint, and it puzzled her that she didn't have a glimmering of what it was.

"When you've finished fannying around," Streak said in a businesslike way as he dragged some bags to the nearest door. "Do the honors, guv."

Michael unlocked his door on cue. "I have one or two calls to make, and then I think it's an early night. But we need to plan what we're going to do tomorrow," he said to Geraint.

"Fair enough. I think a Ministry interest in the remarkable engineering work of the city would be entirely appropriate. I need to call the consulate office here as well, go and flatter some egos," Geraint replied. "Okay, let's get organized. Chop chop."

"We're going out," Kristen told Serrin. It was anything but a question.

"I kind of got that impression," he said with a smile.

The two of them dumped their bags in their room and strode down the stairs and into the night. The square was uncluttered with drinkers at tables, the ordinances of the city forbidding this in the square before the palace itself, and only small knots of tourists like themselves occupied the piazza, save for the guardsmen stationed decoratively before the basilica itself. They walked across the mosaics of the piazza, through a night that seemed to be hushed before the magnificence of the buildings.

They went quietly toward the basilica, stopping ten meters or so before the central doorways. The horses, underlit with small spotlights, reared into the inky night sky, and the black-and-silver-dressed guardsmen stood impassively before the colonnades of the doorways. The huge frontage of the basilica, with its astonishing statuary and frescoes, stretched out on both sides of them.

"Can you imagine building this?" Serrin asked softly. The wonder of the place had struck him too. Flags and pennants hung down from atop the doorways and alcoves, and as he looked at them he saw they were portraits and paintings. He stepped a little closer to examine the nearer of them.

They were, he guessed, reproductions of paintings by the many artists whose work graced the city's buildings; and that had been most of the greatest artists of the Renaissance, that time in human history when art and science had not so much progressed or flourished as exploded in the minds of so many men of brilliance. It had been an era when the shackles of a corrupt and authoritarian church had begun to be loosened, yet so much of the art of the era had been sacred, and used to decorate many of the churches and cathedrals of Europe's great cities.

By sheer coincidence, the first painting he saw on its lightly fluttering flag was Leonardo's *John the Baptist*. Opposite it, across the doorways, was a greatly smoothed and polished reproduction of another of the artist's surviving works.

"The Last Supper," Serrin said. "Christ and his disciples. I don't think the original looks quite as clear as that."

Kristen looked at it curiously, stepping closer to examine it.

"I can't see Judas," she said.

"I'm not sure where he is. I can't even remember if he was there or not," Serrin said. "I didn't pay enough attention in Sunday school."

"He's got to be there, but the arm is wrong," she said, pointing to the left of the picture.

"What?" he asked, stepping forward himself to see what she was talking about.

"Look. There. Someone is holding a knife at that man's stomach, but you can only see the arm. Whoever the arm belongs to you can't see. And he isn't pointing it at Jesus," she added, a little confused. "And why are they all accusing him? Look at their hands."

He squinted, unsure, but with a strange sense of disquiet and anxiety. Something was terribly wrong with this painting.

"Look, they're making daggers with their hands. Look, he is," she said urgently, pointing to the left of the painting. "His hand is a flat dagger across that woman's throat. That's it! Those two on the left hate her, not him," she said, urgently now. "Serrin, what is this? Look at his face, that man with the pointy gray beard, his hand is cutting her throat, and she is so sad, look at her. Who is she? Is that Mary?"

"I think so," he said uncertainly.

"But she's too young," Kristen protested. "That can't be his mother. And look, it's her again. The Mona Lisa. I'm sure it is. It's her eyes, even though they're closed."

Serrin was struck by half a dozen insights in the same instant, and he felt horribly cold and even a little sick.

"It isn't his mother, it's Mary Magdalene," he told her, remembering what he'd read in the book he'd bought. "And I hadn't seen it, but I think you're right. The book only says that Leonardo painted himself as one of the disciples. Here," and he pointed to the other side of the painting, one from the right. "That's him. Talking to the bald man, there at the end."

"And why is the young man at his side turned completely away from Jesus?"

"That I don't know," Serrin muttered, but his eyes returned involuntarily to the woman in the picture. For a moment he realized that the apparently central figure of the painting, the open-handed Christ staring slightly vacantly at the viewer, almost as if he was shrugging his shoulders, was not what this painting was really about. His eyes were drawn to the Magdalene, and the accusing hands of hatred directed at her by the disciples around her.

It is she who suffers, he realized.

This man painted a blasphemy.

"I want to read your book," she said suddenly.

"Hmmmm? What? What book?"

"The book on the man who painted this. And the *Mona Lisa,* and the other things you look at," she said simply.

"That might not be a bad idea," he said. If not for Kristen, he surely wouldn't have noticed any of the strange things about the painting. He made a mental note to come back after they'd toured the square a bit so he could scrutinize every last detail of every painting and etching.

"But now I want to go on one of the boats," she announced brightly.

"Gondolas," he corrected her.

"I know," she said testily. "I want to go on one. Now. Come on!"

He laughed and hugged her, then let himself be pulled along. In some people, such a demand would have been childish petulance, but with her it was a genuinely childlike enthusiasm and desire to learn and experience what seventeen years on the streets of Cape Town had given her no inkling of.

"Yeah, let's do it," he said, and they walked through the piazzetta to the Molo San Marco and down to the Giardinetti, where they found a host of men only too ready to take their money and promise to sing into the bargain.

It's a tourist thing, he grinned to himself, but what the hell? There actually are stars in the sky tonight, we can drink wine, and the canals really don't seem to stink as Michael said they would. The guy propelling this thing has seen untold lovers clamber aboard his boat and he's probably given them all pretty much the same patter about how beautiful the lady is and how her face shines

in the light of his lantern—after all, he's an Italian—and
I still don't care.

Leaving the disquiet of the painting behind him, Serrin
grinned broadly, paid the man a good tip, whispered in
his ear and got a broad smile in return, then settled down
among the cushions of the narrow boat for the ride.

"What did you say to him?" she asked, suspicious.

"That you were an African princess and I had eloped
with you," he whispered into her ear. She was about to hit
him when he put up a hand in self-defending protest.

"It's true! We did elope—after a fashion. We had to
smuggle you out of the country," he pointed out. She
drew back from her playful slap.

"And you are a princess to me," he said with an absolutely straight face.

Then she slapped him anyway.

24

Kristen was so full of the delights of it all at breakfast the
next morning that even Streak didn't have the heart to
puncture her mood with something sarcastic. The lanterns
and cafes of the night had enchanted her, and the eerie,
smooth passage of the gondola across the waters had
seemed like gliding across silk. Appraising Serrin at the
breakfast table, Streak decided that the origin of the slight
shadows under his eyes was fairly obvious. He resisted
commenting about men with younger wives especially
since, after all, Serrin was an elf like himself and there
was some fraternity involved on that count.

"Our friends will be with us shortly after lunch,"
Streak told Geraint. "Earlier than they'd originally
planned, which is all right, innit?"

"Just as well," Geraint fretted. He was fretting a lot,
and fretting all the more because he really wasn't sure
why. "I have to leave you for a while, I'm afraid. I promised to take breakfast with some ghastly little secretary at
the consulate. It's necessary if we're to have backup for
our enquiries at the Doge's offices. It will look odd if

they check and find I haven't actually been in touch with the consulate. Plus I really should get some hints on who to avoid among the paper-pushers."

Getting up, having drunk only some much-needed coffee, Geraint made an excusing gesture of farewell and bolted for the door.

"He isn't well in himself," Kristen observed.

Michael nodded agreement. "It may be what happened yesterday."

"That woman? That Countess? It might be that, but I don't think so," she said.

"You're an expert on that now, are you?" Streak enquired, not passing up some chance for a bit of mischief.

"I can tell when a man's got a woman on his mind," she snorted derisively.

"And it's not that?"

"It's more than that, trust me."

Claudio approached from the door to the kitchens, beaming happily.

"Yes, our breakfast is great, thank you," Michael said, heading off the enquiry.

The man waved his hands in a slightly dismissive manner. "Oh I know that. You English always say that. I could serve you the cloths we use for washing the plates in a sauce made from the scrapings from our trash bins and you English would say it was fine, thank you very much please may I have some more? Have you heard the news today?"

"News?"

"The Doge's wife," Claudio said with much satisfaction.

"Um, what about the Doge's wife?" Michael asked, wishing he'd checked the news, unhappy that someone else had information before him.

"The Doge has wanted a son for the six years they have been married," Claudio said with a slight trace of disapproval. Clearly, the Doge's wife had not been all she should have. The image of the silver replica axe crossed Michael's mind. "And now he is not without a male heir!"

"Oh, they've had a son? Well, um, excellent," Michael mumbled, not entirely sure what he was supposed to say.

"Better than that, she has given him *two* fine sons."
Claudio stood beaming with his arms crossed, as proudly
as if he had fathered the pair himself. "They would have
known, of course, the doctors, but it was kept quiet during the pregnancy. But now she has given birth, and all
Venice will be so proud."

"I'm sure," Michael said. "Well, that's splendid."

"So I wondered if you would want me to arrange your
costumes? My cousin Franco, he has a very fine collection. You can choose from the catalog. I bring you a
copy." He turned to go.

"Excuse me, Claudio, just a minute. What do you
mean, costumes?"

"There will be a carnival, of course, for today and tonight. Everyone must wear one of the costumes. You will
not be able to go out without one, not after noon. It will
be very bad manners."

"Rakk off!" Streak hissed under his breath.

"They are splendid," Claudio said, either not hearing
him—or ignoring him. "It is usual to wear only an eye
mask and light costume for the day, but for the night the
full costume will be required, of course. There will be
wine and song and feasts everywhere, but you eat with
me, yes? You will look fine. For the signora, white silk
for that wonderful skin, yes? And the gilded masks for
the men. You ask Lucrezia to pick the costumes for you."
He waved a finger at the males.

"I think that's an excellent idea," Michael said. If
Lucrezia was to be unleashed on them, they had better
take it in a fully compliant spirit.

"Just don't argue with her," he said to Streak, who was
bristling a little. "I don't care that you have all that
chrome. She could flatten you. I've seen her in action.
You could be decapitated with a dinner plate."

"What is this drek? Carnival? We're not here for a
fragging carnival," Streak replied. "That's what you're
paying me for? To dress up and prance about like some
ponce?"

"Look, if we get what we need from the Doge's offices
we may be out of here after lunch," Michael said, "so
don't grumble. Maybe we won't have to worry about it at
all."

"Well, then, let's bloody hope that his lordship gets some joy out of the pen-pushers," the elf said flatly.

"Yes, let's hope indeed," Michael agreed fervently.

Geraint was back by ten, his stock of forced good humor exhausted by an extraordinarily tiresome underling who'd spent most of breakfast whining about his low salary and complaining that London never paid any attention to anything he did or reported. Geraint had had to utter scores of emollient sentences and gotten little help in reply, since the disgruntled secretary clearly loathed everyone on the Doge's staff fairly indiscriminately.

"When I get back home I'll make sure the little sod gets transferred to a ghastly posting somewhere hot and humid and riddled with malaria and that nice endorphin-destroying virus that's been sprouting in southeast Asia," he growled to Michael. The Englishman smiled, brushed away the last crumbs of an ample breakfast from his lap, and padded toward the exit.

They headed through the piazza and decided to make their way to the palatial offices via the basilica itself. Though they'd allowed plenty of time to make the appointment Geraint had fixed for ten-thirty, they were nearly late. The basilica simply offered too much for them to look at, whether it was the treasury built to hold the spoils of pillage from Constantinople or the mosaics of the atrium, the Pentecost dome or simply the opulent decorations of the aisles themselves. They found themselves on Rizzo's Giants' Staircase, the broad, vast steps leading to the landing where the Doges were crowned, with barely a minute to spare. They didn't even have time to stop and gaze upon all the wonders of the palace itself.

Flourishing the insignia of His Majesty's Government and announcing himself as Lord Llanfrechfa got Geraint past the clerks and paper-pushers faster than he'd hoped. He found himself, with Michael, seated across a desk from someone who gave every appearance of being quite a senior functionary in the Doge's Office of Works. The office was, after all, barely ten meters from the *sala dei tre capi*, the chamber of the Doge's Council heads, and proximity to such exalted men was a reasonable sign of seniority and influence.

"So what can I do for Your Lordship on this happy

day?" the man asked with the unforced good humor of someone who's been told he's getting the afternoon off as a public holiday.

"I represent His Majesty's Government," Geraint said with due ceremony. "We are most interested in the reports dealing with pollution of the canals and lagoon of the city. If I may say so, judging from this and my past visits, Venice is more beautiful and cleaner than I have ever seen it."

The man was obviously pleased to see that Geraint was, apparently, a regular visitor, and he seemed to bristle with a certain pride.

"Well, we like to think so," he said cheerfully.

"His Majesty's Government is most interested because we have similar problems with rising pollution levels in the Thames, which flows past our own seat of government just as waters flow around the palace here," Geraint continued.

"Well, this is a global problem," the clerk said, his brow furrowing a little. "I have had calls from as far away as San Francisco about this matter."

"Indeed," Geraint replied evenly. "Well, His Majesty would be most delighted to learn of any help you could provide regarding this remarkable and fascinating success. Naturally, my government would be only too ready to remunerate the Doge for such expert consultation and assistance."

"That would be in the normal course of events," the clerk said, smiling slightly.

"We had heard," Geraint said, his voice dropping a little, "that remarkable developments in magical techniques were involved. Naturally, we would not pry into such matters."

"Naturally."

"However, we have heard of work with water elementals."

"You have?" the man said innocently.

"We have indeed," Geraint said a little more strongly.

"Well," the man said slowly, "I would like to help you. I myself read history at your university of Oxford, you know."

Gotcha, Geraint realized with utter joy. The Oxford-Cambridge university cabal and old-boy network had a potency all but unequaled in the history of European civilization.

"Ah! Your college?"

"Balliol," the man said with some pride.

"My private secretary is a Balliol man," Geraint said authoritatively, "and so is my boss. I've dined there many times. Well, well."

"I must ask you to respect confidences," the man said, his manner more businesslike but still cheery.

"I can absolutely assure you that—"

"Very well," the man cut in. "It's going to be obvious before very long so I think I can trust you, Lord Llanfrechfa." He then looked at Michael rather pointedly.

"Ah, my friend. He is my traveling personal secretary," Geraint lied. "And, of course, the very soul of discretion."

Michael did a splendid job of looking blank but alert.

"Unfortunately, Lord Llanfrechfa, I cannot help you because I do not know how the work was done," the man said apologetically.

"Is there someone—"

Again he was anticipated. "I regret not. You see, no one really knows. This man came to us and said he could help with the problem of pollution. Of course, we thought he was just a, em, a time-waster. We have paid magicians for many years to deal with it, and the pollution simply returns time and time again. So we took no notice of him."

"And then?"

"The following day, this was only last Wednesday, the man brought us a tray of bottles that he claimed were samples of water from the lagoon, the Grand Canal, and half a dozen tributaries. At first we ignored him, but then we had them tested. We were astounded by the results, so we sent our own people to conduct some tests. They confirmed that the pollution levels had fallen by an average of sixty-two percent. By Friday, the pollution levels were down to ten per cent of what they had been only three days before. The Doge's magicians confirmed that there was intense elemental activity throughout the canal system of our city. A small group of our magicians attempted to conduct a ritual to investigate the exact nature of this activity and its source." The man paused.

"And?"

"They are expected to be in the hospital for some time."

"Good heavens!"

"We are astounded," the man said simply. "Our fellow did not even give a name."

"You must have a picture of him, surely?" Geraint insisted, as gently as he was able.

"Incredibly not. Of course, when we came here he was filmed by the security cameras."

"That's exactly what I was thinking."

"Unfortunately, the films did not, ah, turn out correctly."

He decked into their system and deleted everything, Michael thought. Obviously, this man doesn't want to tell us that. It's tantamount to saying that the Doge's Matrix system was taken to bits. Not something a city functionary will want to admit.

"But you saw him," Geraint said. "What did he look like?"

"That is the extraordinary thing. Everyone's description is subtly different. It is as if, somehow, everyone saw a different refraction of light from one facet of a prism. Everyone saw something slightly different."

The metaphor struck Michael at once. How apt, he thought: an optical metaphor for our Leonardo-freak.

"There is a general picture that emerges, though. He is tall, with long gray hair, balding at the front, and he is fairly lean. It is very strange, though, that no one can agree on his age. Some think he was old, others that he seemed fairly young.

"And he was seen with someone else in his company, and the witnesses do at least agree on that ... with a young man, with long fair hair tied in a pony-tail. This is not an unusual fashion in certain Italian states," he said with faint disapproval.

Blondie, Michael thought. It sounds like the man who saved Serrin back in Florence.

"And the man is still here?"

"Friday was the last day anyone saw him."

"He was not tracked or traced?"

"I can assure you, Your Lordship, we had him followed. Unfortunately"—the man coughed with embarrassment—"it was somehow not possible to track him for any distance. Observers seem to have become confused and disoriented. And after the unfortunate business with the magicians, ritual magic was not deemed a wise approach."

"I can certainly appreciate that." Geraint smiled sympathetically. "Well, I hardly think you are at fault. This extraordinary fellow sounds as if he would have eluded the best efforts of His Majesty's finest."

The reassurance seemed to make the man a little less unhappy, if not exactly cheerful.

"Well, I must thank you for your time, signor," Geraint said. "I very much appreciate your frankness. You have saved me and my government much time. Should this man ever return, I would be delighted to be informed. I hope that you will allow me to send you a small token of my esteem and gratitude when I return to London. I really do appreciate your openness and honesty."

He meant it. The man had revealed a state of affairs that might, indeed, have become obvious sooner or later. But with so little time left to them, it had to be sooner, and his honesty might just save them enough time to find their quarry before the world's computer systems crashed.

They shook hands and departed, wandering slowly back through ever more crowded streets to where they were staying.

"This is extraordinary. That they couldn't film him and that everyone saw someone different. And they couldn't track him . . . What kind of man is this?" Michael was shaking his head in wonder.

"Someone bloody extraordinary," Geraint said. "But now we know for sure Blondie is with him."

"I just don't see how he could have done it," Michael said. "They must have had the police out after him. They probably still do."

"Of course they did and he gave them the slip," Geraint grinned.

By now, they were back in the piazza, and saw Serrin and Kristen just leaving the campanile. The *marangona* bell was tolling already, announcing the public holiday for those still not apprised of the Doge's blessing, and crowds were beginning to build in the square. A few people already wore the black eye masks and dark cloaks of day attire for the celebrations, and tables were being brought into the square, though no more than a few from any of the cafes. The city ordinances were relaxed, but guardsmen were quietly checking that the square was not unduly cluttered. By midnight a huge crowd would be expected here and obstructions were going to be kept down to a minimum.

"Enjoy your sightseeing?" Michael asked Kristen.

"It's amazing, you can see all over the city. Serrin says you can see Padova on a really clear day." Kristen was beaming.

"Possibly a slight exaggeration," Michael teased. "But it's a great place to view from, that tower. If you can climb all those steps, that is."

"Tell me about it," Serrin croaked.

"At least I've got the excuse of a bad back," Michael chuckled. "You're getting old." He poked the elf playfully in the ribs.

"And I have the excuse of a leg shot to hell," Serrin reminded him.

"Sorry," Michael apologized. "I'd forgotten that."

"Wish I could."

Streak waved cheerfully to them across the piazza. He sat, narrow-eyed, scanning the square, his jacket perhaps a little bulky for the morning's warmth.

He's keeping watch, Michael realized, and he's got his usual armory inside that jacket. But it doesn't seem like he's going to need it today. Our man is, or at least was, here. We were right to come. But why was he doing what he did? How did he do it? And most of all, what does he want to do now and how do we find him? He remembered what Kristen had said. *What would you do if you were Leonardo?* The problem with that is he simply didn't know. The genius had every interest imaginable and picking which one might apply right now seemed impossible.

He wandered over to the painting of the Last Supper that Serrin had mentioned to him. It didn't disturb him as much as it did the elf, but there was no doubt something was drastically wrong with the scene. The accusing nature of the disciples on the left was obvious. The seemingly disembodied dagger-wielding hand was obviously wrong; it belonged to no body portrayed.

How on earth did no one see this? Michael thought. How did he get away with this with the Inquisition around, with vicious and venal churchmen all around, all too ready to accuse a talent of whom they had the petty envy of the professionally self-righteous? Whatever this is all leading to, it isn't small beer. And, somehow, I think I can see how the collapse of the Matrix is, like Merlin said to Serrin, actually not the most important thing.

So what is?

His reverie was shattered by an extraordinary sight. Trundling into the square, northward from the piazzetta, was the most peculiar vehicle Michael had ever seen. It looked like a medium-sized armored snail on wheels, and it was decked out with a mass of flags. The flags bore what appeared to be abstract designs, but as it got closer they seemed to show flowing waves of water and arcs of light. The people in the square assumed this was some early part of the carnival celebrations and cheered at its approach.

Behind them, Streak's hand reached into his jacket pocket. As he did so, the gesture was matched by that of two men standing, cloaked and masked, just outside Florian's, the cafe almost directly opposite Quadri's.

The vehicle stopped.

Streak's silencer kept the sound of the missiles down to an absolute minimum. Behind him, a maid was vigorously using a vacuum cleaner on the cafe floor and carpets. He hoped it would cover the noise.

As the first of the men in cloaks dropped to the ground, the vehicle began to fall apart a few meters from the campanile. Guardsmen were rushing to the area now to see what was happening.

A bullet missed Kristen's ear by no more than a few centimeters. Serrin heard the sound and flung her to the ground beneath him, looking around wildly for the unknown assailant. Streak nodded his head with satisfaction as the second cloaked man hit the ground. Next to him, a puzzled and obviously terrified middle-aged tourist woman was beginning to develop the first symptoms of what would undoubtedly turn out to be a suitably histrionic hysterical fit.

As the armored snail disintegrated, its metal plates appeared to evaporate as they hit the surface of the piazza.

A young man stood up inside the vanishing wreckage, utterly immaculate in black jacket, pants, and cloak, with the full gold face-mask of the carnival. A long pony-tail of blond hair hung down his back. He bowed low to the cheering crowd, kissed an utterly bewildered guardsman on both cheeks, and skipped away eastward. Geraint shot after him like a greyhound after a rabbit.

Serrin crafted a barrier spell for himself while Streak's eyes darted everywhere among the crowd. Around the two men on the ground at Florian's a knot of people was gathering and guardsmen were rushing to the scene. Michael could do little. Unable to keep up with Geraint because of his bad back, he could only bustle toward Serrin and Kristen.

The snail had completely vanished. The illusion had been allowed to decay.

The youth sped like the blazes, laughing as he went. Geraint knew he couldn't catch him, and was about to abandon his forlorn pursuit as his quarry headed for the bridge over the Rio del Palazzo. Then he turned suddenly and called out to his panting pursuer.

"My master sends his regards and trusts he will continue to enjoy the game," the stranger called out cheerfully and then vanished across the bridge into the labyrinth of streets beyond. There was nothing for Geraint to do but return to the piazza.

Streak, staying put, was dismayed to see that the fallen assassins were being taken inside the cafe from which they'd appeared.

They were going to be taken away by friends, and there wasn't much he could do about it. The crowd of people in the way were slowing the approaching guardsmen sufficiently that any backup inside the place—and surely they must have some—would get them out in time. If only that damn stunt hadn't had the police all going the wrong way! What the blazes was that thing?

Still, no one saw the narcoject. Better bet than the Predator here. You could always plead self-defense with a non-lethal weapon.

Frag it, he told himself, maybe I should have used the Predator after all.

Having scanned the square enough times, he risked

walking over to Serrin and Kristen, back on their feet now, and Michael.

"You okay?"

"Who the hell—"

"Couple of guys over at Florian's," Streak told them. "I dropped them with some dozies. Keep them out of action for a while. Didn't think I could risk the real thing. I might have been wrong."

"Owe you one," Serrin asserted with real feeling. "I don't understand why my spell lock didn't pick them up."

"You got an enemy detector?" Streak had worked with combat mages long enough to know the basics. Serrin nodded.

"Then they weren't after you, was they? They was trying to whack Kristen," Streak said cheerfully.

"Why?" Serrin was appalled.

"Don't ask me, I'm just the guy who stopped her getting filled with lead," Streak said. "Oh, and what was that thing that just rolled into the square and where the frag is it now?"

"It must have been an illusion," Serrin said. "I didn't have time to observe it closely. Not with being shot at, hitting the dirt, that sort of thing, you know?"

"Next time," Geraint said as he returned to join the conversation, "shoot at that little blond bastard. Know what he said to me?" Without waiting for the obvious reply, he told them.

"The game?"

"I knew it was something like this," Michael mused. "We have to learn to play his game somehow."

"That thing," Serrin said slowly, as if searching through his memory as he spoke, "that tank thing, it reminds me of something. I didn't get long to look at it, but I think it was like one of Leonardo's designs. I think I saw something like that in the book I've got."

"Part of this game?" Geraint wondered.

"So what's next?"

"What's next, guys and gals, is that we ought to get indoors in case there are any more prats in cloaks wanting to take a pop at us. We've got to consider our options, and make some plans instead of farting around out here," Streak said. "Unless you'd like to be shot at again, that is."

"Let's get inside," Serrin said at once. "And let's consider how the frag we play this game. Some game, if my wife's getting shot at."

"I think," Streak said, "that those guys were playing one of a very different kind. The kind where there's guaranteed to be tears before bedtime."

25

They decided not to move elsewhere in the city. Though their whereabouts were obviously known, it would be easy enough to trace them if they moved. Michael also pointed out that Claudio was someone they could trust, and he could alert them if strangers came snooping or asking about them. Serrin decided to conduct some rituals to protect them against magical assault. They didn't know who'd attacked them that morning, but the Jesuit fundamentalists were the most obvious possibility and their mages would hardly be weaklings.

"Now we've got to make an active move. Do something to show our man we're playing his game," Michael said.

"Like what?" Streak asked. "This is your kind of thing, Michael matey. I just shoot people."

"Speaking of shooting people," Geraint said with a wince, "when do Juan and Xavier get here?"

"Any time now," Streak said. "I was right, eh? We're going to need 'em."

"Looks like it."

Before Michael could return to his deliberations, there was a knock on the door. Streak had his Predator in his hand at once, but Michael waved him away.

"For God's sake, no assassin is going to *knock*, Streak."

"Don't you sodding believe it," the elf said, but sat down and reluctantly picked up a magazine and kept the gun leveled behind it as he pretended to be reading. To his disgust, the magazine seemed to be full of lavish illustrations of Italian gardens. Streak had many interests, but gardening was definitely not one of them. If the magazine didn't have guns, military hardware, or members of the opposite gender in states of undress, he was definitely not interested.

Lucrezia popped her head around the door, her mane of flaming curls as prodigious as ever.

"I come to see about your costumes, Mister Michael," she said. "And there is a card for you."

"Thank you very much," Michael said. He took the card, read it, and his eyes widened. He passed it to Geraint without comment.

"I take the lady separately from you gentlemen?" the woman asked, clearly a little puzzled to find them all crammed together in the same room.

"Perhaps you can measure me and my wife," Serrin suggested, seeing that Michael obviously wanted to discuss whatever was on the card. The two of them left with Lucrezia for their own bedroom.

"Please be in the square at midnight, when a most interesting event will take place," Michael read aloud for Streak's benefit.

"Signed by one 'Salai'," Geraint said, looking over his friend's shoulder.

"Very neat. He was the closest to what might be called an apprentice of Leonardo's. Traveled with him for many years. As I recall, he was something of an asshole. According to the history books, that is."

"That seems about right," Geraint said with feeling.

"So this is when he makes another move. The question is what we do until then," Michael said.

"Whatever it is, it's got to communicate with our target," Geraint said.

"That means something public."

"Post a message on the BBS?"

"That would be logical, I suppose. What do we say?"

'Mona Lisa wishes to meet Leonardo'?" Streak suggested. "That's the kind of thing I usually browse."

"I'm sure it is," Michael said disapprovingly, "but I hardly think—"

"Maybe it's not so totally off the wall," Geraint said. "I mean, it probably should be something like that. It's got to be jokey, I think. That damnable farce out in the square was supposed to be some kind of entertainment."

They started to throw ideas around without really getting anywhere, and it was almost a relief when Lucrezia arrived with her catalogue and measuring tape. She dealt with the elf last.

"Watch that inside leg, signora," Streak said slyly. "I'm a red-blooded elf in my prime."

Grinning, not taking offense, she slapped him playfully in the ear. The elf reeled back, a shrill singing tone ringing inside his head.

"Frag me, missus, I wouldn't want to argue with you for real!" he complained and became as meek as a lamb, politely accepting the costume she suggested for him.

When Lucrezia left, Geraint and Michael burst into the laughter they'd been choking back after the elf's chastisement.

"Serves you right. I warned you," Michael sniggered.

"Rakk it, what a right hook," Streak said as Serrin and Kristen rejoined them.

"Everything gets delivered after lunch," Serrin said. "What happened to you?" He peered at the elf's deep red ear.

"Nothing," Streak mumbled.

"Our Lucrezia disciplined him for being a cheeky bugger," Michael told Serrin with a smirk. "He's going to be awfully well behaved for a while."

"Right." Serrin grinned. "Now what about business?"

They told him what they'd been discussing, then picked up the thread where they'd left off.

"It needs to be something more pointed," Serrin said. "Oh, by the way, here's that thing we saw in the square." He opened the book at the appropriate page and showed them the design for the military machine, which did indeed look extraordinarily like a primitive First World War tank.

"I wonder if we might not try something like asking Salai to attend a supper," Serrin said. "And maybe call it 'Mary's supper'."

"You're thinking of the painting in the square," Michael said.

"Yes. I'm convinced that the Magdalene is actually the subject of that picture. It's so obvious when you really look at it."

"It's certainly not what it appears to be," Michael agreed.

"And if we included a line from that apocalyptic essay by Leonardo, the one about the floods, for good measure, we'd show that we understood more now than maybe our man thinks we do."

"It's worth a try," Geraint offered.

"We need to post it on as many BBSes as we can and leave a drop," Michael said. "We can't know if he'll be monitoring, but—"

"Surely he must be. If what he does for fun is wipe his traces clean from the Doge's system, routine BBS scanning ought to be pretty simple," Geraint said.

Michael sat down with his deck. "Okay. Consider it done. I'll leave Smithers to plant it."

"Smithers? Who the frag is Smithers?" Streak demanded.

"One of his frames," Geraint told him. "This one does the routine clerk stuff so he calls it Smithers."

"Don't ask about Tracey," Serrin said.

"I wouldn't dream of it," Streak replied. "What a weird bloke he is."

"I won't take that to heart," Michael said cheerfully. "Better than being boring, eh?"

It took less than a minute to post the message they finally composed, make the nominal payment transfer, and arrange the email drop. Now all they could do was sit back and wait.

"Now what?" Streak was becoming restless, agitated because he was still feeling the adrenaline rush that shooting people always gave him.

"Apart from this I'm not sure there's much else we can do. We know something's going to happen in the square tonight, so—"

Michael's words were interrupted by a signal from his deck that Smithers had observed and located a reply to his posting. Eagerly, he downloaded it.

"Slot, that was fast," he said. "Let's see what we've got here." They all crowded around.

" 'Your understanding is superior to what we had expected. We look forward very much to further developments. Yours respectfully, Salai.' Hmm."

"Respect, indeed," Geraint growled.

"Don't be touchy," Michael said. "Look, he's pleased with us."

"Are you a toy poodle or something?"

"It seems to imply that we're being invited to get closer to him. 'Further developments'."

"We should post a reply to his reply," Serrin suggested.

"Good idea, but what?"

"The flood. That apocalyptic flood." For some reason, the idea suggested itself to him. "That's so final. I think that's a key, somehow. Maybe it's just because he's been here and been doing weird stuff with the canals, I don't know. Let's post a chunk about the flood. Maybe ask if it can be averted."

"All right." Michael settled to work with Serrin's book open at the right page of text.

Again the reply came back within minutes. Michael read it aloud.

" 'Salai and his master congratulate you on making an intuitive leap that is beyond your understanding at this time, and express their admiration. They respectfully suggest no further communications are necessary at this time. Wait until midnight,' Well, thank you, gentlemen."

"Midnight tonight doesn't leave us much time," Geraint said.

"Look, we've got our channels open now. He knows about us and he's said we understand some stuff. We'll have to live with that for now."

"It's the best part of twelve hours until midnight in the square. What do we do until them?" Streak was pacing up and down the room now.

"Look, when Juan and Xavier get here, why don't you take off and get some exercise?" Geraint told him. "I can see you need it."

"Yeah, okay, I'm just getting a bit stir-crazy. Too much hanging around and I start to seize up," the elf said with a grin.

Right on cue, a loud knock at the door announced the arrival of the samurai pair. Streak opened it to find them already kitted out in full carnival regalia. The gold masks made them look even more sinister than usual.

"Ludicrous," Juan snarled. "But it covers the arms up."

"Juan mate, good to have you on board again. And

Xavier, my man," Streak greeted them. "We've already had some unfriendly fire this morning."

"Great," the ork said, cheered up no end. "Just tell me who we're here to kill."

Kristen sighed. Serrin took her by the hand, off to their own room.

"Bleeding hearts," Xavier growled.

"Disgraceful, ain't it? And it was her they shot at," Streak informed the troll, obviously somewhat embarrassed of the company he was keeping these days. "Anyway, guys, I need some fresh air. I wanna take off for an hour."

"Now that Juan and Xavier are here, we all could," Michael suggested. "I'm not sure I need twelve hours cooped up either."

"I'll go off alone if it's okay. Meet you later," Streak said.

"Sure, but—"

"Unless you really want to meet some ladies with highly nuyen-soluble virtue," the elf said bluntly.

"Oh, right, well, no I don't think so," Michael spluttered. "Thanks for the offer, I suppose."

"We could take Serrin and Kristen down to the Rialto," Geraint suggested. "That'll be the liveliest part of the city right now."

"Sounds good to me. Let's hire a gondola and just do the Rialto for a couple of hours."

"If you don't sink it," Geraint said to Juan, laughing. The ork had enough metal to sink something less fragile than the gondolas appeared to be.

"If you'd seen those Texans loading up this morning," Michael recalled from observing a tourist group heading out of the piazza, "you wouldn't worry. They had to be two hundred kilos each, and that was without all the vids and cameras."

They spent the whole afternoon sampling the city from their vessel, and if anyone was watching or following, they caught no sign of it. Even the Spanish mercenaries, apparently unused to leisurely sightseeing, seemed to be impressed by some of the sights. The cafes and street theaters were in full swing as they sailed past the House of Desdemona, the palatial dwelling named after Shakespeare's character, past the monumental baroque church of Santa Maria with its vast dome and million-timber supports, past the royal gardens built by Napoleon, beneath bridges both tiny and magnificent, until they had gorged themselves on the colors and textures and shapes of Venice. It was after six in the evening when they returned, hungry for dinner, having resisted the dubious pleasures of canalside stalls that all offered an extensive range of remarkably poor fare.

"We'll take a corner table," Michael said diplomatically. "Juan's arm will be less obvious in such shadows as there are."

"Bad news for you, having to eat with an ork, huh?" Juan growled.

"No problem with that. It's all that metal that's the problem. Scares the customers, old chap," Michael grinned.

Streak didn't share the general good humor.

"Raoul's been here," he told them.

"Huetzlipochtli?" Juan asked. It was more of a teeth-baring snarl than a question.

"The very same, large as frag and twice as ugly."

"We know him," Xavier said, his tone leaving no doubt that previous meetings hadn't involved sipping cocktails and discussing the latest developments in modern theater.

"You guys will wear body armor underneath those costumes," Streak told Geraint and friends.

"A fat lot of good that will be against the head shot any sensible hitman will want to take," Juan observed.

"Yeah, so let's reduce the size of the target," Streak replied.

"You could fit them with head shields if they wear the cowls with their cloaks. I saw lots of people doing that," Xavier suggested.

"Good one. Then we can't see much because of the masks and we'll be able to hear bugger all. Then they can sneak up behind us and give us an APDS enema from five fragging meters," Streak said. "I seem to remember discussing this with you guys somewhere else. Was it Swazi?"

"Yeah," Xavier said in a bored voice.

Kristen's ears pricked up. It wasn't that far from her homeland, though the bandit- and warlord-infested petty fiefdoms of the Trans-Swazi Federation were a very different place from Cape Town. She'd known some escapees from the Swazi, as most people called it, and they'd been hard, mean souls.

"So we'll skip the headgear, right?" Streak said.

"No, man. Better if they wear it and we keep watch from different angles," Juan offered. "Then we can cover them."

"What do you reckon, Your Lordship?" Streak appealed to a higher authority.

"I think" Geraint said, "that Kristen should wear headware. She was the one shot at this morning. I'll take my chances. I can use a Predator. Not as well as you chaps, of course, but I can use one."

"I can't," Serrin said. "And I won't use headware. I'll have to see and hear if there's any need for magic."

They debated the pros and cons and finally decided that, of all of them, only Kristen needed the additional protection. Juan had brought the appropriate item with him, though it was far too large for her.

"It's too heavy and I look ridiculous," she complained.

"If it saves your life you're not going to bloody care. Listen to your Uncle Streak," Streak said playfully. "He stopped you getting your bonce shot off this morning. He knows what he's doing. He says the little girl should wear the funny thing on her head."

He dodged her punch easily.

"Come on," he said. "Really, you should. No bollocks now. We'll take our chances, this is our profession. You're not like us. You've got to take care now."

There seemed to be genuine concern in his voice and he looked a little embarrassed for a split-second before quickly resuming his normal sarcasm.

"And as for you, gray-head, you'd better make sure you've got us covered magically. If Raoul's in town he's bound to have some poxy combat mage or two in tow, and what those guys can do isn't pretty. I've seen a blood spirit, and you don't want to get one of those fraggers in your face. One of us will stick real close to catch you if you drain-and-drop, but you give any heavy spell you need every ounce of juice or we could be fragged senseless."

"We've been there before," Serrin reminded him. "On the hill."

"This is different," Streak insisted. "Blood magic. It's like, I don't know, it's like biological weapons. Below the belt, right? Good clean firefight, that we like. Biokillers stink. Combat mages, they treat blood magic like it's bio."

"I get the picture," Serrin said. "So let's go eat."

The hours before midnight passed easily. They ate well, and avoided drink, but the throng of customers packed around them drank themselves silly. Everyone was resplendent in the costumes of the carnival, with silk and satin and velvet and gold threading, masks of silver and gold and bronze, cowls and capes and cloaks, everything a whirl of color and texture and the mystery of it all, with everyone masked and few who they appeared to be.

"Just don't chat up the women, Michael," Streak advised him. "Half of 'em will be transvestites, with a sausage surprise you don't want to get your teeth into, know what I mean?" he leered.

"It hadn't occurred to me to do so," Michael replied evenly.

"You should have come out with me this afternoon," the elf said cheerfully.

"Perhaps not," Michael said.

"God, you're a joyless bugger sometimes," Streak groaned.

"I enjoy myself in different ways," Michael informed him.

"You're about the only person you will enjoy," the elf said tartly.

"It's ten before twelve. Let's go," Juan told them. "What are our positions?"

"I'll cover left, you behind, Xavier goes right," Streak said. He leant over to Kristen and lowered his voice. "Now, little lady, go powder your nose and put your hard hat on."

Kristen disappeared into the ladies' room and returned three minutes later, looking distinctly large-headed.

"I don't think it's going to make the runways of Paris this season, but it'll do the job. Come on, everybody, I'm dying to see what our man has arranged for us at midnight," Michael said. They pushed their way slowly out into the crowd.

Trumpets were already giving periodic fanfares to announce the imminent arrival of the Doge and his wife as they stood among the multitudes. Their watches showed five minutes to midnight.

At four minutes to the hour, as the crowd began to hush slightly in expectation, a slim and lithe, dark-haired South American man and half a dozen servitors idled toward the basilica from the south, pushing past indignant people in the piazzetta to get where they wanted to go. Xavier, his line of sight partly blocked by the campanile, did not see them. They had covering magic anyway.

At three minutes to midnight, from east of the basilica half a dozen Spanish men in costumed attire pushed their way forward in like manner. Streak saw them first. He didn't now who they were, but he knew they weren't coming to enquire why he hadn't posted tax returns for the past five years. He coughed to alert Juan and rubbed the nose of his mask, to direct the ork's attention in front of him. The ork saw the men and began to edge forward. Their attention locked on the men from the east, they too did not see the imminent arrivals from the piazzetta.

At two minutes to the hour the Doge's Council began to troop through the central doorways of the basilica. The crowd cheered, realizing the Doge himself would soon appear.

The Jesuits from the east had no clear line of fire. Neither did Streak or Juan, and neither did the men to the south, but that didn't bother them. They'd have been perfectly ready to kill everyone between themselves and their target if necessary. But it wasn't. All they needed for their blood magic was to kill one person, and that victim had already had his throat slashed.

Serrin got an instant shiver of warning and knew instantly that a magical assault was upon them. He threw up the barrier just as the thing began to shimmer into form among them.

The materializing spirit stank of decay and rotting entrails, and it had only a partial form, vaguely humanoid in shape. It was composed of semi-coagulated blood, or at least it appeared to be. From the center of the thing, a fountain of purulent gore squirted hotly at their faces.

Serrin's barrier barely held it. The liquid corroded the mana barrier like acid dissolving metal, hissing and releasing a reeking cloud of toxic gas. People on either side of them began to panic and scream, some fainting, others being trampled down.

The men to the east pushed forward and drew their guns.

Streak and Juan did their damndest to get a line of sight on them, not realizing the direction of the real threat. Xavier had, at last, done so, seeing the bloodied victim of the Aztechnology mage's sacrifice. His SMG was already beginning to chatter.

Streak saw the gun barrels ahead of him and thought, Oh frag, I can't stop them in time. No, not head shots. Come on, you sods, aim low, aim low. You're going down.

He reached for a grenade. Above his head, one was already arcing toward its target. But it wasn't the guns that mattered. They were mostly for self-defense and they weren't being used yet. One among the crowd of Spanish arrivals unleashed a streak of blue fire that raced south and exploded among the Aztechnology crew.

When it hit the ground, it burst like a nuclear cloud, rising up and around the heads of the men like a gaseous, electrified halo. The brilliant fire burned the flesh from their heads down to the bone, and incinerated the upper halves of their bodies, smashing through the mana barrier of the Azzie mage like it wasn't even there.

Serrin, reeling back from the blood spirit even as it sputtered out of existence with the death of its summoner, saw the devastation left behind by the Jesuit mage's spell. He didn't even want to think about what would happen if the mage's next target was them.

Then the grenade burst among the Jesuits, paralyzant gas surrounding them. But they didn't stop moving.

The bastards have internalized respirators, internal air tanks, nose filters, something, Streak thought, his combat-hardened brain assessing the situation coolly. Okay, frag you, guys. Here comes the acid. If it isn't too late.

Of course, it was.

Serrin could see the mage clearly, impossibly. The man was, after all, shrouded in gas. And yet somehow he could see him. The mage was saying, quite clearly, "And now you die, heretic."

The spell was one-tenth of a second away from doing to him what it had done to the Aztechnology samurai and mage.

And then everything stopped. Stopped dead, and everyone was absolutely still. Everyone was seized by an emotion somehow unknown to them, and their heads were turned to the doorways of the basilica as if gripped by hands they could not resist.

A figure moved forward through the doorways. Whether it was a real person, or a spirit, or an illusion, was not obvious at first. It walked in midair, perhaps three meters above them, shining slightly. It was a woman, and Serrin saw her at once as the Magdalene. In her hands she held out to the crowd, on a gold platter, the severed, bleeding head of John the Baptist. A terrible cry of lamentation went up all around, a soul-scouring wail as if from hell itself, and it was all they could do to stay upright. Geraint managed to put his hands to his ears as if to try and force out the agonizing sound.

In a panic the Jesuits looked as if the devil himself had just appeared among them. They were utterly unable to move or act. They were virtually catatonic.

Streak recovered his senses first and pushed through a crowd of fainting and screaming people and grabbed Serrin.

"For frag's sake, let's get out of here!" he screamed. Serrin grabbed Kristen and began to run. Geraint had to be half-dragged away by the elf, Juan moving in to help him, Xavier getting to Michael. The Jesuits were still standing utterly stunned. They looked as if they were going to be completely beyond the help of the best psychiatrists money could buy for a very long time.

Despite the urgent need to flee, Serrin couldn't resist the urge to turn and look back. He still couldn't identify the image as real or illusion or spirit, but he was astonished to find an intense feeling of grief welling up inside him, as if some terrible wrong had been done, and the woman was there to face everyone with the tragedy and awfulness of that wrong. And although he did not know what that was, the grief was painfully real to him and he did not want to run away from her, to abandon her. But his wife was in his care and people had tried to kill her twice today, and he turned away to Streak.

"Where to?" he asked.

"I don't fragging care," the other elf said. "Out of town. Get to the airport, get on a plane. Let's just get the frag out of here before any more drek starts. I don't know what this is, but it's not something we can handle right now.

"Let's just get out, frag it!"

It really was all they could do.

26

Getting out of the city was a nightmare. Panic radiated out from the square like a tidal wave, and they were trying to outrun it. The mayhem was fueled by the trid broadcasts from on-the-spot camera crews expecting to be showing the proud Doge to his people. The drunkenness of the carnival added to the propensity for hysteria, and the lurid trid report of the blood spirit even had wild rumors of the return of the Red Death and numerous variants on the same theme circulating within minutes like wildfire through a tinder-dry forest in August. Venetians and tourists were running everywhere. In their costumes and masks they made the streets, bridges, and canals of the city look like a labyrinth peopled by the escaped, deranged inmates of an immense asylum.

They couldn't just take Streak's advice and run like the blazes. Michael had a million-nuyen cyberdeck at Quadri's and much of their research notes were there. Sneaking in through the kitchens at the back of the building, they got in without being seen and stuffed everything into bags faster than they'd ever done in their lives. Michael gave Claudio a vast tip by way of thanks. At the sight of all of the money, the man's eyes widened and he grew suspicious.

"Are you a part of this? What has been happening to our great city?" he growled.

"I think we were intended to be victims of what happened to your great city," Michael told him, "and we're running for our lives, and that's no exaggeration."

That disarmed Claudio immediately. He kissed Michael on both cheeks and wished him good luck.

"You, too, and when this is all over we'll come back for some quieter times," Michael said.

Streak was impatient to get moving. "Look, bugger the sweet goodbyes and let's just get in the car."

"Oh, God, we don't have one," Michael suddenly remembered.

"Yes, we do." Streak was dangling some keys on a Lancia keyring in Michael's face.

"Thank heavens you had the sense to hire one," Michael said with a sigh of relief.

"Who says I hired the fragger? Come on, move your hoop. There's no telling if we can actually get through the bloody streets," the elf said.

"I'll just hang my arm out the window and they'll get out of the way," Juan said laconically.

"We can get seven people in the car?" Geraint wondered.

"It means some people sitting on others' laps in the back, but don't waste my time and yours making no jokes. Now move your rakking arses!" Streak yelled at him.

Geraint might be the employer of the pair, but he wasn't going to argue. They ran out the back of the cafe, piled into the car, and started what was obviously going to be a tortuous and uncomfortable journey to the airport.

"Just exactly where are we going?" Serrin asked.

"I don't know, and it doesn't much matter," Streak said. "Nnnngh," he added suddenly, wrenching the wheel sharply to avoid a stray pedestrian who fell into their path from one of the packed sidewalks. "We can hop across to Padova, it's only twenty klicks or so, and collect our thoughts there."

Geraint nodded. "We'll find an airport hotel and figure out what we're going to do."

And that is what they did, though a drive that should have taken a few minutes took almost an hour, with some streets so jammed with hysterical people that backtracks and detours became inevitable. The longer the journey got, the jumpier everyone became.

"I think we're being followed," Michael said anxiously, looking out the back window for the umpteenth time.

"No, we aren't," Juan informed him. "I've been watching in the mirrors. It'd be impossible to follow anyone anyway. In all this, I mean."

"We could be astrally traced."

"I don't detect anything, and believe me I've been trying. I'm actually quite good at that sort of thing," Serrin said, grim-jawed. "Years of practice."

"Sometimes paranoia can be a definite advantage," Michael said more happily.

"It's only paranoia if it isn't real," Serrin grumbled and said no more about it. Kristen was looking dubiously from one to the other as they spoke, but made no comment of her own.

"Poor Raoul," Xavier chuckled. "Boy, did he catch it in the hoop. What a frying."

"You know," Streak said, "we were amazingly lucky the Azzies turned up."

"Yeah, right, their bullet missed Kristen's head by a hair. Real lucky," Serrin shot back.

"Nah, think about it, you pillock. If they hadn't been there the Inquisition would have had you on toast. We didn't have a line of fire and you didn't see them. But the Inquisition boys saw the Azzies and they came first in the firing line—before us."

"I hadn't thought of it like that," Serrin said.

"To those guys that blood magic stuff is *real* heresy. Big-time bad stuff. They wanted the Azzies even more than they wanted us. Or you."

"Yeah, but they did want me," Serrin said, "and that isn't paranoia. I heard the mage's words."

"Yeah, that was big-time," Streak replied. "Some stunt, that barbecuing across the square. Now why don't you frag people like that?"

"I don't have years of training with the Inquisition, if that's the right term. It still seems odd to me."

"Oh, you can call them the Inquisition all right," Xavier declared with some feeling. "We know those guys, yes. Don't forget they got their start in our back yard. Nadal, Acquaviva, all those guys with Ignatius. The Jesuits got damned near ninety per cent of their membership from Spain in the early days. It was politics that said they had to go to the Pope and have their central place in Italy, but it was originally a Spanish deal."

"You do know these boys," Streak said.

"Yeah, and not just in Aztlan. Seen 'em in the South American states too," Xavier grunted. "They don't care much for the Amazonians either. And they don't care for their own brethren."

"Nothing like a bit of that ole-time religion for making people kill each other in exciting, brutal, and deeply imaginative ways," Streak declared gleefully.

"I thought that was your number," Serrin said.

"Hey, be fair!" Streak protested, absolutely seriously. "The name of our game is to take out your enemy as quickly as possible—before he does the same to you. With these Azzies, its torture and outright bloody sadism. Take a look at some of the stuff those people invented as torture instruments sometime; there's a museum in Amsterdam where they've collected a lot of it. Makes me shudder just to think about it. Sick frags. Real gratifying to know God guided their hands as they crafted them so exquisitely."

"Point taken," Serrin acquiesced.

At long last they managed to reach the outskirts of the airport. Despite the lateness of the hour, the place was flooded with people panicking to get out of the city. If they'd been wanting to book a regular flight out of there they wouldn't have had a prayer, but with their own aircraft all they had to do was dispense several large sums to the officials by way of flight clearance and get themselves whisked out of the VIP lounge and on to the runway verge.

"You wanna make the hop to Padova or just frag off somewhere else?" Streak asked. He was almost the only one, save for Juan sitting next to him in the front of the vehicle, who didn't have to stretch his legs from the discomfort of being crammed into the car, which was not really designed to take seven adult passengers.

"Let's take the shortest option," Geraint decided.

So they stayed within the Veneto and made the short haul, Michael booking rooms in an airport hotel as they

went, and the journey was a lot faster than the car ride
through the narrow streets of Venice. But with the clock
showing a quarter to two, fatigue was beginning to catch
up with them. There had certainly been enough excitement for one day. But though tired, they wouldn't get to
sleep easily and they knew it. Adrenaline was still cours-
ing in veins too fast.

"Tomorrow's May Day and another bloody public
holiday," Michael lamented. "And the deadline's fast
approaching."

"So, let's order up fifteen gallons of java and start
chewing the rag," Streak said cheerfully. "We'll listen,
eh, boys?"

"For what you're paying us, you can talk about collect-
ing postage stamps and we'll listen," Juan said, a grin on
his face.

"Yeah, I'll even take notes," Xavier agreed, adding a
few mineshaft-deep chuckles.

The combination of relief at being away from the threat
of imminent danger, some light-headedness from tired-
ness and travel, and a swiftly delivered caffeine rush had
them more bright-eyed and lively by the time the clock
had passed two. The hotel room was small, Michael having booked the first on the list without worrying about details, and the air quickly grew stale from the scent of
bodies and cigarettes. To Streak's delight, Juan had also
brought some rather fine export produce of Jamaica, and
he knew how much could be inhaled without feeling useless in the morning. He settled back happily and breathed
out with an expression of sheer delight.

"I think I have that munchies feeling," he said. "What
do you say? Let's order a bucket of choccy biccies."

"I don't think Italian room service would be quite up to
that. But the airport's full of malls," Michael said. "I bet
you could find something."

Slowly and more languidly than usual, the elf got to his
feet and almost glided to the door, to search for the essential sustenance he craved.

"We haven't really discussed what happened in the
square," Serrin said.

"Just a bunch of assassins fried alive and we had to run
for our lives," Geraint said sarcastically.

"I didn't mean that. I meant the point of it," Serrin replied quietly.

"The point of what?"

"Not them, not the idiots and fanatics with the guns and the spirits and the death wishes. I meant the demonstration."

Geraint looked incredulously at him.

"The figure that appeared," the elf said impatiently. "The woman."

"I thought the severed head was pretty gross," Michael said with some disgust.

"A very potent image. Outside the church of St. Mark, our man creates an image of real blasphemy. The Magdalene with the head of John the Baptist, that's who she was. No wonder the Jesuits were so stunned."

"I don't get it," Michael said.

"That figure was the Magdalene. I'm certain. I saw her in the painting outside, the *Last Supper*. It's her, and there's something very, very strange about that painting."

"That's for sure," Michael said.

"And the painting of John is so odd. So androgynous. It's the same thing as the icon he left: the Shroud with the black woman's face. These images are highly powerful," Serrin said deliberately, as if admitting something to himself and being surprised in the process. "I just don't understand what they're actually saying. They're obvious blasphemy. But it's not being done just for shock value. There wouldn't be any point in that, and I don't think our man is up for pointless demonstrations. I just wish I could fathom exactly what it is he's saying."

"So he maybe has a thing about the Magdalene," Michael pondered. "I certainly agree that she's the central figure in the Last Supper painting."

"And unless I'm much mistaken, there are references in the Bible to the disciples being jealous of her and disliking her," Serrin said, reaching for the bedside table. "And for the first time in the history of this planet, someone somewhere is about to find the Gideon Bible in here of some actual bloody use."

He leafed through the pages for a moment, found the relevant passages, and nodded a couple of times.

"They protest to Christ that she's a whore and a bad

woman, and they clearly don't like his consorting with her. Read," he told Michael, tossing over the flimsy book.

"It's a long time since I did this," Michael admitted as he scanned the New Testament references.

"All right, so they do, and the painting shows that. But why have her show up with the head in the square?"

"That's what I can't figure," Serrin said. "It was Salome who brandished the head, as I recall. But our man has something about heads. The head on the original Shroud was separate from the rest of the body. And our man replaced it with another severed head, if you will."

"The Priory," Michael said slowly, clenching and unclenching his fist in an effort to reclaim a memory hidden deep inside his subconscious. "I remember something from my research on them. The Priory of Sion, our chummers back in Rennes. They claimed some descent from the Knights Templar, and the Templars were accused of worshipping a severed head that talked to them. At least, that's one of the things they were accused of."

"Along with sodomy and tax evasion, insider dealing and breathing in and out in a heretical fashion," Serrin said with a grin. "I rather think the Pope drummed up every charge he could possibly think of apart from lesbianism."

"They were men!" Michael protested.

"That's what I mean," Serrin said dryly.

"So what's our man doing playing with these images, and why is he so fixated on Leonardo?"

"That's the million-nuyen question," Serrin concluded. "And we don't know the answer." He paused while another thought slotted into place. "We also don't know where he is."

"Blondie was in Venice yesterday morning," Geraint reminded him. "If he was, then so was whoever he refers to as his master."

"That's logical."

"And I bet they aren't there now," Geraint reasoned.

"That also seems pretty likely."

"So where have they gone, and have we any clue as to where and how they're going?"

"Nope."

"So we have to stay passive and wait for another move

in the game, dammit!" Geraint growled. "I really don't like this. We're back where we were again."

Michael flipped open his laptop. "Now that they've made a move, I wonder if there might be some information for us. Ah, right. Good one." His face broke into a smile. Then he looked puzzled, even a little angry.

"Consider the Hejira," he read from the email drop. "That's it. Drek."

"The flight of the Prophet," Serrin said. "Mohammed fled from Mecca to Medina, wasn't it?"

"Yeah, you got it, but what's that got to do with all this? Don't tell me he's converted to Islam all of a sudden."

"Think metaphorically, Michael," Serrin said exasperatedly. "Mohammed left one city of divinity. Our man has left Venice."

"So he's saying he's some kind of prophet?" Michael sounded as if he disapproved.

"Maybe he is."

"And maybe he's suffering serious delusions."

"Maybe," Serrin smiled. "But we know he can sure as hell move mountains."

"All right. So he takes a flight and—" Michael looked astounded at the idea that had just leapt unbidden into his brain. "No, it can't be as simple as—"

He was already reaching for his traveling cyberdeck.

"As simple as what?" Geraint asked, puzzled.

"As simple as taking a flight," Michael muttered, stabbing keys.

"Well, of course not, you wouldn't mention the Hejira just to tell us that," Serrin said.

"Maybe not, but maybe it actually is something as simple as that and then something more, so let's find out. And maybe we can get a proper look at our man. God bless them, the Italian states routinely keep photodata on all arrivals and departures at their airports for a year after the flights. Originally for security reasons."

"Would that have included us?" Geraint fretted, implications tumbling into place.

"Sure would," Michael said. "So let's have a look."

"It's going to take forever to scan every passenger into and out of Venice today," Serrin lamented.

"Not necessarily," Michael said. "He'd have been with

Blondie, right? I feed a description of Blondie into Smithers and he rattles through, checking for anyone similar, and presto, all done in a couple of minutes. Smithers is very good at this sort of thing."

Juan and Xavier, who'd been quiet up until now though clearly engrossed in a discourse they didn't fully understand but whose logic they could appreciate, gave each other mystified glances.

Serrin threw them a grin. "Don't ask."

Just then, Streak came through the door, a pair of huge paper bags stuffed with snacks cradled in his arms.

"You greedy pig," Kristen said happily, snatching one of the bags as he passed her "You had a huge dinner."

"So why are you stealing my food?"

"I stole some of your dope," she explained with a giggle.

"Oh, well then, help yourself," the elf said cheerfully, depositing himself on a bed and wrenching open a large bag of chips.

Michael sat back and drummed his fingers on the table as he waited. Then the image began to form on the screen, increasing its resolution with every split-second pass.

"Actually we may not even get him. Remember how he fragged the Doge's scanners?" Serrin said.

Michael shook his head. "Not this time." He watched the screen carefully. "Oh, very clever. Very amusing. You bastard."

The ID was on the screen now, the unmistakable pony tail and cheerfully smiling young face of the man they knew as Salai, accompanying an older, equally slender but taller figure.

It was a serious face: a furrowed brow beneath a rather incongruous beret, an aquiline nose, and a chin neither weak nor exceptionally strong. The gray eyes were gentle and academic in appearance. He had that ageless look some middle-aged men acquire when their heads turn to silver or the gray of his long, flowing, slightly wavy hair. Around his lips a slight smile seemed to be playing. For all the world that smile reminded them at once of the Mona Lisa, the smile that had intrigued and bemused scholars of the ages.

Which was not surprising, since the face was unmistakably that of Leonardo da Vinci, younger than his surviving self-portrait showed him in his old age, but him nonetheless. Michael leaned back and laughed, to all appearances on the verge of clapping his hands and stamping his feet.

"Very clever, very good. So he decked the ID archive and changed the image. Neat, neat. I like it, my dear fellow. And now let us see where you've gone, on your Hejira.

"To Ahvaz," he said, mystified, after a few moments. "Our man took a flight to Ahvaz, on a chartered plane. At just after midnight."

"Tonight?"

"Of course tonight," Michael said testily.

"So where the frag is Ahvaz?" Streak asked through a mouthful of Growliebar.

"In southwestern Iran on the border with Iraq," Michael said, having already referenced the archival data.

"That's real bandit country, chummer," Juan informed him from across the room. "A hundred petty warlords and half of 'em still shoot last-century guns off horseback. Really damn primitive."

Serrin was staring closely at the printout that had now appeared of the image on the screen, but no one was taking much notice of him, apart from Kristen, who stood doing her best to peer over his shoulder. He was looking for something, or, rather, he knew something was in the image and he couldn't see what it was, where it was, what it meant.

She showed him.

"Ah," he said, with a low sigh of enlightenment. "Yes, of course."

"What is it?" Michael asked, breaking off from trying to find out more about Ahvaz and what kind of airport it had, if indeed it had one at all.

"His finger. The index finger on his right hand. Look."

"It's pointing upward. So what?"

Serrin struggled through his bag, cautioning an impatient Michael to wait, and extracted the book of paintings he was looking for.

"Look, John the Baptist, look. The picture is just his face and this image. Of the raised finger."

"So? One picture and—"

"It's in his painting of St. John-Bacchus as well. Look," he pointed out, as he flipped the page over to the following plate.

"All right," Michael said, taken aback now. "What's he saying?"

"Remember John?" the elf wondered aloud. "I'm not sure. But I know he didn't make this gesture by accident."

"A raised finger, eh?" Streak said. "I know what I mean by that."

"It's the index finger not the middle one," Serrin said impatiently.

"Ahvaz," Michael read. "It has a small airstrip built by an exploratory team from an oil company late last century. It's apparently reasonably stable at the present time, which means that the same bandits have held it for a year or more and no one has actually been shot out of the sky during that time, and I think we have to go there."

The samurai looked at each other and smiled, the lizard-like leer of all hired hands that says, "The price has just gone up!"

Geraint read the looks and the minds.

"Yes, you're on overtime and bonuses," he told them. "We're going to need you."

"We sure are," Streak said cheerfully. "Yessir, mad guys with big guns."

"I didn't mean—"

"I meant them," Streak said. "Out there in the desert. By the way, you guys got jabs for all the diseases you can catch?"

"Drek," Michael groaned. "I hadn't thought of that."

"We professionals get regular shots all the time," Streak said happily. "You never know where you might have to go next."

"We haven't got time," Geraint fretted. "We'll just have to buy several gallons of insect repellent. And water purifying tables. And—"

"Don't worry, Your Lordship. I was only pulling your pud, a wind-up. We've got all we need. Don't we boys?"

"Sure do," the ork grunted.

"Well, then, that's it. It's now three-twelve A.M. and I for one need some sleep," Michael said wearily. "Tomorrow we go to Ahvaz and we get our man." He flipped his deck off.

But, for once, Michael hadn't been secure enough. It would have appalled him at the time, as it did later when he realized it, to know that he'd been decked himself. The saturnine man responsible gave the information to his master without emotion.

"Then it is so," the man said as if expecting what he learned. "He has gone back to the heart of heresy. Like a dog returning to its own vomit. It is always so."

He considered his options. Of his best men, half were still recovering from the events in Venice. He doubted now whether hermetics or assassins would do the job for him. They had pursued their quarry long enough, and it had eluded them every time. He could no longer trust to the work of his juniors.

He reached for the private line and told the Vatican secretary that, despite the lateness of the hour, he would have to speak with His Holiness in person on a matter of most unique urgency.

Across the Mediterranean, in a fertile land spreading over the wide, lazy valley of the Karun River, a young man was shown through the underground part of the building, having already seen for himself the dome and the observatory above, extraordinary constructions for so poor a people in such a ravaged place. He smiled, and hugged the dark-eyed man who had showed him around so nervously, obviously desperate for his approval.

"It is so fine," Salai said. "It is exactly as it was designed. You have done so very well. This is a wonder to me."

The Arab smiled with relief, his beautiful, even white teeth gleaming in the soft light.

"And the Prophet will be here soon?"

"Within the hour, Tariq. He has only stopped to attend to one or two pressing matters along the way."

"This is such a great day for us," the man said with real fervor. "We had never thought to see such a day."

"And he will bring such great riches, and the greatest artists and scholars in his wake," Salai said cheerfully.

"We have been downtrodden long enough," the man said with some feeling.

"Indeed you have, and no longer. The Great Work will be done here and you will be exalted among men," the youth said soothingly. "You have already been rewarded for your faithfulness—"

He was cut short as Tariq sought to prevent any suggestion of ingratitude or impatience.

"We could not have built this without the money you gave us," he said at once, "and we have a fine hospital and school for the children. We know the Prophet's generosity to his people. It is simply that to have him among us—" His face was literally one of rapture.

"And here is the center," Salai said as he turned the final corner. "Ah, Tariq, this is a fine rendition.'

The mosaic must have taken the men of the place many years of painstaking work. Untold thousands of tiny fragments of gleaming, polished stone and crystal shone in the gentle light from the alcoves. The strange, haunting androgyny of Leonardo's *John the Baptist* was perfectly reproduced in the round shrine at the heart of the labyrinth.

"Wonderful. And then there is the deeper mystery, Tariq, but we shall not speak of this now."

"We await," the man said simply.

27

"So we breeze into a bandit heartland with a photo-ID and say, 'Excuse me, gun-wielding bandit-type fellow, but have you seen these men?' when we know one of 'em doesn't look like this anyway," Geraint pondered over a junk-food breakfast. The airport didn't seem to offer anything better, but at nearly noon—by the time they'd managed to wake, bathe, dress, and pack everything again—they didn't fancy the lunchtime menu and the junk was all they could face.

"We've got Blondie and he's impossible to miss with that pony tail," Michael replied.

"He could tuck it inside his jacket."

"Ever seen him do that?"

"He still might."

"Yeah, right, and that's why when his master fragged the photo ID, he left him so clear-as-day to make it hard for us," Michael replied with some venom. "Sorry. I'm still tired. I really do think he actually wants us to find him."

"That's bizarre."

"Is it really? Look, the guy has to have *some* ego. He's a genius—look at what he's done. He must have some desire for recognition. He must want someone to say 'look how clever I am'. He's just picked us, that's all."

"Fair enough, I suppose, but why us? I mean, there have to be a dozen teams out after him."

"There are. Matter of fact I caught a glimpse of Denison from MCT Frankfurt in Venice, unless I'm much mistaken. But I think we're closer to him than anyone else. After all, Renraku was the only corp that got the Shroud icon," Michael finished, pensively. "Still not sure why he did that."

"Well, we have nowhere else to go," Geraint said. "And if the Matrix crashes I lose a bundle, so let's get the fragger."

"We're actually going to have a day to spare," Michael said. "If this was the movies, we'd only get to him five seconds before he pressed the button, and you'd see the time display counting down the time before—bang!"

"Hmmm," Serrin said for no reason in particular. He'd been lost in his own thoughts for most of the morning, gazing at pictures of paintings and reading notes. It was obvious he wanted to be left alone until he'd worked out whatever he was wrestling with. Kristen was more than familiar with these moods by now, and had learned just to be around when the elf came back to the real world.

"I got permission to cross the relevant air space, so far as that goes," Streak told them. "Mind you, it's bound to be pretty dicey passing over Iraq, so frag that. We'll take the southern route over Saudi. I don't fancy the Turkish route, not with heading down the Caspian past Azerbaijan. They let off SAMs for recreation down there. Saudi's okay."

"Have we got everything we need?" Geraint asked him for the tenth time that morning.

"Your Lordship, you're already dosed with quinine and KZT and half a dozen other drugs, which is why you're so happy stuffing your face with the kind of drek you wouldn't dream of eating back home. Kind of frags your body that way." Streak grinned. "You'll sleep ten, twelve hours a night for a week or two as well. Trust me. Oh, and it'll turn your piss green, but that's always a good party trick if you can do it. If I was a bug, I'd avoid you like the plague."

He leant back and laughed loudly. "Whoops, mixed metaphor. You know what I mean."

"Fine," Geraint said, having indeed swallowed a disturbingly large number of oddly shaped tablets at Streak's behest before breakfast and then wondered whether he should show such naive trust. The hypo, at least, he knew had come from a hermetically sealed pack; it was the same pack he'd used a few times previously, prior to business jaunts to the Far East.

"Then let's go. No point in wasting any more time."

They paid their bill, headed through the small concourse to the VIP and private-passenger lounge, and made their way slowly to their small plane. The last week of their lives had seemed to hold so many plane journeys, taxi rides, and car trips that they were beginning to get homesick in their various ways—not that any of them was actually aware of it. What they all felt more than anything was relief that, at last, they were going to meet the man who'd caused them, one way or another, so much trouble.

They'd already been followed by more than one group of people, and been attacked by at least two of them. They'd also eluded at least two other groups of runners set on their tails by other corps who knew that Michael and his friends had some kind of head start. They'd missed only one tail, which was not entirely surprising for he did, after all, get immediate updates on all information Michael sent back to Renraku. Since Michael had already extracted a six-figure sum in expenses and fees from Renraku, he thought he had to give them some justification for that, and some account of his work. So it hadn't been too difficult to trace him.

The spy made his report and asked for instructions. He was told to wait for reinforcements and told which plane to wait for.

"Frag, that's military issue. I don't know if we can land in that thing," he balked.

The voice on the other end of the line was calm but steely. "Not to worry. We have records of the construction and very recent satellite confirmation of structural integrity," his boss said in the strangled vocabulary of the corporate executive. "Three craft will be despatched."

"Three?" The spy was incredulous. That meant the best part of two hundred paratroops and auxiliary military being flown into the place. Since they were supposed to be hunting a lone individual, this seemed to be overkill, to put it mildly.

"The locals may be hostile."

"Oh, come on, they're just primitives with bloody hunting rifles!"

"Don't be so patronizing. You know, your last profile suggested you might have latent racist tendencies."

"Don't sell me that crap," the man said with some feeling. "Twenty of these guys could take out a bunch of hijackers on a Boeing and you're sending in two hundred? What the frag is going down here? What are you sending me into?"

His suspicion was not unjustified. His superior paused for a moment before reassuring the man and smoothing his ruffled feathers.

"Don't worry Johanssen. We're just taking all due precautions. You do know, after all, something of what is at stake here."

"But what about Sutherland?'

"Don't harm him unless it's absolutely unavoidable. The same for the Welshman. He's a Brit noble and any trouble there could be extremely bad publicity."

"The others?"

"If they get in your way, remove them."

A pause. "I need formal warranty of all negotiating latitude that I have," Johanssen said at last. "What we can offer the man, if force fails."

"Force is not going to fail."

"Of course not. Fifty tons of black ice failed but two hundred goons will work. You know, it just might now."

"We'll deal with that if the need arises. You have this direct encrypted link to me and I'm available twenty-four hours a day."

Johanssen tapped off the telecom. He'd thought that tracking Sutherland, having managed to find him in Venice after losing him twice before, was all that he'd be asked to do until the call had come through from Chiba this morning. Now he was going to be accompanying two hundred or so Renraku troops on what looked like an orthodox single-target strike, and he just *knew* it was going to be a total disaster.

"It's going to be near eighty even at this time of year, and thank your lucky stars the town's on a river so it isn't even bloody hotter," Streak shot back at them over his shoulder from the pilot seat.

Though they'd taken the medicines they needed, had the sunblock they needed, and the weaponry they hoped they wouldn't need, they didn't really have hot-weather clothing. The elf had, however, given them copious amounts of talcum powder with which to dose themselves to prevent what he unpleasantly termed 'bollock rot' from excessive sweating. Exposing flesh to the sun to keep cool would mean more insect bites, despite the best efforts of all the repellent one could smear on, and some risk of sunburn for the fairer among them.

"Just what are we going to say when we get there?" Geraint mused, staring down at the featureless sands of the Saudi Arabian desert.

"That's a good question," Michael said. "My guess is that our man is going to have some kind of agenda of his own. He's going to want something."

"I thought we knew what he wanted," Geraint put in. "A very, very large sum of money."

"That's what he asked for, yet it doesn't make sense that it's all he wants. Why are we playing this game?"

"Hmm," was all the Welshman could manage.

"So when we get out of the plane and find our Leo lookalike, we've got to figure out a way to make sure he's not holding all the cards."

"What do we have?"

"Little more than our native wit and intelligence, I'm afraid."

"We're buggered then," said Streak cheerfully. "ETA twenty minutes. Not a rocket in sight. Thank heavens for that. No worries."

"We don't have parachutes," Michael observed.

"Yeah, but we've got some antimissile rockets. Never fly without them."

"Do they work?"

"Yup. Or, I should say they worked on this baby the couple of times they were needed."

"Do you really think we're going to get shot at coming in?" Michael asked earnestly.

Streak laughed heartily. "Nah, I don't think so. Latest update from Jane's says there's nothing too close to where we're going. It's lively down in Basra, but we're well away from that drekhole."

Events proved him right. As they began the descent to a runway that was little more than a parched strip of red-dened soil, everyone in the group felt the tension knotting inside them. It wasn't fear for their safety, but the excited hope that they might at last be at the end of the trail.

The wheels of the small plane bounced a few times along the bumpy runway, Streak deliberately perpetrating some mischief among his passengers with cries of "Whoa!" and "Oh no!", as if something serious might actually be happening. Finally, somewhat shaken and apprehensive, his passengers tottered out of the aircraft. To their surprise, a Rolls Royce, gleaming silver and gray in the brilliant sun, was standing by the huts that passed for airport buildings. With his arms crossed, dressed for all the world like an English chauffeur, the man they knew as Salai was lounging against the front door of the car. He waved to them cheerfully, as if welcoming old clients.

"You are expected," he said.

Streak drew his Predator from his jacket and advanced on the man.

"Now, you little fragger, let's see who our blackmailer is. Take me to your master," he growled.

The young man laughed. From the buildings behind him, forty or fifty men, armed with positively prehistoric carbines and rifles, emerged to form a very wide circle.

"My friends have slightly antiquated technology, but I

think you will find that, by sheer force of numbers, they exceed your capability," Salai said evenly. "There really is no need for this whatsoever. Demonstrations of such puerile machismo on your part only leave you lower in my estimation than you previously were, if that is possible. Now do me the honor of getting into the back of this extremely comfortable vehicle, which is far better than you deserve, for you all have a meeting to attend."

Streak shrugged his shoulders, pocketed the weapon, and called out rather needlessly to the others, who'd been in full earshot.

"He says get in the car. What do you reckon?"

"I reckon we get in the car," Michael decided for them all.

Everyone followed him. This time there was no problem fitting the seven of them into the back of the spacious limo. A thick glass partition separated them from Salai, and it appeared to be entirely soundproof since he did not respond to their queries. However, a loudspeaker in the back of the limp permitted him to pass messages of his own.

"Your journey won't be long and I trust it will be comfortable. No iced champagne in a silver bucket for Lord Llanfrechfa, I fear. You must understand the difficulties one encounters in such a remote location."

When they asked him why they were in such a remote location, they got no reply and swiftly realized the young man wouldn't respond to interrogation.

"I'm not at all happy with this," Streak bristled. "We could be going anywhere."

"If he'd wanted to harm us, he had all those guys at the airport," Michael pointed out.

"True, but I still don't like sitting around on me arse waiting for ten tons of crap to fall on me head," Streak announced.

"I could have handled them," Juan said evenly. He had dispensed with the usual heavy jacket and his almost grotesque cyberarm was all too apparent.

"Well, maybe," Michael said in an irritated tone, "but we're here to talk."

"Well, bulldrek away, Mister Negotiator," Juan said evenly. "Better than getting shot at, I guess."

As they made their way along the appalling road, the

car bumped and bounced far less than it should have, providing excellent testimony to the skill of the Rolls Royce engineers and their suspension systems. Now and then they passed straggles of people, with their donkeys and carts and baskets and homes, until eventually they saw the building in the distance.

The dome structure had what seemed to be silvered or smoked glass atop it, and it looked like an observatory some corporate or military interest might have constructed on the moon. Its futuristic and hi-tech appearance contrasted startlingly with the humble, simple nature of everything else in the place as they reached the outskirts of the town itself.

"What the frag is that?"

"And how the hell was it kept secret?"

"It was kept secret," Salai announced to them, proving that he could converse with them when he wished to do so, "because the local people are very, very loyal and do not speak to outsiders."

"But satellite systems would have detected this."

"They can be dealt with," Salai said offhandedly. "It's not difficult to crack them."

"I suppose if you can crash into the megacorps, then that wouldn't be so difficult," Michael tried as a gambit. This time he got no reply.

"This seems too easy, too quiet," Michael fretted after their attempts to grill Salai got them nowhere. "We can't just turn up and meet the man here. Something's got to go wrong somehow. It doesn't feel right."

"Feel right?" Kristen smiled. "I don't usually hear you talk like that, Michael."

"I'm not usually in this kind of situation."

"Where you're not in control."

"When I have no control whatsoever."

The conversation was cut short as the car came to a halt before the domed structure, and Salai hopped out to open the rear doors for them.

"Oh, and don't wave that silly gun at me," he told Streak in a bored voice. "I don't need men at my back here. One false move and you'll have the flesh stripped from your bones by spirits in a second."

"He's not lying," Serrin said flatly. He'd been as self-absorbed and quiet as he had been all day, thoughts and theories spinning in his head, but he took note of the presences here and warned Streak not to step out of line. Geraint, too, could sense the strong magical presence of the place. Though no magician, he had some latent psychic gift, and something this strong he could sense. He was uneasy.

The automatic doors of the building opened, but before Salai could show them in, a small group of local men rushed toward them, one of them grabbing Michael's arm as he walked toward the door.

"Is this not a great time? Are you with the prophet?" the man said eagerly, his eyes wide with near-rapture. Astonished, Michael could only mumble some inane pleasantry and bolt for the door like a rabbit for its hole.

"What the frag—"

"This way," Salai said with no word of explanation. They got into the elevator and descended some unknown distance before the doors swished open again to reveal the neat, cool, air-conditioned corridors of a subterranean complex.

"How the hell did you build this out here?" Michael asked, astounded.

"These people have been working on it for nearly twenty years," Salai said slowly. "They really are faithful. They have been for a very, very long time."

"The Mandaeans, you mean," Serrin said lightly, as if it were an offhand observation.

"Yes," Salai answered him with a gleam in his eye. "So you have begun to form a picture."

"I think I finally realize the importance of the image outside the basilica."

"Ah, that was a fine work. My master can craft great illusion—illusion that is great because it reveals the truth. So you think you know, then."

"No," the elf said slowly, "but I think I've learned not to ask the wrong questions."

Salai stopped and looked at him hard. "I may have underestimated you," he said. "Perhaps you will be ready for the move beyond. You've put your finger on the Johannite heresy."

"I read about it," Serrin confessed. It had only been a recent acquaintance.

"What on earth are you two talking about?" Michael demanded.

"It's the belief that John the Baptist was the true divine figure," Serrin said. "The people here have always believed that. Their sacred text is the *Book of John.* It was the image in the photo ID from the airport, the raised finger. 'Remember John'. It's something to do with this belief. That's why we're here. It's the only thing about Ahvaz that's singular. The cult is very small."

"Good, you're still only halfway there," Salai said with the relief of someone who's found that a bright and thoughtful child was not, after all, more intelligent than he or she ought to be. "And they may be few in number, but one faithful and loyal man is worth more than a hundred fainthearts. Isn't that true, Mister Mercenary?"

He looked at Streak and the elf saw him as someone not half so foppish and supercilious as he'd taken him to be.

"Too true, mate," the elf said. "Well, now where?"

"To meet my master. But I cannot permit any form of weaponry. That means, I regret, that our fine friend here"—he looked disapprovingly at Juan—"will have to remain outside. I cannot allow that thing," and he pointed to the cyberarm, "inside a room with my master."

"Of course," Michael said. He handed over his own gun, and told the others to do the same.

"I don't like this," Streak growled. "I feel naked."

"Get used to it," Michael told him. "We have no choice. We're not here to be threatened or harmed."

"Far from it. You are called as witnesses," Salai said with a returned air of annoying superciliousness.

"Bugger that. When they knock on the door it's definitely time to get the Predator out," Streak growled.

"I hardly meant Jehovah's witnesses," Salai said impatiently. "Nothing could be less apt, under the circumstances.

"And now enough of this. If you're ready, it's time to meet my master and behave with the deference he deserves."

Michael already had whoever they were going to meet tagged as a serious nutcase. Brilliant, obviously, but the man gibbering about the Prophet outside made him think they were about to meet someone with some very serious delusions indeed. He couldn't know that the belief was

useful to that very person, and one he allowed to remain
unchallenged not least because it gave comfort to simple
people who had, in return, given him sweat, labor, and
love for many years now.

The internal doors down the corridor swung open.
They were made of smoked glass and revealed nothing
inside the room, so when what lay beyond them was revealed, the newcomers did not have the benefit of fore-
warning, and they were astounded by the scene before
them.

The figure sat with his back to them in a high-backed
chair, only the long, flowing gray hair visible to them,
save for his long-fingered hands resting on the arms of
the chair. The walls were covered with designs and
sketches, finely rendered, apparently blueprints for optical systems of extraordinary complexity. On the desk before the figure was what had to be a cyberdeck, though it
was unlike any they'd ever seen. It made the finest customized Fairlight look like a child's toy. There was not a
right-angle on it. It was sculpted, apparently of ivory or
something similar, and had fluted edges and the eerie, un-
real hyperreality of some alien artifact. It looked like it
could only ever exist inside the extreme geometrical perfection of the Matrix, not out here in a real world of chaotic imperfections. Pearly light glowed around it, and in
the near-darkness of the room it seemed for a moment
that a reflection of that light covered the head of the
seated figure like a halo. The nimbus winked out of existence and the figure turned around, the chair swiveling
through a hundred and eighty degrees.

My God, Michael thought, this is the finest cosmetic
job I've ever seen in my life. Forget the supermodels and
the simsense stars, this is an absolutely perfect replica.
Younger, of course. The photo ID wasn't decked at all.

Staring at them, quietly and gravely and with his hands
folded gently in his lap, was a person who for all the
world was the perfect image of Leonardo da Vinci.

28

"I must commend your plastic surgeon," Michael said. "It's a magnificent job."

"Shut up," Serrin said swiftly. He knew, although the others—including Streak—had not realized it, that the figure was an elf. The long, flowing hair concealed the most obvious distinguishing feature, the ears, and the looseness of the figure's simple robed garment hid his body shape. But Serrin could tell instinctively that the man was elven, and that he was not the kind of person to trivialize himself with cosmetics. And all the implications of that made Serrin very worried indeed.

"I'm glad you are here," the figure said in English, in a quiet voice that struck them all with the unstated force of its serene dignity. Seated simply in his chair, there was an aura about him that stopped wisecracks and levity in their tracks.

"Why are we here?" Michael asked, hoping to get the edge by doing the questioning.

The elf regarded him levelly, unblinking. "For different reasons, actually. In your case, because I expect to deal with Renraku through you. I also hope you may come here on a more permanent basis, but we can talk about that later."

Michael ignored that last, surprising gambit. "Who are you?"

"You can see who I am."

"I can see who you appear to be."

"You can see who I am," the elf repeated, without any impatience, but with a slight sadness instead. "I am who I appear to be."

"No. Impossible."

"Why?"

"Leonardo da Vinci has been dead for more than five hundred years."

The elf smiled slightly. "We've grown used to such

subterfuges," he said simply. "There are times when it becomes necessary."

"I don't believe you."

"Perhaps at the moment you can't," the elf said sadly.
"It doesn't matter at this time. Are you interested in
this?"

Michael looked longingly at the deck the man indicated
with a wave of his slender hand.

"Come and see," the elf invited him.

"I don't see any hitcher 'trodes," Michael said uncertainly, his curiosity struggling with his fearful confusion.

"You won't need that. Shall we see what your friends
are doing in Chiba?"

"Are you serious? No, I'm sorry, that was a stupid
question. You've done it before, haven't you?"

"Very simple," the elf said. "Anyway, you need no
jack. Just sit down."

Michael sat in the chair next to the elf while the others,
unsure of what they should be doing in this ritual, kept
quiet and waited to see what would happen.

Michael had heard of the otaku, of course, the
cybershamans who needed no deck to run the Matrix, but
claimed some mystical communion with it, a union that
let them use strange, singular skills in their autistic minds
to work within it. And the elf worked in the same way,
but he also channeled whatever he was doing through the
deck, save that he used no physical link with it. He
guided Michael's persona—in itself an impossibility since
Michael's own deck was still in their plane, back at the
airstrip—deep into the very heart of the Renraku Chiba
core system. Everything within it, the icons of company
deckers and reactive ice, was moving at a snail's pace.
They traveled through the system and the elf accessed
some personnel records of Renraku's top executives and
danced back out of the system as easily as he'd pene-
trated it. To Michael, leaving it was like waking from a
dream.

"How is this possible?" he said in utter wonder. "Are
you otaku?"

"I have their skills," the elf said, "though they aggre-
gate with this deck. It works on paraoptical principles. It
interfaces with the mind more or less at the speed of
light."

"Impossible," Michael said, knowing he was wrong.

"You seem to be saying that a great deal, Michael Sutherland. Do you not believe your own senses? No matter. I will go into the details with you later," the elf promised. "However, unless my information is much mistaken, we have some rather urgent business at the moment which is more pressing. In about eight minutes a missile is due to hit this building and, unless I am much mistaken, it will probably bear a tactical nuclear warhead."

"What?" Geraint almost exploded. This was all too much to take.

"Oh, there's plenty of time," the elf said calmly. "It will be shot down automatically. However, one of the reasons I wanted you here was to witness the event. You can go and take a look at the wreckage and verify the details for me. Actually, it means that the military men who accompany you will be useful additions to your number. I hadn't expected them, but the unexpected can be rewarding."

"Whose missile is it? And why?"

"The nuclear missile belongs to the Vatican," the elf said. "And they hope to prevent me letting the world know a great many things they don't want anyone to know."

"I simply do not believe this," Geraint protested. "This must be some kind of illusion or lie."

"Which is why I very much want you to go and see what's left of the wreckage when it's shot down," the elf said very earnestly. "I want independent witnesses to prove to the world that the Vatican took what I knew seriously enough to try to murder several thousand helpless, innocent people around this place in order to keep it all from reaching the ears of this hungry world."

"I'll scan it out," Streak said. "And I'll find out where it was manufactured and whose it was. He can't con me on that kind of thing."

"That's what I hoped," the elf said, really in earnest now. It struck home. He needed them for this, and they had to take him seriously.

"But why? What do you know? How can it possibly be worth a nuke? And what does it have to do with your run-

ning the Matrix and threatening every corp out there?"
Michael asked in a flurry of queries.

"As to that, I just want the money. I need it. I have
work to do on a scale beyond what I can manage to earn
from what I do quietly here and there. Such funds got this
place built, but now I need much more."

"Twenty billion each from eight megacorps?"

"Well, I didn't think I'd get it from all of them. Actually, twenty billion would be a good start. I think I
can persuade Renraku to accommodate me," the elf said.
"On balance, I deemed them the best option for negotia-
tions. They'd get a lot in return."

"They'd bloody well have to," Michael said, amazed.

"Well, there is this," the elf said, indicating the deck.
"Is this worth twenty billion?"

Michael was stopped in his tracks. He stared wildly at
the elf, his breath coming hard.

"Frag me, it is. I reckon it is."

"Well, it's only a toy," the elf said, "so perhaps I can
hold out for more than that."

"Isn't this eight minutes getting a bit, well, shorter?"
Streak suddenly asked. He ignored Michael's expression
of sheer disbelief at the elf's comment that the deck was
only a toy.

"Yes, yes, Salai will deal with it," the elf said impatiently.

"Antimissile rockets can't be counted on with a nuke if
it's smart," Streak insisted.

"It won't be done with such primitive things," the elf
told him.

"So, how?"

"Well, as I think they put it these days," the elf said
with a slightly sad smile but a smile nonetheless, "it's all
done with mirrors. Focused lasers. The warhead will be
vaporized. The man casing will remain intact, though, for
you to inspect and identify. There will also be sufficient
radioactive material for you to collect a sample of and
trace. I have suitable protective clothing available, I believe. That's the kind of thing Salai handles."

"Who is Salai?" Kristen asked suddenly, her tongue
working at last.

"You'll have to forgive the name," the elf said. "An affectation when I adopted him. He's otaku, but a very ver-

satile young fellow and far less antisocial than most of them. He does, however, have some of the more negative traits of his historical antecedent."

"He gambles, spends too much, and is rude to his master," Serrin said, almost smiling. He'd studied the biographies carefully.

"Yes, all of that," the elf said. "You have done some homework. I expected that of you from the reports. I could not be certain that Mr. Sutherland would recruit you, but when he did, I was pleased. Merlin thinks well of you, I know."

"You know Hessler."

"Oh, very well. We have known each other for, shall we say, some years. I must add, though, that he did not tell me anything of what passed between you. He simply allowed me to know that you were someone who could be worked with. That was important knowledge. I very much hope he is right. We shall all have to."

"Look," Serrin said, "we're almost totally in the dark. We have to know what's going on. You say too much we can't understand."

"You had to start from the icon in the Matrix," the elf told him.

"Yes. It identified Leonardo. It's also heretical, and in some sense fraudulent. The Shroud is a fake."

"Of course it is," the elf said. "Pope Innocent wanted it done. Innocent! Hah! It had a history, entirely superstitious and unconfirmed, but he thought it would make an excellent inspiration for the gullible. He really was an unprincipled old bastard, even by the standards of the times, and that's saying something. Since it seems some, many, still believe in that ridiculous cloth, it's plain that he knew what he was doing."

They all realized the elf was talking as if he'd dealt with a Catholic pope dead for more than half a millennium, but Serrin didn't seem fazed at all. He continued with his line of thought, each question marking another faltering but significant step in his reasoning.

"The Shroud's face is Leonardo's. So is that of the Mona Lisa, and you put her on the Shroud icon, except that you made her black."

"Forgive me," the elf said. "I never could resist a little self-advertisement."

"You've come among a heretical cult that believes John the Baptist is the true son of God. Why?"

"They're wrong, of course," the elf said evenly, apparently unaware that he wasn't answering Serrin's question. "But they're one step closer to the truth."

"Why is the Magdalene the real focus of the *Last Supper*?" Serrin suddenly shot at the elf. Gray eyes met him firm and full, and the elf looked as if some weight had fallen from his shoulders. Serrin was suddenly shot through with a chill, a realization and understanding that hit him full in the heart and guts.

He is Leonardo.

And that is not all he is.

"So, now we come to the truth," Leonardo said, rising to his feet. He had a sweep of grandeur about him that impressed itself even on the samurai, who stood stock-still looking at him with near-awe on their faces.

"You must understand, the Mandaeans were not taken in by the Pauline propaganda. They knew all the reasons why the older stories were true; the significance of Paul arriving in Corinth and Ephesus claiming himself to be the first Christian missionary and finding churches already there, as the *Acts of the Apostles* so foolishly gives away; and the churches were those of John. They also grasped the deep significance of baptism, and the Muslim people hereabouts regard their long adherence to that practice as very, very strange. The central significance, of course, is that the baptizer always initiates the baptized. He is senior to him, more initiated, more acquainted with the mysteries. He is no follower. He is the bearer of the knowledge, not the acolyte in search of it. How that managed to turn into a tale of John being little more than a spiritual warm-up act is one of history's more endearing little tales.

"John, indeed, was a messenger and a prophet, but not for who most people think. The politics of what ended up as what are laughably called the canonical gospels is, again, an intriguing historical study. For he served someone quite different. As I do too, in my way. And that way grows very important now."

"This is madness," Michael said. "You speak as if—"

"I know, as if I'd been there," the elf finished impatiently. "You won't believe me so I won't bother with that. Not now. There's an easier way to let you know."

"The Magdalene," Serrin said insistently. "The Magdalene figure. The face on the Shroud. The face at the supper."

"Yes," the elf whispered. "Now, Serrin, I could tell you to go to the cathedral at Notre Dame, or in a hundred other cities throughout Europe and Asia Minor—though Notre Dame is the best example because Paris is the city of love—and gaze on the Black Madonna looking out over her people. It is an image they have never been able to replace with their wretched medieval Virgin, no matter how many times they mistranslated that one, simple little word. Because a virgin is barren and joyless, a symbol only of fear and body-hating revulsion, and the true Madonna is close to the lives and hearts and souls of all people and her spirit infuses them instead of denying the rightful wholeness of their souls. The Magdalene was her priestess, and John her initiate. *That's* the heresy. That's what's worth a nuclear warhead bearing the Papal seal. And it's the secret I seeded into all those designs, and I laughed at the popes and their venal servitors who paid me to create those idols of false worship. The secret has always been there for anyone with eyes to see, right in front of the noses of those who would deny her."

The air in the chamber started to acquire the tang of metal and ozone. A figure began to manifest behind him. Tall as the elf seemed to be, risen with exaltation, the woman behind him seemed to be of unearthly height and fullness, richly dressed in satin and pearls and the gems of an ancient potentate's treasury of pillage of far-flung, exotic lands.

Serrin knew from experience that it was the materialized form of a Great Spirit, but it seemed to him to carry an emotional charge far greater even than that he'd known on the very, very few occasions he'd met such a being.

"She is Isis," the ancient elf whispered, the only one able to speak at all. "This is my mistress and my passion. This is the truth. What you have been told until this day is lies. It is now time that this truth be known by all the people of this world, and many people are very, very afraid of that."

The woman was impassive, the ebony of her skin perfectly smooth, her eyes closed, her hands folded into her lap. She stood utterly still, and when they looked upon her they felt an indescribable yearning, a longing for her presence to stay with them and for much more. The incarnation faded, impassive to the end, giving no recognition of either their presence or their existence.

"There is an occult belief that has persisted, though it has never been widely held," the elf said finally, once they were alone again in the chamber, "that Biblical events are merely a retelling of the story of Isis and Osiris. In such beliefs, Osiris is identified with Christ. There is a darker understanding and knowledge of this.

"If you want the simple translation, for Osiris read John; for Isis read the Magdalene; for Salome read Nephthys; the rest you can fill in for yourselves. If you don't know, you'll learn, soon enough."

"If you go to the world with this," Serrin said slowly, trying to regain some composure, "you'll be regarded as simply another nut."

"I think not," the elf said evenly. "For a start, it's time I showed them all how I made the Shroud for Innocent. There will be the debris of the missile you are here to verify. Then again, I do have something of an advantage when it comes to dealing with the lies history has told us.

"After all, I was there."

"I can't take this in," Michael said, shrugging in helplessness. By the looks on the faces of the others, neither could they.

"You doubt? I can identify with that," the elf said, suddenly grinning. "The gospels do manage to record my presence with that tag, after all."

"But what are you going to do here? Why so much money? For what?" Serrin pressed him.

"Because of the Works," the elf told him. "I want to bring some of the better minds of the world here. I remember the old times, all those great artists and engineers at the behest of the Medicis and the Borgias. Ah, such times! I want that again.

"Indeed," he continued, suddenly almost humble, "I hoped that I might invite some among you to join me. I think you, Mr. Sutherland, would enjoy working here."

Michael looked at the cyberdeck and wondered. Fine,

he's glitched, but by hell whatever that thing is I wouldn't say no to looking into it. Just a few weeks, maybe . . .

"And you, Serrin, you I would be glad of for the Great Work."

"And that is?"

"That is something deeper and darker, a greater mystery," the elf said without the pretension such words might well have carried from anyone else. "There are times in the history of the world, Serrin, when mana rises and falls. When it is potent and strong, many wonders and glories arise. An Awakening, some have called it. We are in such a time now. But dangers come with such times, dangers all but beyond imagining. I must work with others to counter those dangers."

"That sounds both vague and paranoid," Serrin told him.

"It may, but you are noted for your paranoid nature and at times you, too, are rather vague," Leonardo said tartly. The sharpness of his voice was so unusual that Serrin almost startled, and his mouth formed into a smile for an instant before he reassumed his usual grave appearance.

"You know of astral quests, of the threshold, of the dangers of the metaplanes—or you think you do."

"I know something of such things." Serrin wasn't sure where this was leading.

"There are dangers beyond which are very great and real. At this time, the barrier between us and those dangers is eroding and must be shored up. To do so will take immense effort. That is the Great Work. However, I ask only that you spend a month, perhaps, learning of such things and deciding whether you are willing. Then you may—"

The elf broke off without warning. He cocked his head to one side for a moment, as if listening to something inaudible to anyone else.

The moment's respite gave Streak the chance to tell Serrin about something whose significance he'd finally realized. "You know, I saw something in that book you had on the Shroud," he said. "Did you realize the face doesn't have any bloody ears?"

Serrin had missed that. He'd seen the presence of things that had remained hidden or at best obscured, but he'd missed an absence of something. If this elf was really who he said he was, or rather if the face of Leonardo's was one he'd worn, then the missing detail was perfect. A self-portrait with the identifying characteristic carefully omitted.

And, of course, what irony there must have been in the gullible of the centuries worshipping an image of himself.

"There may be some trouble," Leonardo informed them. "Several military aircraft have landed at the airstrip. I think that Renraku may have been overenthusiastic in their approach to potential discussions with me, which is not wholly unexpected. Michael, I would very much appreciate it if you would mediate here. I am very eager to speak with them. I had hoped we could come to some arrangement, as I suggested to you. Will you help me?"

"I'll do what I can," Michael said nervously.

"By the way, Salai tells me it is now time you went out into the desert with him," the elf said to Streak. "The missile has been brought down safely, and we have the protective clothing and measuring instruments you will need."

"Show me to it, unless you'd rather I took up a position in the bunker and helped you blow away these yobbish gatecrashers for you," Streak said cheerfully, his good humor recovered after seeing Serrin surprised by his insight.

Michael and Streak got into the elevator with the young man, and as they ascended Michael wondered what he was going to say. Outside the building, the Renraku military had taken up their positions and were clearly ready to begin any bombardment deemed necessary.

Michael thought about it, and walked out into the hot air of the afternoon with his palms out, announcing who he was and the fact that he was working for Renraku too. Johanssen told the commanding officer to hold fire, definitely and absolutely.

"Em, hi, guys. Look. I don't know how to say this, but you really don't want to blow up what's in there.

"Frankly, at twenty billion you'll be getting a bloody bargain."

Johanssen looked at him, reconsidered his order, then picked up the phone to Chiba.

29

The second of May was the day when eight megacorps were scheduled to have their Matrix systems blown to frag and back. Midnight came and went and nothing much happened. At one o'clock, seven of them got a message informing them that their tardiness in making the due payment was reprehensible and that as a result their systems would, periodically, be subject to complete surveillance—and that all of their future operations would have to be conducted with this fact in mind. Only four heart attacks were recorded among the relevant personnel during the following hour, which, given their usual bad habits of smoking, drinking, and eating far too much expense-account drek, wasn't much more than par for the course. Moreover, given their natures, it was probably more or less what they deserved.

The eighth corp was trying to figure out how the frag they could possibly manage to justify such a transfer of funds to the shareholders. Two of their best researchers had been dragged out of bed, piled into a plane, and despatched to Ahvaz. Within an hour of their arrival they'd agreed with Michael that twenty billion was a pittance.

"We can call it a sponsored R&D lab, write it off against taxes as profit reinvestment and retooling," was the best the accountants and marketing people could come up with.

"And who's going to be in charge of it?" came the obvious reply.

"This elf who calls himself Leonardo. Barking mad but he's a fragging genius according to our to computer guys, and we pay them enough to know shit from salami on rye. Anyway, he says he can do it anytime he likes. Bust our systems, that is."

"What's he offering for twenty billion?"

"The deck. Training for some of our top people. Priority access to research findings. Look, our military guy got a peek at a defensive laser system he had in there. Said it was awesome. Not only that, nobody but *nobody* picked it up on sat. He's got to be good. Think about what we could do with this kind of stuff."

Management thought about what it could do with it all, and a lot of them fantasized about screwing the frag out of everyone else on the block.

They began to talk about payment in installments.

Back in London, a group of recent arrivals were trying to shake off an all-encompassing exhaustion and put the pieces together for themselves. Much of what had happened was still taking its time sinking in.

"Renraku looks like they could buy into it," Michael told them. "Pay the guy hefty doses and get the research works. He says it's all toys to him anyway. It's that Great Work he's really into."

They'd had an hour or so with Leonardo after the arrival of the Renraku squad, and then the elf asked them to leave and think over his offers. There was so much to do, he said, and too much urgency to spend longer with them.

"They may come next week, or it may be ten years from now," he'd told them, though his words were mostly for Serrin, "but come they will, unless the work is done in time."

"I wonder, I really do," Michael mused. "I mean, that deck. It was incredible just hitching. The chance to study it . . . and Renraku would pick up the tab. They're talking about building him a huge lab out there. They'd love him in Chiba, obviously, but he won't go. He won't leave the people of Ahvaz. And I don't think Renraku will try to kidnap him, and they'll sure as hell go to extreme lengths to make sure no one else does."

"It was funny hearing him talk about Venice," Kristen recalled. She had a smile on her face nearly all the time these last few days.

"Yeah. Just something he wanted to do, get rid of all of the drek in the canals. 'Couldn't bear to see it like that, so filthy.' "

"I wished we'd had more time with him," she said wistfully.

"Do we really believe it?" Geraint was still turning the impossibility of it all over and over in his mind. "Do we really say to ourselves, this is Leonardo in the flesh, alive after half a millennium?"

"I don't know, and it troubles me," Serrin said. But he already had something else in mind, and was eager to find a pretext to take himself off.

"Not to mention all that slot about John and Isis and what not. What on earth is anyone going to make of that?"

"The Vatican took it seriously enough to try and nuke him," Streak pointed out. "It was their missile, no question. I just sent him the full ID. Got some dosh back too. Working for two masters these days, boss."

Geraint grinned back at him.

"I'm not sure whether what he was saying was true," Michael said slowly. "I know he believed every word of it, of course. But, even if it's true, I reckon that religious belief and reason are sworn enemies. He may have the evidence, he may have alleged firsthand accounts, but I reckon blind faith won't bow to that. Many still believe in the Shroud, even long after science has proved it a fake. I think he overestimates the reasonableness of people."

"He's got a good precedent for that," Streak chipped in. "Let's hope nobody nails this bloke to a tree for doing it."

"Yeah," Geraint said. "But do we believe it?"

There was a long silence. Michael broke it.

"We were there."

"Sure."

"And we got it from the horse's mouth."

"So what are you saying?"

"I think . . . I believe him," Michael said, as though weighing every word. "And if that means that I think history is a lie and a lot of people have suffered and been deceived for two thousand years because of that, then I think . . . I think I believe that too. But don't quote me."

"I wouldn't dream of it," Geraint gave a small, surprised laugh. "I reckon, however that I just might agree with you."

Serrin got away with Kristen in the early afternoon and began to drive westward. He didn't know if he'd be expected, but when he arrived at the end of one of those English early-summer afternoons of real beauty and pleasantness, the cat, at least, was waiting for them. He'd known it would be.

"Hello, puss," Serrin said. "I have the same gift for you as before, but this time I shall retreat at once so that you can enjoy it without being embarrassed." He knelt down and placed the catnip-stuffed cloth mouse before the cat's front paws, got up, and walked away without looking back. The cat dragged the mouse off under a lavender bush and began to savage it.

Merlin opened the door and looked out uncertainly, even slightly fearful, his eyes darting from one of them to the other.

"Are you all right?"

"I think so," Serrin said, patting him on the shoulder. It might have seemed odd to him once; this was not a being of flesh and blood, but the spirit had a naive kindness rarely found in beings so made. The old elf was at the foot of the stairs, about to ascend them, and he turned at the sound of visitors. When he saw Serrin and Kristen, he smiled faintly and waved them in.

"He was telling the truth, wasn't he?" Serrin asked, hardly waiting to be seated before beginning his questions. "History records him as Leonardo. I have no idea what other names and faces he may have worn."

"He has had many but, unlike some of us, he's always been very careful about that," Hessler agreed. "Often he has lived very quietly, especially when the mana was low, but he always becomes restless after a time. It's been hard for him to disguise himself. He is known among us for his brilliance. It is reflected in his true name, but I could hardly tell you that." The old elf smiled at the appropriateness of his expression. Reflection was the ideal word.

"I'd begun to wonder, for some time now, about how some of our people have beliefs about the return of spirits and the paths and the wheel of existences," Serrin said. "And it has somehow never seemed quite right to me."

"It is a belief carefully fostered," Hessler said deliberately.

"It is not that we return to other lives. Some of the People live very long lives indeed," Serrin said quietly. "Once or twice I have heard whispers, less than rumors really. I did not take them seriously at the time. They seemed, well, so wild."

Hessler smiled. "I am glad to hear it."

"You are one such," Serrin said. It was a statement rather than a query.

"I am," the elf affirmed. "But, of course, I trust that you will never mention this to anyone. I have seriously misjudged you if you do."

"Of course not," Serrin protested. "I just needed to know. For myself."

"Then you should consider carefully the offer that was made to you."

"By Leonardo? I still can't get used to calling him that."

"Get used to it. It is who he was and how he wishes to be known still."

"The other things," Serrin said slowly. "His belief. What he called his passion. Isis. What of her?"

"Now that," Hessler said carefully and in measured tones, "is something about which I cannot instruct you. That is an understanding that comes only through initiation. Some things one cannot give to another in words, because words are not enough to express their force and true nature."

"But was it true? Is the history of the West such a lie then?

"No, wait, I know." Serrin laughed after his flash of intuition. "You're going to tell me that it depends on what is meant by truth."

Hessler joined in the laughter for a moment, and then looked serious once more.

"It is so. If you want to know his truth, then you had better go to him. Only he can tell you."

"But his so-called Great Work. Is it a lie or an illusion? Would I be wasting my time?"

"Oh, no," Hessler said, very swiftly it seemed. "That you would not. The danger he speaks of is all too real. I wish more of us would come to terms with it. But some are dilettantes, some are resigned, some have lost the will after so many years, and as for one or two of those who were once among us—" He broke off with a slight shake of the head. "No, we won't speak of that . . ."

"They have been here before," he went on, "and lain waste to every living thing they could ravage. No, Serrin, this is no illusion nor lie. That is why he calls his inventions toys, why Merlin told you that wrecking those computer systems didn't matter. Oh yes, I know he did, he's been rather indiscreet." He laughed again. "But I expect that of him. The wonderful thing is, he's always indiscreet within my own limits of indiscretion."

They both laughed now, and Serrin sat quietly with his hands wrapped around those of his wife, thinking deeply.

"So you think I should go."

"Not least," Hessler said, "because you did inadvertently make some enemies once or twice and I know that some powerful mages have a mark on you."

"Those of Tír na nÓg, Yes." Serrin wondered how Hessler knew about that old skirmish, then realized he'd have been more surprised if the other elf hadn't known.

"Go to him and such troubles will vanish like dew on the grass this morning," Hessler told him. "If Kristen agrees."

"I had thought of asking her, when we got home."

"You missed it, you know. Merlin said something to you. He told you that she was important, and you missed it. The Black Madonna." Hessler regarded Kristen with a gaze as old as Europe. "Your face, my dear, could have told them all they needed to know, if they hadn't been so preoccupied with reason."

She blessed him with a heavenly smile.

"I suppose that is so," her husband agreed. "I have to know. Is it really true? You evaded me."

"You want me to take responsibility for telling you whether two millennia of history is a lie?" Hessler asked him.

"I do."

"I have lived long enough not to be lured into replying to such questions."

As Serrin and Kristen strode hand in hand back down the path, Serrin's mind was far away in Scotland, down along the rugged coast under the gray skies, the cool of even a summer day, of the quietude and solitariness of the land. He needed time to think.

"Do you want to go?" Kristen asked.

"Michael's going to be there, I'm sure of it. He mentioned a few other names to me. There will be some re-

markable minds there if he manages to persuade only half
of them to come."

He was obviously still wrestling with it, but she
pressed him.

"Tell me. Do you really want to go?"

"Half of me does, but the other half is very unsure," he
confessed. "There's also the matter of what you think.
Damn it, I'm so happy just to be at home with you. Walking along those stony beaches, wrapped up against the
weather. I've gotten used to the place. It suits a part of me
so well. But maybe you'd like a place in the sun again.
Tell the truth, Kristen."

"I think," she said playfully as he opened the passenger
car of the door for her, "that anyone who calls the Black
Madonna his passion is all right by me. Even if he's
crazy. Maybe especially if he's crazy."

It was in her face then, it passed through his mind. The
dark face was the biggest clue, the face on the icon.
Kristen was with us every hour of every day and we just
didn't see it. I just hope that isn't a rebuke to me. Looking at her face now, I think I know the answer.

"Why don't we try some sun for a month or two and
see what happens?" she said for him.

They got into the car and buckled their seatbelts. She
turned and looked earnestly at him.

"Anyway, Merlin says we really ought to go."

"You crafty little *skullie*." He poked her in the ribs. "I
thought you were just saying goodbye to him in the
kitchen."

"He'll be there from time to time, he says. He told me
that Leonardo can get rid of the mark those Irish mages
have on you. When they took blood from you, when you
crossed them. You'd be safe. No more bloody long hours
crafting those rituals to protect yourself."

"It isn't just for me, you know that," he protested
rather weakly. He felt himself accused of spending too
much time on his own, and what made the accusation hurt
was that it was true.

"I know," she said, slipping an arm around his waist.
"But wouldn't it be great not to have to worry anymore?"

"Yeah, it would." A sudden spasm of hurt and regret
passed through him, and he couldn't hide it. She leaned
across and hugged him hard.

"Darling," she said.

"Yes, frag it, it would be such a bloody relief," he said in a thick voice, gritting his teeth to steady himself. It hurt to admit it.

He turned the key in the ignition and they headed for the highway.

Michael and Geraint sat drinking brandy together in the early evening, Streak having taken himself back south of the river with a hefty payoff ruining the smooth lines of his black jacket. That they would see him again they had little doubt.

"Well," Michael said after the final phone call, "some kind of deal is being worked out. It's just down to the details really. Apparently, our friend wants me to act as liaison for future arrangements with Renraku."

"Why didn't he just go to them with the deck and ask?" Geraint said. "Why all this fuss and games?"

"Part of it, for sure, was his beliefs," Michael said, having pondered this long and hard. "He wanted witnesses. You have to admit that a lot of powerful people went to a frag of a lot of trouble to find him and try to erase him from the history books once and for all. People who weren't involved with the Matrix thing. The Jesuits. The Priory.'

"Yeah, the Priory? What of them?"

"From what I can make of it they believe they're the protectors of the Magdalene's bloodline. And their initiation secret is his, the sacredness of the Magdalene rather than the Virgin. Their line, I think, is that they just didn't want that being blown open. I've made some enquiries," he told a surprised Welshman. "They're only a small group now and when they got fragged at Rennes, what survived wasn't organized enough to follow or hassle us.

"And I've been wondering, you know. What if I'd been alive for six hundred years or more? What if this guy isn't lying? And what if I had a mind like his? I'd be bored as hell. Would I play games? You bet I would. But it was only partly a game. Partly it was bloody real. That bullet came within a few centimeters of Kristen's head, remember."

"We all got close enough at one time or another," Geraint agreed. "I don't think it was a game in play. It was a game in earnest."

"And let's just entertain the possibility that he really has been around that long. Let's say he is or was Leonardo. Can you imagine talking with him? About Michaelangelo, Verrochio, the great artists and designers? About the Borgias and the Medicis? Not to mention all the times he's lived through since! Let's say he really was there. Talking with him would be incredible!"

"You're taking his offer seriously."

"With the Renraku money I am. Part of a second Renaissance? You bet I will. I could use the regular employment."

Michael put down his glass, and changed tack.

"Those cards," he continued, wondering now. "Back in Florence. All those women. I thought you were reading something else."

Geraint shook his head, realizing Michael had thought it had something to do with the Countess. "I knew a woman was on the mind of our target. So many of the major arcana, it was as clear as crystal. Unfortunately, I had no way of knowing just how that could be. And I damn well should have with that deck. Hang it, it was allegedly based on Egyptian designs. A fraudulent claim, but we were after the designer of a fraudulent shroud, and Isis is an Egyptian figure.

"It was bloody perfect," he said. "And I didn't see it."

"You couldn't have seen it."

"Maybe not. Aw, sod it, Michael, I can see this bloody bottle of five-star and by God we're going to finish it tonight."

Hessler and Merlin took an evening stroll around the Tor, just as they were in the habit of doing at this time of day and at this time of year, weather permitting.

"Don't you dare tell him the truth," the elf said to the spirit. "He can find it out for himself."

Merlin looked crestfallen.

"And you shouldn't have told him to go. He needs to work that out for himself too."

"I didn't say anything to him," Merlin protested.

"You said it to her," Hessler retorted.

"Well, they should," Merlin said with force. "They

would be free then, after a fashion. Look how tight he's locked up sometimes. It's not fair to Kristen. Three months there and he'd be completely changed. I think he'd turn out to be a more fervent follower of Isis than our friend is, if that's possible. With her as his inspiration, I couldn't blame him."

"A veritable Questor," Hessler said quietly. "You might be right."

"I can see into hearts more easily than you can sometimes," the spirit said a little grumpily, as if justifying his right to an opinion.

"No, but you see the simpler things more quickly," the elf said evenly.

"Sometimes that's enough," Merlin said firmly.

"You are rather rebellious this evening," the elf said, and for a moment the spirit looked downcast, like a child faced with a parent's disapproval. And then he saw the smile playing about the edges of the elf's lips, and he mirrored it with one his own.

They walked into the beginnings of dusk, the long-striding spirit and the elf with the walking stick he leaned upon more heavily than he once had. And as they did so a cat, having abandoned the remains of a chewed cloth mouse, cast aside in the brambles with its stuffing torn asunder, followed close behind them, its amber eyes glittering in the golden light.

ABOUT THE AUTHORS

Carl Sargent was born in Wales in 1952, and has a background in academic psychology, with four non-fiction books on aspects of the paranormal to his name. A long-time writer of roleplaying games, he has had published over five million words of books, articles, reviews, games, and gamebooks.

Marc Gascoigne was born in England in 1962 and has been a freelance author and editor for almost a decade. He, too, continues to add to a lengthy catalogue of fiction and non-fiction books, games, and articles.

Together they have written *Streets of Blood* and *Nosferatu,* two other novels in the Shadowrun® series. *Shroud of Madness,* the duo's first Earthdawn® novel, was published in July 1995 by FASA.

Buckled into the open cargo bay of the Fiat-Fokker
Cloud Nine amphibian plane, Jack Skater felt the cool
night air whip around him, carrying the wet taste of the
approaching storm front. He trained his nightglasses on
their prey. "Have you got a positive lock, Wheeler?"

"Ninety-two percent probability of a hit," the dwarf
rigger called back from the cockpit. "According to the
targeting deck, that's the best you're going to get."

Skater scanned the freighter cutting through the angry
waters of the Pacific Ocean, increasing magnification and
blinking through the re-imaging process. The words *Sapphire Seahawk* were emblazoned on her stern in English
and Sperethiel, and she flew the flag of Tir Tairngire. The
night made it hard to see, and the crawling dark of the
storm made it even worse. Her running lights were at a
minimum.

Pocketing the nightglasses, Skater grabbed the lip of
the cargo bay and hoisted himself back inside the amphibian. He unbuckled the safety harness and let it drop.
At twenty-five, he was dark and slim, just under two meters, with high cheekbones, dusty skin, and thick, close-
cropped black hair that showed the influence of Salish
blood. Dressed in black and wearing combat rigging that
supported an Ares Predator II in shoulder leather, a mo-

nofilament sword sheathed down his back, and a variety of other weapons, he looked like someone more at home on the streets than in a plane.

"How far?" he asked.

"About a minute and we'll be within range."

Skater looked up at Elvis. "You done?"

The samurai troll had been connecting the Connor grapple cannon to the firmpoint under the belly of the amphibian through the access port. He was nearly three tall meters of hard muscle and broad mean. The flat planes of his features showed a cruel history of challenges, reflected in a silver-crowned tusk and a twisted left horn. Like Skater, he was dressed in black and prepped for a savage run. "You betcha," he rumbled in deep bass.

Sliding his hands over his gear to take a final inventory, then glancing over the rest of his team, Skater said, "Ten seconds' warning, Wheeler, then fire at will."

"You got it."

Skater looked at Quint Duran and, though the ork was fearsome, he didn't soften his tone when he spoke. "Bloodshed's to be kept to a minimum. Those fragging elves hold a grudge as long as god and don't mind having to geek anyone, particularly where profits are concerned."

Duran's thin lips scowled, looking like a bent dagger edge. Rough and rugged to begin with, the ex-mercenary's face was a map of past violence. Silver tainted his bushy dark hair, and gold hooped earrings dangled from his elongated ears. His leathered black armor looked war-worn and scarred, but well cared for and serviceable. He carried a pump-action Ares Blastmaster 12-gauge shotgun in a gnarled fist. "I read you."

Skater nodded and walked back to the cargo bay. Under control from the cybernetic uplink melding dwarf and machine into a hybrid of flesh and steel, Wheeler Ironnerve heeled the amphibian over and glided down for the kill like a swooping hawk. The rigger was squat and broad, with an immense nose and slightly pointed ears, one more so than the other as the result of a keen blade some time in the near past. His hair was dirty chestnut and braided into a single length, only slightly lighter than his full, bushy beard.

The uneven planes of the ocean rushed up at the Fiat-

Fokker. Skater knew they were only meters above the water, racing along in the same northeasterly direction the *Sapphire Seahawk* was taking to Seattle. Despite the wind and the cooling system in the amphibian, he felt the shadowrunner's edge come over him, filling him with a burning fever of anticipation. If his information was correct, the profits from the raid could set them all up for months, maybe even as much as a year.

"You holding up, Cullen?" Skater asked.

The combat mage stood on the other side of the cargo bay against the bulkhead, outfitted in a roguish black one-piece and a heavy kevlar cape with a high collar that made the most of his slender, intense build. Thin beads of gleaming perspiration, ignited by stray strands of moonlight spilling through the amphibian's windows, dotted Cullen Trey's handsome face. "Stacking both these invisibility spells to mask this craft's approach from organic as well as technological detection isn't my idea of a slotting good time, chummer. Not to mention keeping a major sleep spell on tap for our boarding party."

"We've got one shot at this," Skater said. "However it goes, we're out in minutes. Just hang in there."

"Got to," the combat mage said. "I let go now and you're right about this vessel, we'll be geeked in a heartbeat."

Skater knew it was true. He unclipped the D-ring from his combat rigging while leaving the other end secured, and leaned out the cargo bay. The wind was a hammering force, the water an uneven surface less than twelve meters below.

"Ten seconds," Wheeler called out.

Lowering himself outside the door, fighting the wind, Skater clung to the plane and watched as the grapple cannon spun on its turret, locking on target. He felt the shiver course through the amphibian when the charge of compressed air suddenly fired the grappling hook from the cannon's mouth toward the *Sapphire Seahawk*. The wire spilled out behind it, whirring in a high-pitched scream above the noise of the amphibian's single pusher-propeller.

Skater didn't see what it struck, but he watched the line go taut, managed by a deck-assisted tension governor built into the grapple cannon.

"Locked on," Wheeler crowed triumphantly. "It's taking the full test weight. We are go."

Reaching out, Skater attached the D-ring and let go of the amphibian. The governor allowed just enough slack to send him sliding toward the *Sapphire Seahawk.* Less than three hundred meters separated the plane from the freighter. Even with the amphibian throttled down as low as Wheeler could manage, it was rapidly overtaking the ship. The window for the approach was only heartbeats long. Accessing the cybercom built into his head, Skater activated the Crypto Circuit HD to scramble all transmission along the two radio and two telephone channels open to him.

"Count off," Skater called out. He shot across the open expanse of water, shedding altitude as he dropped toward the freighter. He remained loose with effort, one hand on the combat rigging where the D-ring was secured.

The five members of the boarding party responded rapidly. Only three people per hundred meters of line could be held at a time without snapping. They had to stagger their approach accordingly.

Even in the few seconds it took to reach the *Sapphire Seahawk,* the D-ring was already smoking and glowing cherry-red from the friction. The whirring song it sang along the cable changed pitch, becoming more shrill.

"You're made, kid," Duran warned gruffly.

Scarcely forty meters out from the freighter's starboard side, Skater saw the shadows pull free of the deck and advance toward him. If there'd been a way to return to the amphibian, he'd have done it. But they were committed the instant they'd locked onto the cable.

The elven sailors were dressed in the ship's yellow and red, and evidently had no constraints about shooting first and asking questions later. Given that, Skater figured a seance was the only way any interrogation would ever take place. But it let him know that whatever they were protecting was obviously worth a lot.

Bullets sliced through the air around him. Some of them were phosphorus tracers, burning purple blurs past him.

Two of the elves raced for the grappling hook buried in the wooden coaming of the upper deck while others prepared to meet the boarding party.

"Jack," Wheeler called out, "you people are running out of wire."

Skater didn't attempt an answer. If the line came loose at either end, the team was going to end up in the water and be shot like fish in a barrel. At the edge of the freighter, he unclipped the D-ring. His momentum carried him over the heads of the elves as he fell. "I'm on."

He pushed himself to his feet as hands reached for him. Razor-honed reflexes born from a lifetime of fighting for his own took over. He grabbed an outstretched hand and twisted it viciously, snapping the elbow behind it with an audible crack. An agonized moan followed immediately. No bloodshed didn't mean no maiming. A vatjob and a few weeks of recuperation, and the elf would be as good as new.

Slipping by two awkward blows aimed at his face as the press of elves swarmed toward him, he kicked another sailor in the groin with enough force to double the guy over. He broke for the fallen elf as bullets chopped into the wooden wall behind him and the thunderous explosions rolled out over the water.

"I'm on," Elvis roared.

Skater saw some of the elves break from him, moving to repel the troll. Taking advantage of the respite and knowing the other elves were closing on the grappling hook imbedded overhead, he took two quick steps and sprang onto the fallen elf, using him as a footstool to leap up and grab the coaming overhead. He arched his body and flipped, landing on his feet in a squatting position just as one of the sailors advanced on the grappling line with a sword.

Pushing himself up and forward, Skater reached over his shoulder and ripped the monofilament sword free of its scabbard. The second elf shouted a warning in Sperethiel and launched himself at Skater.

There wasn't much room to maneuver on the lip running around the upper deck. It had been built for maintenance at sea, not fighting. Skater moved with grace, though without finesse, grabbing the leaping man's hair in his free hand and bringing his knee up into the elf's face. Bone crunched. He dropped his unconscious foe and lunged over him, monofilament sword extended.

The elf's sword swung toward the cable with enough

force to easily sever it. Instead, Skater's sword sheared through the metal near the haft, leaving the elf with only a stub fronting the ornate basket hilt. The blade went spiraling loosely and clattered to the deck.

"You scrod-scarfing brainwipe," the elf snarled, his pale face spotted with anger. He reached for a pistol at his hip.

Skater flicked the blade once, removing the holstered piece and a section of the belt, then stepped in and gave the elf a mouthful of the sword's knuckle bow. Squalling in pain and anger, the elf went backward and over the lip of the deck, crashing down among the crowd attempting to stop Elvis. They'd have done just as well trying to slide naked through killer IC in the Matrix. The troll was a rolling dreadnought of Arnie-Awesome cyberware unleashed in full frenzy. Still, Skater was glad to see that none of the attacks were lethal, though a fair number of the elves ended up over the side.

"I'm on," Quint Duran dropped into an easy standing position only a few steps from the elves. Without hesitation, he waded into the thick of the battle, swinging the Blastmaster like a staff. Elves flew in all directions.

Looking out over the sea, Skater spotted the three bunches of sparks sliding along the line that announced the impending arrival of the rest of the team. "Cullen," he called softly, scanning the rest of the freighter as more hands poured on deck.

"I'm ready," the combat mage responded.

"I'd say we're about up to standing-room-only. Time to say goodnight."

"Done." Abruptly, a shimmering spewed from Trey's hands as he slid along the grappling line. Whenever they touched the *Sapphire Seahawk* elves, the sailors fell in crumpled heaps.

But not all of them went down, evidently protected by wards. Duran and Elvis were making short work of the survivors as they surged across the deck.

"I'm on," Shiva, the flame-haired bounty hunter dressed in skin-tight black, joined them when she hit the deck. At just over two meters and possessing skillwires and vat muscle, she wreaked havoc among the elves immediately, a whirling blur of nunchuks.

Trey dropped aboard next and whipped out his polished

wooden walking stick. Among other nasty little surprises, the cane also powered up as a stun baton. The combat mage parried a sword thrust, then brought the walking stick up into his opponent's crotch and triggered the stun charge. Visible electric current sizzled blue-white veins through the air. The elf went down like he'd been pole-axed. Trey move on, gripping his cape in one hand. He hadn't been born to street-fighting, but he had a natural aptitude.

"Drek, I'm out of line," Wheeler warned.

Skater heard the deep-throated *sproing* of the cable separating as it hummed past his ear.

"Jack."

He turned, recognizing Archangel's voice. The elven decker had been almost three meters out when the grappling wire snapped. Dropping the sword, taking the sweep and roll of the freighter into account, Skater grabbed the line, his hands partially protected by the fingerless gloves he wore. He gripped and yanked with everything he had. "I've got you."

Archangel came over the side and joined him on the second deck, miraculously keeping her balance with his help. She was as tall as Skater, but slender and small breasted, almost childlike. Her hair was normally platinum and cut in street fashion, but was now tucked up under a tight black skull cap that left the impressions of her very elven pointed ears in highlight. Almond in shape, her bronze eyes held orbiting gold flecks that were strangely hypnotic. The gleam of the datajack on her right temple had been masked by the same camou cosmetics that streaked her beautiful face. She wore her deck on a shoulder strap, counterbalanced by an Ares Light Fire 70 in a crossdraw holster on her left hip.

She pushed herself out of his arms, nothing personal Skater knew, but the elven decker liked her space, didn't like being touched at all. Archangel wasn't her real name, but he'd never been given anything else to call her.

Skater took the lead, knowing they were working on borrowed time. The storm was overtaking the freighter and rain was starting to fall, making the deck slippery. He raced to the stern with Archangel a few steps behind him.

A trio of elven sailors met them at the companionway

leading down into the private quarters of the *Sapphire Seahawk*.

Skater threw himself backward, flattening against the wall as bullets ripped long wooden splinters from the coaming. "Frag and hellblast," he swore. Sheathing the sword, he drew the Predator II and palmed a flash grenade.

The first elf around the corner met a side-kick with Skater's full weight behind it. A howl of pain erupted from the man as he tumbled back among his companions.

"Elvis," Skater called out over his headware.

"Yepper," the troll responded.

"Fall back stern."

"You got it, chummer."

Another elf out on the deck stitched the side of the hold with a ragged line of machine fire.

Turning, Skater instantly brought up the Predator and unleashed a pair of heavy slugs that crashed into the elf's chest and sent him reeling backward. "Doubledrek," he said softly. All he needed was an elf vendetta from Tir Tairngire looking to slot him over. Business was one thing, but family could be a fragging lifetime of looking over a guy's shoulder.

"It's okay," Archangel said. "He was wearing armor."

Glancing at the man he'd shot, Skater saw that the elf was moving but stunned. He breathed a sigh of relief and peeled the pin from the flash grenade. Counting it down, he tossed it toward the companionway, then closed his eyes and told the elven decker to do the same.

As soon as the brunt of the explosion was over and the flare had died away, Skater ran toward the companionway. Looking over the side, he saw two elves beating embers from their clothing and coughing hard enough to hack up a lung. He moved without warning, leaping over the side and dropping on them. Swinging the Predator in a vicious arc, he caught one sailor alongside the temple and put him down. Managing a sleeper hold on the other elf, he choked him into unconsciousness.

"Elvis," Skater cried out as he tried the door at the bottom of the companionway and found it locked.

"Here, chummer." The massive troll suddenly blotted out the dark sky above with a silhouette blacker than the night.

"The door."

"Step aside, stringbean." The troll came down the stairs, fitting tight with the armor and weapons strapped around him.

Skater flattened himself against a wall as the troll drew back a hobnailed boot and drove it forward. The door was made of ceramic and steel and didn't give, but it was mounted in wooden framing which did. With a squealing shriek, the door slammed inward and released an oblong of yellow light that spilled out over the steps.

Without hesitation, Skater dove through the door, the Predator gripped in his fist. The room was a private berth, filled with a bed, desk and chair, and a short sofa.

One of the four elves inside came at him, firing pointblank. The bullets smashed against Skater's armor and felt like hammer blows, knocking his breath away. Skater grabbed the man and drove him backward, firing as fast as he could over the elf's shoulder.

He put three rounds into another guard's knees and cut his legs out from under him, tried to home in on a second man, but had to turn his attention to the elf he held when the guy brought his pistol up. Headbutting the elf in the face and breaking his nose, Skater stripped the Ceska vz/120 from the man's grip and threw it to the floor. He spun and caught the guy with a roundhouse kick that put him down.

An elven female dressed in street leather, looking as slender and unthreatening as Archangel, suddenly bared two sets of forearm snap-blades. Coolly and dispassionately, she rushed Elvis.

Setting himself with difficulty in the belowdecks room, the troll samurai met her attack with a series of blocks and parries that were too quick for Skater to follow. Flesh slapped flesh, and three lines of blood appeared like magic over Elvis's left eye.

Another man had been moving near the massive deck against the wall, pulling the snap-jack out of hiding and toward his temple. Skater fired a round without warning, putting it through the man's thigh while Elvis and his opponent fought.

"Move away from the deck," Skater commanded, holding the Predator in both hands.

"Slotting runner," the elf said, ignoring the wound in

his thigh that was sending crimson streamers down his leg. "Your life expectancy has just moved into negative numbers."

A wintry smile seasoned on Archangel's lips as she moved toward the deck with her own system. "We've been living there for a long time, skell. And quite well at times, thank you."

Keeping the elf covered, Skater glanced back to check on Elvis. The troll obviously had his hands full with the elven gillette, and was bleeding from another cut on his cheek and two on his left arm. But a cruel smile raked his lips back. Without warning, he popped out of a defensive posture and backhanded the woman with a paw the size of a gallon jug.

The razorgirl flew backward and struck the wall. She struggled briefly to get to her feet, then gave it up as unconsciousness claimed her. Elvis moved in to secure her with disposable cuffs.

"Down on the floor," Skater told the man he'd shot. The guy moved slowly, looking for an opening, but the shadowrunner didn't give it to him. By the time he and Elvis had cuffed the other elves, Archangel was jacked into the deck, her eyes turning to frozen ice as her mind went far away.

"Done," Elvis said, breathing hard. "Fragging dandelion-eating catskinner was slotting good." He touched his bloody forehead and gazed at the wet crimson staining his fingertips.

"You going to be okay?" Skater asked.

"I been cut wider and deeper," the troll replied.

Nodding, Skater moved over to join Archangel at the desk. "Any chance of simply ripping out the drive and going?"

She shook her head. "It's wired for self-destruct if anyone tries to move it. I tripped to the sensors already, but whoever hid them really knew what they were doing."

"Get what you can." He instructed Elvis to search their prisoners for ID while he tossed the drawers and traveling packs. In less than two minutes he knew they weren't going to find anything. They were dealing with professionals. None of the clothing held labels, and there was no paperwork to indicate from where in Tir Tairngire the team had come.

"Skater."

Looking up at the sound of the voice, Skater saw Quint Duran standing at the top of the companionway. The ork's armor had fresh scratches.

"We're in danger of being overrun," Duran said. "The elves are reorganizing, getting ready to make another try at us. Trey's sleep spell didn't affect as many as we'd hoped."

"Stay with her," Skater instructed Elvis as he dropped a lockbar into place over the other door in the room. He figured it led down into the major holds aboard the *Sapphire Seahawk.*

The troll nodded. "Nothing and nobody's gonna touch her without touching me first.

Skater went up the steps at a dead run and breathing hard. His ribs ached from the impacts of the bullets, promising bruises—if he lived another few hours.

Shiva was nestled comfortably behind a narcoject rifle, taking advantage of the cover provided at the side of the cabin. Trey was at the other side, a lime-green mana bolt just leaving his fingers, blistering the air.

"The sleep spell worked fine," Trey grumbled. "These people came from belowdecks where I couldn't see them. There were more hostiles onboard than we'd been led to believe."

"Two minutes," Skater said. "Then we're out of here. Archangel's into their system."

"You don't have the two minutes," Wheeler said over the cybercom. "We have bogeys coming up from the east, and they're riding hard."

Skater spun, searching the wine-dark sky. Then he spotted them, a tight trio of helos aimed straight for the freighter. They were on the *Sapphire Seahawk* in seconds, and .50-cal machine gun fire started smashing into the decks.

"Damn," Duran swore. "We're about to get our hoops jammed, hard and dry."

Skater had the cold, hard feeling that the ork's words were deadbang on target as he took cover from the hammering bullets.

ENTER THE SHADOWS SHADOWRUN®

YOUR OPINION CAN MAKE A DIFFERENCE!

LET US KNOW WHAT YOU THINK.

Send this completed survey to us and enter a weekly drawing to win a special prize!

1.) Do you play any of the following role-playing games?
Shadowrun ———— Earthdawn ———— BattleTech ————

2.) Did you play any of the games before you read the novels?
Yes ———————— No ————————

3.) How many novels have you read in each of the following series?
Shadowrun ———— Earthdawn ———— BattleTech ————

4.) What other game novel lines do you read?
TSR ———— White Wolf ———— Other (Specify) ————

5.) Who is your favorite FASA author?

———————————————————————————————

6.) Which book did you take this survey from?

———————————————————————————————

7.) Where did you buy this book?
Bookstore ———— Game Store ———— Comic Store ————
FASA Mail Order ———————— Other (Specify) ————

8.) Your opinion of the book (please print)

———————————————————————————————

———————————————————————————————

———————————————————————————————

Name ———————————————— Age ———— Gender ————
Address ————————————————————————————————
City ———————————— State ———— Country ———— Zip ————

Send this page or a photocopy of it to:
FASA Corporation
Editorial/Novels
1100 W. Cermak Suite B-305
Chicago, IL 60608